MW01531241

FAMILY ASHES

0955-CHEA

FAMILY
ASHES

A Novel

Dave Cheadle

0955-CHEA

Copyright © 2000 by Dave Cheadle.

Library of Congress Number:		00-190194
ISBN #:	Hardcover	0-7388-1591-8
	Softcover	0-7388-1592-6

All rights reserved. No part of this book may be reproduced or transmitted in any form or by any means, electronic or mechanical, including photocopying, recording, or by any information storage and retrieval system, without permission in writing from the copyright owner.

This is a work of fiction. Names, characters, places and incidents either are the product of the author's imagination or are used fictitiously, and any resemblance to any actual persons, living or dead, events, or locales is entirely coincidental.

This book was printed in the United States of America.

To order additional copies of this book, contact:
Xlibris Corporation
1-888-7-XLIBRIS
www.Xlibris.com
Orders@Xlibris.com

CONTENTS

PART I

PART II

0955-CHEA

To those who meet in caves,
pancake houses, and church basements...
seekers, survivors, promise keepers,
hogmen in spirit, if not in name.

0955-CHEA

PART I

PROLOGUE

Indian Summer, 1975.
Grand Haven, Michigan

"May I help you?" The man behind the desk dropped a magazine into a drawer and rose to his feet.

"Flowers?" asked Jim.

"For the funeral?"

Jim nodded, then turned to inspect the store. The entire shop had been rearranged. The T-shirt rack was shoved against the east window and buried beneath folded tapestries, and the wall where Jim's father busted a drill while hanging a menu marquee was now covered with poster samples of orange sunsets and bright sailboats slicing the Lake Michigan horizon. The island of ice-cream freezers had been replaced by two sets of refrigerated flower cases.

"Sorry." The man shook his head and sighed. "Our selection is kind of low right now. Even after my special order. Seems like the whole town must have known the girl. Pretty sad, huh? Between Karen's funeral today and yesterday's services for Randy, I'm pretty much cleaned out. Only a few things left."

The man stepped to a case and looked through the glass. "I suppose there's a couple of bouquets here that might do. Did you know her from school?" He reached to open the case.

Jim shrugged and stared through the glass. He felt the man's eyes. The damp ooze beneath Jim's pants, near his groin, suddenly felt sticky and cool. He instinctively glanced down. Still dry. Thank God. The burning had stopped and the bandages were holding. Jim quickly looked up.

The man was studying him, blinking, turning pale. "Oh . . ."

0955-CHEA

The clerk's hand slipped on the door's handle. "I'm terribly sorry. I didn't recognize you at first. There have been so many new faces to learn. . . ." He opened the case and removed the largest arrangement. "Here, why don't you take this one. It's on us."

Jim glanced at the arrangement.

"Do you have any others?" He met the man's eyes, then looked away. "Anything smaller, with some yellow? Karen was kind of partial to yellow."

"Right here," said the man. He moved toward the windows facing the lake. "I think there is yellow in a bouquet on the other side of this case."

Jim shuffled around the end of the coolers. His toe groped instinctively for the bulge of a warped floorboard. The old hardwood slat creaked lightly beneath his right foot.

He quietly examined the remaining selections.

"This will be fine." He carefully withdrew a modest corsage of three tiny yellow roses, a delicate black shell, and a spray of baby's breath.

"Are you sure? That's not really a funeral arrangement. I have another. . . ."

"She would have liked this. But thanks." Jim reached into his back pocket. "How much do I owe you?"

"Nothing. It's the least I can do."

Jim placed the corsage next to the cash register and examined the price tag dangling from a string. "Twelve dollars," read Jim. He removed a five and a ten from his wallet. "Plus tax. That makes twelve forty-eight."

"Half price," said the man. "Those were leftovers from homecoming. The roses have already begun to fade."

Jim handed the man fifteen. "I'd rather pay the full price," he said. "These are the only flowers that I ever got around to buying for Karen. It wouldn't feel right to get them cheap."

Jim accepted his change, left the store, then began to walk.

The service was across town and he would need a long stride to arrive in time. He could stop by his house to ride with Ben and his mother, but he didn't feel up to talking. He made his way south along Harbor Drive, staying parallel with the waterfront and one block inland from the beach.

Karen would have liked the flowers, even if they weren't quite traditional or fresh. She would have smiled, satisfied that he remembered her favorite color, happy that he found something with a shell. She collected shells, the pretty ones that she found in the sand along the lake. There were two rows of them in her bedroom, above her books and below a shelf of hand-blown glass unicorns.

Jim turned east on Harrison. The gash in his groin was beginning to burn again beneath the thick patch of gauze and cloth tape that he had cinched around his lower hips. He should have gotten stitches. But then some doctor would have asked questions, would have found out.

He glanced left and right. No one.

Fortunately, the wound was more wide than deep. It would probably leave a scar. Jim looked down. Still no signs of blood. Good.

A block later, he crossed the slowly rising street to seek the shady refuge of larger trees. The smell of damp sand ripening with algae and dead fish began to thin as he moved inland, though the air grew more stifling and thick. His shirt clung to the growing spots of sweat on his chest and lower back. Jim shortened his stride and tried to slow his heart.

Trash cans lined both sides of Harrison, some with lids, others too full to close. Ahead, beneath the heavy branches of a walnut row, two squirrels chattered among piles of crumpled refuse. Limp lettuce and dried chicken bones lay strewn in a semi-circle around a toppled bag.

Randy had hated squirrels. "Nothing but rats with bushy tails," he said. One of Randy's favorite tricks had been baiting them onto the back fence with a smear of peanut butter. Then he'd knock them off with crab apples sidearmed from the back steps. His buddies used to sit on the porch, cheering and betting on when he'd miss.

From atop a squashed milk carton, one of the squirrels studied Jim, then, with surprising vigor, began ratcheting something within its paws. Its sharp teeth tattooed lopsided orbits around the object, though its eyes remained fixed ahead.

Jim never understood why the squirrels kept coming back. They could see his brother right there, smirking, ready to throw, yet they always returned. It was as if they were as addicted to the habit as Randy. Once, when Jim was seven, he took a black eye from Randy for banging pots to scare them away.

Jim shook his head. Randy could be a real jerk.

But that was over. Randy would never bother the squirrels, or anyone, again. Not from the grave. No, not a grave. An urn. Nothing was left of his brother but ashes in a vase.

Jim shifted Karen's flowers back to his right hand, then resumed his walk to the church.

He slipped in through the side door, sweaty and late, his flowers wilted, and the funeral already in progress.

He stood for a moment among the palms and ferns in the foyer, gazing through the glass wall in back, trying to adjust himself to the restless solemnity of the service.

The church was packed. Hundreds of classmates, teachers, family, and friends were shuffled and pressed shoulder-to-shoulder in the pews. Soft wooden groans creaked down from the maple benches in the balcony overhead.

Up front, a frosty-browed pastor in a dark robe swayed gently behind a small microphone, gently stroking scriptures with a thin finger like an old phonograph needle tracing the worn grooves of a favorite song. His soft Dutch accent converted black lines of ancient text into the soothing promises of the prophet Isaiah.

Near the communion table, a closed casket drew lingering, wet-eyed stares from around the sanctuary. The dark coffin lay like a swamped boat, half-submerged in waves of green foliage and the bright frothy blossoms of irises, white orchids and red roses.

Jim scanned the congregation. He leaned, pressing his knuckles to the cold glass, searching for a gap in the sea of mostly blond heads, hoping that Ben and his mother had somehow managed to save him a seat.

The pastor glanced over the top of his bifocals and caught Jim's eye. His creamy voice never broke from its comforting cadence as he acknowledged the high school junior with a slight nod and continued reading from the old Bible cradled in his right hand.

> Thy dead shall live, their bodies shall rise.
>   O dwellers of the dust, awake and sing for joy!
> For as the sparkling dew refreshes the earth,
>   so shall the Lord revive
> those who have long been dead.

The pastor lowered his arm, then nodded at the organist to alert her of a change.

"Please rise," he said, addressing the congregation. "And turn with me to page eight so that we may sing together words of assurance from Psalm 90, 'O God, Our Help in Ages Past'."

The organist located the unscheduled number and launched into the familiar refrain. People rose to their feet as the pastor tipped his head again, this time to a short man in pinstripes who quickly joined Jim in the narthex. Jim listened as the man whispered, then followed the usher forward to the second row.

Mrs. Vanderspyke looked up from her hymnal as Jim slid next to her in the pew. Ben inched to the left to make room. His mother smiled softly, sadly, then offered Jim the thick side of her hymnal. There was a blackness about her eyes that frightened Jim, and he quickly looked down to the words of the familiar hymn. They held the hymnal together, her right hand resting lightly against his left beneath the book's spine. His other hand clutched the drooping corsage.

Jim looked past his mother to Ben. His brother stood tall, muscular in his dark tie and white short sleeves, unflinching as he silently mouthed the opening words of the song. Hundreds of voices rose and fell around them in a ceremonious profession of faith.

Jim glanced down past the hymnal to the legs of the soloist in the front pew. Mrs. Vickers stood erect, her hymnal outstretched, her elbows locked as her broad shoulders rose and fell with each breath. Her dress hung high in back, snagged up several inches by her ample rear. The dress slid up another two inches as she raised her book to reach for a note. Jim closed his eyes against the sickening web of varicose veins that crept eerily through the white flab behind her knees. Not pretty. Not at all like Karen's.

Karen's legs had been firm. In coconut oil, her legs glistened appetizingly on the beach. In autumn, her legs flashed smooth and strong beneath her uniform's skirt. Vaulted her into mid-air splits and wild jumps whenever he broke free of the line for another six points.

Karen's legs were now stiff and empty of life. Never to be seen or touched again. Soon to be shriveling, caving in upon themselves like fruit abandoned beneath a neglected tree.

Jim became aware of the corsage pin biting into his right palm. The sharp prick in his hand was a welcomed distraction from the headache rapidly spreading from his eyes back toward his neck. He squeezed harder and savored the pain. He rolled his knuckles and crushed the greens beneath the flowers into fiber and thin juice, then relaxed his fingers and looked down. Several drops of wet blood mingled with the pulp in his open palm.

He had dated Karen for three years. And he had played, wrestled and fought with Randy all his life.

Both had been disfigured beyond recognition. Jim glanced at the sealed casket only a few yards away. He closed his eyes. Game day. Karen squirming in her uniform, her knit sweater billowing and stretching, her beautiful legs crossed beneath the desk beside him in their Honors English class. She was looking at him, smiling. Her eyes sparkling in the excitement of the approaching game,

in anticipation of another victory dance. Eager for quiet time together later when they would stop on the way home. . . .

The gash in Jim's groin throbbed.

His plans to attend college with Karen were ruined. Their
dreams of marriage would soon be packed under six feet of dirt.
No more dates, no more quiet walks beneath the stars in the dunes.

Damn you, Randy. Jim looked at the hymnal. Still the third
stanza. The song was taking forever.

Where was Randy, anyway? Heaven, probably. Randy and
Karen were probably together at this very moment. Keeping each
other company until they got used to the place. Maybe walking
around laughing and holding hands and introducing each other
to strangers. Maybe giving each other friendly pecks on the cheek.
People supposedly weren't married in heaven, so a guy could probably kiss any girl he wanted. Randy would like that. He'd kiss
Karen for sure. Maybe even try to cop a feel.

Jim could picture Karen, a golden halo hovering over her long
black hair, kneeling at the edge of a cloud, smiling down at him.
Trying to reassure him as he stood in church squeezing pins into
his hand. Randy was there, too. He was smiling over her shoulder,
nestling right in behind her, his hands disappearing into the folds
of her robes. For Randy, that alone would be worth dying for.

Would Karen put up with that crap from Randy in heaven?
Jim stared at the hymnal. Two more stanzas to go.

After football season, then what?

Time to get a job. Time to forget about Karen and Randy. He
could work in a store. All of those years in a family business should
be good for more than the stack of bills his mother dumped into
bankruptcy court last year when they lost the gift shop. He could
work at Seinner Family Books. Jim knew a lot about literature, and
he loved to read. After Karen and Randy's deaths, Mr. Seinner
would give him a job for sure.

Jim flexed his hands.

Karen and Randy were dead—he wasn't. He needed to get on
with his life, to get his mind on other things. Needed some major

distraction and the discipline of a schedule. In a year or two, he could probably work himself off to college, away from Grand Haven, and away from the mess and memories forever.

Jim looked down. It was the last stanza, finally. He lowered his small arrangement of yellow roses into the pew rack in front of his thigh, then closed his eyes. From the darkness, the words flowed as he finished the hymn.

> O God, our help in ages past,
>> Our hope for years to come,
> Be Thou our guard while troubles last,
>> And our eternal home.

CHAPTER 1

Friday, March 15, 1996. Denver, Colorado

"Grrrrrr."

A blonde pre-schooler giggled through a missing tooth.

"Grrrrrrrrrrr," Jade growled again. He flashed teeth and jerked his hand from the book in his lap. He looked at his hand, then let his eyes grow big as invisible claws sprouted from the ends of his fingers. He spun back toward the girl with the missing tooth.

Her lips tightened.

"Who," Jade roared, "has been eating my porridge?"

The girl gasped. A boy in shorts buried his face in his mother's skirt.

Jade's eyes narrowed menacingly as they moved through the children on the Book Nook carpet near the front of his store. Jade fixed his glare on the tallest of the boys, "WHO has been eating my porridge?" He lowered his finger toward the boy's freckles. "Was it you, Samuel?"

The boy shrugged hesitantly. He clutched his knees and glanced at his mother, who grinned as she leaned against a nearby shelf.

Jade's finger moved back to the girl.

"Or was it you, Katie? Have you been eating my porridge?"

"I don't think so," she whispered.

"Well," he bellowed, turning to the others, "whoever ate my porridge left something behind."

They held their breaths.

"What?" gasped one of the youngest. "What did they forget?"

Slowly, Jade reached into his pocket and withdrew an invisible something as small and precious as a diamond. He held the imaginary object between two fingers, then studied it from all sides.

"What is it?" whispered Samuel.

Jade adjusted his wire rimmed glasses and examined it more closely.

"If I'm not mistaken," he whispered, "this clue was left by someone in this room." He growled. "It was inside my porridge bowl." He slid the book from his lap and shifted the object to his other hand.

"It's not very big."

The phone rang. Fifteen feet away, Chris sprang to the counter, met Jade's eyes and lifted the receiver before the second ring. "Seinner Books," she said softly. "May I help you?"

Jade turned back to the children. "I almost didn't see it in my spoon."

A plump-faced child in a Disney shirt pulled Jade's hand down for a closer look.

"I don't see it." She held his thumb. "I can't see no anything." One of the mothers laughed.

"Oh, it's there, Sarah," said Jade. "I can feel its sharp edges." He let Sarah tug his hand so close that her Minnie Mouse nose nearly disappeared into the cup of his palm. Others stretched and shuffled tighter for better views.

Jade looked up. In a single, practiced visual sweep, he took inventory of the store's activity. Chris leaned at the register, nodding her head, the phone lost in a nest of beautiful black hair. Beyond Chris near the store's wide entrance to the mall, a young man loitered among the magazines. To the far right two women fidgeted among cookbooks. Nearby, young mothers watched their children and glowed.

Except for two; two of the mothers looked past their children to Jade, who they absorbed in appreciative grins.

Women grinned that way a lot around Jade. There was something about the forty-ish bookseller, something in his good-natured intensity and his self-assured professionalism that drew reflection and respect. It was the charm that got him elected to the Merchants' Board in the mall as easily as to the Board of Deacons at church. He was not tall, but his neck and shoulders were full, and his thick forearms with their blond wisps created an impression of both strength and vulnerability. And Jade's eyes. . . . At a poetry reading, a divorcee once murmured that his eyes caught smiles like sails catching wind on a summer's lake.

Jade drew Chris' attention, then nodded in the direction of the women by the cookbooks. Chris nodded back.

"I think I see it," shouted Samuel.

"No you don't," said another.

"Do too!"

"Hush," growled Jade. The children moved back.

"Hush before I fling my hand to the sky and this treasure disappears from the earth forever." He leaned toward the child in the Disney shirt.

"It's okay, Sarah," he smiled. "Don't worry if you can't see it. But we both know it's there, don't we?"

Sarah shook her head, then frowned, "Yes, but what is it?"

"I'll tell you," he said softly, "but first, you must promise not to laugh."

"Ahh, come on," groaned Samuel. "Just tell us."

Jade straightened, curled his lips, then growled. "I think that I know who has been eating my porridge."

"It wasn't me," protested Samuel. The boy cowered slightly, freckles bunching around his eyes.

"No," said Jade. "It wasn't you." He turned toward Katie and smiled. "It was you," he asked gently, "wasn't it?"

Katie looked back and forth between Jade and her mother. The little girl said nothing, but she seemed pleased by the attention. Several children turned to see what Katie would say. Instead, she waited.

"Katie," Jade grinned, "I know it was you who ate my porridge, and I have proof. I have what you left behind in my bowl. And here it is."

Jade thrust a closed hand in Katie's direction.

"Open it," he said, "and take back what is yours."

The girl hesitated, then reached forward. Carefully, one by one, she peeled back his fingers. When only one finger remained, the entire group leaned and held its breath.

The young girl pulled, but the finger would not budge.

"Wait a minute," growled Jade. He scrunched up his nose. "Katie, let me see you smile."

She beamed.

"Yes, this belongs to you." He threw open his hand.

"In my porridge this morning, I found . . . your tooth!"

Several children gasped, then moved closer to make sure. It certainly looked like a tooth.

Katie studied the object, then giggled.

"That's not my tooth," she blurted. "That's a Tic-Tac."

Jade feigned bewilderment. Children started to laugh.

"What?" he gasped. "This isn't your tooth?"

"No," she giggled again. "It's just candy."

"If this isn't your tooth," he jerked his head from face to face, "then whose tooth is it?"

"It's not a tooth," laughed Katie. "It's candy!"

Jade acted as if he hadn't heard. "Are you missing a tooth?" he asked another child. The girl laughed and emphatically shook her head. "How about you?" he asked a little boy in the front row.

He looked at the mothers. "Sorry to bother you, Mrs. Hunt, but would you please smile? I'm looking for the person who lost this tooth."

The children rolled in laughter as Jade pinched the white candy between his fingers and lifted it high above their heads.

"Whose tooth is this?" he shouted.

"Nobody's!" they shouted back. "It's not a tooth. It's only candy!"

"Oh, noooooo," cried Jade. "I found this tooth in my porridge, and if it doesn't belong to any of you . . . then . . . it must be . . . MINE!"

Jade flipped the candy high into the air, then caught it between his lips.

The children squealed as the phone rang for the tenth time that hour.

By eleven o'clock, the children and their mothers were gone. The phone had begun ringing almost as fast as it hit the cradle.

Jade looked up and sighed as it rang yet again.

"Chris," he called. "Could you please get this one?" He bumped a fingertip against the bridge of his glasses. "I'll take the next two."

He turned back to the woman who had drawn him to Health and Nutrition.

"As I was saying," he continued, "this book is generally recognized as the definitive work on nutritional low-fat diets. The critics agree that. . . ."

"Yes," said the woman, "but what about *Frying Fat-Free?*" She wet her lips and shot glances to Jade's left and right. "Do you stock *Frying Fat-Free*, or not? Because I'm not interested in. . . ."

Jade sighed. He raised his left thumb to prop his jaw, then hooked his right wrist behind his left elbow. She was the eighth walk-in during the past hour to ask for the same title.

". . . and since Mary and I have both been having the same problem with our ankles, I thought that this book might. . . ."

Jade's left index finger began moving slowly back and forth over his teeth, his knuckle lingering and slipping as if lost in some pensive harmonica tune. He had discovered the harmonica routine 20 years earlier in college in the back row of his first semester of philosophy. The pose served him well in the book business, where customers preferred to imagine their salesman as thoughtful and attentive rather than as bored.

". . . and so that's why I need to find a copy of *Frying Fat-Free*. . . ." She paused and looked at him. "So do you handle it or not?"

The invisible harmonica dropped to Jade's thigh. "Of course," he said, shaking his head no. "Of course we handle it."

He hated these moments. He leaned toward the woman, smiling, sailboats flashing in his eyes. Hating these times when he had to say things that were not, technically speaking, true.

"*Frying Fat-Free* is about to become one of our best sellers. The thing is," he assured her with a smile, "we don't have a single copy left. The book was reviewed this morning by a newspaper columnist and. . . ."

"That's how I heard about it. In this morning's Denver Post."

"Well, what do you know?" Jade stroked his smooth square chin, shaking his head as if amazed, instinctively sucking his knuckle for another two bars.

"Anyway," he continued, "all I can tell you is that we have a shipment of *Frying Fat-Free* due any day. Perhaps even this afternoon. In the meantime, now that I have a better idea of what you're looking for, let me recommend this wonderful title over here. . . ."

Five minutes later he tallied up three titles.

Jade grinned through a headache as he waved her away. Sales were lagging behind his goal for the month, and every turn-around sale like hers would help. He was aiming for his best March on record. Mr. Seinner liked numbers, and a set of solid figures for a traditionally mediocre month like March would cinch a transfer for sure. He looked around.

A middle-age woman stood talking with Chris in Hobbies & Crafts. Chris was smiling, tucking her thick hair behind a naked ear. Chris frowned and dropped her brow. The woman sighed again, then continued.

Otherwise, the store was empty. But not unusual for this hour of day. He needed the break anyway. Jade removed the phone from the hook—a rare breach of his own policy—and sighed deeply. He drifted west, then disappeared into the Reference section.

Five minutes later, a road atlas cradled in his right arm, Jade felt himself observed. He sensed Chris. Did not look up.

Page numbers flashed beneath his fingers as his attention ricocheted between maps, mileage charts and the index. He felt Chris approaching, loosened his grip, then met her gaze.

Cream-sweetened coffee steamed from the mug in her hands. Within Jade's hands the United States Federal highway system lay winding across a double-page spread. His thumbs were pressed to the blues of the Atlantic and Pacific oceans. Some 80 pages below, his right index finger twitched expectantly in the pale blues off Coos Bay, Oregon.

"What's up?" he asked.

"Not much," said Chris. "Just taking advantage of a lull to catch my breath. It's been so busy this morning that I haven't had a chance to say hello." She tucked a loose twist of hair behind her ear. "By the way, Jim, great job with Goldie Locks this morning. The kids loved it."

Chris was the only one who called him Jim. She had spotted his full name—James D. Vanderspyke—on some legal documents and it had caught her imagination. He explained how "Jim" became "J.D." in college, then "Jade" later, but Chris insisted that "Jade" sounded too much like a rock. Calling him Jim was one of her private ways of teasing him when nobody was around.

"Thanks." Jade met her eyes. "I enjoy these weekly readings. It reminds me of years ago with Mark and Carla. I really miss those times with my kids. We used to read together almost every night. Now, we hardly even talk." He shrugged and grinned. "Besides, these readings sell books."

Chris nodded at the atlas. "Going someplace?"

"Uh, just checking a few things out about Portland. I thought maybe I could find a shorter route for my next road trip. I might be making another run up there in a couple of weeks."

Chris looked down at her mug. She raised it to her lips and blew softly at a swirling curl of gray steam. Jade glanced awkwardly past her shoulder to the front of the store, then scanned the mall's corridor outside the entrance. Empty.

"Do you know," he asked, "what bothers me the most about this morning? It's that in spite of how busy we've been, our sales

have been off. All that activity, but hardly a thing to show for it."
He shifted the atlas entirely to his right hand, his fingers still
marking several pages.

"It bugs me when publishers fail to deliver on schedule. Like
those *Frying Fat Free*'s that still haven't arrived. And then customers blame me for the screw up." He shook his head. "As a shift
manager, I'm sure you know what I mean."

"Sure." She lowered her cup. "I know exactly what you mean.
I hate being caught in the middle. It takes the fun out of selling
books." She hesitated. "Jim, are you okay?"

He shrugged. "I'm fine."

"Those new books," she sighed at last, "should have been here
by now. I can see why you're a little upset. But up until a few
months ago, something like this wouldn't have fazed you in the
least. Nothing fazed you. You could handle anything."

She studied him for a moment.

"Jim," she said softly, "pardon my saying so, and I hope that
I'm not overstepping the line, but it doesn't seem like you've been
very happy lately. You don't kid around like you used to. I'm afraid
to crack a joke. Even an innocent one." She smiled.

She was right. Until recently, they had teased and joked a lot.
Lately, not at all. He tried to smile back.

"Yeah, I know." He ran his left hand over his chin. "I've been
feeling a lot of pressure about this NightLight Books decision.
Damned if I do, damned if I don't. I grew up in the book business—family bookstores—and now they want me to close down
my Children's Book Nook to clear floor space for another rack of
semi-pornographic sleaze. Then yesterday my mom called and left
a message on my machine. It isn't like her to call. She said it was
about my dad. Something serious."

"Your dad? I didn't know he was even alive. You've never mentioned him."

"Yeah, well, I think he's still alive. It's hard to imagine him
dead. I haven't seen him in 20 years. So now that's on my mind.

Not to mention the sleep that I've been losing over this Portland move."

"Well," said Chris, "don't add to your stress by taking this Fat Free fiasco so seriously." She laughed. It was an ironic, compelling laugh.

He returned a wobbling grin. Their eyes locked. Her laugh grew. Grew hot.

All morning, Jade had stayed clear of Chris' heat. Suddenly, it came to him in waves.

She wore a smoldering combination. Her taste in clothes was maddening. A thigh-high skirt, sharp black heels, a loose white blouse. The dramatic curves of her tiny frame, an open collar and a missed button revealing a dot-to-dot of three moles, a partial constellation of stars plummeting in an arch into the folds of her blouse.

Jade looked back to her eyes and focused on clouds. Blinked away the stars.

"You're right," he said. "It's nothing to obsess about."

She relaxed. She leaned her shoulder against the bright dust jackets of the dictionaries on the reference shelf, then lifted her coffee and carefully sucked her first draught.

Her mouth jerked. "Whew," she said. "Still hot."

A half-kiss of moist lipstick clung to the cup's rim.

In an instant, the familiar twister was upon him, swifter than logic, more complex and powerful than tides. The cyclone enveloped his senses and spun him off the floor.

Jade dropped from the sky onto the beach of another world.

Within the swirling vapors of Chris' mug there now stretched a path of forbidden white sands. Chris faced him from the water, her hair blowing and body leaning into the press of a wave. As the wash withdrew, she straightened, smiling, her freshly-drenched blouse flowing translucently over white, quivering air bubbles that rolled beneath her breasts. Two sharp, pebble-sized nipples stressed her crepe blouse. . . .

Jade turned. Focus, he thought, focus.

When he looked back Chris was still smiling, her lips again pursed barely above the steam.

"I'll be leaving before lunch today," he said. "In fact, in half-an-hour. I've got to go downtown to relieve Sally. She has a doctor's appointment at noon. I promised her that I would cover the rest of her shift."

"What a gentleman," laughed Chris. "So helpful. The kind of guy who would give a girl the shirt off his back if she needed it."

Suddenly, she needed it.

Jade closed his eyes. When he opened them, she was fully clothed, extending her arm.

"Here," she winked. "You look like you could use a nip of coffee." She stretched her hand farther, then paused, the mug hovering several inches beyond his grasp. "It's been a rough morning. Tell me, though, what is it that's really bothering you? Something is wrong. We're friends. You can tell me. What is it, Jim?"

It occurred to him that he should insist that she stop calling him by that name. Instead, he leaned forward to receive her mug.

"Oh, I don't know." Their hands brushed as he took the mug. Chris smiled.

Jade looked down and took a shallow sip. The thick coffee was hotter than he expected. He blinked and focused on the cup, not trusting himself to look up past her blouse to her eyes.

He rushed a second, larger swig, then held a mouthful of the burning brew, letting it smolder like lava on his tongue. He swallowed, relishing the fire as it raked a sweet raw swath down his throat.

"My wife," he said, glancing into the mug, "has been a little hard to live with lately."

Jade rolled his tongue in the white ash of scalded nerves. Why did it have to be Chris, instead of Alice, that he dreamt of meeting on secluded sands? His wife was still attractive. He still loved her. He was sure he still loved her. These shifts at the store were becoming hell.

He took a half sip.

"Alice," he looked away, "is threatening to boycott my Port-land plans. Mark and Carla swear that if she stays in Denver, then they're staying with her. It's like they want me to move, but with-out them. Like they want to get rid of me. I don't know what to think."

The side of the mug still glowed from the red imprint of Chris' lips. Her scarlet gloss appeared several shades deeper on the edge of the cup than it did upon the soft edges of her mouth.

"I don't know," he said. "Maybe I can eventually get Alice to come around. My marriage is one of the most important things in my life, but if it comes down to that. . . ." He shrugged. "Once Seinner sells the downtown store, I don't know if I'll have an option."

"I wish," said Chris, drawing his gaze, "that I could help. But if the store sells, I'm not sure what I'll do myself."

Jade sighed. "Things were going so well. Now it seems like everything is falling apart. At home . . . and even here at work." He looked away.

"I guess," said Chris, pulling away from the shelf, "that about all we can do is stick together and hope that things work out." She reached hesitantly toward his shoulder.

He saw the white cuff of her sleeve dissolve, revealing an in-credibly slender wrist. His eyes seized the wrist and slid up her bare arm to an exposed shoulder. The twister. . . .

Jade sank a molar into the side of his tongue.

He winced.

"You okay?"

"Yeah," he said, licking his lips and stepping back. "Just a crick in my neck. Anyway, I wish that I could promise you some-thing. But as far as I know, when Seinner sells that store you and I will both move on. Or else take big cuts in pay. Sally will want to transfer out here to run this store, and she definitely has seniority over you. I'll have to give her your job."

"What about you?" asked Chris. "Wouldn't you want to hold

the manager's position open here for yourself, just in case the Portland transfer falls through?"

"No, I barely make enough money as it is. And that's as a regional supervisor. I could never cover my house payments and support my family," he hesitated, then smiled, "on the pittance that a manager makes."

He helped himself to a final sip from Chris' mug.

"Besides," he said, "Seinner has already made it clear what he wants. He wants to dump the downtown store and for me to move to Portland to open two new mall locations by the end of the year. Another four next year. I'll be Seinner's West Coast regional supervisor. Within a decade, I'll be overseeing stores all the way from Seattle to San Diego. There's no way that he's going to make it easy for me to stay in Denver. He's got plans for me elsewhere."

She smiled sadly, then stepped nearer.

"If you end up moving to Portland," she said, reaching with both hands to retrieve her coffee, "then I really will miss you. Somehow," her fingers wrapped around his, pressing his palm against the hot mug, "I hope that you can figure out a way to stay right here." Her eyes remained fixed on his, her hands steady.

Something shuffled behind him.

Jade turned as a rusty barge of a woman reached to tug his elbow.

"Excuse me," spluttered the stranger. "I hope that I'm not interrupting anything important here, but I could use some service."

Jade's face reddened. Chris took back her mug.

"Yes, ma'am," he said. "How may I help you?"

"It's only that when a person makes the effort to come all the way to the mall to find a book," she shifted her considerable freight toward Chris, "it's not unreasonable to expect a little attention." Jade fought to keep his eyes from Chris. "I've been looking for help, and I've been virtually ignored since I got here."

The barge belched vapors of breakfast burrito, then rebuilt steam.

"It's not," she moaned, swinging a massive arm aft to scratch, "as if I'm asking for much. But a person has gotta eat, and for a person who's on the go as much as me. . . ."

Jade sized the breadth of her hull and estimated that she would hit less than a knot headed anywhere except over Niagara Falls. After the five minutes he had just spent ogling Chris' little skiff, this scow seemed huge, repugnant.

". . . so when I got my paper this morning and read that there was this new book. . . ."

Jade nodded his head and smiled.

Chris drifted back toward the cash register at the front counter. He glanced briefly, longingly, as she moved away. He redirected his attention to the woman breathing in his face. This customer needed to be humored and docked. He needed to land two more sales before he could leave.

". . . not to mention the fact that my doctor, who I've been seeing for several years, ever since my operation, he says that I should look for foods with whole wheat grains, vegetables and fruit, especially fruit, because. . . ."

Jade's fingers and hand tingled where Chris had cupped them around the hot mug.

". . . chocolate cake, mind you, so long as. . . ."

The timing of the interruption was perfect. Perfect to save him—or cheat him—from another plunge down the throat of the whirlpool. He curled his damp fingers and drew forth his harmonica for a melancholy tune.

He cleared his head of Chris. He imagined himself outside on a crisp day, his heart pounding and muscles flexing. Mountain biking down the rugged spine of Dakota Ridge.

The customer's rambling monologue and wobbling cheeks blurred as his head bobbed in time with the erratic bumps of the pits and rocks of the trail. A dramatic descent in the familiar trail lay just ahead. Below at the base of the slope was a beautiful spot for a water break. He would park his bike. . . .

Jade's stomach surged.

He gasped and jerked. His hand dropped to his side. The customer paused, stared.

"You okay?"

"Yes."

Jade's tongue flicked across his lips. He took a breath. Where had that come from? Weird. Nothing like that had ever happened before. He'd been thinking about the trail, picturing a nice place for a break. . . .

It hit again. This time shorter, less severe. He shook his head and wiped his mouth.

"Sorry," said Jade. He met the woman's eyes. "Just a twinge of something. I'm fine, really. You were saying?"

"Are you sure you're all right?" She frowned. "Because if you're sick, I'd like have someone else's help. I'm highly susceptible, you know?"

"Don't worry, I'm not sick. Really." He fixed his gaze on the woman's barnacled lips and forced himself to focus. "Please, continue. I'm all ears."

"Well, then, as I was saying, it's a proven fact that certain processed starches. . . ."

Images of the ridge started to return. Jade pushed them aside, willed himself back to the broken texture of the customer's swollen lips. He strained past her lips to her stained teeth and bloated gums. He refused to consider anything else.

"Do you have . . ." she asked at last, having apparently exhausted the quips of every doctor and tabloid she knew, "the latest book, which, from what I hear. . . ."

"No," Jade snapped. He felt a sudden urge to stuff an apple into the woman's mouth. To go home, to grab his mountain bike and to head for the foothills. To find that spot in the trail.

He re-shelved his atlas and turned toward the front counter.

"But I. . . ."

"Leave your number," he said, facing her once again. "I'll call you as soon as the *Fat-Free's* arrive."

The woman coughed, collected herself, then pointed a chipped red fingernail in the direction of his nose.

"If I have a heart attack while waiting for this book," she blubbered, "I'll hold this store financially responsible."

She rattled a thimble of congestion free from her left nostril, then daintily tapped the corners of her mouth with a paper napkin from the food court up the mall.

"And you'd better believe me," she puffed. "I got me a good lawyer."

"I'll call the very second they're in."

"Or?"

"Sue me."

"Can I have that in writing?"

"Good day, madam. Talk to you soon."

CHAPTER 2

Jade crammed a small box with books and paperwork for inventory transfers, then said good-bye to Chris and stepped through the dark back door into the eye-burning Colorado sun.

He was angry with himself. Very angry. And with Chris. The woman played him like a chump. But he always came back for more. This morning it had cost him at least one sale. Chris' damned smile and open blouse completely blew his poise and left him too edgy to think. He lost it with his last customer, and that wasn't like him at all. He never blew sales. They were his life.

And what was the lurch in his stomach when he pictured that spot on the Dakota Ridge trail?

Jade hoisted his pants and began high-stepping through the parking lot's ridges and troughs of slush. March needed to be a good month. A record March would cinch Portland for sure.

Jade glanced ahead. Hundreds of vehicles stretched in haphazard rows, parking lines obscured by the slush. The mountains lay beyond, hazy dun heaps absorbing the spreading brown cloud of commuter fumes.

A splash of icy slop washed over Jade's thin sock.

Damn.

He shook his foot.

New shoes, half ruined already. And how could he afford another pair? Where did the money go? Everything was so damned expensive.

He glanced ahead at his car.

Perhaps they ate out too much. Carla's teeth were costing a fortune and Mark's changing taste in clothes and music was driving the whole family nuts. And then there was Alice's speeding ticket. What was she thinking, anyway? Speeding on the way to a high school band concert, for crying out loud. Just a band concert.

The box slipped.

Jade caught it at the last instant.

Damn.

Fifty bucks worth of books. That wouldn't have helped his March figures a bit. He reached his car and fumbled with the lock until the keys rattled from the door and dropped into the slush. Jade angrily tossed his box onto the car's roof. He yanked his coat sleeve, then stooped to grope for the keys with his bare hand.

He found the icy keys, lifted them gritty and dripping, then shook them at the sky. With his clean hand, he searched his pockets for one of the monographed handkerchiefs Alice had given him on his last birthday. He wiped the keys and then worked on his wet fingers. A dark ringlet clung beneath his wedding band. He removed the ring, wiped it, then slipped it into his front pocket. He glanced at his watch. Sally would be waiting.

Jade loaded the car and dropped in behind the wheel, then re-examined his keys.

The keys were fine; the photo inside the worn plastic key-ring charm was ruined. A dark stain ran through the faces of his family. They posed sludge-soaked in the photo, stiff and cold in front of a pine tree at the mall's Santa Claus Village.

Jade shook his head, which throbbed. Alice, Mark, and Carla stared in disapproval, as if in pain. He looked closer.

What was happening to them? To him? Their smiles flickered sadly, forced and thin, like Christmas tinsel recycled one holiday too many. Jade closed his eyes. Tried to focus.

When his eyes opened, the stain remained. But the strangers were gone. He recognized the smiles, including his own.

Gently, feeling ridiculous, Jade touched a finger to each face.

"Sorry," he whispered. "It was an accident."

He turned the old charm over and read the back. "The family that prays together, stays together." A gift from Alice, from when

Mark was born, right before their second apartment in Grand Rapids. She updated the photo every Christmas.

Alice had been collecting such trinkets for almost as long as they'd been married. Lately, more of them than ever. Key-rings, refrigerator magnets, bumper stickers, pens with scripture verses for his briefcase. . . .

Each with some trivial or overly-simplistic maxim indelibly stamped or embossed. And she always managed to find new ones. Jade glanced at the air freshener dangling from his mirror.

"Good days begin with good attitudes."

Good grief.

He shook his head and started the engine. He found reverse and backed away, then spun west and headed for the exit. Thirty yards from the outlet, the light changed.

Jade stopped, glanced at his watch, then swore.

Beyond the stop light, the mountains appeared strangely unfamiliar. They looked grayer, browner, more alien than he could remember.

A cold shiver swept down his arms. He shook his head.

Probably from the slush. And the odd weather. He glanced again toward the distant peaks. It was avalanche season in the high country.

Jade cranked his heater.

And wondered if there were avalanches in Oregon.

CHAPTER 3

Supper that night was a pork chops affair.

Mark was staying after school for band rehearsal and Carla had theater. Alice said the kids would be stopping for fast food on their way home around 7:00. She had given them each five dollars from the tin box atop the refrigerator, and the food fund now needed restocking.

Jade glanced above the refrigerator. The empty tin box pictured fruit, bread, and a Bible verse in black letters:

> "And having food and clothing, let us be therewith content.
>   I Timothy 6:6."

He shook his head and tried to remember how much money was left in his wallet. The kitchen swirled in puffs of sautéed onions, and he couldn't focus, couldn't remember whether he had used money that afternoon for lunch. Couldn't remember if he had even eaten.

His eyes slid from the food fund to the note taped on the window over the sink. Against his will, he skimmed the familiar words:

"There are two ways to be rich. One is to have more . . . the other is to want less."

Alice stepped into view, dropped a sizzling fry pan into the sink, removed her apron, then sat.

Jade prayed.

"Our Father," he recited softly, "We thank Thee-for-this-food, this-day, and-Thy-love. Please-forgive-us-of-our-many-sins, and-may-Thy-grace-enable-us-to-sin-no-more. Amen."

The meat was tender, and Jade grunted so, as was the salad. Alice acknowledged the observations with a polite thank-you-please-pass-the-vinaigrette, and they chewed their meals like old fishing companions who had taken to dropping their cinder-block anchors in opposite coves.

"By the way," said Alice at last. "Terry called this afternoon."

"Was I supposed to call back?"

"No. He said that he would call you. He's having trouble with Wednesday. One of his clients wants to do an insurance review Wednesday, and now the day is looking pretty full."

"Thanks."

"Don't mention it."

He looked at Alice. This had not been one of his better days, and it was only getting worse. It had not always been this way. He shook his head. He hated such nights. What was the problem? They still loved each other, didn't they?

He studied her, trying not to stare.

Alice was still attractive. She still drew glances at the rec pool, and her faint traces of uncolored gray only made her appear more of a prize for her age. Nobody in his right mind was throw her out of the sack. Jade closed his eyes and felt himself between her legs.

He opened his eyes and reached for milk. Alice adjusted her fork and met his gaze. He smiled, faintly.

A waiter once spilled wine while glancing down the top of Alice's dress. She had blushed. They laughed, then later made love. Twice.

He tried to remember, and did. Vividly. Forcing it. Trying to turn the memory into love as he met her eyes.

Alice rose to scrape her plate.

Jade cleared his throat. "My mom didn't happen to call today, did she?"

"No. Not as far as I know." She returned to the table and sat down. "There wasn't anything on the machine."

"Well, I was just wondering. My mother might call tonight.

She rang the store today before I arrived, and Nancy said that Mom would try to catch me tonight at home."

"I thought you left early this morning?" Alice searched his eyes. "How did Nancy beat you to work if you left early?"

"Nancy works downtown. You know that. I opened at the mall this morning." He pulled away. "I didn't make it downtown until noon."

"Oh." She looked at his ring finger, which was bare.

Jade followed her gaze. "It's right here." He stood and pulled it from his pocket.

"I had to take it off in the parking lot. I dropped my keys in some slush, and I had to take it off to clean my hands. I guess I forgot to put it back on."

She nodded.

"Alice," he frowned. "Believe me. There's nothing going on." Beyond his wife, he could read the calendar proverb of the day, a quip about many strokes and falling oaks. "I believe it," he sighed.

"What?" Alice raised her head.

"Nothing."

They adjusted their silverware and napkins.

"I saw an interesting bumper sticker today," she said, hunting for his eyes. "It was on the back of an old Volkswagen beetle."

"And?"

"Make love, not money."

"That's it?"

"That's all it said. Make love, not money."

"Oh."

Jade looked at his plate. He lifted his fork, then bumped a pork chop toward the last of his applesauce. A nibble or two of gray meat clung to the bone, daring him to gnaw. He thought about leaving the table and sitting behind his computer to reread old e-mail. Or to write some fresh notes. Maybe to download some graphics from the internet.

He bit his tongue, lightly.

No. No more e-mail, no more graphics. Bad habit.

A hard workout would be better. He could climb on his bike and pound some rocks off the Dakota Ridge trail. Jade cautiously allowed himself to recreate the scene that had triggered the gut-lurch in the store. The familiar slope with the flat spot at the bottom. He could see it again in his mind.

Nothing. Good. Not even a twitch. That had been the strang-est thing. Jade glanced back at the window over the sink. Still plenty of light.

But if he went biking, he would miss his mother's call.

From Texas?

What was she doing in Texas? Nancy said his mother called from Texas to tell him something about his father. Alice had never met Harry. Maybe he should warn Alice, tell her a little more about his mother's call and Harry. The guy was probably in trouble. He might be begging for help.

Let him beg.

A distant siren rose and fell, and a large dog howled two or three times through a neighbor's fence. Then the dog and Jade lost interest and the sounds faded into the dark.

The bleak silence was gradually filled by Alice's old wall clock in the other room. It was a wedding gift, an heirloom passed down for generations. Its steady beats had echoed within its box for over a century.

Jade listened to the clock.

The ticks were predictable, balanced, familiar. He could al-most feel them pulsing at the stem of his brain. Tick. Tick. Tick. Tick. Back-forth-up-down. Like calisthenics. One-two-three-four. Jade closed his eyes and felt the throbs in his arms, shoulders, and legs. His neck and chest tightened to match the strokes.

A scuffed wooden metronome tapped its cadence near his ear. It was 1974, and he'd bought the beat-keeper at a garage sale to pace him through a hundred pushups a day. The first week clicked off at the slowest speed. The second week, a little faster. Then faster, stronger, and more methodical each week. Jade's mind and shoulders gradually melded into the powerful, addicting rhythm of the full-body repetition. 100 pushups became 150, then 200, 250. His arms had become pistons, his entire body a finely-tuned high performance machine.

The pendulum clock in the other room, however, perpetually ticked at a single speed. An endurance pace.

Jade imagined himself raising and lowering his body in time with the clock. He wondered how many minutes he would last if he synchronized himself to the clock's restrained beat. If he locked the ticking in his head at 2-4 time, the pace was relaxed. Unhurried. Almost slow enough for good love.

He felt himself rising and falling above a woman.

Alice.

Not Alice. Chris. Tiny, curvaceous Chris. Beneath him, undressed, rolling her hips to meet his, gasping on each beat of the clock. He felt a familiar stirring beneath the table. The pulse of the clock helped. He could feel the strokes, could feel her slick warmth. . . .

He shook his head free of the alluring rhythm, back to the numbing silence of Alice's gaze.

"What?" he asked.

"Where were you?"

"When?"

"Just now."

He thought for a moment. The kids were gone. He could tell her. Maybe it was time that he did.

"Where," he wet his lips, "where do you think I was?"

Alice reached for her napkin. "From that look in your eyes, I'd say that you weren't at a ballgame with the kids." She shook the napkin open. "And you certainly weren't with me. You haven't grinned like that with me in a long, long time."

She wiped her hands, then returned her napkin to beside her glass.

"I was listening to your clock."

"Uh-huh. And thinking of me. Or my mother, perhaps? Right."

He was a pig. A bum. A sad excuse for a husband. Thinking

about Chris across the table from his wife. He should at least respect Alice enough to wait until he was alone. Behind a locked door. Maybe in the shower. Chris would face him, kneeling. . . .

He bit his tongue. "Sorry," he said, feeling the blush of shame.

"For what?"

"I don't know."

She leaned toward him over her glass, not blinking, nothing in her eyes.

"You don't," she asked, "know why you're sorry?"

His mind went blank. His stomach knotted. He looked down at the bone on his plate, then up at Alice.

"For daydreaming," he said. "At the table. It's impolite."

She sighed, closed her eyes, and shook her head. Her eyes opened, but slowly.

"Talk to me," she pleaded in a whisper. "Tell me what's going on. Let me in."

Jade shrugged and looked away. "I'm just trying to eat in peace. I've had a rough day. I hope it's not too much to ask to just be allowed to relax at the end of a long day?" He forced a taste of applesauce.

The kitchen reverted to the serenity of a morgue. Alice stooped to itch an ankle, and Jade looked back at his now tasteless food.

Carla's gray cat wandered into the kitchen from the new carpet in the other room. Smoky stopped between Alice and Jade, then sat. She looked up expectantly. Jade leaned from the table, and the cat leapt into his lap in a graceful bound.

He checked his watch and scratched Smoky's ear. The numbers flashed 6:22 pm, Friday. He lowered Smoky to the floor, then patted her bottom in the direction of her dish beside the door.

The kids would hang around school after their rehearsals. On a Friday night, they certainly would not come home at 7:00 the way Alice hoped. Mark would likely drop his sister at the front door, then hurry off to some party where he would drink until someone threw up. Tomorrow, he would sleep until noon.

Alice stared blankly at her napkin.

Jade closed his eyes. Twenty-some years ago, as a teenager, he had been far more disciplined than Mark.

He could smell the big lake. It was a quiet, late summer night. The hot dogs were gone, and the last of their driftwood fire was floating in orange embers among the black coals in the fire pit. Friends had paired and retreated to the shadows of the hidden hallows in the dunes.

Beer cans clinked as Jade kicked his way down to the packed sand at the damp ribbon marking the farthest reach of the lake's soft-licking waves.

He had not dated since Karen's death.

Several girls flattered him with come-ons, but he politely brushed them aside. From the edge of the cool black water, he faced the darkness of night, alone.

He removed his sneakers. The beach at the edge of the water felt firm, yet spongy, like the special asphalt on the new track at school. He tossed his shoes back toward the ice boxes. Far to the south, a red lighthouse beacon pulsed steadily, calling boats home to the tranquil slips of Grand Haven's quiet marinas.

He turned north and began to jog.

He jogged along the water's edge for a long time, sometimes fast, sometimes slow. Eventually, he came to a gash in the beach where a small stream cut through the sand to bleed the nearby dunes and inland woods. He stopped.

Beyond the inky waters of the icy stream, an empty shore stretched north, then bowed west and blurred into the ebony abyss of the great lake. Shadows made dark snakes of the ripples in the sand along the stream, and low clouds conspired silently to smother the stars. Jade stood in the rising breeze on the beach, his toes curling lightly into the suddenly cold sand. He could ford the stream, swimming if necessary, and continue his run. Or he could return to his shoes, collect his things and go home.

Jade splashed into the black waters, then resumed his run on the other side.

Alice cleared her throat.

"And this time?" she asked.

"What?"

"I was just wondering where you were this time. Honest to God, Jade, it's getting to the point where even in the kitchen, you're still never home. It's almost easier when you're at work. Or when you're off at some convention or sales meeting. At least when you're not in the room, you're not rubbing my nose in it."

"In what?"

"What do you think?"

"Fine," he sighed. "If you prefer it when I'm gone, then maybe I'll go back to the mall. It's Friday night. Lord knows, I've got plenty to keep me busy there."

"Lord knows."

"And what is that supposed to mean?"

"Whatever."

"Come on, Alice. Don't give me that 'whatever' crap. It's bad enough when I get it from Mark. I sure as hell don't have to take it from you."

Alice glared.

He found himself glaring back.

"No," said Alice. "I guess you don't have to take anything from me. Not when you can shut me out at a moment's notice. Not when you can escape whenever things get tough. In fact, I'll give you a 10-count right now. I'm sure that's more than enough time for you to leave. One . . ."

"Alice . . ."

"Two . . ."

"Come on, cut this out . . ." Jade's throat tightened.

"Three . . . Four . . ."

"This is bullshit . . ."

"Five . . ."

"Fine then. It's your own damn fault."

"Six . . . Seven . . ."

"That does it!" Jade stood, pushed his chair, then turned toward the back door.

"We'll talk again," he said, "when you can act more civilized. When Mom calls, tell her to try me at the mall."

"Eight," she whispered.

The door slammed, and he was gone.

CHAPTER 4

"Seinner Family Books. May I help you?"

"Jimmy! It's so good to hear your voice. This is your mother. I'm calling from Texas."

"Mom!" Jade set aside a publisher's spring catalog. "How are you? What in the world are you doing down in Texas?"

"One thing at a time, please James." She laughed. "It's been a while since we've talked. Alice said that you were working late tonight. She sounded a little upset. I hope that you're not having money problems again."

Jade pulled a stool to the counter.

"No, nothing like that. Business is good. Very good. I'm just trying to get in a few extra sales. I'm shooting for a record-breaking March. I've got my eye on a major promotion. Lots more money."

"Alice said that the kids were out tonight. That she was home alone."

"Yes. I guess so."

"On a Friday night? You used to love going out on Friday nights. But now you work. Are you sure that nothing's wrong?"

"Mom. . . ." Jade turned his back to the sales floor. "Is this why you called? To lecture me about how to spend my Friday nights? Because, really, I'm just trying to make sure this promotion goes through."

"Another promotion. In other words," she paused, "another move?"

"Well," Jade lowered his chin, "I guess so."

"Where to this time?"

"Portland. Oregon."

"I know where Portland is. What does Alice think? What about the kids and their friends?"

"There's a Portland in Maine, too, you know." Jade snapped the phone cord, annoyed.

"Of course there's a Portland in Maine. But you don't do east. You always move west, Jimmy. You've had your eyes on sunsets ever since you were a little boy."

"Grand Rapids was east of Grand Haven." He snapped the cord again. "And Lansing was east of Grand Rapids. What are you talking about, that I don't do east? And the name is Jade, not James, not Jimmy. Nobody calls me James or Jimmy any more."

"Jimmy, James, Jim, Jade, whatever you want to call yourself, it's all the same."

"What's the same?"

"You. Your life."

"What is that supposed to mean?"

There was a long pause.

"Jimmy. I didn't call to talk about your moves. Or, for that matter, to fight."

"Sorry, Mom." Jade slowly swiveled back toward the sales floor. He shifted the phone to his left ear and slid a wrist beneath his left elbow. He glanced at the empty aisles, then down to the next catalog on his stack.

"I'm in Texas," she sighed, "because of your father."

"And?"

"He's dead."

Jade sucked his lips, wet them, then shifted the phone back to his right ear.

"How?"

"Suicide. A shotgun. A real mess."

Jade reached down with his left thumb and began flipping through the pages of the catalog, waiting for something to catch his eye.

"I see. How did you become involved, Mom? How did they know to call you?"

"Your father left a letter. A short one. And a few other things.

The note said where I lived and that I should be the one to tell his sons. He didn't leave any money or anything. In fact, I had to sell his car to reimburse myself for your father's expenses. Almost a thousand dollars. The rest of his stuff went to Goodwill."

"Expenses? What kind of expenses?"

"His cremation. He requested a cremation. His rent and utilities were already paid, thank goodness, through the end of March."

The catalog blurred. Cremation.

Like son, like father.

"I put the cremation on my credit card over the phone. They called right after he did it. They wouldn't cremate him without money up front. But I couldn't get down here right away because I was in the middle of planning a trip with Gretta to Florida. I'll be leaving here, from Houston, in the morning. Gretta and I are flying to Florida. I know that I've never been one to go anywhere, and now all of a sudden I'm visiting Texas and Florida in the same month. It's amazing. Gretta's sister has a time-share condo on Marco Island, and we're going down to check it out for two weeks."

"I'm sure you'll have a good time."

"I hope so."

Jade pushed the catalog aside and leaned into the counter.

"I thought that dad remarried?"

"Two or three times, from what the landlord says. I guess the man talked with Harry once a couple of weeks ago."

"So why you? Why did you have to be the one to straighten out his affairs? Where were the other wives?"

"There really wasn't that much to straighten out, Jimmy. I make it sound worse than it was. Your father's note even said where to sell the car."

"And the other wives?"

"Who knows. I think one was from New York. One was from Los Angeles. But there weren't any addresses or anything. And his note said not to bother calling them. He never had kids with any of the others."

"Why did he do it?" Jade closed his eyes. "Did his note say anything about that?"

"Cancer, I guess. Prostrate, and something else. The note said that he was in a lot of pain and that he was ready to end it. It didn't sound bitter or anything."

Jade rubbed his temples.

"So I guess you didn't attend his funeral?"

"No, that was a few days ago, before I arrived. And there really wasn't much of a service anyway. Just a few words at the chapel. Then they set his ashes aside for me to pick up. I guess he hadn't been in Houston long enough to make many friends."

Jade looked up as a young man in blue jeans approached the counter. "Mom, why did you wait this long to call?"

"I wanted to see if there were any problems down here, you know, before I bothered you. After all these years, I knew that another couple of days wouldn't make much difference."

"And, well, were there? Any problems, I mean?" Jade held up an index finger at the young man, gesturing for a minute of patience.

"Just the ashes," she said. "I don't know what to do with Harry's ashes. I sure don't want to drag them to Florida with me. You know how Harry's mom and brothers felt about him, and Ben won't touch them, either. Ben said that he'd throw them away if I sent them there. So I thought that I would send them to you."

"To me?"

"I'm sure that you'll think of something. I'll also include a few papers and a couple of other things. Documents that I'm not sure if I should throw away or not."

"You're sending Dad's ashes to me?" Jade again held his finger in the direction of the young man, who stood looking at his watch. "Is that even legal, to send something like that in the mail?"

"Hmm. I don't know. I'm not sure if it's legal or not. Tell you what I'll do. I'll disguise them. I'll pack the ashes in something inconspicuous and nobody will ever guess."

"But Mom. . . ."

"Listen, Jimmy. I've got to go. This call is probably costing a fortune. I'll mail the package on my way to the airport in the morning. You should get it in a couple of days. In the meantime, don't work too hard."

The young man turned to leave.

"But Mom, what am I supposed to. . . ."

"Good-bye, Jimmy. I know you'll think of something." She hung up.

Jade held his temples and shook his head.

Harry's ashes? What would he do with them? He raised his eyes as the young man disappeared into the mall.

CHAPTER 5

Summer, 1966. Grand Haven, Michigan

Clouds had drooped in soggy grays since Thursday. Jimmy watched the billows rise from the great lake like muddy cotton candy until they filled the sky and rolled inland to settle over the beaches, orchards and cornfields of western Michigan.

It was a bad weekend to catch a tan.

Jimmy Vanderspyke knew all about tans. From behind the cash register, his mother complained all summer about not having one. And from May to September, his dad eagerly bobbed his nose at every woman who did.

Ladies in snug swim suits and loose plastic thongs would flap into the Vanderspyke Gift, Snack & Pop Shop from the beach two blocks away. They would peel their clothes and proudly present their dark bodies in a parade of lip-smacking caramels, chocolates and bonbons, then make odd selections from the silk-screened shirts and trinkets that cluttered the shop's aisles and walls.

Jimmy's dad displayed an unusual amount of patience with these customers. He would nudge Ben, his oldest, and wink and nod at Randy and Jimmy whenever one of the tanned ladies appeared, even naming the foods each brought to mind as he studied them from behind his elbow-worn counter. Harry often struck up conversations and offered assistance, even when his assistance was unrequired.

Saturdays brought the shop's busiest times. Teenagers and tourists flocked by the thousands to Grand Haven, where they spent hours diving through waist-deep waves, tossing frisbees and stretching beneath the sun. As night settled, many unfolded towels onto the waterfront bleachers and snuggled beneath blankets to listen to the music and watch the dancing lights and pumping geysers of the world's largest musical fountains. Rows of enormous sprinklers and high-pressure hoses sprayed soaring jets of water through brilliant beams of colored lights. Each movement was synchronized to the music and narration of the evening's theme.

This weekend, though, people were avoiding the lake. A few carloads of visitors pulled into the shop's parking lot to kick gravel and wait for the lowering of the drawbridge across the channel to Ferrysburg as tall-masted sailboats left the marina, but otherwise, it was a good time to catch up on chores.

Harry scratched his elbow and surveyed the deck. Jimmy watched his dad, waiting for the bad news.

"Wait here." Harry pointed to a board on the deck. Harry sometimes looked heavier than he was, especially on holidays when mingling with the thin Dutchmen of his clan. Still, even cousins in drab dresses whispered that he was much better looking than most.

He returned with a butter knife from inside.

"See this, Jimmy?" Harry stooped with the knife and poked at a black spot on one of the deck slats. "It's ugly. Look at it."

He swung his hand in a wide fan of the deck. "Folks see these bubble gum smears all around our place and then they lose their appetites. They go up the boardwalk to the Dairy Queen, where they don't have to look at this kind of filth."

Harry straightened.

"Have at it." He handed Jimmy the knife.

"Huh?"

Harry frowned.

"Here," he said. He took the knife back. "Watch."

Harry lowered himself to his hands and knees. He slipped the blade under a bubble gum and pried firmly, quickly working the wad free.

"See. That's it. Now you try."

"Ah, dad, I hate working on my hands and knees."

"That's okay, Jimmy." Harry stood and passed the knife. "That's good. Hating this kind of work is perfectly normal. I'm glad you don't like crawling around on the ground. I would have been worried if you said that you did."

Harry was always reassuring Jimmy about how normal he was, which only added to Jimmy's concern that maybe he wasn't.

He reluctantly dropped to all fours. He zeroed in on the first wad that looked easy. Mr. Vanderspyke watched, nodding encouragement and offering suggestions until the sun peaked out and a young woman with a poodle approached the deck in tight shorts.

"You're doing good," whispered Harry. "Keep it up. I'll be back to check on you in a little while. We've finally got a customer, and I don't want to lose her."

Jimmy was half through with his fifth wad when a station wagon pulled into the lot. Five doors opened. Two women spilled out with a small tribe of boys.

The boys were decked in the regalia of a birthday celebration, complete with headbands, feathers, and the kind of paper noise-makers that rolled out like a snake's tongue when given the right sort of blow.

From his hands and knees, Jimmy watched, poking his head around the corner and prying half-heartedly at the gum.

He didn't have many friends. It was hard to have friends, having to work and hang around the store all day. He wasn't sure if he wanted friends anyway, at least not ones like these. The boys were growing wilder by the minute, jumping on the picnic tables, yelling and charging in and out of the shop's front door as if they owned the place.

Two of the boys discovered the crab apple tree at the far end of the deck. They pulled themselves up several limbs and found branches to sit on. Almost immediately, they were picking and throwing fruit as fast as they could.

Jimmy grew more indignant with each volley.

The two boys were making a mess. Gum wads were bad enough; now he would have to start scraping smashed apples as well. He should tell them to stop it. He had seen his dad tell kids how to behave a hundred times.

Jimmy started to lift himself from his knees.

Suddenly, the birthday chief crashed in from around the corner. He tumbled over Jimmy in a tangle of arms and legs.

Jimmy struggled back to his knees. The stranger was bigger than him. Much bigger. Their eyes locked. The boy squinted, then smirked. Jimmy hesitated, then cleared his throat. "Listen, kid," he said, "you should watch where you're going. You could have. . . ."

The boy jumped to his feet. "You should watch where you're farting, fat boy."

"What? I wasn't. . . ."

"Watch where you're farting, fat boy!"

"I wasn't farting. I was. . . ."

The boy laughed. "Hey guys!" He brushed back his headdress. "Look over here. Looks like I found us the fat-boy cleaning lady."

They bounded in from all directions, shoving and elbowing until Jimmy was trapped within a suffocating ring of jokes, laughter and knees.

Jimmy bit his tongue. Fire burned in his cheeks. He started to rise. Someone kicked him lightly on the butt. Then someone else. "Leave me. . . ."

Then another kick, this time really hard. Jimmy coughed in pain.

"What's a matter, fat boy, cat got yer tongue?"

"He's got his own tongue, any idiot can see that. He must be the cat."

"Yeah, a pussy."

"Here pussy. Here pussy, pussy, pussy."

Jimmy seldom heard that word. Cats were called cats in Grand Haven, and the word pussy, when said like that, meant something else. Something dirty.

"I guess," said another, "that's why he's crawling around on the ground. He's just a big old pussy looking for something to eat."

"Here pussy, pussy. Here pussy. . . ."

Jimmy hung his head.

"Is this yer piece of junk?" demanded the chief.

He was walking toward Jimmy's small red bicycle, which stood balanced on a single training wheel near the customer's drinking fountain a few feet away. Jimmy rode his bike every chance he could. All summer, he begged his dad for a real kickstand. Money was too tight, he was told. The left training wheel was all the kickstand he would need until Christmas.

"Hold it. . . ." said Jimmy, trying to catch his breath and stand. "Leave that bike alone."

"So it is your bike!" The boy laughed.

One of the boys put a hand on Jimmy's rising shoulder and shoved him back down on the deck.

"You know," said the chief. "This kid really is a pussy. Look at his bike. It's still got training wheels."

They all laughed.

"Yeah, but I only see one training wheel. He must be only half a pussy."

Jimmy started to rise again, but again was knocked to his hands and knees. He closed his eyes and shook his head.

When his eyes opened, their voices were very far away, and he was shrinking small, like an ant. Soon, he would be tiny as an ant, small enough to crawl between the boards of the deck and disappear forever.

All he could see was legs. Legs in cuffed shorts. Legs above fancy shoes with new laces free of repair knots and frayed ends. He tried to speak, but couldn't.

The shoes stepped closer. With the shoes, came knees. Hard knees. Knees that bumped his hips and sides.

"Listen fat boy."

It was the chief again, yanking Jimmy back from his shrinking escape. "If you ain't a pussy, what are you?"

He couldn't answer.

"Maybe," laughed one of the others, "he's a ground hog. He's on the ground, and he sure as heck looks like a hog to me."

They laughed harder.

"A pig or a hog?"

"Same thing, ain't it?"

"He's a hog-boy."

They laughed again.

"Naw, he's no hog. They've got him tied back here because he's a horse. A dwarf pony. They just keep him around to give customers rides."

"Is that right, fat boy? You here to give us a ride?"

"I'll ride him first."

"No, me."

"Me!"

And then they were on him. All of them joking, piling on at once. Jimmy's arms and legs collapsed and his cheek jammed against the half-pried gum.

He couldn't breathe. Elbows and knees pinched his soft flesh into the deck. There wasn't enough air to sob, though tears squeezed through his clenched eyes and across the wet dust on his face. Something was in his nose and throat. Maybe blood. Jimmy started to choke.

Then a foot slipped from the back of his right hand, and he realized that at the end of his pinned arm, he still held the hard steel handle of the butter knife.

Somehow, he managed to turn his wrist.

He raised the blade perpendicular to his arm, the butt of the knife planted solidly against the deck.

Moments later, the knife twisted and there was a scream. Rising above the ensuing chaos of scattering boys came the shrieks of two panicked mothers. Above their voices came the thunder of Jimmy's dad.

"What the hell is going on here?" he shouted. "What the hell is going on?"

Jimmy had never heard his father swear in front of any woman other than his mother, who suddenly appeared behind Harry with a look of frightened concern. Jimmy began shaking, sucking ir-regular gulps of air, the knife still clutched in his trembling hand.

Then another voice cut through the tumult. It was the voice of the little chief.

"That boy jumped us," he said.

"What?" The tone of Harry's bark silenced the din. "What happened?"

"That maniac jumped us."

For the second time in 10 minutes, the birthday chief pointed at Jimmy like he was some kind of animal. "We were just playing and all of a sudden he came charging at us with his knife."

Harry shook his head. "Jimmy," he demanded. "Is that true? Look at me. What happened?"

Jimmy tried to meet his father's eyes, tried to say what happened. Then he felt himself again fenced in by legs. Cuffed shorts, fancy shoes, new laces. Moving toward him, ready to fall upon his back. Sobs rattled in his chest and shook his throat and limbs. The knife slipped from his fingers as he buried his face in shuddering hands. There was no place to hide.

"We should press charges," snapped the lady in the pink dress.

"Boys," called the other. "Get in the car. Kevin, stay right there. I'll get some paper towels and we'll wrap your leg and see if we can find a doctor."

As if ordered, Jimmy's mom disappeared in the direction of the bathroom for the first aid kit and several clean rags.

Harry approached the woman in the pink dress. "I'm terribly sorry," he said. "Jimmy has never done anything like this before. The boys must have been teasing him or something."

"Save it," she said. "I'm not calling the police. I'm not pressing charges."

"Thank you. This is all very embarrassing."

Harry spun on his son.

"Jimmy, tell this boy that you're sorry. I don't know what happened, but you are to never, I repeat, never, do anything like this again. Now apologize."

Jimmy lifted his face from his hands and looked at the other boy, who was also crying.

"Jimmy! I said to apologize. You tell that boy that you're sorry."

Jimmy looked back at his dad, too weak to stand. He began sobbing again, unable to stop. Harry reached him in four steps. He stooped low and swatted him on the back of the head.

"Apologize!"

He struck him again, harder.

"Stop whimpering," he said, "and you stand up like a man."

Harry frightened Jimmy more than the legs, more than the other boys, more than anything he knew. He started to rise. His body ached and the bones in his right hand throbbed from where they had been crushed into the deck. With all of his strength, he willed himself up from his knees, his eyes fixed upon his father's frown.

"Well," said Harry. "We're all waiting."

He looked at his dad, and then at the boy, who was still sprawled backwards on the deck. Harry hit Jimmy again. This time, Jimmy felt the swat coming and braced himself. For some reason, instead of hurting, the swat seem to glance off him and hardly sting.

The boy was about Jimmy's age, with tear streaks down his face and a trickle of blood draining from his leg into a tiny dark pool on the deck. The boy looked much smaller from this angle.

Jimmy suddenly realized that it would be his job to hose off the boy's blood. He looked back at his dad, expecting another blow, yet turning his face to take the shot. Harry's hand stopped mid air, then dropped to his side. A peculiar smile flashed across Jimmy's face, and he unexpectedly found his voice with ease.

"I'm sorry," he said turning back to the boy, "that I hurt you so bad." The boy winced. "I promise," Jimmy continued, "that I'll never hurt you again. Even if I run into you someplace and remember who you are."

The boy's mother shook her head in disgust.

"Pathetic," she said. "This whole thing makes me nauseous. If my boy was retarded, I'd keep him locked up where he couldn't hurt anyone. You should be ashamed of yourselves, all of you."

Harry trembled.

"I'm terribly sorry," he said. "Really. My boy is a strange one. But he's never hurt anyone before."

"Then you've been lucky." The woman softened, apparently drawing solace from Harry's sincerity. "From now on, you'll have to be more careful."

"Yes," said Harry, shifting his posture and nodding back. "I'll have to watch him more closely. I'll definitely keep a better eye on him from now on. In the past, though, he's always been harmless. Really."

Jimmy stared at his father. He couldn't believe it, Harry was agreeing with her, practically telling this woman that she was right, that he was retarded or something.

"It must be awful," said the women, ignoring Jimmy altogether. "I can't imagine the burden of having a child like this."

"Yes. It's a burden all right. But what's a father to do?"

Jimmy watched his father's mouth and eyes.

"Still," said the woman, "you do have a responsibility to protect the public."

"You're right, of course. But as I said, the boy has never done anything like this before. Now. . . . Well, I don't know what we're going to have to do."

The woman turned to her son and inspected his injury. It appeared to be less serious than first imagined.

From behind her, Jimmy saw his father's eyes plucking hungrily at the back of her thin dress.

The lady stood and turned back to Harry. "Have you considered hospitalization? I understand that mental institutions are sometimes for the best."

"Yes," said Harry, meeting her eyes, "we've talked about it. But such places can be very expensive. . . ."

Harry pulled the rags and first aid kit from Jimmy's mom, who had just returned, and carried them over to the woman in the thin pink dress. He passed them over without looking back. "Here, maybe these will help."

"Thank you," she said, smiling faintly.

Harry turned to his wife. "Honey, would you mind running back into the store and getting a sucker or something for this boy? He's been through a lot and he's being awfully brave."

Mrs. Vanderspyke gave her husband a long, disgusted look, then abruptly retreated without a word.

The lady in the thin dress dabbed at the boy's leg and spoke over her shoulder. "Does that son of yours embarrass you often? I mean, can you even go out with him in public?"

"Oh, sure, we still go out sometimes." Harry's eyes grew greedy as the lady continued to bend and dab. "But we do have to be very careful about the kinds of places we take him." His voice nearly cracked as she bent lower. "For example, church is safe, but most restaurants are out of the question."

Jimmy glanced back at the shop as his mother slammed the screen door. With the sound of that slamming door, a powerful wave of something like anger, yet something unfamiliar, washed through Jimmy's body. He wasn't sure what it was, but it made him feel stronger, as if another blow to his head would be nothing.

"Perhaps," the woman offered, "a State-run institution? I hear that the one in Traverse City has sliding fees for families that qualify."

"You don't say?" Harry leaned for a better view.

"Yes. If you don't make enough money, perhaps the State will help pay to keep him there."

Harry tipped his head.

Jimmy leapt forward.

"Bad lady!" he shouted.

The woman stiffened and spun to face him.

"Bad lady!" Jimmy's finger was aimed at the face of the horrified stranger. "Bad lady!" He shouted it again, this time slurring the words like an idiot. "Yer a bery, bery bad lady!"

The woman turned red. Harry's hand lashed toward Jimmy,

but the blow brushed painlessly aside as Jimmy squirted beyond reach.

"Bad lady!"

"Shut up," barked Harry.

The woman scooped her son from the deck, then cantered toward her car.

Furious, Harry stepped toward Jimmy and loaded his fist for a more serious blow. Again, to Harry's bewilderment, Jimmy dodged, then took off running.

Jimmy found himself chasing the stranger toward her car. Halfway there, he dropped to all fours, then surprised even himself by turning up his chin and howling at the sky.

He glanced over his shoulder. Harry stood frozen in disbelief. Jimmy howled again. This time, the sound came naturally, surging from some hidden place deep within his stomach.

The sound felt good in his throat and cheeks. It even tasted good on his tongue. He tried it again. "Yaooowwwwl!"

The woman jumped into her car and spun stones without looking back. Jimmy closed his eyes.

After a moment, he rose to his feet, grinning. His shocked father stood too dumbfounded to yet unleash. Jimmy's grin widened against his will.

"What was that?" Harry stuttered at last. He took a hesitant step in Jimmy's direction. "What in God's green earth was that all about? What were you thinking?"

Jimmy shrugged. "I don't know." He looked back and forth between Harry, the wet blood stain, and the spot where the woman had bent so low.

"I don't know why I did it." Jimmy snorted, darting off to fetch the hose. "Maybe I'm just retarded."

Harry's beating would have to wait.

CHAPTER 6

Saturday, March 16, 1996.
Dakota Ridge, Colorado

Small patches of soot-caked snow clung to the dark lees of schist outcroppings on the northwest face of the ridge. Otherwise, the hogback was clear, baked dry by the desiccating rays of the Colorado sun.

With each driving thrust of his right leg, Jade sucked a lungful of thin air. With the downward thrust of each stab with his left, he exhaled. He imagined himself as an ironman boxer, pounding and crushing sandy shale in unrelenting jabs delivered through his legs and feet.

He tightened his grip on the mountain bike's handlebars, then quickened the punishing tempo of his right and left leg combination. The rock-strewn trail took his abuse. Jade smiled as the next familiar pitch beckoned him for more.

His bookstore stocked a locally-published guide to the hogbacks. When business was slow, Jade often stood in the Regional Interest aisle, thumbing through the guide's detailed maps and illustrations, imagining himself attacking each bend in the trail.

The front range hogbacks served as a transition zone between the High Plains and the foothills. The plants and animals found along the trail traversing its spine included everything from short stands of cactuses and low rugs of lichen to rattlesnakes, rabbits, coyotes, and an occasional mountain lion. Juniper, mountain mahogany, sumac, and Gambel's oaks provided cover for the small prey that drew the birds that earned the region its reputation as a major raptor flyway.

In most parts of the country, the ridge's dramatic formations and the dinosaur fossils embedded along its face would have drawn stampeding crowds of gaping visitors. But in a state littered with dinosaur remains and in a location overshadowed by 14,000-foot snowcapped peaks, the hogbacks were largely ignored, even by the residents of the developments that encroached several places into the ridge's base.

Which suited Jade fine. On a crisp morning, he could look up from his driveway six miles to the east and trace every major feature of the Dakota Ridge trail—where it surged, where it dropped, and how it ebbed along the hogback's jagged crest. And three days out of four, he could ride the hogback trail alone.

If he moved to Portland, he would miss the hogbacks.

Jade landed with a double bounce. The trail leveled and was clear for 30 feet.

He glanced at his watch.

11:03 am. Perfect. He'd make the final summit by 11:30, then be home and showered by 1:45. He would arrive at the mall to relieve Chris by 2:00 pm as scheduled.

Ahead, an unfamiliar chunk of siltstone lay in the fine white sand beneath a stunted ponderosa pine. It must have dislodged during the recent thaw and run-off.

Jade tapped his brake and popped his front end as his wheel collided and bounced over the football-sized rock.

A bluejay flashed above from the shadows of the ponderosa, then disappeared into a clump of junipers 40 feet away.

Below him, beyond a few hills to his right, Denver and the plains rolled flat and brown like an endless sea. To his left, the ridge dropped several hundred feet to an asphalt road and the quiet intersection at the north entrance to the Red Rocks Amphitheater and park. Above the sandstone monoliths of Red Rocks Park rose Mt. Morrison, and beyond Mt. Morrison loomed the white peaks of the Continental Divide.

Sweat streaked from Jade's helmet. It stung his eyes in salty trickles that drained into his grinning lips.

He dropped a hand to the sloshing water bottle clamped to the bike's frame. Three quarters full. Still cold. Good.

Time for a break.

He could see the horse-head slog just ahead, 20 yards past the next cluster of sumac. He would stop between its ears.

Jade had named the mini peak 'horse-head slog' because of its appearance through his binoculars from his back yard. Thick juniper clung like a horse's mane to the east side of the unusually long and straight incline. The trail flattened briefly between two enormous ear-like rocks at the summit, then dropped quickly down a steep shale grade that was as hard and smooth as the forehead of a mule. At its base, the descent broadened into a wide hollow trough of thick vegetation, as if the mule was submerging its mouth into a gigantic black bucket.

He would have named it mule-head slog, but he didn't care for the connotations.

Jade crowned a short grade, passed the sumac, hopped a shallow wash, then peddled furiously up the approach to the steep pitch of the horse's neck.

The horse's neck was always rough, but early spring run-off had compounded the challenge of the steep climb by eroding an erratic eight-inch rut that was nearly impossible to get a line on. The staircase of gravel and sandstone ledges that began half way up the grade was so water-torn and rock-littered that he was forced to abandon his saddle and revert to granny gear to negotiate the chaos of the ascent.

Jade's firm hold on his bar became a death grip. His jaw and neck tensed, and his breathing became forced and irregular as the tension extended into his chest.

His bike lurched wildly as a large stone squirted from between his rear tire and a half-buried slab of shale. The bumpy gulch of the trail narrowed, forcing him to bounce and careen over jutting rocks that stressed his suspension fork and body into a grueling slow-motion ballet of spine-grinding grace.

He felt the tautness of his quads and glutes spreading to pings of cramps in his hamstrings and calves.

He could dismount and easily walk it up the last 50 feet. No one would know. The strain on his body and the pressure on his legs was becoming excruciating. He could stop.

No way. Full out, no regrets.

Every muscle in his upper body tightened as he yanked on his bar and brutally rammed his feet through each cycle of each groundward stroke. His chain and derailleurs strained and the laws of physics stretched as he hoisted his body and bike upward through castigating stabs of his weight downward through his pedals.

His eyes darted over the trail in front of his fork rake like a mine sweeper whose life depended upon his detection of each charge.

He glanced to the side. The ridge had become a spiny highwire near its peak; the banks to his right and left were now precarious palisades dropping half a hundred feet before catching themselves and slopping outward at less deadly angles.

The last 10 feet of the assault were nerve-wracking torture. Maintaining his balance required years of experience and the attention of all of his strength. He began counting his strokes. Another four should do it.

One . . . Two . . . Three. . . .

Jade grinned as he passed between the rocky ears of the summit. He resumed his saddle and shifted gears, then picked up speed.

Change of plans. Too good. He'd take his water break at the bottom of the horse's snout.

He plunged downward from the ears, the trail's slick shale surface shimmering more like a alpine slide than a bike path. The slope looked familiar from a hundred wild and successful rides.

Familiar from yesterday at work. From the fat lady's monologue.

Jade's stomach lurched.

He licked his lips and shifted another gear. Reflections and sensations quickly vanished in a flood of adrenaline induced by the immediacy of his surging momentum.

Committed, he finessed his front and rear brakes along the insane pitch, grinning as the knobs of his tires skidded and clung tenaciously to rock. He eased his brakes and picked up more speed. His drenched face and sweat-soaked spandex burned in the cold whip of the rushing air.

Jade hit the gravel at the foot of the slide with raw cheeks and a tight-lipped smile.

He jammed his brakes, dropped a leg, and spun his back wheel in a half pipe that sent small stones and dust shooting in a bowed spray that took several seconds to settle.

He wiped his lips.

"Not bad," he muttered.

He checked his watch. Yes, time for a break.

The sweeping vista from the base of the slide was spectacular. Jade glanced around, swung his leg from the bike, then walked it a short distance from the trail. Carefully, he leaned the bike against a crumbling obelisk of red and gray shale near the western face. He unzipped his fanny pack and removed a white rag and a small plastic case of tools. He knelt and began his inspection and clean up.

The tires were fine, but the tension of several spokes required a quarter-turn of fine tuning. The brake pads still showed plenty of groove. He straddled his front wheel and gently pushed and pulled on the bike's headset and cables. Pretty tight. He loosened his stem binder bolts and adjusted the screw atop the stem anyway, just to make sure there was no extra play.

He completed his inspection, unclamped his water bottle and stood up.

The first cool squirt from the bottle disappeared into Jade's rag. Within moments, the damp cloth was flowing over the bike's frame and saddle with the firm tenderness of a lover's experienced hand.

The bike had cost nearly a thousand dollars, and the shop only allowed three hundred bucks on his trade-in. But on a day like this, the bike seemed worth every penny. Besides, he had a full year over which to stretch the payments.

He finished and backed away to inspect his work. She looked good. It would be a pleasure to remount.

He carefully repacked his wrenches, then looked for a perch with a view. Ten steps later, he plopped himself on the shallow ledge above a sheer cliff.

Far below his swinging shoes, past the talus at the base of the cliff, the hogback sloped gradually for several hundred feet, then flattened at the bottom of the valley near the banks of Mount Vernon Creek. Horses grazed among the budding willows, cottonwoods, and wild plums along the stream. Beyond the creek, Mt. Morrison showed its first signs of green.

Jade sighed.

A quiet breeze whispered through the nearby crags and trees. He took several deep breaths, filling his senses with the thin chafed fragrance of juniper and sun-dried sandstone.

God's country. Finally, he lifted the plastic bottle to his lips for his first drink. Moments later, his second.

The water was good.

He loosened his chin strap and carefully raised his helmet from his caked hair. He looked at it, then grinned. The helmet showed hard use, scuffs in the design and inside stains from rain and sweat. He flexed his fingers against the helmet's texture and strength.

As hard as the helmet was, when nestled behind his head, it made a good pillow. Jade rubbed his neck and chin, wiped his face, then leaned back, the helmet pressed to the base of his neck.

High over head, a eagle circled in serene spirals and an airliner scratched its stark signature across the blue-slate sky. Jade checked his watch, then closed his eyes.

Time to relax for a few minutes.

Chris would not be expecting him before 2:00.

Chris would be looking for him then, though. She would be

glancing up as he entered the store. As always, Chris would be dressed well. She would smile broadly as he approached her at the cash register. She would look very good in some perky spring ensemble, tempting for sure. A little cleavage perhaps. . . .

Jade squeezed his eyes. Until they hurt. Focus!

Mom had called last night at the store.

Dad was dead. She was sending him his father's ashes. His father's ashes, for crying out loud.

He tried to picture Harry, alone in Houston, sick with cancer. Eager to die. The barrel of a shotgun in his mouth.

Mom said that she had taken care of everything. Except for the ashes. A man's whole life cleaned up during a layover on the way to a Florida condo. Nothing left behind but dust. His few possessions dumped or strewn across a strange town according to the whims of a couple of sorters working part time for Goodwill.

He should have told Alice about Harry's death.

But Alice was asleep, or pretending to be, by the time he finished his paperwork and crawled into bed. She would have been sympathetic if he had told her, despite their recent fight. She would have set aside her hostility and tried to be supportive. She was still a good woman.

Too good. She would have asked all kinds of questions. And she would have pressed him to 'open up' and talk.

Jade was in no hurry to talk about Harry. But the ashes could be trouble. Randy's ashes had been troublesome enough. If an uncle hadn't offered to spread them on Lake Michigan, who knows what would have become of Randy's ashes.

Jade opened his eyes and studied the eagle, whose spirals were drifting south along the ridge.

Maybe his friend Terry would have an idea Wednesday about what to do with Harry's remains. Or maybe Chris would have a suggestion. He would see her in a little while, and he would ask her then. She would find the question intriguing. It would be easy to talk with her. She would understand. Chris would be sympathetic. Her big eyes would look sad. . . .

Jade's stomach tightened. He felt his pulse racing, felt the sucking of the familiar whirlpool, an exciting matrix of swirling dark waters. Felt the physical stirring. Fought it.

Then let go. Was swallowed body and mind.

She would lean toward him and touch his arm with compassion, would want to comfort him. She would be wearing a thin white blouse, an extra button carelessly unhitched. Silver combs tucked above each ear, almost lost back deep within her black hair.

He saw her, behind the register, punching in numbers and ringing up a sale. She turned toward him, winked over her shoulder . . . naked except for black spiked heels. She looked down, smiled, then ran her hands over her tanned stomach. She cupped her hands beneath her breasts and closed her eyes, then gently squeezed. A moment later, her lashes flickered open, and she smiled.

Hey, Jim, she whispered. Jade felt himself blush upon his helmet. Do you like what you see? She squeezed again. Would you like in on this? I think there's enough to go around, don't you?

Jade bolted upright.

"No," he whispered. He sank a molar into the back edge of his tongue. "It isn't fair to Alice. Or to the kids. It isn't right."

He squirted a mouthful of water.

It was sinful. He had to stop thinking of her that way. Just last Sunday in church, the sermon. . . .

He felt his body wilting away from the fantasy.

Jade squished the water over his bleeding tongue and shot another six ounces into his face and hair.

Below him, the valley was serene, beautiful. He wiped his face with his sleeve. Views from this ridge once filled him with peace, with a sense of awe, even of God's presence. Now, it felt like the hogback was becoming just one more place to bleed. The whirlpool followed him wherever he went, even up here.

And he liked it. Despised it and lived for it at the same time. It was exciting, fast, dark, forbidden and wild. The struggle quickened his heart, challenged his thoughts, made him feel strangely potent and alive. Powerful.

And dirty.

His thoughts of Chris made him feel filthy. Like a pig. He did not enjoy thinking of himself as a pig.

What was wrong with him?

Was he some kind of pervert, or what? Did he enjoy making himself suffer? In the back room at the store, he skimmed dozens of books about sexual obsessions, shame and guilt, but none of them helped. The whirlpool could not be contained. It rose from inside of his stomach with a life and logic of its own, and he sensed that it drilled deep into his past, deep into who he was.

He closed his eyes.

The whirlpool was again churning inside, tugging his mind toward Chris. Like the Cheshire cat, Chris' smile, face and body were taking form, her naked. . . .

"Please, God," he whispered. "Help me. Lead me not into temptation." He opened his eyes, took another swallow from his bottle, then started to rise.

The sharp crack of smashing glass jolted Jade to his feet. The sound came from over the rim of the cliff.

Again. Directly beneath him. It sounded like an anchor dropped into a barrel of crystal.

No one brought glass to the hogback. Too heavy, too dangerous. A violation of the code of the trail. Again, a deep shattering crunch. Jade looked around.

A few yards away, a faint trail disappeared into dense scrub growth near the cliff's edge. He glanced at his bike, then back at Mount Vernon Creek several hundred feet below. The drop-off was abrupt, save for a narrow ledge of juniper 25 feet down the face. Jade made his way to the small trail and ducked into the brush.

The trail wound along the lip of the ridge, snaking through thick tangles of juniper and occasionally out onto the loose rocks at the top of the cliff. Fifty paces in, where the hogback again sloped upward, the trail abruptly sawed back south in the direction of his perch, then dropped steeply down the cliff's weathered face.

Jade looked back through the brush. He could no longer see his bike. He placed a tentative foot on the trail, stepped over the brink of the cliff, then began his descent.

As long as he kept his eyes fixed on the trail's inside corner, between the cliff and the path, he found the route less difficult to manage than he expected. The trail was as wide as his hips and often wider, and although it was steep, for the most part it was no more difficult to navigate than the main trail that ran along the ridge. He glanced up. The trail had wormed itself beneath rock; it now clung to the cliff hidden within a recessed bow. He had taken his water break perched on a thick overhang.

The trail disappeared into the same huddle of dark trees that he had spotted from above.

He was almost at the ledge when he again heard the sound of breaking glass.

He held his breath. Jade pressed his left hand to the sandstone cliff and inched his way downward toward the trees. Ten feet from the ledge, the cliff curved slightly outward. He reached the outcropping and slowly moved his head around to the other side.

Jade found himself staring past the edge of the cliff into a shallow, gallery-like cave. A man stood inside the shadowed chamber, facing the back wall. In his hands, raised in outstretched arms, was a rock.

CHAPTER 7

The man did not throw the rock. He merely dropped it, exploding into a thousand pieces what appeared to have been a liquor bottle.

Jade squinted into the dim cave. The rock and the crushed glass lay within a bird-bath indentation on the cave's floor. The man stooped, picked up a dry juniper branch, then began sweeping into the basin the few bottle fragments scattered beyond the basin's rim.

The man waddled in a slow orbit, whisking the broken glass with surprising effectiveness. He was a short black man, overweight, and perhaps 45.

From the other side of the basin, the man glanced up, saw Jade and jumped.

It was a remarkable leap for a man of such diminutive stature and expansive hips. He hit his head on the cave's back ceiling.

"Holy shit," he sputtered. "Where the hell did you come from?!"

Jade stepped from beside the junipers into the fragmented shadows of the chamber walls.

"I came from the top of the ridge." He jerked his head somewhat hesitantly toward the trail outside. "Sorry for the scare. I didn't mean to sneak up on you. It's just that when I heard the sound of breaking glass, I thought maybe some teenagers were screwing around."

"Teenager, I wish," the black man grinned as he rubbed his head. "Screwing, I double wish." He narrowed his eyes and peered at Jade's silhouette among the trees that hid the chamber's entrance. "Okay, now that I'm breathing again, show me what you brought."

"What I brought?"

"Yes, your sacrifice. For the cairn." The man's gaze drifted down to Jade's feet. "Good grief," he said, pointing at Jade's shoes. "You should know better, pilgrim. Please, remove those synthetic abominations immediately. You're standing on holy ground."

Jade looked at his feet, then at the stranger's. "You're wearing shoes," he challenged.

"Look again. Leather moccasins. There's a world of difference."

"I don't see much difference. Besides, I'd cut my feet on all of your broken glass." In addition to his moccasins, the man wore a headband, a sleeveless sweatshirt, and an old pair of khaki shorts.

"First time here, eh?"

"Yes."

"So then you didn't bring any sacrifices for the altar?"

"What altar? Who are you, anyway?"

"I'm the self-appointed Keeper of the Cairn."

"Uh huh." Jade surveyed the shallow cave. In the far corner was a large mound of crushed plastic, metal, ash, and glass. Near the black man's feet, two empty pint flasks lay on their sides, still intact. Nothing else. Certainly no mound of cairn stones.

"Are you safe?" asked Jade. "Or should I get out of here right now while I can?"

"Safe? That depends." The man hiked his knuckles to his hips with a grin and squared himself over the basin. "What do you mean by safe, stranger? When you get down to it, safe is, at best, only a transitory illusion. A car wreck, cancer, lightning bolts, rock slides, frayed elevator cables, chickens with rabies. . . ."

Jade laughed. The man continued.

"But, more to your point, if you've wandered in here from the cush suburbs to flaunt your fancy spandex and to prove your manhood against this innocent rock," he patted the cave's wall, "then you're probably the enemy. In which case . . . I might have to kill you." The cairn-keeper smiled. "'Fess up, and I'll tell you if and where you should go."

Jade grinned and stroked his neck. "Well, I gotta admit that I like the feel of my spandex. And I love the challenge of the hog-back. And, as you guessed, I live in the suburbs." He opened his hands and shrugged. "But otherwise, I'm pretty much a regular guy. I mow my own lawn, shave my own chin, and go to church most of the time. All that I do for a living is sell books in a couple of Denver stores. Great prices, by the way. We're having a sale next week. Perhaps I can help you find a special title?"

The man laughed. It was an honest, straight-from-the-belly laugh. A laugh Jade sensed he could trust.

"May I," asked Jade, "be so bold as to inquire what you do when you're not keeping the cairn? By the way, where is the cairn? All I see is a little pit and a pile of trash."

"Looks can be deceiving, my friend. The cairn is here, but you must use your imagination. As you know, things are not always as they seem."

"That trash is the cairn?"

"Bingo."

Jade crossed the broad-but-shallow chamber in 12 steps. Television components, records, tapes, videos, radios, a camcorder, the charred remains of several adult books and magazines, even a toaster oven, it was all there, mangled, pulverized, and stirred together in one grotesque heap. Jade looked back at his host.

"No," sighed Jade. "I've got nothing to sacrifice today. How about you? What did you bring to the cairn? Your empty liquor bottles?"

"Yes, as a matter of fact. Mine and a couple of extras I found in the ditch when I parked my car. But that's between me and my God. It's not your job to judge. God lets me do what I need when I come here. I expect the same mercy from you. Even if this is your first visit to the cave."

"You say that as if you think that I'll be back."

The man studied him for a moment.

"I know you will," he said at last.

"Uh huh. Both a cairn-keeper and a prophet. And again, what do you do for a living?"

"Why is it that we always ask such a question? Wouldn't it be more telling if we asked our strangers what they wished they were doing for a living? As for me, I teach humanities at Foothills Community College."

Jade shook his head and grinned.

"As I said," the man chuckled, "looks can be deceiving."

"And," asked Jade, "by what name does the Keeper of the Cairn preferred to be hailed? Since you seem to believe that I'll be seeing you again, I might as well know what to call you."

"Hosea. You may call me Hosey Moses for short, if you're so inclined. Some pilgrims do. It's up to you."

Jade smiled. "Is Hosea your real name?"

"Does it matter?"

"I'm not sure. You tell me."

Hosea looked at Jade thoughtfully. "No, Hosea is not my legal name. It's my cairn name. Several of us have taken on cairn names. You will probably eventually have one yourself."

"Is this place a religious cult site, or what?"

Hosea laughed again, deeply.

"Goodness no," he smiled at last. "Some of us have never even met. Organized, we are not. Once in a while, we do accidentally bump into each other, and a few of us occasionally rendezvous. Especially when someone is going through a hard time and needs support. And, as might be expected, we occasionally leave notes. But for the most part, this is a fraternity of anonymous, anti-establishment social misfits."

Hosea stepped toward Jade, then stopped.

"We each were led to this cave by a different path, and we each offer our unique libations for reasons sometimes clear only to ourselves. All that unites us in this chamber is our sense of guilt, this crushing stone," Hosea nodded at the rock resting on his broken bottle, "and our shared thirst for personal repentance and divine mercy."

Jade laughed. "Oh, well, if that's all, then count me in. It sounds easy."

His eyes finished adjusting to the cave. Hosea's complexion remained as black as when Jade first spotted him as a rock-wielding phantom among the shadows.

"Why," asked Jade, "did you pick the name Hosea?"

"I've always liked the prophet Hosea, from the Bible you know. There was something about his message of suffering, repentance and restoration that I'd always found moving. And then, a year ago, when I found out that my wife was a whore, I couldn't resist completing the identification. Hosea married a prostitute, of course. On purpose."

"So I've read. Her name was Gomer. How about you? What makes you think that your Gomer is a whore?"

Hosea's face grew somber.

"One day," he said, "when I wasn't looking, being caught up in myself as I was, my wife done got herself seduced by a white man with an eight-inch bankroll. Mine was only five. Hell, the joke is on him, though. I know for a fact that every time she strokes that big bankroll of his, she palms herself off another $100 bill."

There was an uncomfortable pause.

Jade reinspected the debris of the sacrifices heaped against the wall. He sensed that these mangled pieces were intimate things, the bewildering heart-felt confessions of men he'd never met.

"You puzzle me," said Jade, at last turning to confront Hosea's gaze. "I can't figure out your point of view. Or your language; it's coming from all over the place."

"That's me," Hosea sighed, "from all over the place. An incarnation of disparate discrepancies. One big walking contradiction. But then, aren't we all?"

"I guess." Jade thought of his lust for Chris and of his troubled love for his wife. He felt his stomach knotting.

"Philosophers and theologians," said Hosea, "speak of self knowledge as the beginning of wisdom. I say that self knowledge is the beginning of depression. Who really wants to examine the hypocrisy and contradictions within one's own head and heart?" He looked at the cave's ceiling, then down to his feet. "I despise my booze, and I curse my fat. Yet I indulge both and remain a slave of each. I judge the man that stole my wife, even as I imagine myself in bed with the daughter of a friend. I condemn consumerism, but I traded up from my old Pinto to a Buick to impress my friends at work."

He lifted his head and met Jade's eyes. "Such inconsistencies can be pretty depressing when faced. Most of us would prefer to talk about a speck of dust in a brother's eye rather than to confront the logs stuck in our own."

The cave fell silent.

Jade cleared his throat. "If self knowledge," he offered, "is the first step toward wisdom, then there's got to be a second step. Maybe once a man faces the depressing garbage inside himself, maybe then he gets humbled. Perhaps getting humbled, finding humility, admitting to ourselves how messed up we are, maybe that's part of the journey toward wisdom."

Hosea smiled. "Exactly. If a person has the courage to take such steps."

Hosea glanced at the altar, then back to Jade's eyes. "Of course, some the messes inside of us make sense. You asked about my inconsistencies in language." He smiled. "My daddy was obsessed with upward mobility. I learned to ride a bicycle on mean streets where there weren't no whites, and then I ended up with a classic education in a private suburban school where there were no blacks. I've spent most of my adult life lost somewhere between the two worlds, raging against middle-class superficiality and pretense, while at the same time feeling repulsed by inner-city brutality and ignorance. I wander as a stranger in strange lands, with two languages and conflicting points of view. With no place called home."

Hosea turned his head and slowly surveyed the cave.

"Sometimes," he continued softly, "this place is the closest thing to home I can get. I drive to this hogback in my suit, park

my Buick, duck behind a bush to change into these rags, climb to
this cave, and finally, I get to stop worrying about what other
people will think. About whether I'm doing it right in the middle
class, whether I'm selling out the brothers, about whether the fa-
cades that I erect are helping or hurting the so-called black cause."

Hosea sank to his knees beside the altar, staring into its depths.

"I smash a few of my empties, I swear at the shards, I shout,
cry, gnash my teeth, and then fall to my knees. 'Dear God,' I pray,
'forgive me. I keep doing the very stuff that makes my life hell.
Show me the way. Help this suffering nigger do what's right.'"

He shook his head. "And then I go home." Hosea's eyes closed
as his voice faded into the shadows.

Jade looked aside. For several minutes, he stared blindly at a
jagged fissure on the wall beside the mound of sacred tailings.

He tried to clear his head—kept picturing Chris, naked, willing and eager.

Hosea was right. Doing the very stuff that we hate. Mentally
stripping and gaping and fondling and penetrating. Over and over,
hating it, but unable to stop. Like a shameless animal. But filled
with shame.

Obsessed.

Was it the same for all of those who came to the cave, those
who came to crush their videos and burn their magazines? What
else lay hidden within the rubble of the cairn? Candy wrappers
and cigarette cartons? Decks of cards? Telescopes? Baseball mitts?
Women's clothing?

An hour ago, he would have smirked at the thought of some
suburbanite smuggling up a pair of silk panties into a cave in the
hogback.

He sighed, felt a strange sadness for them all. For himself.

"What kinds of books do you sell?" asked Hosea.

"You name it." Jade turned. "I run a couple of Denver stores
for a bookstore chain out of the midwest. Seinner Books. We're
located downtown and at Westwood Mall."

"Your stores carry it all, huh?"

"Pretty much."

"Even that pop-culture mind-rotting poop?"

"If you're referring to our best sellers, the answer is, of course we do. That's how we do enough business to stay open. Otherwise we wouldn't be able to offer the good stuff. You know, inspirationals, classics, religious titles and that sort of thing."

"Man, you are the enemy!" laughed Hosea.

"I thought that you said you wouldn't judge?"

Hosea grew quiet.

"Right," he said. "Sorry."

"But," confessed Jade, "you're onto something. I'm wrestling right now with a new line of books that the home office says I've got to carry. Except that the books are all trash and I don't want them in my store. I feel like I'm caught in an ethical dilemma."

"Don't sell the books."

"Wait a minute, you haven't even heard. . . ."

"I've heard enough. Your heart is saying no. That should be all that you need to hear. Nothing punishes so severely as a sin against one's own conscience."

"You said it," sighed Jade. "But still, a promotion could be on the line with this. If I say no to. . . ."

"What does it profit a man to gain a promotion if it costs him his very soul?"

Jade clamped his jaw in anger. Who, he wondered, was this stranger to paraphrase scriptures at him?

"It must be hard," Jade snapped, "to always have to carry the burden of God's inspired word. But, I've got to ask, why is it that your inspired words flow forth so hackneyed and clichéd? My wife can match you quip for quote from her old Ziggy calendar on the family room desk."

Hosea stepped back. "Sorry," he said, looking genuinely pained. "I know I get carried away. You're right, I'm way out of line."

Jade turned toward the cave's entrance. Through the junipers came the rustling movement of air rising along the sun-warmed face of the cliff. He glanced at his watch. There wasn't enough time to complete the trail ride and relieve Chris by 2:00. If he eliminated the Red Rocks Loop and headed south down the hogback the way he had come, he could spare a few minutes more. But why linger? He had barely met this man and they were already arguing.

He turned back to Hosea, who stood patiently waiting.

"My crack about clichés," said Jade, "was uncalled for. You punched a button. Your words started hitting a little too close to home and I lost it. My turn to apologize." He smiled at his own string of clichés.

"What can I say?" Hosea grinned. "I like proverbs, popular quotes and clichés. A sharp old saw is often an effective tool for cutting through the thick skulls of those of us who might otherwise get lost trying to grasp an abstraction from scratch."

"Well put," grinned Jade.

He thought of Alice, wishing it were so easy to survive a tense moment with her. To accept her clichés. He felt ashamed of how he had slammed the door on her last night to run and hide in the mall.

"I believe," said Hosea, "that it was the theologian John Calvin who said that God was willing to use baby talk with us, if necessary, to make Himself understood. A simple cliché, like a vivid metaphor, can often reduce the imponderable to a truth that is at least felt, if not fully understood."

"Don't," laughed Jade, "bother to quote Calvin at me. My degree is from a religious school called Calvin College. I had to study that stuff for four years."

Hosea whistled.

"Yeah," said Jade, "I was raised in western Michigan, in a mini-Dutch Bible belt world of its own. Pastors there couldn't talk about the corn or the World Series without quoting scriptures and referencing their opinions to something John Calvin once wrote. My last name is Vanderspyke. Jade Vanderspyke. Pedigreed Dutch Reformed. Both sides." He shook his head. "At least until they excommunicated my dad after his divorce."

"Well," said Hosea, stepping around the altar to extend his hand. "I'm a pedigreed mutt. All the same, would you care, Mr. Dutch-Calvinist Vanderspyke, to put it there?"

Their hands met. Hosea's grip was as firm as his gaze.

"Welcome, Jade, to the Fraternal Order of the Confused Men of the Hogback Cairn. Hogmen for short."

"Thank you, Mr. Hosey Moses. It's an honor."

They stared into each other's eyes another moment, then released their grips.

"So," asked Jade, "what made you say that I'd be coming back? That I'd even be interested in this place, or you for that matter?"

Hosea studied his eyes.

"Do you believe in God," he asked, "or do you just like to dabble in Dutch theology?"

Jade thought for a moment. It was one of the strangest, most personal questions he'd ever been asked.

Hosea smiled. "Well, I believe in God," he said. "And God believes in me. That's why, once in a while, God let's me in on something. Today, it was you. I woke up this morning with a sort of premonition, a prophetic vision if you will, that something important was going to happen here today at the altar. That I would not be smashing this glass in vain. You're not exactly what I expected, but then, hey, nothing is."

Jade closed his eyes. He believed in God. But Hosey Moses, he was not so sure about.

"Yes," said Jade. "I have faith that God exists. At least most of the time. And I pray. Probably not enough. It doesn't feel like God answers, but I keep doing it anyway."

"What makes you think that God doesn't answer?"

"I didn't say that God doesn't answer. I said that it doesn't feel like God answers."

"I see."

"You see what?"

"What do you think I see?"

"I have no idea what you think you see. You're the alleged prophet, not me."

Hosea laughed. "Now I'm an alleged prophet, huh? And is your God now suddenly an alleged God, as well?"

"I've known God," said Jade, "a lot longer than I've known you."

"Have you?"

Jade shook his head in frustration.

"Tell me this," asked Hosea, "what would you expect it to feel like if God answered one of your prayers?"

"How would I know? I'm not sure that He ever has."

"Interesting. What do you mean, not sure that He ever has? What would it take for you to be sure that something was of God? Isn't that one of the greatest questions of all religions? The epistemological dilemma of faith and experience?"

Jade sealed his eyes and shivered his head. "This is too weird. Here I am, debating philosophies of knowledge in a cave with a self-proclaimed prophetic hogman."

"Can you imagine a better place for such a discussion?"

"No." Jade could not keep the edge from his voice. "Nor can I imagine a more pointless discussion to have. This is not why I came to the hogback today."

Jade checked his watch.

"Then why," asked Hosea, "did you come to the hogback today?"

Jade considered the question. He contemplated it more carefully than he intended.

"Answer me this," said Hosea. "When was the last time that you prayed?"

Jade laughed. Hosea was trying to shame him, to make him feel like he wasn't very spiritual, as if he didn't really take God seriously. Jade felt almost smug as he answered.

"For your information, I prayed just a little while ago. Right here on this ridge, 25 feet above your head. Probably less than a minute before I started hearing you break your bottles."

"And?" Hosea did not appear taken aback.

"And what?"

"And what was the nature of that prayer? What exactly did you and God talk about?"

Jade thought for a moment. He remembered his impassioned "Please God. . . ." Felt his mouth go dry. Couldn't answer.

"That's okay," Hosea said softly. "This is your first time here. Trust me, it'll get easier. Easier to ask the tough questions, and easier to find the strength to answer them with the truth. This place, and those who you'll meet here, will do that for you, if you can handle the mystery and the power. If that's what you're after."

They were again silent.

Hosea studied Jade, then stooped and finally returned to sweeping his liquor shards.

Jade glanced at his watch.

"I've got to leave in a few minutes," he said. "Someone is counting on me at 2:00. But if you don't mind, I'm curious about a couple of things."

Hosea looked up. "Go ahead, shoot."

"Well, for one thing, you act like you've been using this cave for a long time. I've been riding my bike on this ridge for over five years. How come I've never seen you on the trail?"

"I don't use the trail." Hosea dropped his juniper branch and stepped toward the trees. He thrust his hand into a nest of spidery gray roots. "I come up this way." When he straightened, he held a thick coil of blue climbing rope.

Jade joined Hosea at the lip of the cave and looked down. The drop-off was a good 50 feet. Jade leaned back from the edge and refocused his attention upon Hosea.

"These," said Hosea, transferring the coiled rope to his other hand and reaching for more equipment among the roots, "come in handy as well." The belt dangled a dozen aluminum carabineers and assorted chucks that clanked together like a string of out-of-tune sleigh bells.

"Pretty fancy looking gear there," said Jade. "Every bit as high-tech as my shoes."

"Nobody's perfect."

"And you scale this wall yourself?"

Hosea deftly shouldered the belt, threw a large figure eight in the rope, then offered Jade the opportunity to place his wrist within the knot.

"No thanks," Jade laughed. "I trust you. It's just that you don't exactly cut the profile of a sherpa."

"Actually," said Hosea, carefully returning his equipment to the roots, "the climb is far less technical than it looks. The broken west face of the hogback is cake climbing on almost any pitch you pick. It's perfect for beginners." Hosea laughed and patted his stomach. "And for heavy-duty climbers like myself."

Jade laughed. "That answers one question," he smiled. "Here's another. How many guys did you say were using this cave? As I said, it's hard for me to believe that I've never run into any of you guys up top before."

"Tough question." Hosea squatted at the ledge's lip and looked out over the valley below. He raised one hand to the trunk of a juniper, then turned to face Jade.

"Beneath the 20th-century debris of our cairn lies a deep hole filled with rusty gun barrels and flattened gold pans. Below that, Apache arrowheads and Ute beadwork, then pre-Columbian ax heads and pottery. That much I've learned from my own probing. Somewhere beneath that, I supposed one would eventually start hitting samples of the kinds of early vegetation and dinosaur fossils that we find scattered everywhere throughout this ridge, though I've never bothered trying to bust up any rock to find it. My point being, this place is old."

Jade glanced back at the odd cairn.

"Men have been coming here," said Hosea, "practically forever. At least as far as I'm concerned. Right now, I'd guess that there are about a dozen of us who get up here a couple of times a year or more. But we don't flaunt it. None of us does. This site is really a sacred place and we wouldn't care to see it defiled. I suspect that if one of the other hogmen were to see you on the trail, he would hide. Or maybe he would pretend to be out for recreation, just like you."

"Hmm." Jade raised his invisible harmonica to his mouth, touched his knuckle to his lips, then played several slow, thoughtful bars.

"My last question," he said, breaking the silence. "Would it be a breach of hogman etiquette if I were to ask you when you'll be up here again?" He grinned, awkwardly. "God, I feel like I'm asking you for a date or something. This has been one of the strangest days. . . ."

"I told you that you'd be back."

"And?"

"Hogmen don't worry about etiquette. Just the truth. We're sticklers for the truth. As you know, it is only truth that can set a person free. And Lord knows, we all want to be set free of something. You can come up here any time you want, with or without a date." He laughed. "We don't own this ridge, so legally speaking, we couldn't keep you out even if we wanted to."

"So," said Jade, "do you think that you'll be back up here again in the near future?"

"Next weekend. About this same time. In fact, expect me at 10:00 am. I make it every Saturday that I can. Other days, I come as I'm able. As Keeper of the Cairn, I like to stay on top of things. And to keep the sacred temple clean."

Jade glanced at his watch.

"I've got to go," he said. "Hopefully, I'll see you next weekend."

"A question for you," said Hosea, "before you leave."

Jade paused.

"How does a pedigreed Dutch Calvinist like you, blond hair and all, end up with a name like Jade?"

Jade scratched his neck. "I'm not sure. I guess it just sort of happened."

"Okay. That's fine for now. One last thing. Are you sure," asked Hosea, nodding at Jade's wrist, "that you don't want to leave that watch here on the altar? The cairn could use a good high-tech crunch like that timepiece of yours. If you lack the nerve, I could smash it for you myself."

"Naw," Jade smiled. "I gave up a watch once. I just had to go out and buy another one."

He smiled again, waved, then stepped out onto the ledge and hurried back up the trail toward his bike.

He shook his head. Weird place.

But yes, he would be back.

Why not? It could be interesting.

CHAPTER 8

Sunday, March 17, 1996.
Bear Creek Canyon, Colorado

"If we moved to Portland," said Jade, "maybe we could afford a new house like one of those."

He nodded out the car window in the direction of the latest foothills development. The sign facing the highway read: Starting in the Low $220's.

"Please," said Alice. "Let's not talk about Portland."

"Are you two going to fight again?" asked Mark from the back seat. "Because if you are, you can let me out right here."

"Sure," said Carla. "And you're going to walk home, right?"

"No, I'd hitchhike. Dad is always bragging about how he used to thumb around when he was young. I think maybe it's time that I gave it a try. Sort of a rite-of-passage experience. A he-man thing. Right, dad?"

Jade eyed his rear-view mirror. The boy had no respect. At least he had changed his ridiculous pants for church, though there wasn't much that could be done for his hair.

"Mark," said Jade, "I did my hitchhiking in the 1970s. Things were different back then. Lots of young people were thumbing all over the country. It was accepted back then. And it was safer."

"Sure," smirked his son. "No perverts then, right? Charles Manson and Jim Jones and all of those other wacko's were only interested in California hippies, right?"

Jade re-checked his mirror. Mark was snickering toward Carla, who sat in a new dress, one shoulder against the door, grinning and tugging a long curl of blond hair.

"For one thing," said Jade, "Manson's primary targets were middle-class women, not boys."

Jade flicked the turn signal to pass a muddy pickup. A black dog stared from the back of the truck, tongue and ears flapping, eyes white.

"For another, Manson had been in prison for almost five years by the time that I started hitchhiking in 1975."

The dog barked twice as Jade passed. "And, just to set the record straight," Jade merged back into the right lane, "the Jonestown massacre of 1978 took place in Guyana, not California."

"Sorry, dad." Mark met his dad's eyes in the mirror. He didn't blink. "How stupid of me. I guess this is going to be on the test, then, huh?"

Jade avoided the mirror. He looked down and double-checked the Sable's gas. Three quarters full. More than enough.

They had repeated this outing for years. A leisurely drive to Morrison, then another 20 minutes of winding turns and steady grades up Bear Creek Canyon to the outdoor tables at Dick's Hickory Dock. The trip was a Sunday afternoon ritual, like an extension of their 10:00 am service at South Suburban Community Church. The rustic mountain barbecue was once an important part of their lives; the end of another tradition was probably around the next curve.

They drove north along the foothills in silence, then turned off C-470 and hooked west through the hogbacks at the Morrison exit.

Jade tried to imagine when or how he would raise the subject of his father's ashes. So far, Alice and the kids had no clue that Harry was dead. Not that any of them ever met Harry when he was alive. Jade had worked hard to protect them, and himself, from any such unnecessary rehashing and pain.

The handful of shops in Morrison, the restaurants and bars and antique stores clustered between Bear Creek and the west face of Dakota Ridge, all bustled with their usual assemblages of pa-

trons. Jade slowed for three blocks, then picked up speed at the
west end of town.

Several hundred yards ahead was the south entrance to the
Red Rocks Amphitheater. He had studied the amphitheater yesterday from the unusual angle offered by the cave's entrance. He
wondered if Hosea was up there in the cave this afternoon. Probably not. At church, maybe? Did Hosea even go?

Alice would find it hard to believe that such a cave existed.
Especially the part about the hogmen and their cairn. He should
tell her. It was kind of a big deal, particularly Hosea's claim about
having a prophetic vision of Jade, or someone, showing up at the
altar. If Jade brought it up now, Mark would turn it into a joke.

They passed the Red Rocks entrance without a word.

He could bring the subject up during lunch. Right before he
told them all about his father's death. And the package that would
be arriving in Monday or Tuesday's mail.

Falling rock signs and yellow caution warnings announced the
narrowing of the canyon's walls.

"This new car handles well on these tight curves, doesn't it?"
said Jade. He glanced right. Alice's seat was partially reclined, her
eyes closed. He checked his mirror. Mark was fussing with a yellow pair of headphones and fumbling with a case of CD's. Carla's
headphones were black; her CD was already in spin. Jade reached
under his seat and groped for a CD of his own. Something soothing to keep him company for the rest of the drive. He found a new
title, then slipped it in.

He had completely missed the morning's sermon. Instead,
Hosea's penetrating questions and sorrowful prayer rolled over and
over in his mind, haunting him until he could think of nothing
else. Hosea nailed it in a whisper. "I do the very thing I hate."

Chris, Alice, his kids, the bookstore, they all suffered because
of his weakness, his inability to do what he knew was right. His
wobbling knees whenever he faced or fantasized about Chris. Most
of his adult life, he took pride in living like a man of discipline and
strength. Lately, he was proud of very little.

Hosea's words sounded familiar. Like something from the Bible, but not the sort of verse that one found plastered on the kinds of sticky notes that Alice posted around the house. Jade looked the passage up using the pew Bible's concordance during the sermon.

Romans 7:15. I do not understand my own actions. For I do not do what I want, but I do the very thing that I hate.

Alice gave him a strange look, watching him bent over a Bible in church for the first time in years.

But now what? So the saints had problems, too. What was the answer? The Bible also said that if your eye or your hand caused you to sin, you should pluck it out or cut it off. Better to grope in the dark than to burn in hell, it warned.

Jade slowed for a sharp turn.

Maybe he should find a knife and whack his testicles, since that's where his problems seemed to rest. Put his nuts in a plastic bag and toss that onto the pile in the cave.

Jade slowed for a concerned white Cadillac with Nebraska plates. He squeezed the wheel. The next passing stretch was almost a mile away.

Other men, of course, had done that. Not in the hogback cave, maybe, but elsewhere. Monks and priests, during the dark ages and before. Eunuchs for Jesus. Jade could revive the old cult. Initiation rites: final.

The road straightened for several hundred yards. Jade punched it, the car gathered speed, and the Cadillac disappeared behind him at the next curve.

Harry could have been helped by such a cult. On his own, Jade's father was unable to break from his rut: church on Sunday, sluts on Monday. A quick castration and Harry might have been a better man about the house.

Jade applied his brakes for another curve.

Alice should have been told the truth about Harry a long time ago. Someday, he would have to tell her. Like it or not, Harry had been his father. And his ashes would be arriving all too soon.

Jade parked the car on the dirt pad beside the restaurant. Several creek-side tables were available. By force of habit, the four of them marched single file beneath three ancient cottonwoods, then slipped beneath the umbrella on the picnic table at the far end of the gravel patio. Jade unrolled his silverware from a red cloth, then cleared his throat.

"So Alice," Jade draped his napkin over his left thigh, "you never used to be able to sleep like that while driving up the canyon in our old car. This new Mercury handles very well, doesn't it?"

"I wasn't sleeping. I was thinking."

Mark laughed. "Sure. Thinking about your dreams."

"As a matter of fact, I was," she said. "When I was young, I used to dream that one day I would have a job helping people, and that I would live in a nice house with a wonderful family."

"Two out of three," Mark chimed, "I guess that ain't too bad."

Alice looked at him. "It's good to dream when you're young. I had a teacher in eighth grade who kept a sign over the chalkboard." Alice spelled the sign out with her hands. "It read: 'If you aim at nothing, you're bound to hit it.' I liked that sign. I found it inspiring."

"Back when I was in fifth grade," said Mark, dropping his voice, "I once found an inspirational message inside a fortune cookie on the sidewalk. I folded that missive into my wallet and kept it there for years." He traced the message with a finger that inched across his palm. "It read, 'One day you'll be so rich, you'll never have to work again.'"

Mark and Carla laughed. Jade and Alice frowned.

"That," said Jade, unable to stop himself, "is the trouble with kids today. You all want something for nothing. When your mother and I were young, we knew that if we wanted anything worthwhile in life, it was going to take hard work and sacrifice."

Mark added, "Maybe it's time for another sacrifice. What works best, dad? A goat, a virgin, or a child?"

Jade closed his eyes, then turned to Alice. "A meaningful job, a nice home, and a happy family, those were good goals. We've been there and we'll be there again. I'm sorry that things have been so rough lately. Hang in there. We'll figure a way through this."

Alice smiled, faintly. Perhaps she had found hope in his reading of the Bible at church. That sort of thing would impress her, though he had not thought of impressing her at the time.

"I hope so," she said. "Our family is too important to throw away."

Carla leaned forward. "Throw away? You two haven't been planning a divorce, have you?"

She twisted a thin wisp of light sideburn between her finger and thumb. "When I said that I would stay in Denver with mom, I wasn't agreeing that you two should break up. I was only making my point that I was against another move. You're not really going to get a divorce, are you?"

"Of course not," said Jade too quickly. He looked from Carla to Mark, trying to reassure them. "Your mother and I are not planning a divorce. It's just that I've been under a lot of pressure with the Seinner Book company over the past few years. All of the stress and changes have taken a toll on our home life. With Mr. Seinner deciding to sell the downtown store, it's only gotten worse. Mr. Seinner has done some research, and he's confident that with my experience, we could have two new stores thriving in Portland within. . . ."

"We know the story, dad." Mark was fiddling with his knife and fork.

Their waitress arrived for their orders.

She appeared to be in her late twenties, with coarse black hair tied in a loose bun. She wore an oversized 'Dick's Hickory Dock" T-shirt pulled over a blouse and brown slacks. A green plastic St. Patrick's Day four-leaf-clover was pinned above her right breast and a hand-printed name badge identifying her as Wanda was pinned over her left. Jade did not recognize her.

"Where's Janet?" he asked.

"St. Louis, I think." The waitress turned a page and flipped the cardboard invoice buffer up from the bottom. "Janet got married two weeks ago. Her and her new husband had to move the next day. I think he was an engineer or something. Anyway, he had some great job offer out of state."

Jade glanced around the table.

"That's funny," he said. "I knew she was engaged, but she never mentioned anything about moving."

The waitress looked at Jade as if he was crazy.

Alice scratched her ankle and tried to explain. "We've been eating here for over five years," she offered. "We've come to know her very well. I remember when they first hired Janet. She was always spilling things. That's why they assigned her to the tables outside, so that they wouldn't have to worry about mopping up the drinks."

Alice laughed.

"I see," said the waitress. "I'll try not to spill anything."

She briskly took their orders, then tucked her pencil behind an ear and headed back inside.

"Nice lady," said Carla.

"Real personality," added Mark.

Alice shook her head. "Let's not be mean. She's obviously new, and she probably hasn't gotten the hang of it yet."

"Speaking of getting the hang," Mark leaned into his elbows on the table, "when am I going to get some hang time off the moguls up at Steamboat? It's been so warm the past week that folks are up there skiing in their bathing suits. The season is almost over and I've hardly done any down-hilling all year."

"Mark," said Alice, "You've gone skiing at least a half a dozen times."

"Yeah, but I've got friends who go snow-boarding every weekend. You wouldn't even have to drive me there. I could ride with them."

"So," said Jade, "we know what Mark wants to do when he graduates. He wants to become rich and to ski from September through April. And not to have to worry about some annoying job that might get in the way. Did I forget anything, Mark?"

"Just the fast car and the five beautiful babes."

"Uh huh. Very noble indeed. How about you Carla, what are you dreaming of these days?"

"Nothing exotic," she replied. She thought for a moment, then smiled. It was a pretty smile for a girl of 15, the kind of smile that usually got its way.

"I'd like to marry a guy with a good job. You know, something that pays more than you two make so that we wouldn't have to ever be uptight about money. And then I'd like to have a couple of kids. It might also be nice to do some volunteer work at the kids' school or something."

"That's nice," said Alice.

Mark laughed. "Same as me. She wants to be rich, and she doesn't want to have to work."

Alice ignored him. "If you could live anywhere in the world, Carla, where would you choose?"

"Right where we are, in Lakewood, Colorado. Lakewood seems perfect to me. I like the malls and the schools, and the view of the mountains. And there's always so much to do in Denver. But by being in the suburbs, you don't have to put up with the street people and the gangs and stuff."

Carla again leaned over her plate. "Dad, I don't want to move to Portland."

"Nothing is final," he said. "And we need to plan a family trip to check out the housing and schools there. From what I hear, Portland might even be nicer than Denver. I know that moving sounds like a drag, but I just don't know how much choice we will have in this. When Seinner sells the store, I either relocate, or I'm out of work."

"Can't you find a different job?"

"I've been with Seinner for over 20 years. I started working for Jeffrey back when he only had three stores. I was just a teenager, but he gave me a job and let me work all the hours that I needed, and I needed plenty of them back then. I can't just walk away from the company. They've earned more loyalty than that. Not to mention my benefits and pension."

Mark's fork dropped to his plate. "If you've been working for the same company for 20 years," he said, "it seems like you've earned a little more consideration than having your store sold out from underneath you and being told to pack your family off to another city half way around the globe."

Jade shook his head.

"Portland is only 1,300 miles. We can drive it in two days."

"Sure," said Mark, "Only 1,300 miles. That means that we can zip back to Denver on weekends to see our friends."

"You won't have to zip back. There's plenty of skiing near Portland."

"Right."

Carla twirled her hair, then let it spring. "Dad," she asked, "you never had to move when you were growing up, did you?"

"Not exactly. We moved out of a trailer when I was five. And I moved into a smaller house with my mom after my dad left when I was 11. But I spent my whole childhood in the same town, if that's what you're getting at."

"How about when you got older and went to college and started moving around to manage different stores? Did you ever miss anybody then? You know, the friends that you left behind?"

"Jade, speaking of friends," said Alice, "I keep forgetting to tell you. Terry called this morning while we were getting ready for church. He says that your get-together is back on for Wednesday. His appointment was changed."

"See," said Carla. "That's what I'm talking about. Aren't you going to miss Terry if we move? You two have been doing that mid-week happy hour thing of yours for years."

Jade glanced at Alice, then back to Carla. "I guess you're right. I'll miss Terry. It's probably always hard to leave some people and certain places. On the other hand, I've always looked forward to moving as a chance to start over, a way to make new friends and to find a fresh beginning. As long as your mother and you two kids have been with me, it hasn't been all that hard."

"Not for you, maybe," said Mark.

Jade sighed. This didn't feel like a conversation that would work its way around to Hosea and the cave, let alone to Harry's ashes.

"Try this," said Jade. "Pick the three things that you hate the most about Denver. Then think of some people in Colorado that bug you. Now try to imagine how good it will feel to leave them all behind."

Mark began silently pointing and counting his way around the table. Carla punched him on the arm.

Jade took a sip of water. It tasted cold. Too cold. The sky was clouding. They should have brought their jackets.

"Your father's right," said Alice. "It helps to focus on the negative things about staying, at least when you know that you've got to go. I'll never forget when we sold our house in Lansing. It was such a relief to get away from our leaking garage roof and the neighbor's rottweiler."

Carla folded her arms in defiance. She turned to her mother. "Do we really have to move? Can't you see what a bad idea this is? I like my school and I'm finally making some good friends."

"Yeah," said Mark. "Like Bill McDalley."

"Who is Bill McDalley?" asked Jade.

"That football gorilla who wears his jersey to church. He's from South Platte High School. Rumor has it that he's having some trouble with his eligibility. His shop teacher is trying to cut him back to four hours a day. Him and Carla have been sitting knee-to-knee in youth group for weeks."

Carla glared.

"Is this true?" asked Alice. "Are you interested in an older boy?"

"Oh mom," she said, tugging her hair. "Bill is such a sweet guy. His dad owns an appliance store. Bill helps his dad and everything. He makes appliance deliveries every Saturday."

"Why haven't you mentioned Bill before?"

"I don't know. It's not like he's asked me out yet or anything. We're just friends."

"My goodness," said Jade. "Carla, you're only a sophomore.

And you're talking about dating an older boy who plays football at another school?"

"Dad, you used to play football."

"That," Mark imitated Jade's voice, "was back in the 1970s. Things were different then. That was back in the good old days, when boys respected girls. Back when boys kept it zipped unless they needed air."

"Mark," said Alice, "that is hardly Sunday table talk."

She turned back to her daughter. "Yes, Carla. Your father played football. He was very good. There's nothing wrong with dating a football player per se. It's just that you're only 15, and if he's an older boy who. . . ."

"I don't see what everybody is getting so excited about. If you met Bill, you would see that he is as gentle as a lamb."

"Sure," said Mark. "When we played his school last fall, I got a good feel for how gentle Bill is. He embraced me quite tenderly, just before he buried me six feet under the 10 yard line."

"What about you, Mark?" snapped Carla. "You're in love too, aren't you?"

"What are you talking about?"

"Pamela Anderson, that's who."

Jade lifted a brow. "Who is Pamela Anderson?"

"From Bay Watch," said Carla. "The TV show."

Mark threw Carla a threatening stare. She continued. "Pamela Anderson is that blonde who bounces down the beach and can hardly stay in her bathing suit, even in slow motion. Mark has been collecting pictures of Pam for some time. Naked pictures of Pamela laying with her. . . ."

"Carla!" said Alice. "That's enough of that. Have you been going through Mark's personal things?"

Mark continued to glare.

"Mother, of course not. I would never violate the sacred trust that exists between a sister and her brother's things." Carla ran her thumb and fingers down her hair. "Actually, I discovered Mark's collection one day while doing some innocent research on the computer. I was rummaging through the Finder, trying to locate a literature report of mine on Sherwood Anderson. And up from nowhere popped a folder called 'Anderson.' That didn't seem right, but I thought that I'd better check it to be sure. And guess what I found?"

Mark looked away.

"I found a whole stack of Pamela Anderson photos, all downloaded from the World Wide Web. And believe me, some of them were pretty nasty, huh Mark?"

"Okay," said Jade. "End of discussion. What Mark does in private on the computer is none of our concern." He paused for a moment, then added, "I mean, if he prefers computers over real girls, that's his own business. At least we won't have to worry about him getting any diseases. Except maybe a virus." He grinned.

Mark spun toward his father, face red. "Very funny, dad. And how about you? How's your collection of e-mails from Chris coming?"

Alice gasped.

Jade shot her a quick look, then wheeled on his son. "That's it." He rose and leveled a finger, his lips thin and jaw taut. "You're way over the line. You know that your mother and I are having enough trouble right now without any help like that." He dropped his hand. "Now you tell your mother it was a joke. A bad joke."

Mark shrank. They all waited.

Jade turned to Alice. "Yes, I occasionally get e-mail from Chris. Mostly questions and reminders. She sends them from work when I'm away from the store. E-mail is less intrusive than phone messages, and it's strictly professional." He turned back to Mark. "Am I right?"

"It's okay, mom," said Mark, looking down. "Dad's right. I had no business looking at his e-mail, and there wasn't anything there anyway. It was a dumb joke. That was a stupid thing for me to say."

Alice closed her eyes.

"I'm sorry," said Mark.

She rose quietly and excused herself to the restroom.

Later that night, after Mark and Carla were in bed, Alice caught Jade's attention in the mirror.

"What," she asked, brushing her hair, "what was Mark talking about. . . ." She cleared her throat. "What's going on with e-mail . . . and Chris?"

Without turning, she glanced briefly at his eyes, then back to her hair.

"Nothing," he shrugged. "Like I said, strictly professional."

He reached to pull off a sock. "Mark has a twisted sense of humor. He was trying to embarrass me, that's all. I probably had it coming. I never should have made a joke about his sex life. He's a typically insecure teenager. He's still just trying to figure it all out. I must have hit a sore spot."

Jade tried to look nonchalant, dropped the sock and met her gaze in the mirror. "But there is something else that we need to talk about. A couple of things, in fact." He reached and pulled the sock from his other foot. "My mom called the other night about my dad. We had a nice talk, but she said. . . ."

Alice cleared her throat. "It's just that there seemed to be more to it than that. At the time, it didn't seem like a joke at all. I could have sworn. . . ."

"I said it was a lie." Jade stared at Alice in the mirror. He threw his socks at the hamper, then stood up.

"What's the matter, don't you trust me anymore? I don't care what Mark says. The truth is, I'm not fooling around behind your back. I took my ring off Friday afternoon because my hands were wet and dirty. Now let's get some sleep. I'm exhausted."

Jade abruptly hit the light.

They crawled into bed in silence.

Back-to-back, an arm's length apart, neither slept for an hour.

CHAPTER 9

Summer, 1970. Grand Haven, Michigan

The morning's thick heat reminded Jimmy of the bathroom after one of his father's 30-minute showers. The air was so steamy a person could hardly see or breathe. An out-of-state tourist muttered that such humidity could choke a fish, then complained that the afternoon forecast called for more of the same.

Jimmy's mom was out on errands, and Ben was tending the register. Randy unpacked a shipment of driftwood figurines by the window, and Mr. Vanderspyke scooped ice cream while blending shakes for tourists too hot to eat.

The little bell at the front door tinkled lightly.

Jimmy paused on his broom and looked up as the woman entered. She was pretty, but a little on the heavy side, though plump mostly where guys never seemed to mind. Lively red hair fell from an enormous floppy hat with bright flowers and tiny yellow bows. Beneath an unfasten beach robe, she wore a swim suit of a style seldom seen in their store. An embroidered canvas bag dangled from the crook of her freckled arm.

"Hello," she said. She glanced around, then approached the ice-cream case in uneven steps. "Mr. Vanderspyke?"

"Hello," said Harry. He wiped his hands on his stained apron and cast his boys a nervous glance. "Do I, uh, know you?"

"I believe we have met."

Harry looked more closely, then grinned. The woman smiled broadly.

"My name is Marsha Fenton. Friends call me Mars. We met a few weeks ago at the musical fountains. I was with my husband at the time. We were visiting from Chicago and you recommended the Sand Castle Hotel on the south end of the beach."

"Ah, yes, Mars. The Sand Castle Hotel. I remember now." Harry reached behind his neck and unfastened his apron. He lifted the garment over his head and hung it on a nail behind the counter. "And how is your husband? I believe he had an allergy or something, right?"

"Yes, an allergy. The rag weed was terrible that week." Mars glanced around the shop and counted the boys, then discovered the postcard rack to her side. The rack wobbled unevenly as it turned, lopsided with beach scenes, fountain views and Holland tulip photos. Mars selected a card, then held it at arm's length.

"They were beautiful," she said. "I think I remember this part of the exhibition. It was during Hello Dolly." She turned the card over. "The fountains shot up like this near the end of the performance. The colors, as I recall, were tantalizing."

She put the card back. "My husband decided to stay home this time. He had work. I'm only up here for the day."

That struck Jimmy as odd. Chicago was almost three hours down the coast. Several beaches were much closer to Chicago for a day outing, and they were all almost as nice.

"Well," said Harry, "it's too bad you can't stick around until after dark for another round of our world-famous fountains. I think I saw where tonight's show was going to be a medley of Aaron Copland tunes. I'm sure that you would enjoy our interpretation of 'Fanfare for the Common Man.'"

"Really?" she smiled. "Copland? I'm a huge fan of his. I've always been particularly partial to his adaptation of the Shaker's tune, 'Simple Gifts.'"

"'Simple Gifts?'" he smiled back. "That's always been one of my favorites as well. But then, I guess I'm just a simple man."

Mars laughed. "You do not strike me as all that simple."

"No? Perhaps not. Perhaps just easy to please."

There was something about the way that Harry began to laugh, to enlarge his laughter over and through the woman's laugh, that made Jimmy uneasy. Tourists walked their dogs along the beach, and Jimmy had seen how one dog would sometimes tug its leash to get a better sniff of another. His father was leaning his laughter toward this city woman as if for a better sniff. After a moment, Harry seemed to notice the stares of his sons, and his laughter quickly subsided.

"Since you, too, like simple gifts," grinned Harry, "I have something for you." He stepped around from the back of the snack counter and brushed his hand past Mars' robe to the center of the card rack.

"Here," he said, plucking a post card showing a blonde child chin-deep in tulips. "Call this is a simple gift from me to you. I'll even inscribe it with one of my favorite lines from the tune. Are you still sure that you can't stay for the show?"

Mars smiled and nodded no.

Harry turned to Ben. "Hand me a pen, would you?" Ben took a green one from the cash register and passed it somewhat reluctantly to his father, whose eyes were already fixed again upon Mars. "I'll just write it right here on the back."

Harry scribbled for what seemed to be forever, then handed the card to Mars.

She read it, smiled, then said good-bye. The boys looked at each other and shrugged. She hadn't bought a thing.

Ten minutes later, Harry announced that it was time to clean the customers' restroom. He called for volunteers, got none, then for once offered to clean the toilet himself.

"Ben," he said, "watch the store for a few minutes. This shouldn't take long." The door to the customers' restroom was located outside the store on the south end of the building. Harry lifted the bathroom key from the wall, patted the counter and disappeared, almost whistling as he stepped through the front door.

Jimmy stared after his father, sensing that something was wrong. It took him a few moments to figure it out. His dad had forgotten to collect the cleaning supplies from the storage closet at the end of the hall.

Jimmy looked around. Randy and Ben were busy, apparently oblivious to their father's blunder. Jimmy thought, then decided to get the brushes, pail, and mop, and take them to his dad himself. He could save his father a trip back inside. Besides, he liked to watch his dad work. There were times when he didn't understand his father, but when Harry was working, everything made sense. Harry's hands and arms were strong, and he tackled scrubbing around the store the way Jimmy imagined a sailor scouring before a captain's review.

Their storage room at the back of the building had a large utility sink that shared its plumbing with the bathroom on the other side. It was gross, but Jimmy discovered that if he put his ear to the sink, he sometimes could hear when a customer was using the toilet. Jimmy opened the door to the dark little room, then stepped inside.

He reached for the light, then paused, holding his breath. Someone was definitely over there. He began to lower his ear to the cold gray sink, then hesitated. It seemed like a dirty thing to do. Besides, it was probably just his dad straightening up the wastebasket. Jimmy again reached for the switch. Then, for the first time, he noticed a pinhole of yellow light. He looked closer. The light was poking through from a small gap beside the hot water pipe that serviced the customers' sink. A week ago, the gap had not been there. Plaster must have recently crumbled away from the pipe on account of moisture and neglect.

Curious, Jimmy moved closer, letting the door shut behind him. He slid his hand from the light switch, knowing that the hole would be easier to peer through in the dark.

Muffled whispers and bumps sounded from the tiny bathroom on the other side of the wall. It sounded like two people.

A strange sound, a velvety purr, rose and fell. It was almost scary. From the laugh that followed, Jimmy knew the noise came from the lady in the floppy hat. Mars. Marsha Fenton.

Jimmy stood for a moment, unsure what to do.

He inched closer, then pressed his cheek to the warm pipe and lowered his eye to the hole. The hole was bigger than he expected, and there was a clear view through to the other room.

Facing him, swinging forward and back, forward and back, were two frighteningly naked breasts. Each of the gigantic sagging mounds was cupped from behind by thick fingers, each nipple barely exposed, pinched between the thumbs and hands of sailor-sized paws.

Above Marsha's bowed head grinned Jimmy's dad.

Jimmy gasped and recoiled, then conked his head on the dust pan dangling above the sink. He lost his balance, knocked over the mop bucket and dragged down a shelf of soaps and cleansers in a swirling snowy crash.

"Shhhh . . . don't move."

Jimmy slumped into a dark corner and held his breath.

"Someone is on the other side. . . ." More whispers and frantic rustlings leaked through from beyond.

Then footsteps, hurried ones, padding down the hall and stopping outside the closet door. The knob turned and the door jerked open in a blast of stinging light.

Glaring down was Jimmy's mom.

"Jimmy! What are you doing in here, banging around in the dark and making a mess of. . . ."

He instinctively glanced at the pinhole by the pipe. His mother followed his gaze.

"Were you spying on a someone? A girl?"

His mother looked furious. "What a sneaky, shameful thing to do. Why I ought to. . . . " She lowered her voice. "Is she still in there?"

"I, uh, I'm not sure. I mean, maybe I scared them out. . . ."

"'Them?' There were two people in there?" Jimmy's mother sidled through the door. "Move aside!" She leaned to take a look for herself. Only at the last possible instant did the pinhole disappear as a finger popped in from the other side.

Mrs. Vanderspyke straightened, never shifting her gaze from the hole.

"Who is in there, Jimmy?" she demanded.

Jimmy thought quickly. She would pound it out of him if he didn't answer soon.

"I'm not sure," he said. "I couldn't see. The hole was so small that the lady's tits filled up the whole thing."

"Tits?" She shot him a quick squint. "Were they the breasts of a woman or a girl?"

"How should I know," said Jimmy. "Do you think that I'm an expert about these things?"

A muffled snicker rose from the adjacent room.

"Were the breasts this big," Mrs. Vanderspyke held out her hands, "this big," she widened them, "or this big."

As long as his mom didn't ask about the man, his dad might be safe.

"That big," said Jimmy, indicating the extra-large.

"Damn. I knew it." She turned back to the wall.

"Harry Vanderspyke," she yelled. "You come out of there this instant." She did not wait for an answer. She stooped to the floor and snatched her purse. Moments later, she opened a safety pin and leaned toward the tiny hole, then rammed the point with all the force her angle allowed.

Jimmy jerked at the screech from the other side.

But before Mrs. Vanderspyke could reposition her eye, a lump of toilet paper was crammed deep into the hole.

"If that don't beat all," she muttered. "Well, we'll just see how long they can last." She straightened.

"Harry," she shouted, "I know you're in there. I gotta tell ya, it's an awfully hot day, and I'm pulling the fuse for the bathroom fan. You might as well brace yourself, because sooner or later, you're going to have to come out."

She reached down and lifted Jimmy by the arm. "You stay right here," she ordered. "And if it starts sounding like they're doing it again, you call me. I don't want them enjoying themselves while I'm waiting."

Mrs. Vanderspyke shouldered her purse. She propped the door open with a bottle of Clorox, then disappeared into the pantry opposite the open closet door. Harry kept a handgun in the pantry, and Jimmy feared the peculiar look in his mother's eyes. When she finally reemerged, she wore a hat, sun glasses, and a foamy white skin of fresh tanning lotion. Cradled in her right arm were Twinkies and fruit. Her other hand rested upon the flap of her purse, her fingers folded stiffly over a large squarish bulge. She slammed the front door, then plopped herself in a lawn chair under the crab apple tree outside the bathroom door.

Jimmy sighed.

Over the ensuing hours, several unsuspecting customers approached her lawnchair, each claiming an urgent need for use of the facilities. She dispensed them in short order, urging them in so many words to haul their needs elsewhere.

The last of the musical fountains were drained, and the last of the stragglers from the bleachers had found their way home when Jimmy heard Harry and Mars quietly begin discussing how they would like to die. Jimmy discovered that despite his father's dark side, Harry possessed the working vocabulary of a religious man. At the sound of prayer, Jimmy sensed he could leave his post, though what he really wanted was to use the stool on his father's side of the pipes. He exited through the back door, uncertain where to go. His mother was still waiting in the lawnchair.

It was nearly midnight when Harry and Mars finally unbolted the lock to their love nest and slithered out into the black of night. Jimmy was hiding outside, watching from behind the crab apple tree, unable to go home and unwilling to leave.

There was no gun. Only the blinding white explosion of an instamatic's flashing bulb.

"I'll need this shot," said Jimmy's mom, "for the divorce."

CHAPTER 10

Monday, March 18, 1996.
Dakota Ridge, Colorado

Jade leaned his mountain bike against the same ragged wedge of shale that he had used two days before.

This time, he did not clean or inspect his equipment, nor did he linger to admire the vistas from the trough at the snout of the horse-head slog.

After several hurried gulps from his water bottle, he caught his breath, then made his way down the trail to the shallow cave on the face of the cliff.

Hosea was not there.

Nor was anyone else.

The morning had been tense, wondering when Harry's ashes might arrive, not knowing to which address they would be sent.

His mother had forgotten his home phone, so Jade worried that she wouldn't have his home address, either. She would need to get a zip code from the post office, and then she would have to bluff the street number. That made the mall store a likely choice for where the ashes would arrive. Unless she could remember his house address from her occasional letters.

What if she thought she remembered, but then she scrambled some of the numbers and the package proved to be undeliverable?

Jade pictured a box of Harry's ashes gathering dust, gnawed by mice, lost in some package bin for 25 years. Unclaimed because his mother had cleverly mailed the box 'Book Rate' with a bogus return address to prevent the box from being traced.

It was maddening.

He should have warned Alice.

Jade had lingered at the downtown store long enough to receive his mail and UPS, then drove home for lunch. No Alice. No packages or messages, either.

He drove to the mall. The only shipments there were two cases of Frying Fat Free.

Jade had finally relaxed. With the threat of the ashes from Texas shelved for the day, he smiled and sold books. Lots of them. Even made amends with the red-chipped-nail lady, who graciously dropped her threat of a lawsuit and thanked him repeatedly for setting her copy aside and calling back so soon. Things were picking up. Jade was back in the groove, on schedule. Headed for a record March.

In the glow of his successful afternoon, memories of Hosea and the hogback cave came easily and fondly. Jade caught himself several times thinking of Chris, and he managed each time to pull himself free from the whirlpool of alluring fantasies. He felt himself in the throes of a moral victory, his life again under control. After work, he changed his clothes quickly and mounted his bike for the hogback. He needed to see the place again to reassure himself that it was real. Perhaps even to meet others who might be there. He reached the horse-head slog in record time.

Hesitating at the mouth of the abandoned chamber, Jade suddenly wasn't so sure.

The cave was darker and quieter than he remembered. More like a neglected mausoleum than the wild hogmen frat house that he imagined it to be while biking up the ridge.

His eyes adjusted to the broken shadows and dingy light. Carefully, he entered the tomb-like stillness, stepping softly, half wondering if he should remove his shoes.

He glanced around.

Not a lot to see.

What little there was looked about the same . . . but somehow different. Perhaps it was the shadows? The different time of day? He stepped deeper into the dark.

He approached the so-called altar, glanced down, then squatted. He placed his palm on the round crushing stone resting at the basin's side, then gingerly ran his fingers from the stone down to the inside of the cold gritty hollow. Hosea had cleaned the bowl of all its broken glass.

What other offerings had been surrendered within the bowl?

Jade rose, dusted his hands, then made his way to the pile of mangled scraps piled against the farthest, darkest corner of the chamber.

The cairn. A cascading mound of twisted metal, broken glass, plastic scraps, and ash.

Jade bent and studied the waste more closely. He was correct the first time. There were pieces of appliances of every sort, including at least one computer and a couple of television sets. He poked the mound. And several charred scraps of clothing.

What kind of man would lug a computer or a television set up the hogback and then down the face of this cliff, only to destroy it, leaving it as part of a growing twisted shrine? He could understand lugging up a video tape or a magazine as a poetic gesture, but a whole television set?

He thought of the smut saved on his zip drive at home. He should erase it all. Or smash it here, symbolically, if that would help him break the habit.

But who would pack in an entire working computer system? Perhaps some of these objects were broken already, before they were smuggled in for their ritualistic destruction. Probably not. These guys seemed serious about what they were doing.

Jade stood, then returned to the altar.

A cloud passed in front of the descending sun and the cave dimmed. Jade tapped the crushing stone with his toe. It tottered weakly in response.

He slowly lowered himself Indian-style beside the rock, his back to the cave's entrance, the altar bowl bottomless within the shadows of his thighs and crossed legs.

The silence of the cave was frightening. It washed over him in musky waves that left him near trembling, eager to leave. Yet, he remained.

"Why," he whispered, "am I here?"

He stared into a choking pool of silence, a pool in some ways like the black mud that once enveloped the dinosaurs that were now embedded within the mountain around him.

"What," he whispered again, "am I doing in this god-forsaken cave?

Images flashed quicker than he could catch, blurred like the wings of a startled jay. Alice. His father. Chris. E-mail. Mark and Carla. The ticking clock. The stores. Sand dunes. Randy. Karen. . . .

"No," he cried, softly, squeezing his eyes. "No."

He tried to open his eyes, to pry himself free, but the black silence sucked and pulled him deeper.

He lost track of his hands. They found each other, then latched together for strength. His eyes remained sealed as he rocked gently forward and back.

The flashes grew in intensity and pounded like relentless waves. He tried to scoop one scene, one image, to ride it, to control it. But the next was upon him and passing before he could tighten his grasp. His wedding. His father gaping at a young woman's tan. A defensive lineman buckling beneath the force of Jim's angry lunge. A young girl shouting capitals and states. A sensuous burning in the palm of his cupped right hand. Randy laughing in a speed-boat. Karen's tan legs and yellow bikini. Chris, facing him, naked. . . .

"No," he sobbed again. "No. . . ."

He opened his eyes.

Jade sat for a moment, staring into the swirling black of the altar pit between his knees.

"God," he whispered, probing the silence of the hole. "Are you in there? Can you hear me? I could use some help. I'm kind of messed up." He thought of Alice. "I don't want to lose her." He thought of Chris. "I can't seem to shake this, this . . . addiction."

He thought of Harry's ashes coming in the mail. "Please, God, help me. What should I do?"

He waited, patiently, for a voice. God's voice. Any voice. If needed, the voice of his own reason.

The sun outside slipped beneath orange, purple, then black clouds, all but disappearing behind the ragged peaks of the Continental Divide. A soft breeze rustled in the junipers at the mouth of the chamber as the hogback cooled and the air of the valley and mountains rose and fell in search of equilibrium.

Jade's legs and neck grew stiff. If he sat much longer, he would have to walk his bike off the ridge in the dark. He tried to summon pious, religious thoughts, but found his mind drifting to images of Chris, his family, and his job. His fleeting moment of rapture was over, perhaps as quickly as it had begun.

No answers.

He rose to his feet, disgusted. Disgusted within himself for his faith, or lack of faith. Frustrated with a God who did, or didn't, have the power to speak.

He kicked the crushing stone again.

The stone wobbled pathetically.

How heavy was it, anyway? He had never actually picked it up. Jade stooped and latched onto it with both hands.

It wouldn't budge.

Jade bent his knees and lowered his hips for better leverage. With a jerk, the rock released its grip from the floor and Jade straightened. It wasn't so heavy after all. It felt smooth, strangely comfortable, even slightly warm within his hands.

He gently lowered it to the altar's side.

Jade checked his watch, turned, then started to leave. From near the junipers, he glanced back at the stone. An odd sensation stirred in his stomach.

He found himself back at the altar, groping for some kind of gesture, however irrational.

He again glanced at his watch.

Without thinking, he knelt and loosened the watch's band.

He placed the straps flat at the bottom of the bowl. Then the crushing stone was within his grip, poised, quivering, high in his hands, stretched above his head.

He closed his eyes and drove the stone crushing through the intricate mechanisms of the watch. Jade sensed the impact of the stone more than felt it. He sensed its imperceptible reverberations sinking through hundreds of feet of ancient strata, deep into the heart of the hogback, perhaps beyond.

He removed the stone from the basin and set it aside.

The wristband and watch fragments scooped easily into the cup of his hand. Jade rose, brought them to the cairn heap, then flung them from his hip like seeds.

Outside in the falling shadows, he began his ride home. The climb back up the smooth face of horse-head slog was comfortable in the coolness of the late hour.

He would have to buy a new watch; he could not manage the stores without one.

The horse's ears stood erect 10 yards ahead.

That watch had been a good one. It cost him over a hundred dollars. He glanced at his bare wrist. What a waste. What madness had seized him?

Smashing his watch was stupid.

Somehow, though, the gesture made sense.

Jade shifted gears and started down the horse's neck.

A paradox. Smashing the watch; buying another. Life appeared little more than a string of incomprehensible mysteries and contradictions. Hosea had said something like that.

Who was it, someone in the Bible, who had tried to make sense of the paradoxes? The man nearly killed himself in despair.

The trail disappeared into black holes. Jade was glad he knew the path by heart.

David? No, Solomon. Ecclesiastes. The Philosopher. "Vanities of vanities! All is vanity. What does a man gain from all his labor at which he toils under the sun? All streams flow into the sea, yet the sea is never full. The eye never has enough of seeing, nor the ear its fill of hearing. For everything, there is a season. . . ."

Jade felt the beat and heard the sounds of the Pete Seeger tune as sung by the Byrds rising and mingling, fetched from some forgotten place, merging with a paper he once wrote in Philosophy 101 back at Calvin College.

He shifted a gear and leaned to avoid a loose stone.

For everything there is a season, and a time for every purpose under heaven: A time to be born and a time to die, a time to plant and a time to uproot, a time to kill and a time to heal.

He squinted ahead at a dark shadow in the trail. A rock? A rabbit? It disappeared.

A time to weep and a time to laugh. A time to mourn—he shifted again—and a time to dance. A time to scatter stones and a time to gather stones together.

The trail veered sharply, then plunged down a bouncy rock-studded pitch. Another few hundred yards, and he would be off the ridge. Where was he?

Stones.

Right. A time to embrace and a time to refrain. A time to embrace. . . . There she was, Chris, reaching out her arms. . . .

Jade hit the back brake and yanked up on his front wheel to avoid cracking into a broken limb across the trail.

A time to refrain from embracing. A time for . . . for . . . a time to tear, and a time to mend.

The final 30 yards of the trail plunged and flattened, then spilled onto the shoulder of Highway 26.

A time to be silent, and a time to speak. A time to speak. A time to speak. . . .

Jade reached the highway, gathered speed and geared up for the cruise home.

He would talk when he got home. He wasn't sure how much he could share with Alice, but it was time to speak. There was too much that she didn't know, and it was hurting them both.

Jade knew that his marriage and family were on the line.

CHAPTER 11

Monday, March 18, 1996.
Lakewood, Colorado

"Welcome home."

"Thank you." Jade took the door from Alice and shut it gently. He removed his helmet and hung it on the back of the rocking chair by the front window, then reached to the side of the window and closed the drapes.

"Your supper is in the refrigerator," said Alice, "on a plate beneath the plastic wrap on the second shelf." She returned stiffly to an open magazine on the floor beside the couch. "Mark and Carla got tired of waiting, so we ate without you. They'll be back home around ten. Until then, you're on your own."

"I'm sorry," said Jade. "I didn't mean to screw up dinner. I had no idea how late it was getting."

"Bull," she snapped. "You knew what time it was. You always wear a watch. Even in bed."

"Well," said Jade. "I usually wear a watch. But. . . ."

Alice looked up.

"What happened?" She glanced at his bare wrist. "Were you mugged?"

"No. Nothing like that. It's a long story." He wanted to tell her. How much would she understand?

Alice found her place in her magazine and slumped back into the pillows on the couch. "I'm sure it's a wonderful story," she sighed. "You'll have to tell me the whole thing some day, when you're not so busy, and when maybe you have the time."

"I have the time now," he said. "If you're not too busy with your magazine, I'd like to talk now."

"Since when has my schedule mattered? Your schedule is the only one that has ever counted in this house. Just ask your kids."

"Please," said Jade. "I said I wanted to talk. I've got some important things I need to say."

"Oh, gosh. I'm sorry. You want to talk. I'd better shut right up. I wouldn't want to miss this once-in-a-decade opportunity to communicate with my globe-trotting, mountain-biking spouse." Alice folded her magazine, dropped it to the floor, then sat straight.

"This is nonsense." Jade wiped his forehead. "Look, I'm sorry. I should never have used that tone." He took several steps in the direction of the couch. "What's happening to us? What's going on?"

She glanced at her magazine.

"I don't know," she said.

"I don't know either. But what do you think? Make a stab at it, give us a place to start." His voice softened. "Please. I want to talk."

She met his eyes.

"I guess," she said, "that I have been thinking about this. A lot. And I do have something to say." Her gaze shifted to the floor, then his eyes. "I'm feeling a lot of anger toward you right now. And frustration. I'm frustrated and mad. It feels like there's so many miles between our worlds these days. You miss meals, work late, make plans without a thought for your family. You don't talk, you daydream or fantasize or whatever it is you do when we're alone. . . ."

She pressed her fingers to her cheeks, then slid them over her jaw and down her neck. Her hands dropped to her lap.

"You've always been aloof at times. I guess that I've always suspected that there were parts of you that you would never share. But other times, you used to be tender and attentive. When you wanted to, you could make me feel like I was the only woman that you'd ever loved. You used to make me happy. Very happy. I even looked forward to sleeping with you, in your arms. Including the sex. It was great sex. I thought that we had something."

She looked at the front door and the closed drapes.

"Now . . . I just don't know."

She closed her eyes.

"Jade," she continued, "you hardly seem interested in me anymore. But I see you looking at others. What are you thinking? And now there's this whole crazy business about Chris, who you've said yourself is one of the most attractive women that you've ever known. More and more, you run from me, your kids, this home. And you hide. It's like you've become infested with some sort of emotional cancer that's growing, consuming you from the inside out. What's happening to the man inside of you?"

The clock ticked.

Then, softly, "I miss the old Jade."

Jade raised his thumb to his chin and pressed a knuckle to his lips.

Emotional cancer. What did Alice mean?

Harry had cancer inside of him. Harry was dead.

His father had just killed himself.

And here Alice was, ragging on him. Telling her husband that he didn't make her happy anymore.

Wasn't a woman supposed to be showing her husband some kind of sympathy after the loss of a parent?

Not that he needed it. What did he care about whether or not Harry blew his brains out? Missing or dead, with Harry, it was the same thing.

But Alice still didn't know. He still hadn't told her. What was wrong with him? Why couldn't he just say things?

"Jade?"

"Sorry." He let go of his chin. "I was just thinking about what you said."

"And?"

"And I agree." He met her eyes. "I've been screwing up a lot lately. And I haven't been treating you as well as I used to."

"Why?" she asked. "Why the change between us? Is the love

gone? Is your work that important to you?" She looked down. "Is there someone else?"

"No. There isn't another woman. I told you that last night. And I still love you."

He started to move toward her, then hesitated. "But," his voice dropped, "I guess that my love has changed. This happens to every couple. Time beats the heck out of love, whether we want it to or not."

Jade looked away, and then continued.

"At first, love is always fresh and overwhelming. That's universal. Ours, too. Who knows, maybe the scientists are right, maybe new love is all mixed with hormones and the instinct to mate. Fresh lovers get drunk on the thrill of flesh, blinded by the newness of everything. It's a high."

He smiled. "That first year, I could have told you that I was Robert Redford and you would have believed me. You could have said that you were the bride of Frankenstein, and I would have loved you and stole you away just the same."

"Robert Redford and the bride of Frankenstein?"

"Sorry, poor choice of metaphors. What I meant to say was that I would have taken on the monster to have you for myself." Jade forced a smile. "As you undoubtedly remember, back then, I thought I could do anything."

"But now you know better."

"That's right."

"And you look at me, and you think of Frankenstein? And you want to tell me that the hormones have run low and chemistry is gone, and that the disintegration of our marriage can be blamed on the tedium of our predictable lives?"

"Alice," said Jade, his stomach knotting. "Please, don't be quoting your women's magazines at me. Let's get back to the subject. I know that you're upset about this Portland move. I'm thinking that maybe, with some concerted effort, when we start over in Portland we can work on some changes. Maybe even get some professional help. Some therapy."

Alice started to rise from the couch.

"Wait," he said. "I'd like to continue to discuss this."

"I didn't know that we were discussing." She spun to face him. "I could have sworn that you just ignored my question and told me that I was moving to Portland. Apparently, my end of this discussion is supposed to be wordless. A simpleton grin and an occasional nod of my empty little head."

"Alice," he glared, "you've become a real fighter. You love these new little brawls of ours, don't you?"

"Fighters do not walk from fights," she smiled, nastily. "Good-bye."

Alice stepped over her magazine, wiped her hands on her thighs, then turned to leave.

"Come on, Alice. This isn't fair. Let's work this out."

She stopped, turned back, and smiled again. "This isn't fair, huh? But is life ever fair? Fair for who, and at whose expense? Now there's an interesting topic for our next little share time."

"What are you talking about?"

"Well," she said. "A share time is when. . . ."

Jade slapped his hand. "Why," he shouted, "can't you just for once just give me a straight answer? I'm getting fed up with of all of your double messages and passive aggressive manipulation."

"Uhm . . . 'double messages and passive aggressive manipulation,' eh?" Alice feigned a posture of thoughtfulness. "Nice combination. Which pop-psychology best seller are you quoting this time?" Alice began tugging her chin. "Really, Jade, I do miss how you used to think for yourself. It's been ages since you've had anything original to say."

Jade stepped to her face. He met her eyes, searched for anything other than anger, found nothing.

"That's a cheap shot, Alie." He hadn't called her Alie in a long time, and he wasn't sure how it came out now. "I think for myself."

"Touchy tonight, aren't we? What's the matter, did I hit a nerve?"

"I know damn well what you're saying and it's not true. I make my own decisions. Seinner Books doesn't ask me to do anything that I wouldn't do on my own."

"Right. Like move to Lansing? Move to Denver? Work 70 hours a week? Like starting to sell the very kinds of books that you once swore should all be shredded and mixed with cow manure to feed the soil for corn?"

Jade ran his fingers through the side of his hair. "I was 19 when I said that. Just a self-righteous book salesman trying to hype religious titles and to sound impressive to an attractive co-ed. You. If you'll remember, I thought you were beautiful. What did I know about literature? I'd never even read half of the works that I was condemning."

"But you have now, haven't you?"

"Your point?"

"You've changed, Jade. And not for the better. There was a time when you believed in things, right or wrong, and you stood up for them. I thought I married a good man, a strong man of faith and commitment."

Jade placed his hands on Alice's shoulders.

"Alie, I still believe in things." He found her eyes. "I believe in this family. I believe that I'm doing the right thing by providing you all with a good home in a good neighborhood. And, if I take this transfer to Portland, I can provide an even bigger house in an even better neighborhood. We'll be able to trade your old Honda in for a new car with air bags and a CD player. I want to take good care of this family. Can't you see that?"

"Baloney." Alice brushed his hands away. "This transfer is for you, not us. You're the only one who wants to leave. You're the only one who has something to prove to the world, to yourself, and to Mr. High-and-Almighty Jeffrey Seinner. And why is it that I get the feeling that you're running from something? You and your secrets. It drives me crazy."

His secrets. What did she know of his secrets?

Right now. He should tell her everything.

Alice glared.

"I've decided," she said. "That I'm not moving again. You do whatever you feel you must." Her jaw tightened. "Portland would be a mistake, and you know it. And it's a mistake that I'm not going to make. Nor are your children."

"Why," he exploded, "can't you ever trust me? Everybody says that Portland is wonderful. And we're not going to make a final decision without checking things out. This will be our last move, I swear it. Our last move."

"As I was saying, it's been an awfully long time since you've spouted anything original around here. 'Denver is beautiful, one of the best cities in the country . . . this will be our last move, I swear it.' Stop me if any of this sounds familiar."

"Oh, this is sounding familiar all right. Here we go again. Drag up everything I ever said, throw it all back in my face."

"The kids have made friends here, Jade, and so have I." Alice returned to the couch and dropped into it, exhausted. When she continued, her voice was quiet, grave. "It's not fair to talk about moving 1,300 miles away from everything we know so that you can imagine that you're moving up the corporate ladder. We don't need a bigger house, and this neighborhood is fine."

"We can't stay, Alie. Staying is not an option." Jade dropped himself into the rocker opposite his wife. "The mall store is doing well, but one location could never support my full salary. You know that."

"So let's figure out something else. If it's the right thing to do, something will come together."

"Things don't just magically 'come together' because we want them to, Alie, no matter how hard we wish."

"I'm not talking about wishing, Jade. I'm talking about thinking, making changes, planning . . . and prayer. Or don't you believe in prayer any more, either?"

"Great. Another cheap shot. What's with you lately?"

Jade rose from the rocker and went to the kitchen. He rummaged in the refrigerator, found part of six-pack behind a loaf of bread. Pulled one free. Returned to the living room with the remaining three dangling like the fish stringers they used to fill together in their boating days in Michigan.

"Want one?" he asked.

"Why not."

They were quiet again for many minutes. Jade finished his beer, then wrenched free another. Their eyes never met, and neither attempted to leave.

"Alie," he said at last. "Please, look at me."

She rolled her beer several times between her hands, then set the can on the cover of her magazine. When she met his gaze, her eyes were dry, but barely.

"You're right," he said, slowly. "I've changed. So have you. There was a time when I thought about you day and night. There was a time when all I wanted was to see your smile, to make you laugh, to take you in my arms. For the past year or so, it's has been easier to stay at work or to ride my bike. And to think about anyone but you." Jade placed his beer on the floor. He hadn't meant to say that. Not yet.

"I come home," he said, "and there you are, sulking around like I just spent the evening getting off with a whore." Where did that come from? "Maybe I've been away too much, but that's part of my job."

"Your job. It always comes back to Seinner Books, doesn't it?"

Thank God. She missed the slips. Or was she afraid to pursue them? He shook his head.

"Alice, what about your job? I can remember lots of lonely stretches when you were working on your nursing degree. I would hardly see you for weeks at a time. But you didn't hear me complain. I understood that it was something that you had to go through. A time to pay your dues before you could get to the kind of flexible schedule and the part-time hours that you now enjoy."

"Do I enjoy my schedule? How would you know? When was the last time you asked about how things were going for me at work, or what my shift was like at the hospital?"

"I ask you almost every day."

"Right. 'Honey,' you say as you pick up the paper, 'how was your day today?' You turn on the game. 'That's nice.' You change the channel. 'Uh-huh, uh-huh.' What kind of conversation is that? Do you really expect me to talk to you while you're doing five other things and not listening anyway?"

"If you want to talk, you have to tell me. I'm not a mind reader, you know."

"Of course I want to talk! I've always wanted to talk. That hasn't changed. The only thing that has changed is that you've stopped wanting to listen. You've become far too preoccupied to listen. Preoccupied with your job, busy with your computer, busy thinking about other women and new cars, busy riding your damn bike, busy with your plans for your next new book store. . . ."

Jade looked at his wife across the room.

There was a strangeness and a hostility writhing beneath her expression that startled him.

She looked tired and old.

What did she see in his face? His age? His slipping strength? His shame?

He looked away.

"Alice?" he asked. "Is it too late? Have we drifted too far?"

"I don't know," she answered. "I don't know."

CHAPTER 12

Tuesday, March 19, 1996. Denver, Colorado

Harry's ashes arrived from Houston in a red, white, and blue Priority Mail carton about the size of a small cake pan. The meter strip indicated the eight pound rate, an even $9.00. The handwritten Michigan return address was accurate, and the Colorado zip code was correct. The box was addressed: 'To Jim Vanderspyke Only,' care of the Seinner Books mall store.

Jade shook the package twice, then replaced it unopened upon his desk. He studied the American eagle printed on the box.

Harry was in there. He was settling like the sand in an hourglass beneath that eagle's wings.

Jade rose. He stepped to the door, opened it, then looked out over the sales floor. Chris caught his eye, smiled, nodded and then returned to her conversation with a quivering thin man in green polyester and oversized pants. Jeremy punched numbers into the cash register for a couple of coffee table gift books. Theresa was quietly restocking paperback best-sellers.

All was well at Seinner Family Books.

He retreated, not pulling its knob, letting the door shut in its own slow time. The door sealed with an iron thunk. Jade reached out and twisted the lock.

He returned to his desk, sat down and again studied the package. Wide plastic tape neatly secured the sides and flaps at each end.

Jade lifted a sharp letter opener, then gingerly made incisions the length of the seam and around each flap. He returned the letter opener to the top right drawer. He looked at the eagle, then opened the drawer again, retrieved the letter opener and shifted it over to the top drawer on the left.

The eagle watched, unblinking.

Harry was in there, and Jade was in no hurry to get him out.

Jade adjusted the neck of his desk lamp, brushed aside several pencils, paper clips and a note pad, then tinkered with the parcel until its bottom edge was in perfect alignment with the edge of his desk.

"Harry," he said, addressing the eagle. "Before I can do this, I think that we should talk."

He looked up, felt foolish, though he knew that no one had heard him.

"Harry," he said, turning back to the eagle. "I don't know how well you remember me, but I've got to warn you that I've changed. I've changed a lot. How long has it been, Harry? 15, 20 years?" He quickly did the math in his head. "Well, I'm sure that over the past 19 years, you've changed some, too."

Jade grinned.

He opened one end of the box, careful to leave the package over his desk for fear that the ashes would gush forth and spill to the floor. He prayed that Harry had been double wrapped.

Nothing gushed.

Jade opened the flap at the other end, then cautiously pried the mailer apart along its lateral seam. He slowly unfolded the sides of the package, spreading them open like wings unfurling to catch the sky.

Facing him was a large manila envelope. The envelope rested upon what appeared to be an inner box wrapped in butcher paper. The envelope was marked: To Jimmy. I'm sure that you'll figure out what to do with this. Love, Your Mother.

He closed his eyes.

"Thanks, mom," he whispered. "I think that I'll change my will. I'll see if I can figure out a way to provide you with some equally sentimental memento. My ashes, perhaps."

When he opened his eyes, the envelope and the box still waited.

So much for the nightmare theory.

Time to dig in, to get it over with. Starting with the envelope. Jade lifted the envelope and undid the clasp. Slowly, carefully, he withdrew its contents.

The top item was a pair of stapled documents. Jade reached for his reading glasses.

The first was Harry's marriage certificate, from when he married Jade's mother. It was dated June 3rd, 1955. The second was the corresponding divorce certificate. Notarized February 14, 1970.

Valentine's Day.

Nice touch.

He hadn't known that they had used that date to make it final. Good old Harry, always a kidder.

The next item was similar. A pair of photocopied documents stapled together. Married April 7, 1972; divorced April 1, 1974.

April Fool's Day.

At least Harry hadn't left his sense of humor in Michigan.

The third pair seemed fresher. Yes, August 12th, 1989, and December 21st, 1994.

Winter Solstice. The longest day of the year.

Jade examined the numbers. Fifteen years with his mom, two years for the second marriage, and maybe five years for the last one.

What about the missing years? Were there other marriages? Other documents from failed relationships, records somehow misplaced?

Jade set the certificates to one side.

The next object surprised him.

It was a collector's item. A 1968 Detroit Tigers program. Jade remembered the game. It was one of the only two games that his father had ever taken them to. They closed the shop and tackled a sweltering three-hour drive across the state. One of Harry's friends couldn't use the tickets, and nobody yet guessed that the Tigers would go on to take it all in the World Series. Jade ate too much cotton candy and peanuts. Half way home, he puked in the back seat.

Jade smiled.

It had been a good day. No yelling, no fighting. Even after he threw up, his dad looked more concerned than angry.

Willie Horton homered for the go-ahead run.

Jade placed the program on top of the certificates.

Beneath the program was a wrinkled and stained menu from the Vanderspyke Gift, Snack & Pop Shop. Written across the top in his father's script was the notation: "Our last one. Summer, 1970."

Beneath that was a small envelope; below that was a yellowed, crumbling news clipping neatly folded into quarters. Jade recognized the clipping immediately. He had read it 21 years ago himself, over and over. A week later, he had thrown his copy away.

Jade pushed the clipping aside and examined the envelope.

There were no markings on the outside, and apparently no documents enclosed. He lifted the flap and reached inside. He removed a single, faded instamatic photograph, obviously taken at night with a flash cube. The images were now reduced mostly to pinks, whites and blacks.

Harry faced the camera in the picture, his mouth open, his eyes spooky red, one hand rising to shield his face. He was stepping through a door. Behind him was Mars.

Marsha Fenton.

All these years, and Jade still remembered her name. He studied the photo a moment, then set it aside. He glanced at the last item, the newspaper, then turned back to the photo.

His father had been a good-looking man. The photo did not do him justice. It wasn't exactly one of Harry's finer moments. Even so, Jade could see why women liked him. He was stepping through the door first, prepared at last to face his wife. Jade could hear his father's voice, whispering in prayer, begging for God's forgiveness, urging Mars to pray along, just in case. Convinced that his wife would shoot them both dead the moment that they stepped through the door.

Jade looked closer.

The white explosion of the flash was frozen on the plate glass window near the bathroom door. The picture was poorly framed, so that Harry and Mars were off center to the right. There, to left of the flash star in the window, Jade could make out the dim silhouette of his mother's left side. To the left of her were the faint lines of the trunk of the crab apple tree.

Jade tilted the photo beneath the desk lamp, leaned toward the light.

And there, in the shadows behind the tree trunk, was the vague outline of a small boy. Jade closed his eyes as the flash exploded again in his mind. Looked back.

Perhaps not.

The lines were too faint, too faded, could have been anything.

He set the photo aside, still looking at it. His father's red eyes stared back. Jade turned from those eyes to the final item from the manila envelope.

It was the front page of the Grand Haven Daily News. Jade checked the date. October, 14, 1975. Two days after the accident. The banner headline read:

Community shocked by tragic deaths of two local teens.

Jade scanned the lead.

Friends, family, and community members were shocked yesterday by the news of the untimely and tragic deaths of two local teenagers, both popular students at. . . .

He glanced at the sidebar. Randy and Karen's front-page obituaries. Randy's school picture at the top; Karen's photo near the bottom. Their lists of accomplishments and activities were recounted in the middle, along with the details concerning their memorial services. Jade realized for the first time that Randy was listed on top because he was older, a senior instead of a junior. Karen was only an underclassman. Two decades ago, Jade had raged at the paper for placing Randy's picture above Karen's.

In his senior photo, Randy smiled his father's smile, thrust the same familiar, confident square chin.

Karen's smile looked almost coy, as if she knew some secret that she might not share. She wore a light turtleneck and a dark vest. A tiny gold cross and chain were barely discernible in the newspaper photo, but Jade could tell that it was there. It was something that she almost always wore.

Reluctantly, his eyes drifted to the front page headline photo.

A tow truck was winding in a long cable. Police officers and emergency crews hovered about the scene. The cable extended into the water, straining to haul up the shattered bow of a partially submerged boat. An expensive motorboat, destroyed.

The boat had belonged to Karen's dad. She was driving it when it rammed into the dock, when it plowed beneath the deck slats. When the steel joist of the deck splintered the top of the bow and sliced off the windshield.

And Randy's head.

Jade felt his stomach lurch.

He closed his eyes.

He turned the clipping over, then leaned into his hands.

"And thank you, dad, for the memories." He rubbed his eyes.

After several moments, Jade gathered the small pile and slipped the papers back into the manila envelop.

"That's it?" he asked. "That's all you left?" He touched the white butcher paper. "Not even 27 cats to grieve your passing."

He warily raised the inner package and shook it gently. The butcher paper was wrapped tightly and secured with two pieces of tape. The box felt flimsy, the contents heavy. The sides of the box bowed out slightly, though it was clear that Harry had been packed with little room to shift.

Jade broke the tape seals and slowly peeled back the wrapping.

Inside was a cereal box.

Frosted Flakes.

Jade smiled and looked closer.

Family size. Jumbo package, fat free.

Harry settled to one side as Jade instinctively checked the nutrition label on the end panel. Jade caught himself and laughed.

Jade returned the box to face him from his desk. Tony the Tiger grinned widely, eyes full of life. Promises of tasty nutrition.

"Welcome to Denver," Jade grinned back. "I hope that you enjoyed your trip, and that you weren't too cramped in there." He laughed again, shaking his head.

His mother had said that she would disguise the ashes, and Harry had always liked Frosted Flakes. It made sense. She probably emptied the box from Harry's own cupboard.

Jade again picked up the box, this time to examine the top and to check for leaks. And to see Harry. He had still not gotten a look at Harry.

There was more scotch tape, and surprisingly enough, no leakage. Jade broke the tape with his thumbnail and folded back the flaps.

A stay-fresh liner. Of course. No wonder Harry had stayed inside.

The ashes were visible through the translucent plastic bag. Shades of gray. Jade reached into the box and loosened the final piece of tape. He worked gently to avoid any tears, then unrolled the top of the stay-fresh liner and peered in.

Harry's ashes. Sand. Thicker than dust, thinner than gravel. Maybe even a little bird shot buried somewhere in there.

But mostly just shades of grays, somber hues not altogether unlike the Michigan sky under the canopy of a building storm.

Jade touched a fingertip to the grays and smiled faintly.

Only drier. Much drier.

He bent closer and sniffed. Faint traces of the cereal lingered within the box.

Too weird.

Jade closed the top and sighed.

CHAPTER 13

Wednesday, March 20, 1996.
The first day of Spring, Denver

"What's the word from the home front?" Terry brushed his cocktail straw aside and sipped from a tall White Russian. "Are you and Alice still at war?" He squared his coaster and returned his glass to the table, a lacquered slice of cottonwood harvested from Eldorado Canyon. At the Grill, every table had its own charm, though their favorite was this one in the corner, far from the street's busy windows.

Jade frowned. "I don't really want to talk about the war." He stirred his drink. "Alice has got me by the big guns."

Terry laughed. "Not good."

"Not good."

"Well, at least you still call the shots at work."

"Right." Jade shrugged. "Work." He looked at his drink. "To be honest, it's getting tougher every day to go in. I'm getting tired of always sucking up to big Jeff Seinner back at HQ." He sighed. "My son says I'm being used. Worse yet, Mark's right."

Terry smiled. "Makes you wonder, huh? One day you look up from the trenches, shell shocked and bleeding, and you ask, Is this it? Is this the rest of my life?" He retrieved his drink. "It's a bitch."

"A bitch." Jade laughed. He saluted Terry with his glass and took another drink.

"Welcome to mid-life," said Terry, saluting back. "The midlife bitch. And I don't mean my wife."

They grinned. Jade's shoe tapped against his briefcase under the table.

Terry sighed. "As much as our bosses bug us, I guess we're lucky. At least we've got jobs to knock. With all the acquisitions and mergers lately, lots of guys our age are out the door. They can really bitch."

"Tell me about it. One of my best sellers is a book called *Planning Ahead: Mapping Your Next Career, Next State, and Next Prenuptial.*"

Terry laughed. "Someone called me today about his insurance. This guy was just laid off, and he wanted to know if his policy covered accidental death if he was speeding."

"A fair question."

"Speeding through his boss's front door."

"Not good."

"Right. Not at all good." Terry touched the sleeve of a passing waitress and requested another round.

"Terry, how about you?" Jade leaned back. "Anything new with the kids?"

"Naw. Sandra says she hates junior high. Diane wants to go to Northwestern to study journalism. I told her to publish a letter to the editor about the idiocy of universal health care, then maybe we could talk." He swallowed the last of his drink.

Laughter erupted from the next table. Three women in tattered jeans and dangling plastic jewelry bubbled and burped like a tight huddle of water coolers. A thin girl with pink-streaked hair struggled with a spoon. She steadied herself, then tested the spoon's balance. She raised it level to a pair of bottle necks, then tried to bridge the spoon between the bottles' lips.

"Oh yeah," said Terry, "Eric is thinking about running high hurdles. I think he. . . ."

Shrieks and giggles cut him short. Jade turned his chair. "How about your wife?" asked Jade. "Is Mary still involved with the truck driver?"

"So they say. He hasn't moved in, but it looks like things are headed in that direction."

"It's got to be tough, thinking about your wife in bed with another guy."

"Not really. Our sex was usually uninspired anyway. She wasn't one to run around, but in her head, whenever we slept together, I'm sure she was screwing other guys. I know I was."

Jade smirked.

"Not other guys, you pervert. Other women. I was thinking about other women when. . . . Sheeze . . . you drink with somebody for six years, and you think you know him. Then all of a sudden. . . ."

Jade laughed. He glanced to his right as their neighbors stood to leave. A large-breasted young woman in a tattered Broncos jersey was taking charge. The shortest girl had a rip in her pants that—from where Jade sat—suggested she wore a G-string or less.

"What do you think?" asked Terry, nodding at the girls. "Are they drunk, or is the Pope an Okie?"

"I've never met the Pope," said Jade, "but I'd say them girls is looped."

The skinny one lost her balance and capsized in Terry's direction. He caught her elbow six inches from his grin, then set her aright.

"Thanks," she slurred. "I needed dat." She giggled. "Say, do I know you?"

"No," said Terry. "I don't think so."

"Then wha's yer hand do'en on my ass?"

"It's not," he laughed. "That's your hand on your ass."

She looked.

"Sure 'nough," she giggled. "Say, yer kinda cute. Would ya like to put yer hand on my ass?"

The other two girls hooted and stomped. Terry looked at Jade and grinned.

"Okay," laughed their leader. "Let's move along. Time to pay our bill and go home. Unless these two guys wanna take us for a spin?"

"I'd love to," laughed Terry. "Except today I took the bus.

Maybe some other time. I'll give you a call."

"And what's your excuse, big fella?" she asked, leaning toward Jade. "You gonna be a gentleguy and ride us a give home?"

Jade felt himself blush.

"I, uh, would," he said. "But my wife has got my keys. If you want a ride, you'll have to ask her." Jade pointed toward an enormous woman at the bar. He had noticed her earlier and had wondered if she had yet bought her copy of Frying Fat Free. The girls followed his finger, then laughed.

"Thanks anyway," blurted the third. "We'll walk. We need the exercise. No offense, but we don't want to end up needing park benches the next time we come in."

There was another round of giggles. As the girls left, Jade confirmed that the torn pants were certifiably panty free.

"Would you look at that," snickered Terry, shaking his head. "What a smut-fest. If those three became regulars, the Grill could hit us with cover charges for the show."

"Say, speaking of smut," grinned Jade, "I've got a dilemma down at work."

"What's the matter, has Chris started leaving notes again?"

"Shhh." Jade leaned forward with a sudden frown. "Keep it down, would you? People come here who know me from the store."

Jade sat back, but kept his voice to a near whisper. "No, Chris has been fine. I laid down the law a while ago, and she's been perfectly appropriate ever since. I miss her flirting, but I'm not dreaming about her every night, and that's what counts. I was scared to death that I'd mumble something in my sleep. If Alice ever got a snatch of one of my dreams, she would go through the roof."

"If Alice really cared about your mental sex life, maybe she'd give you a little snatch of her own to think about from time to time."

"We have sex."

"Sure. New Year's and birthdays, right?"

"It's not that bad."

"Just bad enough that when you doze off, you dream of another woman?"

"I guess. Sometimes."

"Well, if you can't change Alice, you can always change yourself. Go ahead, sleep with Chris. You know she's willing. Maybe after a couple of wild rolls you'll finally get the little tease out of your system."

"No. Sleeping with Chris wouldn't solve anything. I'm not wired that way. Some guys have affairs, but some of us never do. Never have and never will."

Terry grinned.

Jade stirred his drink. His mind flashed to the sweet spot in the young woman's pants, the torn hole that aligned once each step to reveal the coupling of her tan ham with her firm white bun.

"Well," said Terry. "I've never been a choir boy myself, so I wouldn't know. It's hard to believe that a guy could live his whole life without ever probing the mysteries of at least a couple of extracurriculars. But you're the expert, right?"

"I'm not an expert on anything, least of all women." Jade took a shallow sip. "But of all the things that I'm ashamed of, cheating on Alice is not one of them. I've never done it. It's kind of a promise that I made at our wedding, and it's part of a vow that I made with God about my sex life long before I met Alice. I don't think that I could live with myself if I broke those vows and messed around."

"A man might be surprised by what he can live with."

"Maybe. If he has to. But living through something is different than choosing it. And who in his right mind would chose to create his own suffering unnecessarily?"

Jade took another drink.

Chris would have looked deadly in those holey pants. She undoubtedly packed a savory sweet spot of her own. He could imagine. He bit his tongue.

"Terry," he said, "You know about that Promise Keepers movement that started with the football coach up in Boulder? I've never attended any of their meetings, but I think that I'm a kindred spirit. I take my promises and commitments very seriously. I always have. That's the way I am."

"Promises are made to be broken." Terry sighed. "Things change. Jade. Accidents happen. I should know, I'm in the business. That's all I see. Accidents. Unexpected disasters. Broken dreams and crushed bones. The smart guys are the ones who have the courage to admit that bombs go off. They're the ones with the guts to plan accordingly to minimize the fallout."

"No, I don't buy that." Jade leaned forward. "There are choices a man can make that'll have harsh consequences. Hellish consequences that must be suffered, and perhaps appropriately so." Jade paused, thinking of Harry's ashes in the box below. "Like when a guy chooses to get drunk or to have an affair. Eventually, such a man has to wake up and live with the mess that he's made."

Jade realized that his toe was resting against the briefcase, tipping it slightly. He quickly pulled his foot away.

"And then the other—a very different thing—is having to endure the sort of suffering that results from situations that are out of our hands. Like the birth of a sick child, or developing a brain tumor, or getting carted off to Auschwitz."

"I think," said Terry, "that it's all out of our hands. Life is one big string of accidental situations. We are what we were dealt. Fate rules."

"No God?"

"Fate is God."

Jade shook his head. He looked around the room, mostly to avoid Terry's stare. The kitchen help was preparing the buffet table against the back wall.

"Over there," said Jade. "See those appetizers? Fruit, vegetables, cheeses, buffalo wings. . . . The chef in back decides the options, but I get to choose what goes on my plate. Just like I'm not the one who makes the women of this world, but I do get to decide how many or which ones I'm going to sleep with."

"Wrong. You can't sleep with a woman you've never met. And you can't meet a woman who runs because she thinks you're a jerk. And a woman can't help it if she thinks you're a jerk if you look like someone who used to do terrible things to her Barbie dolls. Fate rules."

"Barbie dolls?"

"Yeah. I read about it in Psychology Today. There's a whole national support network of traumatized women who are recovering from the abuses suffered by their Barbies. You know, from brothers and older boys. Amputations, scalpings, acid tortures, dog licks, that sort of thing."

"I'm afraid I hadn't heard."

"Oh yeah. Big news. They've even got a diagnosis for it. Post-Traumatic Barbie Abuse Distress Disorder. My company has already started getting reimbursement requests from therapists."

"Uh huh."

"Yeah, big news."

Jade watched a well-dressed couple settle into a booth near the window. The woman was quite attractive. Even more so when she removed her coat. Jade shook his head and turned back to Terry.

"So," he said. "You hinted a few minutes ago that you thought about other women while you were making love to Mary."

"All the time. I don't think I could have made it without their help. Sometimes women from the past. Sometimes women from the media. Even the wives of best friends."

"Terry, are you baiting me?"

"Whatever do you mean?"

"You fantasized about my wife? Alice?"

"Relax Jade, only in my head. Your precious Alice remains undefiled."

"I'm not angry. Just surprised. You'll have to let me know your secret. I haven't successfully fantasized about Alice in years. Whenever I picture her in bed, I lose interest."

"You dummy! That's your problem. Don't picture her in your

bed. And not as your wife. Picture Alice as my wife, in my back yard, tanning on a lawn chair. She's intentionally entertaining the neighbors, you know, the ones with the telescopes. She's got her suit untied with the strings pulled down. She starts rubbing in the oil, and, well, you can imagine." Terry grinned. "It always works for me."

Jade squirmed in his chair.

"Terry, maybe we shouldn't joke around like this."

"Who's joking?"

Jade sat back, raised his invisible harmonica, then rubbed a knuckle against his teeth. After several notes, he planted his elbows and leaned into the table.

"I know that you're not much into religion," said Jade, "but what do you make of that Bible saying about lust? It's something like: 'Anyone who looks at a woman with lust has already committed adultery in his heart.' Sometimes I worry about that verse. Do you suppose there's any truth in it?"

"Sounds pretty harsh to me. I've heard the saying, and I've always felt that a guy doesn't stand a chance against a saying like that. It makes us all a bunch of adulterers, because there's no way you can keep certain thoughts from popping into your head from time to time. Particularly around beautiful women who like to tease. It's a hormonally and culturally-conditioned reflex thing."

"I'm not sure if the saying is about what pops into a guy's head, or if it's just talking about when a guy intentionally indulges in fantasies. You know, bells and whistles and all of that."

"Bells and whistles?" Terry laughed. "I'll have to try it. Sounds interesting."

"So you're not worried about committing adultery in your head."

"Of course not. How can I commit adultery when I'm not even married anymore? Besides, this whole thing gets way too complicated. Take for example you and Chris."

"Shhh. Come on, I said to keep it down."

Terry smiled. "Okay," he whispered. "Let's take you and this hot tamale that's got your tongue all balled in a knot."

"Thank you. That's more like it."

"Okay. So it's the middle of the night, and this dish comes to you in a dream. It's a tasty dream. Very explicit. And you don't wake up until you're drooling, if you know what I mean."

"I know what you mean. Thank you for being discreet."

Terry leaned forward and barely moved his lips. "So after you wake up and the memories flood back, would that verse say that you just fucked her once, twice, or not at all?"

"Terry!" Jade threw his napkin and shook his head.

"I'm serious. Check the logic. Was the dream an 'accident,' or not? Are we responsible for our dreams? Are we responsible for what happens to our bodies while we dream? For our fantasies and memories? For everything that goes on inside our head? See, this is what I said a while ago. It's all a bunch of accidents. Fate and chaos rule, so don't get too bent out of shape over what you can't control."

"We've already established that I don't buy that philosophy."

"Well, then, what do you do with your accidents? What about the things that have happened in your life that messed you up? The things over which you've had no control?"

Jade tapped his glass. "I guess the best thing is to just forget about the bad stuff. Don't wallow in pain and memories, and don't let them mess you up. Such 'accidents,' as you call them, have probably done more than enough damage already."

"I don't know." Terry, stirred his ice. "When something bad happens, it's impossible to simply forget about it. And even if you do manage to put it out of your mind, the bad stuff is still stewing on the back burner in your dreams and subconscious. You can't really just forget it and move on."

Their waitress arrived with fresh drinks. Terry smiled politely, then leaned forward as she left.

"Probably the best long-term thing about insurance is what most people never imagine. We force our clients to tell us exactly what happened. We provide a structured forum through which they must relive the tragedy, complete with all its vivid details, while the loss is still fresh in their minds. Our questionnaires and claim forms make repression almost impossible. From my experience, if a client leaves something out, sooner or later, it'll come back to haunt him. And then we all end up with an even bigger bill to pay."

"Yes," said Jade, "but what if it's water that's long since passed beneath the bridge, and now there's absolutely nothing a person can do?"

"That's never the case. Never. There's always something that a person can do."

"What?"

"Talk about it, you moron. Break the silence. Speak up. To a priest or a therapist, if no one else. What do you think I'm trying to say?"

"I don't know. I've been considering this for a while. I don't necessarily believe that talking about things is always such a good idea. A couple days ago, I remembered that famous passage in the Bible that was made into a song. You know, 'For everything there is a season.' One of the lines in that passage says there's a time to be silent."

"Right," sighed Terry. "But in the same breath, isn't there a line about a time to talk or something? The way that I remember it, that's the whole point of those sayings, to show the tension between doing and not doing things." Terry shook his head. "And what's going on with you all of a sudden? Why are you bringing up Bible verses today? You're not trying to turn our happy hours into prayer meetings, are you?"

"No, of course not. Sorry."

Jade decided against expanding the discussion to include his recent encounters with Hosea and prayer at the cairn. But he still needed to find a way to bring up the subject of Harry. He needed suggestions for what to do with Harry's ashes.

They were both quiet.

"Well, anyway," said Jade, "here's my problem at work. When

I started with Seinner, the company was a small chain of religious book stores. Family stuff. Then 15 years ago, Seinner added some science fiction and fantasy titles. The next year, he added historical romances, then westerns and detective stories, then bodice rippers. Now he's made a deal with a new publisher called NightLight Books. These folks specialize in nothing but pure sleaze."

"And?"

"I don't want to handle those kinds of books."

"Why not?"

"They're trash. By design, with no apologies offered."

"So?"

"Whose side are you on, anyway?"

"I'm just playing devil's advocate." Terry smiled. "So to speak."

"So to speak."

"And?" pressed Terry.

"For one thing, most of my employees are young women. It wouldn't be fair to subject them to the kinds of situations and clients that would be associated with such books."

"Watching over your virgins, eh, big daddy?"

"Come on, Terry. I'm serious."

"Okay. What else?"

"I've tried to take pride in what I do. I've wanted to believe that I was making a contribution to society and to the lives of those who buy my books. But with this garbage, no way."

"Then tell Seinner no."

"It's not that easy. Seinner's contract with NightLight stipulates that a small publisher's display of their titles will be exhibited in each of Seinner's 25 mall locations. They gave Seinner a special pricing break just for this sort of national exposure."

Jade briefly raised his knuckle to his teeth, hesitated, then lowered his hand. "If I don't toe the line on this, it'll cost Seinner thousands of dollars in wholesale discounts. NightLight is hellbent on gaining national recognition their first year out. Suburban mall distribution is very important to them, and they'll play hard ball to get it."

"I see."

"I've dragged my heels as long as I can. The publisher's regional representative will be by any day to check on the display."

"Not good."

"Correct. Not at all good. Do you see my dilemma?"

"Sure. But you're a bright boy. I trust you'll do the right thing. Now trust yourself."

"Thanks."

Terry grew quiet. "Do you know what your problem is?"

"No. Enlighten me."

"It's your damn high-mindedness. You're getting all tripped up in your prissy ideals and convoluted loyalties. The world is a messy place. You can't traffic in worldly affairs without getting a little mud on your boots. This is the same problem that you're having with your family. You go into these things with such lofty ideals that you inevitably set yourself up for discouragement, failure and guilt."

"Guilt?"

"Sure. Look at how you're beating yourself black and blue for not being good enough to give your wife and kids the moon and Denver too. Look at how you're slitting your wrists over a little compromise at work. And look at your shame over your attraction to Chris. You're drowning, feeling guilty as sin."

"The word 'sin' does come to mind."

"Jade, what am I going to do with you?"

"Help me?"

"Okay. You want help, here's the best I've got." Terry touched his napkin lightly to his lips, then placed it on the table. "You, my friend, are a lost puppy. God only knows how, but you have somehow wandered out the door. You've been roaming around for a long time, and now it's time to find your way home."

"What do you mean, home'? Where, or what-the-heck, is home?"

"How should I know? That's something we each decide for ourselves. For you, maybe home is being in a good space with

Alice and your kids. Maybe it's a job you believe in. Hell, I don't know, maybe it's church. You figure it out."

"I'm not sure I can. Even if you're right, I'm not sure that I'd be able to go home. My wife and daughter are so mad about Portland right now, they'd probably throw the deadbolt if they saw me coming. And Mark. I don't know what has happened to Mark. He's become such a smart mouth, it's all I can do to sit with him. How does a person go home to that?"

"Anyway he can."

"Wonderful."

"I'm serious. A person has to go home anyway that he can. And sometimes, it ain't pretty."

Terry looked at his hands, then back to Jade. "When I was a kid, we had a neighbor who was an alcoholic. He'd stay out until his money was gone. He'd sleep in the gutter until he was sick. He'd knock over garbage cans until his knees bled. And then eventually, when he was sick and hungry and cold enough, he'd find the courage and humility to come back home. I can remember watching him through the window a few times. When the hour arrived to come home, somehow, he would do it. Even if he had to crawl. I guess he was lucky, because his wife never locked the door."

"I'm not much of a crawler."

"Most men aren't. I know I'm not. I think that we're all pretty much in the same boat. We're better at running, screwing and fighting than we are at crawling."

"This is all very encouraging."

"Sorry. As I said, I'm not much of a crawler, either. If splashing through muddy puddles on your hands and knees is not your bag, then hit the high seas like the rest of us. Hoist the sails, brave the storms, and fire your guns. Eat, drink, and be merry, for tomorrow we shall die."

"Good idea." Jade started to rise. "Let's eat. The line at the buffet has finally disappeared."

"That's it?" Terry put his hand on Jade's sleeve. "Come on, hold it. What's going on with you tonight?"

Jade dropped back into his seat. "What do you mean?"

Terry looked him hard in the eyes. His voice became demanding, almost cruel. "Time to cut the crap, Jade. I'm a better friend than that. I deserve more. What's going on?"

Jade met Terry's gaze. He reached beneath the table and found the handle of his briefcase, thankful for the chance to look away. He straightened slowly, then placed the case upon the table.

"I have something to show you, Terry."

"Yes, I figured as much. I've never known you to bring work in from your car."

Jade clicked open the locks, then hesitated.

"I got a call from my mother a few days ago."

Terry did not blink.

"My father, Harry Vanderspyke, is dead. He blew his head off with a shotgun right after Valentine's Day."

Still no response.

"Terry," Jade opened his black leather case, "meet papa Harry."

Jade withdrew the cereal box, closed the briefcase, then deposited the beaming tiger upon their lacquered stump.

CHAPTER 14

Thursday, March 21, 1996.
Lakewood, Colorado

Jade opened his eyes to the sound of optimistic winter birds. Rolling to his side, he found himself rested for the first time in weeks. Alice stirred, then recurled herself in sleep.

The night before, Terry had left him confused, but somehow empowered. Terry was full of humor about the situation, and some of his ideas for Harry's ashes were hilarious. On the practical side, his suggestion to sprinkle the ashes on a mountain top or in a flower bed at City Park made sense. If Jade ever got sentimental, he could return to pay old Harry a visit. Terry was also encouraging about the NightLight display. He told Jade to trust himself, to face the issue and then move on. Full speed, no regrets.

Jade folded the covers down from his chest and swung his feet to the slippers beside his bed. The sun poured fat and unobstructed through the drapes. He rose and parted the curtains farther. A kaleidoscope of colors splashed and bounced from windows and car bumpers and off the delicate ice crystals etched along the curbs by pre-dawn frost.

"Nice," he whispered. "What a beautiful day."

Jade entered the mall through the front entrance. To save time, he normally used his key on the back door, but today he wanted to approach the store like a consumer. He wanted to imagine a buyer's impressions as he walked the mall and entered Seinner Books with an open mind.

He wanted to imagine the effect of encountering a NightLight display.

Jade strolled the expansive gallery, finding the shops and merchandise that usually blurred in the rush of his day now suddenly clamoring in garish urgency. He passed a sneaker store. Black for gym, purple for joggers, red for bikers. Plastic, and canvas, and leather, and tiny brass eyelets. An entire store of options in minutia.

To his left, a cookie shop. A truck-sized case of fresh chocolate chips, pecans, peanut butters, raisins, white chocolates, almonds, coconuts. . . .

Again to his right, a clothing store. An alluring mannequin guarded the window with one hand thrust toward the glass in a stopping gesture he could hardly resist. She leaned into an implied wind as the fingers of her free hand slipped seductively into the waistband of a fashionable skirt. Behind the plastic and plaster sentinel, rack upon rack of young miss, and women's, and full-figure tops and bottoms hung in lavish rows of wanton necessity.

Ten paces to the left, a music store . . . aisle after aisle, classical, alternative, rap, rock, easy listening, western.

And then Seinner Books.

The store looked unfamiliar from this side. Glass windows and wooden racks, metal shelves of stock. Colorful displays identified by bright yellow, blue, and red signs. The store was open, but quiet. Except for the cushions and thick carpet of Jade's Book Nook, his store looked much like all the rest.

Chris was busy behind the counter, silently rifling through a box of book markers. She was oblivious to Jade's appraising gaze.

To Jade's left was a stone planter with a thick palm tree. Next to the planter was a steel bench, a bronze animal sculpture and a large concrete trash receptacle. The objects hung together like a small island in the waters of a vast commercial sea. Jade stepped behind the palm, set his briefcase on the tile, then leaned to watch. Chris continued flipping and sorting.

Jade imagined a customer seeing her for the first time. She

looked 30, comfortably confident and unusually attractive. Standing on the riser behind the counter, she seemed average in height. But if she stepped down, her breasts would drop to below his chest.

She had applied for this job after quitting as a high school librarian. She interviewed well. While answering routine questions, she demonstrated a quick and daring sense of humor. She possessed an impressive command of literature and the English language. She was the daughter of a Denver contractor, had been married once, no kids, and had gone back to college for an English degree after her divorce. She seemed wonderfully tailored for the job. Jade offered her the position on the spot.

From behind the palm, he continued to watch.

She was beautiful, and she moved well. Her whole body moved well. Even her elbows and chin.

What would it have been like to have been her first husband? To have pulled her close every night in bed? Her first husband had been a fool to let her go.

Chris finished organizing the book marks, then began straightening the pens and invoices that were scattered around the cash register.

She was a good manager. Customers responded well to her suggestions, and she did a solid job of motivating and directing the clerks that worked beneath her supervision.

The only problem was the sexual tension between her and Jade. It had started with her jokes about Alice and his home life, then progressed to more blatant flirtations and sexual innuendoes. Around Halloween, the outright teasing began, then rose to dangerous levels.

Finally, there was an incident in the store. It was after hours, and Jade had stopped himself only at the last possible moment. Afterwards, e-mail messages began arriving on his home computer, until finally he told her it must end.

But he felt guilty. He had participated in the escalation of the situation, and he sensed that his problems with Chris were partially of his own making.

Chris finished her work behind the counter and stepped down from the riser. She wore a light-colored top and a tight dark skirt. She walked to the table near the store's entrance and began straightening books for the new day.

The attention of such an intelligent and attractive woman had been exciting. His mistake was not stopping the flirting early on while things were still under control. Fortunately, the move to Portland would put an end to an increasingly awkward situation. Jade shifted as Chris bent to align books on a bottom shelf.

Suddenly, a massive hand clamped itself to the back of his neck.

Jade jerked, nearly upturning the palm tree as he instinctively spun to face his assailant.

"Hold it," boomed the voice. The man towered over Jade in a dark uniform. "I think you've seen enough of the lady for one day." He wore the eyes of a snarling Doberman. Jade recognized him as one of the part-time security guards left over from the holidays.

"I, uh," said Jade, trying to gather his wits. "I own that store. Well, I don't actually own it, but it's mine. I'm the manager."

"I thought," he accused, "that Chris was the manager. She told me so herself."

Jade shifted uneasily. "Well, Chris is the manager, but I'm her boss. A supervisor, actually. I'm Jade Vanderspyke."

He wondered how the man had found time to chat with Chris, but had never found three minutes to introduce himself to Chris' boss. Jade glanced past the security guard to Chris, who now watched with concern from the front of the store.

"Okay, Mr. Vanderspyke." The man stepped back. "If that's who you are. But something seems fishy. You know what I mean?"

Jade knew, and felt ashamed.

"I was walking my beat and there you were spying on her from behind the tree. What was I supposed to think?"

Jade didn't need the man's apology. Just his good-bye.

0955-CHEA

"As you can imagine," the guard continued, "we don't need no stalkers in this mall."

"I understand," said Jade. "But I assure you, I'm no stalker. I just like to check on my employees from time to time, to make sure they're doing their jobs."

"Right. If you say so." He started off, then turned. "Have a good day, Mr. Vanderspyke. And let me know if you ever need some help keeping an eye on her. Got that?"

"Got it," said Jade. "Okay. And you have a good day, too."

Jade turned. Chris was staring, looking confused.

He sighed, shook his head, then approached the store. Dead man walking.

"What was that all about?" she asked, stepping aside to let him pass.

"Just me and Mr. Rent-a-Cop introducing ourselves."

"But what was Bob saying? You looked upset."

So his name was Bob. Chris seemed genuinely worried. She brushed a wisp from her left eye. "It looked like he was trying to arrest you or something."

"Naw, Bob's just a friendly guy." Jade didn't know what to add. He felt like a teenager caught in the garage with a stack of Playboys.

"Okay," she shrugged. "Well, Bob was hanging around the store the other day, and he struck me as a little strange."

Jade frowned. "No, Bob is safe. Nothing to worry about."

"I was surprised to see you in front of the store. I never saw you come in."

"I came in through the mall. I wanted to check the store from the outside." He stepped to the nearest display. "This sign is a little off." He adjusted it several inches left and right.

"I'm sorry, I hadn't noticed." She watched him fidget, then caught his eye. "It's been quiet this morning. You haven't missed a thing."

"Well, it's Thursday, and Thursday's are always slow. A good day to catch up on little things around the store." Jade struggled to slow his heart, which was still pounding from the surprise of Bob's hand.

"I suppose. Is there anything else you want me to work on besides inventory?"

Jade stepped to the counter and briskly checked his planner. "Maybe you could catch up on a little paper work. My big thing today is deciding about the NightLight books. I've got to make a decision before I leave tonight."

"I know," said Chris. "Mr. Seinner called yesterday. He told me to remind you about the display." Chris smiled. "His exact words were," she lowered her chin and furrowed her brows in mock seriousness, "'Chris . . . you go to work on him. That man is starting to make me nervous.'"

Chris laughed. "This is a pretty big deal to him, isn't it?"

Jade felt a rush of anger. He had been with Seinner for over two decades. Now, all of a sudden, Seinner was turning his own people against him.

"Yes, this is important to Jeff. It's stuck in his craw that I might be starting to think for myself. That I might no longer need his constant advice."

"Well, Jade, you've got to do what you've got to do." Chris lifted a Civil War history and tapped the cover jacket flush at the bottom. "But I don't see why you're fighting him on this. Have you read any of the NightLight books? They're really not that bad. A little more racy than usual, but nobody has to buy them if they don't want to. It's a free country, right?"

"I guess."

"And if folks don't buy them here, they'll just buy them someplace else."

"Is this what Seinner meant about working on me?"

Chris smiled. It was the smile that sent him whirling.

"No," she said slowly. "This is a friend offering a simple piece of advice. Cool down, look at the books yourself and give me the go-ahead. I've already picked an inconspicuous spot for the display in the back corner by the sword and sorcery display. I'm think-

ing we can leave the Book Nook there if we double up a bit in
back. Little old Sunday school teachers will never know the books
are in the store. I'll put the display up myself. Your hands will be
clean." She grinned. "And a new lineup of titles this weekend would
certainly help us hit that record March you've been trying so hard
to get."

"What about the other clerks?" asked Jade. "How do you think
they'll feel about handling these sorts of books?"

Chris stepped to the side of the table. "That's what I like about
you, Jade. You're so old fashioned."

She straightened a red sale sign, then rejoined him behind the
counter. "Don't worry about the other clerks. The sex doesn't bother
them at all."

"It's not just the sex scenes. . . ."

"Jeremy read most of the books they sent the first week, and
he thinks they're great. Theresa and Autumn think the books are
boring. They figure that anyone who reads stuff like that is a Ne-
anderthal. And you already know what I think."

"Refresh my memory."

"I think the books are harmless. They're only stories. If Seinner
can make some money selling them, why not? They're definitely
not worth getting into hot water over."

"Am I in hot water?"

"Yes and no. Mr. Seinner likes you, and he's not going to dump
you if you send back the display. On the other hand, as we both
know, the downtown store will be closed within a year."

Chris ran her hand over the side of her hair. "If Portland is
something that you'd like to make happen, now is not the time to
rub Mr. Seinner's nose in a lot of independent thinking." She
stepped uncomfortably near. "I'm worried about you, Jade.
That's all."

Her hair and perfume floated into his senses like butterflies;
he could almost feel wings brushing in the warmth of her body
and breath.

"What about you, Chris?" He inched back as casually as he

could. "Any new ideas about what you'll be doing?"

"Oh, who knows," Chris stepped again in his direction. "Maybe I'll move to Portland. You might need help. I would be happy to give you a hand."

The way she pronounced 'hand' unnerved him. He imagined her hand. . . .

"Let's take this a step at a time. I might not even go myself. Alice and kids are fighting me all the way."

"Of course," Chris sighed. "But you're a great boss, and I'm just worried that I'm going to lose you."

Her eyes softened. "I would miss working for you more than you might think. A guy like you is hard to find. I hope your wife realizes how lucky she is."

Jade felt a flash of panic. Felt the whirlpool gathering momentum. Felt Chris' smiling lips buried in the soft part of his neck. Felt himself stroking. . . .

"Speaking of my wife," he blurted, "I'd better give her a quick call." He looked around Chris to the phone at the other end of the counter. "There were some things that I was supposed to pick up after work, but I forgot the list on the kitchen table."

Chris flashed Jade a knowing smile. "She couldn't pick them up herself on the way home from the hospital?"

"Uh, no." Jade took a small step. "Alice was planning to work late. She said she wouldn't have time to stop."

"Well, you'd better call her then." Chris lifted the receiver and handed Jade the phone, making him reach.

He numbly punched the numbers for the nurse's station at the hospital. He cursed himself as the phone rang on the other end. What kind of man. . . .

The nurse who answered said Alice was busy, but that she would leave a message. Jade said thanks and hung up.

He returned the phone to Chris.

"Alice is with a patient. She'll call later." He felt a blush rising up his cheeks. "When she calls, I'll be in the back room."

He looked at his new watch. "Yes, this would be a good time

for me to check the NightLight books. But don't forget to come and get me when Alice calls."

"Good idea," said Chris. "And if anything else comes up," she winked, "I'll come and get you for that, too."

"Okay. Good." He started to leave.

"By the way, Jade. When Alice calls, I'll just announce it over the intercom. Like usual. I'll even announce what line she's on. That way you can take the call using the phone that's there. On your desk, right where it's always been."

Jade walked toward the door, flustered and more ashamed than he had felt in years.

She had dropped him to his knees with little more than a batting of her eyes.

CHAPTER 15

Jade pulled the components of the NightLight display from the large carton in which they had been shipped.

This display was one of the few things in his store that he had not himself ordered. Mr. Seinner authorized a drop shipment of the package directly from the publisher, having assumed that Jade would simply unpack and assemble the display without question when it arrived.

The cardboard shelves and poster-back advertising of the display were pretty typical. They were pre-cut, folded and broken down flat for shipping, then inserted as dividers and liners in a 40-pound box of assorted books. The various pieces of the display could pop open and be tucked together in less than 15 minutes. The books were pre-sorted so they could be checked into inventory and shelved in a matter of minutes.

The whole business was engineered to consume less than an hour of a manager's time.

Jade arranged the pieces of the display into piles that fanned around him on the stock room floor. He had solicited the input of his employees on the new line, so the seals of the display's boards and bundles were already broken, and the sub-boxes containing the publisher's sample titles were already slit.

Jade nudged the books aside for later inspection. He began with an examination of the cardboard portion of the display. The poster-back advertising of the display followed the usual mixed-medium die-cut formula. Once assembled, it became a near life-size version of the flier that caught his eye months ago. The dominant color of the display was black, with most of the lettering and graphics glowing in Halloween oranges, blood reds and oozing greens.

The top edge of the display was punched to silhouette the profile of a voluptuous scarlet-lipped vampiress, clad in a seductively tattered red and white cheer leading outfit. A pair of plastic ruby-eyes and celluloid fangs were glued to the cheerleader's haunting face. The girl's right arm stretched off the top of the cardboard display and disappeared beneath the shimmering red streamers of an actual pom-pom. She led her hurrah with one shapely thigh raised and the other leg pointing downward to a red-sneakered foot planted firmly atop a gray headstone crudely chiseled to read: "Principal Jack Hoff, May he Rest in Pieces."

Woven around the cheerleader and through the poster was a banner with the company's slogan, "NightLight Books: Horror, Humor, and Erotica, for those who lie awake."

Jade reluctantly conceded that the graphics were effective. The display would undoubtedly move merchandise. He looked again at the cheerleader's strangely familiar skirt, her smooth calves and tanned thighs. They were beautifully done.

He softly bit his tongue.

"Damn."

With some apprehension, he squatted to examine the books themselves.

The first small case was marked "Lovers' Leap, Crash, and Burn." The four books inside were identical, each bearing the same title and illustration. Two young people were depicted flinging themselves hand-in-hand from a jagged cliff into the inferno of a flaming motor home smashed below. The young woman's open white dress billowed above her pink panties as she plummeted; her bronzed lover wore no shirt.

He fanned quickly through the book to reassure himself that there were no other illustrations.

Satisfied, he straightened and stepped to the swivel chair at his desk near the back of the room. He pulled his reading glasses from the center drawer and opened the book a few pages into the first chapter. He picked a spot to check the writer's prose.

> . . . Andrea slithered discreetly through the crowd, her temples throbbing wildly in the awareness that beyond the dance floor lay a cloak room, and that within the cloak room there sat a young virgin who had yet to taste the savory fires of orgasms sealed with blood.
>
> Winnowing her way across the floor, weaving through hot, simmering, nubile masses of gyrating flesh, she passed Jed, captain of the football team. She brushed his infamous #3 jersey with her breasts, a tingling. . . .

Jade closed the book. He smiled, then slid Lovers' Leap to the far edge of his desk. He walked back to the boxes on the floor and reached for another title. The second box was marked "For Your Eyeballs Only." Jade pulled one of the four copies and opened to page 32. He began reading where he stood.

> . . . Dr. Heinsmeier stared confusedly ahead, his eyes absorbing all, but his brain comprehending little. Only seconds ago, she had been an innocent child of nine. Now, under the influence of a mere three drops of his potion, she was changing before his very eyes. The child's closely-cut red hair grew long, flowing, then crimson and writhing beneath his gaze. Her face contorted and shifted from the angelic countenance of youth to the terrifying glow of a gnarled hag suddenly possessed by some savage fiend from the dark side of the grave.
>
> "What have I done!" the doctor screamed, knowing that his formula had somehow loosened the anatomical barriers between human flesh and disembodied spirits, between earth and the demons below.
>
> As he watched, unable to divert his eyes, he witnessed the damned child's tiny fingers metamorphosing upon her lap.

> To the doctor's horror, her fingers quickly elongated from
> young fleshy stubs into steel-like talons with razor tips that
> promised to sear, and pluck, and shred all that they encoun-
> tered. Dr. Heinsmeier found himself powerless to retreat,
> unable to turn his eyes from those sprouting talons. . . .

Jade skipped to the middle of the book.

> Wally gasped in rapt ecstasy. She was a beauty unlike any
> that he had ever beheld. Her flowing hair and full breasts
> glimmered above him in the moonlight like the rippling
> and undulating streaks of silver salmon he had seen fighting
> their way up wild waters to spawn. Her naked hips curved
> in response to his visual caress with the fluidity of mercury
> and the energy of smoldering white coals. . . .

Jade closed the book.

"Okay," he muttered. "No surprises so far."

He shifted the book into his left hand and reached for box
number three. The box was labeled: "Hard Times for Henry." Jade
read the title again.

"Henry," he muttered to himself. "Let's see what's up."

Jade straightened with a copy of the book and examined its
colorful cover.

A cartoon illustration established the book's tone. The cover's
illustration featured an opened-mouthed, middle-aged man at a
diner, who sat peering over a newspaper at a lusty blonde waitress.
The man's drooling tongue rolled out over his teeth and down his
chin like a soggy red carpet. His blood-shot eyes bugged like hard
boiled eggs stewed in Tabasco sauce. The waitress in the cartoon
bent away from the man toward an adjacent table, her blue skirt
hitching provocatively high above white gartered hose. A second
woman, presumably Henry's wife, stood behind the drooling man,
a double-barrel shotgun shoved to within a hair's breadth of the
man's ear.

"That's me," sighed Jade. "Good luck old guy, you're going to need it."

Jade carried the two books back to his seat.

He sat, then tossed the horror-humor *For Your Eyeballs Only* title next to *Lovers' Leap*. He leaned back in his chair and swung his feet to the top his desk.

Jade flipped through the book several times. *Hard Times* for Henry was a collection of short stories, all recounted by a first person narrator named Henry Bittle. The stories were a light-hearted chronicle of Henry's many failures in love and love making. Jade turned to a story bearing the title "My Weekend in Scranton, Pa." He pushed his glasses snug to his nose, then began to read.

> I can't remember how many times the old ball-and-chain begged me to pack the station wagon and tote the family off to her kid sister's place (I had never met Camile) in Scranton, Pa. Last August, I finally caved in.
>
> The kids were about as excited as I was about the whole deal, and as soon as the vacation was announced, every last one of them commenced to work up their excuses for why they'd have to opt out.
>
> Robert came up with a soccer tournament, though I knew for a fact that he had been cut from the team since the second week. (I let him know right off that my silence was going to cost him a thorough cleaning of the garage.) Sandra invented a deathly-discouraged friend who was hospitalized with complications resulting from a liver that had turned sour, and Mike dreamed up a. . . .

Jade skimmed a few pages, then slowed.

> . . . alone. Who would have thought it. With the old ball-and-chain now laid out under an ice pack and enjoying the influence of an extra-strength prescription of I-don't-know-

what, and with the kids all back home 350 miles away, I was
finally free to double-check in on my wife's sister without
having to worry about any more inopportune interrup-
tions.

I quietly slipped from my wife's side and tip-toed down the
hall that led to Camile's bedroom.

Sure enough, the door was still open an inch or two, and
Camile was still going at it on the shag carpet inside. Fortunately, her groaning was sufficient to drown out my heavy
breathing, which under normal circumstances would have
given me away in a second.

Camile's bare feet were strapped in tight, and now that I
had the leisure to study the whole scene more intimately, I
noticed how her glistening shoulders and smooth thighs
heaved whenever she drove herself back in those long sweaty
strokes.

She was in good shape, that was certain. Even so, I was
worried how much longer she could last. I had read in one
of the old ball-and-chain's women's magazines that 20 minutes was pretty much average for a well-trained woman in
good condition, and Camile had probably been pulling
and pushing on her rowing machine for almost a half-hour
already.

Jade lowered the book, shook his head and grinned. Hosea would
love this. What had he called it? Pop-culture, mind-rotting poop?
Jade reopened the book and continued.

Sure enough, Camile was tuckering out and winding down.
Her strokes slowed, then shortened, and then stopped.

I watched as she leaned forward and undid her foot straps.
I could see plain as day that even when doubled over like
that, Camile had less tummy under her black tights than
my old ball-and-chain had floppy stuff under her chin.

As Camile stood, I kind of leaned back away from the door,

just to be sure she wouldn't notice me. I also turned my feet
sort of sideways, getting ready so that when Camile decided
it was time to come out and use the shower at the end of the
hall, I'd be in a position to fly off at a quick hustle. If she
caught me looking in on her, and then told her gorilla husband or my old ball-and-chain . . . well, I shuddered to
think.

But instead, an amazing thing happened. In my wildest
dreams, I had not dared to hope for such luck.

Camile and Bud had a lot of money, so they could afford
something that me and the old ball-and-chain had only
talked about but knew we'd never have. Camile and Bud
slept in what they call a 'Master Bedroom.' That meant that
Camile had, and I never noticed it before, because it's not
like I'd spent a lot of time in there, she had her own shower
right there in her bedroom.

And then, just as casual like as if she was peeling a banana,
Camile skinned off her sweaty clothes right down to her
nipples and pubic. Of course, she had no idea that I was
watching, but it amazed me how a woman of her features
could act so casual in the presence of that degree of breathtaking nakedness.

I desperately wanted to mop the sweat from my forehead
and to clean my glasses, but I feared that if I so much as
twitched, I might wake up from this incredible dream at
home and in bed with the old ball-and-chain.

Still naked, Camile stepped from the crumpled pile that
had recently been her filled tights and stretched underthings.
She moved smoothly across the room, then stopped in front
of the full-length mirror on her closet door. She looked herself up and down, then raised her arms to the hair behind
her head and pulled this ponytail thing free, which let it all
go.

Later, I had to pay a price for that exhibition of sensuality.
But I'd pay the price again a hundred times if I could. There

she stood, long brown hair tumbling as she shook her head,
fingers running back through that hair again and again, her
white tan lines drawing attention to all of the special places
a guy gets to wondering the most about already as it is.
And then, long about the time that I was convinced that life
was about as good as it could get, Camile up and. . . ."

Jade scratched his nose and looked up. He felt embarrassed, excited and a more than a little dirty as he turned the page to see
what happened next to Henry Bittle.

Jade's preliminary assessment of the NightLight book assortment
was mixed. As he had guessed, the writing was uneven. The stories
were classic examples of the sort of hack fiction that sold well within
certain circles, but that was panned by critics as devoid of literary
merit and inappropriate for readers under 18.

Ten years ago, this sort of writing would never have made it
through the doors of a Seinner store. Yet now, dozens of books as
bad as these were already scattered throughout his shelves. The
difference was that NightLight was more direct in their marketing
and more shameless in their commitment to building a reputation
with such trash.

But what was wrong with that? Sex was everywhere in American culture already, and it was always on people's minds. Could he
accuse NightLight of anything other than a shortage of hypocrisy,
of anything other than having the guts to simply deliver the scenes
that men constantly imagined anyway?

Jade wished that he had encountered several brazenly porno-
graphic passages. He could have jotted down the page numbers,
along with a few typed notes, and then returned the whole package for clearly defined reasons.

So far, no such luck.

He would have to read more. Hopefully, worse passages still
lay ahead.

Jade turned another page.

He had been sitting in the back room quietly reading for nearly three hours. The more he read, the more ambivalent he felt.

Hosea had warned him not to cross his conscience, but after several hundred pages of NightLight stories, Jade was no longer certain what his conscience was saying. Immersed in the muck, he felt his vision blurring. He found himself enjoying the stories altogether too much, discovered himself wretchedly leaning toward each disgusting passage he could find.

There was a knock on the door.

"Come in," called Jade. He quickly dropped his book and rose from his chair, then stretched.

It was Chris.

"Hello," she smiled. "I'm glad to see that you're still in here. I was starting to worry that maybe one of those NightLight boogiemen had hauled you away."

She held out a sandwich and chips on a foam plate from the food court. "Here. You've got to be famished. Theresa is watching the register. Jeremy came in early, so I thought I would get you something to eat."

"Actually," said Jade, "after a full morning of this garbage, I think I've lost my appetite. But thanks. I'm sure I'll eat it later. I'll owe you one."

He stepped toward her and extended his hand for the sandwich. She smiled, and their eyes met. Beneath the plate, their fingers brushed lightly during the exchange.

Jade blinked, turned and bit his tongue. He set the lunch on his desk among the books. And fought the whirlpool.

Focus!

"Have you made up your mind?" she asked.

Jade tapped the power button on his computer and listened as the machine surged to life.

"Not yet." He opened a word processing program. "I think I'll put a few notes together, then print something out and see how my reactions look in hard copy. I'm usually more objective once I see something on paper. Whatever I decide, I want to be sure that I can defend my position."

"That makes sense to me." Chris started toward Jade, then stopped. "Well, I suppose I'd better let you get back to work."

"I suppose," said Jade. He wished that she would come closer—was frightened that she might. "But thanks again for the sandwich. Is everything okay up front?"

"Everything is fine. Now you get back to work. I'll check in on you again in a little while."

Chris turned and slipped silently away.

Jade continued to stare at the door after it closed. Once again, he had nearly gone under. If she had lingered. . . .

Jade suddenly felt ravenously hungry. His mouth watered and his lips were dry. His stomach groaned. But the sandwich on his desk did not look good.

Chris had looked good.

He reached for one of the books already flagged with a dozen sticky notes. He turned to a particularly racy paragraph, then began typing the passage onto his screen.

The typing progressed slowly at first. He was concerned about breaking the new book's spine, and he could not find an effective way to keep the pages from flipping. In frustration, he finally cracked the book's spine and dropped a stapler as a paperweight across the pages to hold his place. His fingers began to fly and his thoughts began to churn.

Examined closely, one image at a time, the NightLight stuff was predictable. Yet mysteriously compelling. He knew how some readers became addicted to the escapist fantasy worlds of these insidiously powerful books. He was himself more than merely intrigued. Reading such stories was a lot like his whirlpool fantasies of Chris.

It was mesmerizing . . . and terrifying in its appeal.

He turned to another passage and continued to type.

Jade sensed her presence, sensed the familiar tug of the damned whirlpool. Smelt her perfume. Closed his eyes. Bit his tongue. Felt the wings of her heat brushing against the flush in his cheeks.

The whirlpool closed in, latched onto his lower body and sucked him under before he could catch his breath.

"How long have you been watching?"

"Not long," she smiled.

"I got a little lost in cyberspace for a minute. I never heard you come in "

"I slipped in quietly," she said, "I didn't want to interrupt your work."

"No problem. I needed a break anyway."

"So what's the verdict? Are we going to sell the books, or are we going to send them back?"

"I'm still not sure. If I could pick and choose, there are a few titles in the pile that I'd feel reasonably comfortable handling. The rest," Jade sank into his chair, "I'd rather not stock."

"What is it about these books that bothers you, Jade?"

"For starters, most of the horror stories are exploitative and callous toward violence. The presentation of women in many of these books is degrading, and the passages that pass for humor are often vulgar and mean-spirited. And the books in this stack here," Jade pointed to the erotica titles, "glorify infidelity and promote sexual indiscretion."

"Professor Vanderspyke," laughed Chris. "May I approach your desk?"

Chris walked to the desk and lifted the top book from the small erotica stack. She examined it for a moment, then looked up, apparently happy with what she had found.

"So is this the sort of thing that's giving you a hard time?" She touched her finger to a passage and began to read.

> . . . Chang Lo lifted Ashley's face to his lips. He began kiss-
> ing her forehead and cheeks with the passion of wild grass
> fires teased into steaming clouds by hot Asian monsoons.

0955-CHEA

> His desire had simmered for days, building and burning,
> boiling within. . . .
> His lips found their way to Ashley's mouth, where they
> paused, drawing moist pleasure from her soft trembling
> gasps. His lips lingered, probing the damp crevasses of her
> receptive mouth. . . .
>
> Once again, Chang Lo's lips were sweeping across Ashley's
> face in hot circles, spirals of heat and energy that burned
> their way ever downward, past her smooth chin, down her
> white throat, and into her sweat-drenched blouse.

Chris looked at Jade and smiled.

He stopped breathing. She pushed a few books aside, then sat
on his desk, crossed her legs and continued to read.

> Ashley moaned softly. She wanted to push Chang Lo away.
> He was going too far. Her husband could walk through the
> door at any time.
> She raised her hands to Chang Lo's head, intending to make
> him stop. As her fingers reached his hair, she felt his tongue
> suddenly hot and wet upon her breast, lapping the flesh
> above her brassiere. Ashley shivered, her arms instinctively
> wrapping themselves around his head and drawing him
> deeper into her throbbing chest. His tongue continued to
> knead and explore her soft flesh, more eager, more bold than
> before, driving itself deep beneath the lace of her. . . .

Jade rose from his chair and cleared his throat. "Ah, yes. That's
probably enough to give us the idea."

"Oh, you old puritan," laughed Chris. "Getting a little too
hot for you, eh?"

"There's nothing wrong with a little heat. When the time and
place are right, heat is great. But that kind of heat doesn't belong
on the bookshelves of a family store where any young person can

stumble into it and get burned. And as for the passage you started to read," Jade reached and took the book from Chris' hands, "I wouldn't call it heat."

He returned the title to the erotica stack. "More like an inferno. I skimmed that chapter an hour ago, and those two furnaces of passion were just warming up. In another three paragraphs, even the bed sheets started to smoke."

"Why James Vanderspyke," Chris scolded. "Do you mean to say that you kept reading, but made me stop? How fair is that? Letting me warm up, then leaving me unsatisfied? Shame on you."

Jade blushed.

"I can see," said Chris, "why you don't want to stock these books. You can't handle them yourself. It's a personal issue, isn't it? They embarrass you, don't they?"

"There's nothing wrong with a little modesty when it comes to sex." Jade sat back down. He lifted the previously untouched sandwich and took a token nibble.

"I agree," said Chris. "Sexual modesty is a very endearing trait. On the other hand, is it fair to impose your standards of modesty on others?" She grinned and shifted on his desk. She recrossed her legs and flashed a palm's length of thigh.

"Take for example," she said, "the hypothetical Jade Vanderspyke alter ego. Now here's a man with a college education, a wife, two kids, two cars and a house in the 'burbs. A thoughtful and responsible man of sound body and mind if ever there was one. But let's say this man and his wife are not getting along, not sleeping together to be more precise."

She shifted again, exposing another three fingers of flesh.

"The man is clearly stuck in a painful quandary. One: Does he dump his wife? Two: Does he find a mistress? Or three: Does he buy a NightLight book to facilitate a harmless imaginary liaison in the privacy of his own bedroom while his wife goes shopping for new hats?"

Jade thought for a moment. The question felt aimed precariously close to home.

"I'm not saying," he sighed at last, "that a person can't judge for himself what he should or shouldn't read. I'm just saying that as a businessman of principle, I should also be able to judge what I do or don't put on my shelves."

"That sounds good," said Chris. "But you know as well as I do that by controlling this other man's access to these books, you are in effect censoring his reading and infringing upon his animal rights."

Jade laughed. "His animal rights?"

"Correct. We're talking animal instincts here. After all, some guys need this stuff. They're all steamed with no place to whistle. They're pacing under the moon in a lonely glade."

Chris unfolded her legs, then swung them around, slightly open, to Jade's side of the desk.

"You do agree," she pressed, "that some guys do need these stories?"

"I wouldn't know," said Jade, starting to sweat. She had been close to him unchaperoned like this once before. That encounter had haunted him ever since.

His stomach began to churn. He felt the chaos and closed his eyes.

"Are you sure?" asked Chris. "Certainly, at some point in your life, you must have known a man who was not getting what he needed at home."

"Perhaps."

Chris leaned down, close to Jade's face.

"How about you, Jim? Are you getting what you want at home?"

Jade nearly fell over in his seat. He caught himself, then rolled his chair a couple of feet from the desk and stood.

"Chris," he said, trying to regain his composure. "My sex life is none of your business. I thought we discussed this. No more teasing and flirting. I like you, and I find you attractive. But I don't want to sleep with you."

She laughed. "Look at me in the eyes and say it again."

"Chris, how can you take this so lightly? You're jerking me

around like a toy. Is sex just a game with you, or what?"

"No," she replied. "I know better than to think that sex is just a game."

Chris looked away for a moment, avoiding his eyes, then slowly turned back, unblinking. "You must think I'm a real slut, don't you?"

"No," said Jade. "You're no slut."

Yes you are!, his mind screamed. *You're a dangerous slut. A black widow prepared to destroy.*

"I don't believe you," said Chris. She drew her lower lip within her mouth, held it, then continued. "You think that I'm something dirty, something cheap that might soil your hands. So you avoid me. You think of me as a slut, yet you feel drawn to me, eager to see and touch me, don't you? You step toward me, and then you run."

Chris closed her eyes and laughed.

"Who," she asked at last, "are you the most afraid of? Nasty me, or nasty you?"

Jade bit his tongue in anger. Fought for control.

"I'm not afraid. But I am confused. I wish you would respect the fact that I'm married. I'm not the kind of guy that has an affair."

"I do respect those things."

Chris swung her legs back around to the side of the desk, then smoothened her skirt. When she looked back at Jade, there was a sadness in her eyes.

"Did I ever tell you that I'm seeing a therapist?" she asked. "I've been in therapy since I was 18. It's a long story, but my family life got pretty weird when I was a teenager. I've had problems in my relationships with men ever since."

Jade stared quietly, uncomfortable with her unexpected disclosure.

Chris lifted one of the books from the horror stack, looked at it, then set it down.

"My therapist tells me that I'm attracted to men that I can't have. It's an intimacy thing. The more aloof and distant the man, the safer I feel. That was Don, my ex-husband. Aloof and distant. We lasted a year. But then another woman who needed an aloof and distant man came along, and I was out-maneuvered."

"Is that how you see me?" asked Jade, curious. "Am I aloof and distant, too?"

"No. Not you," she laughed. "You get a little caught up in your work, but you're as warm and kind as they come." Chris smiled. "You're untouchable for a different reason."

She lowered her voice. "I've told my therapist about you. She says that I see you as something that I can never have, and that's what makes you so attractive to me. As they say, nothing is so sweet as forbidden love. My therapist says that I've fixed on you with the passion of a child who desperately craves love, yet who is also a woman unable to handle intimacy and commitment with an adult."

Chris turned again.

When she looked back, her voice was so soft that Jade had to lean forward to hear her thoughts.

"The irony is that I am fixed on you because you're unattainable. My love will never be returned. It's a one-way street, without hope or fear genuine connectedness."

Jade studied her. She was an enigma. And in the yellow light of his desk lamp, she was bewitching.

"How can you be so sure I am safe?" he asked.

Chris hesitated, as if reluctant to share a secret.

"Guilt," she said at last. "I know that you are safe because of guilt. You wear it on your forehead and I can see it in the twitching of your eyes. Sometimes the corners of your mouth twist just so, and I can see it on your lips. You're one of those rare individuals that has yet to learn the art of blocking shame."

"I don't understand."

"Look at me," she said. "Do you remember this?"

Chris raised her hand and placed it upon her own breast.

Jade squeezed his eyes and turned away. Then bit his tongue.

"See," she said. "I'm safe with Jim Vanderspyke."

She swung her legs back in Jade's direction.

"And even if we did make love, it would only happen once or twice. I know you Jim, perhaps better than you know yourself. If you made love to me, and I know that you wouldn't fuck me like Don did, a man like you doesn't just fuck, if you made love to me, you would practically die of shame. You couldn't leave your wife and kids. Knowing you, you would probably become so mired in guilt that you would break down and tell them everything that happened. You could never leave them for me."

Jade closed his eyes.

"Then again," she said, "perhaps you would feel so much shame you would never tell a living soul until your deathbed. Then you would spill it all to some priest or something and finally die in peace."

Chris smiled. It was a sad smile. "No, Jim, I know you, and you are not a dangerous man."

"Why are you telling me this? These are pretty personal confessions and insights to be coming from a woman who supposedly fears intimacy."

Chris dropped her legs and stood.

"You mock me," she said, stepping from the side of the desk.

"I didn't mean it that way."

She turned back. "Do you think it was easy for me to share what I just said?"

"Of course not." He wished he could think of something to add. It was difficult to see Chris so vulnerable and distressed.

"Jim," she whispered, "I was abused. Things happened to me as a girl that I'm still trying to work through." Her eyes began to fill. "I shared that stuff about myself because I want you to understand me. I am not a vamp. I am not intentionally evil. I can't help the way that I sometimes come on to you. I try to stop, but it just happens. Do you know what its like to do something over and over that you swear you'll never do?"

She began to cry. "I'm sorry," she sobbed, "for the way that I've upset you."

Chris had cried with Jade once before. They were doing the year-end inventory late after work. They ordered a pizza and vowed that they would stay until they were through. Sometime after midnight, to help stay alert, they began making jokes from the names of books they read as they checked titles and counted copies. The puns and jokes grew increasingly sexual in nature, until they were laughing and saying things Jade had never said before in the presence of a woman.

Jade had felt an odd sense of liberation, even euphoria, in their abandon and uncensored kidding.

Then, in the midst of their joking, Chris somehow fell into his arms. She laughed hysterically into his shoulders and chest, unable to stop until the rhythm of her convulsions pulsed its way into his core. She looked up, her laughing ceased, and they kissed. Her waist seemed absurdly small in his hands, and the angle of her mouth and jaw produced novel effects upon his throat. Her breasts felt firm and wildly new as she pressed herself into his embrace. She turned within his arms, and his right hand slipped from behind her shoulder to beneath her arm, and finally to her breast.

The memory of that warm unfamiliar breast within his hand had stayed with Jade. It became a constant, frustrating companion. He would reach for a small mixing bowl, and the breast would suddenly be cupped within his palm. He would turn his keys in the ignition, and suddenly he would sense the electricity of her flesh. And he would touch Alice . . . but it would be Chris' flesh beneath his hand.

Chris was right.

He was a man sinking under the weight of guilt and shame. But he could not find his way from the whirlpool, and the spirals seemed to be growing tighter and tighter each day.

The night of the pizza, he had pulled his hand—not quite immediately—from Chris' breast. But not before the burning brand of her hard nipple seared its mark through her blouse and thin bra. Burned its way deep into his tingling palm.

Jade and Chris never finished the inventory that night. They talked, and Chris cried. He had not touched her since.

Nor had he ever let her go.

Now, she was crying again.

Her tears and sniffles were restrained, and Chris seemed embarrassed by her display of emotion. She wiped her cheek with the back of her hand.

"Thanks for putting up with me," she said. "I know that I'm a pain in the neck. You've got to be thinking right now about how nice it'll be when you move and you'll never have to see me again. I admit it, I'm a flake. I look starched and pressed on the outside, yet underneath, I'm a screwed up kid whose best friend is a seventy-five-dollar-an-hour shrink. But, maybe now, at least you'll understand why I am the way I am."

"You're not a flake," said Jade.

He stood and placed his hands upon her shoulders, turning her body to face him squarely.

"Stop cutting yourself down. You're no more screwed up than any of the rest of us. We've all got our pains and secrets, and we all do what we do for reasons that we'd rather not address. If there is a difference between you and the next person, it's that at least you've had the courage to attempt to come to grips with who you are. I respect that, and I'm sorry if it seemed like I was mocking you a few minutes ago. Maybe I was just jealous or nervous. I couldn't handle the fact that you were able to share the deep personal secrets of your past—and of your heart—the way you did."

Chris looked at him, tears again welling in her eyes.

"Thanks," she whispered. "That helps."

Then suddenly, she was crying again. This time her tears flowed freely. She wept as Jade had rarely seen a woman weep, with uninhibited tremors and sobs that drew him involuntarily around her. She buried her wet face in his shirt and clung to him with the desperation of woman drowning in a whirlpool of her own.

Jade, too, began to cry. Softy, for he had very little experience in tears, but he wept. He felt himself resisting, and then gradually uncoiling like a clock spring that had been wound too tight for too many years. Chris' confession was shocking, not because he didn't believe that such things happened, but because he knew that such things did. He closed his eyes tightly against memories. . . .

And became aware of Chris' flesh.

For the second time in their relationship, her hot breasts were pressed to his stomach in convulsions of emotion. Her cheeks and neck were moist from her warm tears, and he could feel the passion of her sobs and breath as she laid her sorrow upon his chest.

Chris was a victim. She had suffered. He had suffered as well. The world was filled with suffering victims. As Terry said, accidents happen. Fate rules. Jade had not planned for Chris to come into his life, yet here she was, vulnerable and sobbing within his arms. Life was brutal at times, and the most that anyone could hope was that the good times would outweigh the bad. And that there would be moments when one did not have to cry alone.

Chris' sobs were abating, though she did not pull away.

Nor did he encourage her to.

Instead, he held her tighter, moving his hand gently up and down her back, allowing her to feel through his pants the throb of his rising passion.

"Jim," she whispered into his chest, "I know that after what I told you, my love for you must seem perverse. But I can't help it, it's what I feel, and it is real."

"Love," he whispered back, "is a beautiful thing. It is powerful and mysterious, and it seems to operate under laws of its own. You needn't apologize or call it perverse."

Chris gently leaned from his chest, her arms still around his waist, her soft belly pressed against his throbs. She tilted her head and looked into his eyes.

"Jim," she said. "What am I supposed to do with my love for you? I'm not sure that I can go on pretending. That I can continue acting like I really care about some stupid book display, when all that I can think about is a chance to be alone with you. Pretending not to notice you when you walk into the store. Pretending to be busy as I watch your every move. I feel like a complete hypocrite, denying the thoughts and desires that raise me from my bed and bring me to this store each day."

Jade looked down at his tiny Chris. He felt himself deep in the whirlpool, deeper than he had ever let himself be drawn. The tips of her breasts brushed lightly against his chest with each breath as she returned his gaze.

He felt tired of swimming against the whirlpool, exhausted from fighting against the sucking hole.

"Perhaps," he said, "the time has come for honesty. You do know me. You were right, I'm not getting what I want at home. And I think about you constantly. I daily relive the memory of the time I touched you, the moment that almost was, that would have been if I had not said no."

He lifted his right hand from her back. He turned to look at his hand, then back to Chris.

"Do you see this hand?" he asked. "I try to forget. But the hand remembers. It burns from where it has been."

Chris reached up and took Jade's hand into her own. She held it for a moment, kissed it lightly, then lowered it to her breast. Jade closed his eyes. The hand had found its way home.

"There," she said. "Welcome back. I've missed you."

Jade felt his breathing deepening and his body adjusting in anticipation of imminent demands. He thought of accidents and chaos, and of the brand that burned in his palm.

He did not withdraw from the searing heat this time. Instead, he savored the scorch of the hot iron in his hand like a masochist grinning under the lash of a whip. His hand began throbbing in time with the primal tempo of their pressed bodies. Once again, their lips met, unabashedly this time, questions and reservations flung to the winds like kites teased into a tempest and then severed from their moorings to fly where they might.

The tempo of their bodies increased. He became aware of Chris' perfume, felt its power stirring deep within his throat.

His free hand began to explore Chris' back, up and down, lazy circles and intense angles. Down to the small of her back, then over the rise of her buttocks. He lifted, lightly, raising Chris to her toes and drawing her body into fresh nooks of his chest and stomach that sent shimmers through his belly and inner thighs.

Chris' body squirmed and wagged in the delight of his attention. Her mouth opened and her tongue began explorations of its own.

Jade's right hand remained upon her breast, though not inert. As she worked her lips down his throat, his hand shifted and circled, then found its way between her bra and flesh. Her nipple was iron again, immediate, responsive, burning unmuted by layers of clothes.

Chris began unbuttoning his shirt, working down from his neck, then over his chest to his belt. She drew the tails of his shirt free from his pants, then parted his shirt with thumbs that slid excruciatingly slowly down his shoulders to his thighs. Her hands drifted, then began tacking back and forth in delicate, probing sweeps that once again forced Jade to squeeze his eyes.

"What's this?" she asked.

Her fingertips traced a broad scar that disappeared beneath his loose belt.

Jade looked down, unwilling to release his hold. He leaned away several reluctant inches to allow her to see what she had found.

"It's huge. What happened?" she asked, running her nails lightly over the region.

"It's nothing," sighed Jade. "I hardly remember how I even got it." As she slipped lower, his grip tightened upon her breast.

Chris laughed. "What's with you and my tits? You're hanging on like you'll never let go."

"I don't think I ever will. You have no idea how memories of this flesh have haunted me since our last encounter."

"Then go ahead, hold them both."

"I'm not sure that I could handle two. One was almost enough to blow a fuse already."

"Well," said Chris. "There's no sense living in fear of the unknown. There's only one way to find out."

With that, she straightened and rotated herself within his arms. She stopped when she faced away, toward the computer screen on his desk. She lifted his second hand until it cupped her other breast.

"How are the fuses doing?"

"So far, so good," he grinned.

"Then let's check them under a full load," she laughed.

Chris caressed his forearms, then pulled his hands tight to her chest, working his hands up and down, massaging her breasts with his fingers in sensuous strokes.

She held his palms clamped tight to her erect nipples, then leaned forward, drawing his chest over her back until his hips cradled her from behind. Jade's eyes closed again as she began slowly wiggling, flexing her buttocks into his lap. He felt himself nearing an explosion, fighting it to prolong the pleasure. Wallowing in his surrender to Chris' power.

One of her hands dropped to steady her against his desk. Her other hand dropped and disappeared to touch herself beneath her skirt.

They both trembled as the motions increased, forward and back, her breasts still firmly cupped within his hands.

Jade froze. A white flash.

He was a child, leaning over, peeking through a pinhole of light into a bathroom beyond a closet wall. Two breasts, each cupped from behind, moving forward and back, forward and back.

"What's wrong?" whispered Chris.

"Nothing," said Jade, pushing the memory aside. "Nothing."

He squeezed Chris' breasts more firmly, almost roughly. He began arching his back and grinding his hips into her from behind.

His temples throbbed as memories pounded against a back room's deep darkness. He released her left breast and slid his hand down her stomach, onto her hip, then around to the front of her thigh.

Whispers, shuffling, the blinding light of an open door. His mother looming, silhouetted by the piercing whiteness of the hallway.

Jade found Chris' taunt hand and damp fingers within her panties beneath her skirt. He massaged her hand, angling his wrist outward to work her panties slowly down her hips.

Whispered prayers about death, about a gun in the other room. He could hear their voices. His mother marching with Twinkies, setting up her lawn chair, waiting them out.

He slid his fingers deeper into Chris' clutch. Felt her hot wetness. Felt his own erection throbbing in near pain.

His mother was waiting. There was something in her purse. Sooner or later, they would have to come out.

Then the blinding white explosion, a camera's flash in the dark.

"No!" he cried. "No!"

He jerked himself violently free from Chris' hot web of thighs and arms.

He scowled in disgust. Bit his tongue. Closed his eyes against her, fell back into his chair and shook his head.

Focus!

He opened his eyes and roughly jammed his shirt back into his pants, then quickly cinched his belt.

He felt angry and weak, resolved and disoriented. He tried to ignore her, but she was too close. And his heart still raced too wildly.

"Please," he whispered, massaging his pounding temples. "Just leave."

He turned away, closed his eyes, sank deeper into his chair. He tried re-reading the text on his screen. His eyes flowed over the blurred words like water streaming over ancient stones. The whirlpool slowed, then ceased.

When he looked again, she was gone.

Jade struggled at the typewriter for several minutes, but he found himself unable to complete a thought.

He shuddered at the awareness of how close he had come. How far he had gone. At work. Was the door even locked? He shuddered again, shamed by his weakness.

He dropped his head forward into his hands. "God," he sighed, "what a loser. I should tie the damn thing in a knot."

He needed help.

God should be helping him. But it was only getting worse. Terry suggested maybe a therapist.

No way.

Who else? Alice?

The thought of sharing everything with Alice terrified him. He should have been honest with her from the beginning. Delaying his confessions only allowed his problems to escalate, his guilt to deepen.

"Shit."

Jade hit the save key on his computer to preserve his jumbled work. Then he opened a new document. He tried again to type. A letter. He would type a letter.

His thoughts returned to Chris. He continued to type.

She smiled again, invitingly. He shook her off.

What would Hosea say? What would a hogman do? The truth?

"I'm an idiot," he sighed. "An obsessed fool." He bit the raw edge of his tongue.

Jade rolled from his desk and stood. He stared at his computer and swore.

He needed to clear his head. To talk to Alice, to tell her everything. To come clean. To be helped, or at least to be understood. Perhaps to be chastised, to suffer, even to pay for his stumbling. But to finally get it out before it strangled him.

"A time for silence," he quietly recited, "and a time to speak."

He was wasting his time diddling on the keyboard. He needed to get out of the store. He mindlessly hit several keys, closed his work, then killed the power.

He adjusted his collar and reached for the briefcase beside his desk.

Gone!

But where. . . .

Harry. Harry was in there!

The store's lights pierced white and harsh as Jade emerged from the back room. He glanced around, fearing that the shame on his forehead and in his twitching eyes would give him away. Panicked about Harry.

Theresa and Jeremy were assisting customers. Chris was at the register, alone.

He approached Chris as casually as he could.

"Well?" she asked.

"I, uh, I need to go home."

"I can see that. You look terrible." She laughed. "You'd better get out of here before you scare customers away."

He was unable to meet her eyes.

"But before you leave," she said, "I do need to know one thing." She tried to catch his gaze, then abandoned the effort.

"What," she asked, "should I do about the NightLight display? Can I put it up this afternoon or not? What did you decide?"

Jade ran his hands through his hair and turned to go.

"Have you seen my briefcase? I've looked everywhere in back. I need my briefcase."

"No." She glanced around the front counter. "It's not here either. In fact, I'm quite sure that you didn't have it with you when you came in this morning. You came in the front way, remember?"

Jade clutched his temples, then suddenly bolted for the store's front entrance.

"The display?" she asked, starting to follow.

"Pack it up," he called, not looking back. "I want that thing out of my store. It's dangerous stuff. It screws with a person's head."

"But what is Mr. Seinner going to say?"

He was gone.

CHAPTER 16

Jade was half way home before he remembered that Alice would not be there when he arrived. She was scheduled to work at the hospital until 4:00 pm. Then it would take another 20 minutes for her commute.

He checked his gas gauge. Almost full.

He had been picturing Alice at home when he returned. He glanced at the oil light, which was off, then switched on the radio.

Where was Harry? It was an expensive case. Any punk could have walked off with it. "Lost and Found" didn't have it, and neither did security. He should call the police. What would he say? They would want to know the contents. What a mess.

He would have a few hours to think while waiting for Alice to finish her day. What would she be doing right now at work? Probably drawing blood or something.

Jade looked in his mirror. He fiddled with the radio, searched for anything other than commercials. Three blocks later, he turned the radio off. He rechecked his gas, then flipped the visor.

He had imagined himself returning directly to Alice, immediately spilling everything. About Chris, about the night they did inventory, about his fantasies, even about what had happened at his desk.

And about Harry. Missing Harry.

Now, facing the reality of several hours alone, the choices that he had made in the back room began stretching themselves intimidatingly through time.

He glanced around the interior of his new car. He imagined Alice beside him on the passenger side. He glanced in his mirror

again, almost expecting to see Mark and Carla in their usual places
in the back seat.

Three blocks ahead was a traffic light, then another signal.
Beyond that, a turn, four more blocks, and then his driveway. He
saw a locked door to an empty house. He imagined himself sitting
in the living room, quietly waiting for hours, the old Regulator
clock ticking louder than ever. Three o'clock, four o'clock. The
kids finally coming home. And then Alice.

What would he would say?

"Hello, honey," he said to the mirror, checking the sound of
his voice. "You're not going to believe my day."

He cringed.

He could greet her at the door, take her coat and tell her that
they needed to go upstairs for a talk. He could suggest a long
drive, just the two of them, to a nice restaurant in the mountains.

It would probably be best to ask her about her day first, to act
as if nothing was wrong. What if she was in a bad mood after a
lousy day herself?

"I'm sorry, Alice," said Jade, clearing his throat. "But your day
is about to get worse."

He would tell her about Harry first. That would get her feeling sorry for him. Maybe he shouldn't bring the Chris thing up
tonight at all. It might make sense to wait until just the right
time, perhaps after a glass of wine this weekend. Or even next
weekend, when Alice had Saturday off.

She would be upset to hear about Chris.

He wouldn't be able to blame her. If she were to come to him
with something like that of her own. . . .

He would try to explain, but she would not understand, and
she would be very angry. Maybe she would rather not know. He
didn't have to tell her. After all, it wasn't like he actually had sex
with Chris.

Or was it?

Jade turned into his driveway and pressed the remote to the
garage door.

Alice's car, thank God, was not there. He would have more time to think.

But the kids. They would be home. They had the day off today, some kind of comp day for their teachers or something.

He parked the car and stepped into the back door.

"Mark! Carla! Anyone home?"

No answer.

They were out. God only knew where or for how long.

The mailbox was stuffed with bills, magazines and bulk. Nothing good. Alice would wonder if there had been any calls. Jade checked the answering machine. There had been no calls. She would ask him why he was home early. What would he say? He decided to get a beer.

He opened the refrigerator and looked on the first shelf, the second shelf, behind the milk, no beer.

"Shit."

On top of the refrigerator was a six-pack of long necks, Pete's Wicked Ale, in a red and black box.

The first thing that he would tell Alice was that he was returning the NightLight display. She would like hearing that.

The long necks were too warm to drink. Jade paced.

Sooner or later, he would have to tell Mr. Seinner about the display coming back unused.

What if the NightLight representative showed up at the mall this afternoon? What would Chris tell him? Would she have the rep call him at home?

Jade pulled back the living room curtain and glanced at the empty street.

The newspaper was on the coffee table where Alice must have left it before leaving for the hospital. He picked it up and began skimming. The stories seemed dull and familiar.

He looked out the window. It had been a good morning. The day had opened glorious. Then gone to hell.

"What a mess," he sighed. He tossed the paper where he had found it.

Mr. Seinner was going to hit the roof. How should he break the news? The thing that he needed to do was to finish jotting some notes, to organize a logical rationalization for his decision, and to put everything down once and for all on paper. Perhaps to write a letter, and then to fax it back to Michigan just before he took Alice out to dinner. It might be best to get it all over with at the same time. Seinner and Alice, both on the same night. What a mess.

He walked to the study. The heirloom clock ticked loudly, accusingly, as he moved by.

His father had left no clock for Jade. Just the envelope and his damn ashes. A Frosted Flakes box, for Christ's sake!

What would the punk think when he opened the briefcase and found a cereal box full of gray sand? He would probably throw the box away in some dumpster. Or maybe pour out the sand in the gutter, checking to see if there were drugs or something hidden inside in a plastic bag. Maybe the kid would think the ashes was cheap cocaine or something.

Jade pictured Harry's ashes up some kid's nose.

He sat, turned on his computer, then drew his rolling chair snug to the desk. He keyed up a blank screen in word processing and placed his fingers on the key board.

At least he didn't have to worry about what to do with Harry. The problem was now off his hands. He should feel relieved.

But didn't.

And he wasn't sure why.

The computer. He could do some work. That would help. Jade adjusted his chair.

Where to begin? He could check his e-mail, then work on the letter to Mr. Seinner.

He leaned back in his chair. Suddenly, Chris was again in his lap, facing him, her breasts in his face.

He blinked his eyes and shook his head. She had not sat in his lap, or even in his chair. But she had been in his lap. Or his lap had been in her. How was it? The sensations came back. The whirl-pool stirred.

Jade raised his invisible harmonica, pressed a knuckle to his teeth.

"Knock it off," he said. He bit his tongue.

He pushed away from the desk and returned to the refrigerator to get another beer. The six long necks were still on top. And nothing was still inside. Jade checked the freezer. No chilled mugs.

He'd run to the store and pick up some fresh cold brews.

The liquor store was in a shopping plaza.

A few doors down from the liquor store was a small bowling alley. Inside the bowling alley, they would have a little bar and frosty glasses and cold beer on tap. A few other guys might be sitting around. Jade thought of the blank screen on his computer back in the loneliness of his empty house and decided to have his cold beer in the company of strangers.

The bowling alley was dark and quiet inside. A small group of men were laughing and rolling spares and splits in the golden light at the far end, but the rest of the lanes were blurred in smoky yellow shadows.

He made his way to the bar, which felt much older than the building.

"A draft," he said.

"What kind?" the bartender asked.

"Whatever."

"You got it."

The bartender was a broad man with a bald, mole-peppered brown and white head. He wore a blue striped shirt and baggy gray pants. The man took his time. He seemed to be shuffling his feet beneath the remembered weight of a hundred thousand beers.

"Been bartending," he said, "for over five decades. Sixteen years in Georgia, four in Virginia, 12 in New York, seven in St. Louis, one—can't remember—and now in Denver."

Jade ordered another draft of whatever.

The bartender's name was Jim. They had a lot in common. Michigan was the other city. Not the state, Michigan City, Indiana. The bartender had worked there.

Jade hoisted his weighted drinking hand and toasted a selection of palatable Michigan memories.

Two of the bowlers came to fetch more nuts and beer.

One was shorter than Jade, the other was beet-faced and tall with wavy red hair. They worked a late-hour shift with their three buddies at the dairy. They really needed another man to keep the lanes even. They wanted to bowl a few more games and then go home for a few hours of sleep. Jade said he wasn't much of a bowler, but they begged him to join them anyway until Jade finally declined them off with a joke and a good-bye wave and ordered another draft from Jim.

Whatever it was, it hit the spot. Jade was feeling better, though the spot seemed much less full than when he'd finished his first.

Much less. Or more? What was he thinking?

Jade and Jim, come to find out, had both screwed up. Chris reminded Jim a lot of Eloise, who Jade said Eloise was just like, and whom Jim had finally broke it off with, but only after it was too late and the damage was done, and Jade had to agree that Chris had probably done some damage too. Jim warned Jade that Chris was the kind of trouble that a sailor gets into when he's been to sea too long and he has begun to wonder whether the choppy weather will take him to Davey Jones' locker. So when this sailor finally hits a strange port, and he meets an Eloise or a Chris and makes a mistake, it turns out to be a mistake that makes going home pretty hard when the home port comes up the next time around.

Yes, that was it. Exactly.

Jade excused himself to take a piss.

So maybe telling a woman about another woman and crap that's been going on inside a man's head wasn't always the best thing to do. Maybe it was best to learn from an accident and to shut up about it, but to make damn sure to wear a safety belt for the rest of the trip. And to take out an insurance policy, which Terry would appreciate immensely.

Shorty and Curly came back and got some more beer and slapped Jade on the back and finally convinced him that he needed some exercise.

They were good-old-boys and quick for some sorely-needed laughs. After a couple of frames, they all agreed that Jade was a man of his word . . . they hadn't seen such a lousy bowler since the night that Al had played the Dairy and Office-Cleaning Tournament with a concussion and a broken arm after a fight with his wife's boyfriend.

They slapped their knees and shook their heads about that for a long time.

Jade bought the next pitcher.

He left the bowling alley around 6:30 or 8:30—his new watch was digital and almost impossible to read—since it didn't make any sense to leave before the rush hour traffic had a chance to work itself through the pike.

Jade found his car pretty easy, but finding a few of his usual turns ended up being a little more tricky than he remembered. He parked once, passed out, then restarted the car. He knew that he wasn't completely drunk, because he felt that his thinking was finally clearing up for the first time since he'd taken a nibble of Chris' sandwich that afternoon.

Things were beginning to make sense.

He wouldn't tell Alice a thing. At least for now. That was for sure.

As best as he could tell.

"Hello, Jade," said Alice. She stood holding the front door.

Jade had decided to park perpendicularly on the curb, on the sidewalk and on the neighbor's grass instead of risking his Willow Green paint job on the lawn mower in his garage.

He took a wobbly step across the threshold of his front door.

Alice looked more beautiful than he remembered. He could

not recall an evening when she appeared so lovely and so young.

"I love you, Alie," he blurted, reaching to pull her into his arms.

He missed her body, but he did manage to catch one of her arms at the elbow. He gave the arm a tearful hug. He fished for the other arm for a moment, then gave up. He kissed the arm that he was holding, slobbering down to her wrist and onto her hand until he tasted something cold and hard and realized that her diamond was clenched between his teeth.

"I'm glad you still wear dis," he said. "Looks dery good on you. Dery shinny. Makes ya look like a married woman."

Alice studied him.

"Jade," she asked. "Would you like to come in and sit down?"

"Love ta," he replied with a half-witted grin.

He staggered to the couch and flopped down, his head rolling like an in-and-out gutter ball until his senses caught up with his rear and settled down.

He looked for Alice. She was sitting quietly in the nearest chair.

"I gotta warn ya," he said. "I may've had an extra drink two or three many." He laughed. "I read that in a novel once. Never had a time to use it before. Get it? Drink too many . . . drink or two . . . drink two or three many?"

Alice switched on the floor lamp that stood between the couch and chair.

"Jade?" she asked. "Are you too drunk to read?"

"Whatever gave ya dat idea?" he asked. "I read so much I can read wid my eyes closed. I musta read 10 books today alone. I don't have to be sober to read."

"Well," said Alice. "If you did, this would probably do the trick."

Jade spotted a sheet of white paper in her hand.

"Wha's that?"

"Your computer was on when I came home. I assumed that you were in there working, so I went in to see what you were doing. It's not like you to come home early, so I was curious. The screen was blank, which also seemed odd. I started to turn the computer off, and then I remembered something that Mark said a few days ago in the car."

"What was that?" Jade guessed what she was referring to, yet he found himself instinctively playing dumb. For days he had been fearing that sooner or later, Alice would settle the issue of Mark's remark.

"About hot e-mail from Chris," said Alice.

"Uh huh." A jolt of electricity shot down his spine. Adrenaline pumped vigorously into his system, producing an immediate sobering effect that partially offset the alcohol in his blood.

"Well," he said, "as you know, Mark has a strange sense of humor."

"Perhaps. Then again, maybe Mark has a good sense of recall." She offered him the sheet in her out-stretched hand. "Or, if you'd prefer to play games about this, then I guess Mark must have a sense of prophecy."

He ignored the paper.

"What are you talking about, Alice?"

"I decided to check the mailbox. Your mailbox. The one on the computer. And guess what? The little computer voice had good news. 'You've got mail,' it said."

"You read my personal mail?"

Alice stood and dropped the sheet into his lap.

"Personal," she said, "is the word."

She watched him for a moment, waiting for him to lift and examine the message.

When it became clear that he was not going to read it with her watching, she turned to leave. She took several steps, then stopped, wheeled and looked him in the eyes.

"We'll need to talk about this when you're sober. Do whatever you want with the letter, I printed two copies. Since you're too drunk to handle the stairs, it's probably best that you sleep on the couch this evening. There are a couple of afghans in the closet. I'm going to bed. Please don't bother me any more tonight. I have a terrible headache, and I need some rest. See you in the morning, Jim."

He watched her leave.

After she disappeared up the stairs, he lifted the letter and leaned toward the light. The words swam in and out of focus. After a few deep breaths, and with considerable effort and several false starts, he was able to make his way through the text.

Dear Jim:

Sorry things got out of hand, so to speak.

I just can't help it. Maybe I'm obsessed, but today I wanted more.

Because I respect your marriage, and your commitment to your family, I will do my best to avoid coming to you like that again in the future. Even though I know how much you like it.

It's a thrill, isn't it? Having me like that? Whenever you need me? Whenever you can't stand it any more? My surrender to your power and your every whim? Your familiar escape, pleasure, and release? I know that your guilt is maddening, but I'm worth it, aren't I?

For myself, I wish that you had finished what you started at your desk.

Feel free to imagine how I'll compensate, right about the time that Alice the Refrigerator falls asleep and you grow restless for something wild, slutty, and hot.

And even if you never call me again, and even if you try to block me from your thoughts, you and I both know that you'll never really forget.

Because "the hand remembers."

Yours forever,
        but never.
                Chris

P.S. If 'Duke' ever gets another itch for a good scratching, and you decide to stop feeling so guilty, you know that I'm as close as a locked door.

Jade did not need to read the letter twice. It read pretty much the way he remembered from earlier in the afternoon.

He sat for a moment, content to surrender any further attempt at sobriety. He welcomed the alcohol as it seeped its way back into his thinking.

He glanced again at the letter floating between his hands. It felt dry and thin between his fingers. Several phrases jumped from the page.

A sudden wave of nausea swept through his entire body. He looked back at the door through which he had chosen to stagger, then again at the note.

It seemed indecent to leave such a vulgar message exposed under the lights and under the same roof beneath which his wife and two children were attempting to sleep.

He folded the note. He tried to get the four corners to match, but two of the corners kept slipping off at unexpected angles. He snickered.

"I'm wasted," he slurred.

So drunk he couldn't fold a piece of paper without screwing the project up and making a fool of himself in front of himself, since no one else was in the room. Thank God.

An old adage came to mind. Maybe one of Alice's from the refrigerator. Except that he couldn't quite remember how it went. He made several thwarted attempts at getting it straight, then belched.

"Oh, what tangent lines we weave," he chanted to the letter with a grin, "when webs we practice to conceive." He knew he had it wrong. He kind of liked his muddled version anyway.

Alice said she printed two copies of the note. Jade looked at his copy. He needed to destroy it, even if there was another. Slowly, he tore the folded sheet into small pieces. The letter scraps were much larger than Harry's crumbs, but the comparison came to mind. He wadded the final remnants into a crumpled ball and lifted himself for the long walk to the bathroom toilet.

The alcohol in his system reestablished its influence upon his legs. A carpet of air beneath his feet cushioned each step. He welcomed the returning numbness as it worked its magic yet deeper into his limbs and brain.

On his way to the bathroom, Jade tottered past the obtrusively-ticking Regulator heirloom.

He stopped, swayed back, then examined the clock. He steadied himself, bracing one arm against the wall, listening to the steady beat. He bent to read the tiny etched inscription in the lower corner of the clock's time-weathered face.

"Congratulations," it said. "May you take the time to make it work."

Jade considered the words.

Then he opened the clock, reached in and blocked the swinging pendulum with his right index finger.

And the ticking ceased.

CHAPTER 17

Friday, March 22, 1996. Lakewood, Colorado

Jade awoke to the sounds of Mark and Carla bickering in hushed insults over the breakfast table.

A flash of panic seized him as he tried to remember what he was doing on the couch. Sunlight from the front window drilled his squinting eyes. His head pounded and his stomach rolled.

With the nausea came the taste of stale beer.

Jade rolled to shield his eyes.

The dispute in the kitchen trailed off. Mark and Carla were apparently keeping an eye on him. They must have sensed that they had disturbed his sleep.

A cool wet spot dampened his neck on the pillow. He had been drooling. He did not move or open his eyes.

He felt ashamed. Utterly ashamed. On top of everything else, his children had come downstairs that morning and seen him unkempt, passed out on the couch like some wino on a bench in Cheesman Park. He could not face them like this. He faked an unconscious stupor, and the act came easy.

His mouth tasted vile. His head throbbed from his eyebrows to the base of his skull, even into his neck and shoulders. Where had he been last night? The memory of slamming frosty mugs with strangers at a bowling alley swam into focus. His right arm and thumb began aching as well.

Jade heard Alice approaching the couch. She stopped, paused, then turned and left the room. Ten minutes later, they were all gone.

He was alone.

He rolled over. A blue sleeve. He was still wearing the same shirt as yesterday. He remembered fumbling with its buttons in the back room at work.

"You've got to be kidding," he mumbled, closing his eyes. "What an idiot."

Other than to adjust the afghan around his ear, Jade did not move for a long time. His head and his arms and his aching legs felt alarmingly heavy, as if pinned by mounds of sand squashing him into the cushions of the couch. He wanted to move, but couldn't; wanted to clear his head, but was trapped in loops of hellish dreams.

Jade lowered his feet to the floor, shook his head and forced himself to the bathroom. Swallowed four aspirins.

His toes ached. He hadn't had his shoes off in over a day. He sat on the stool and pried them loose, then shoved them beside the tub.

He reviewed his limited experience with hangovers.

What would help? A yoga shoulder stand? Pills and sleep. A piece of bread? His stomach was not yet ready for food. Maybe not even for the four aspirin.

He should be showering and getting re-dressed for work. He checked the clock. 9:30.

No way could he go to work.

Before returning to the couch, he called both stores and left messages on the machines. He was sick. Very. He would not be in all day. He would not accept calls for anything short of an emergency.

The phone rang at 10:05.

The digitized voice on the answering machine offered to record a message.

"Hello, Jade. This is Chris." The intercom was set at full volume. Jade did not have to strain to hear the tension in Chris' voice.

"If you're there, could you please pick up." There was a short pause. "Okay, I guess that you're not by the phone. It's Friday morning, and I just opened up. There's a gentleman here from

NightLight Books, and he's asking about the display. I told him that the display is still in the back room, and that you went home sick yesterday before you could finish putting the thing together. I'm not sure how long he can wait around to see you. Please give us a call as soon as you get this message. Thanks."

Jade pulled the afghan over his head and went back to sleep.

Around eleven, he roused himself to use the bathroom for the third time.

He started to reach for the light switch, then saw the mirror. He decided against turning on the light, and left the door open instead. Muted light was amply sufficient. In the bounced rays from the hall, he saw plenty more than he cared to see.

"Pathetic," he sighed. "Don't even want to see my own face."

He eased his aching body back into the cushions, closed his eyes and sought escape in sleep.

But sleep refused to comply.

Images of Chris and Alice and Hosea and Mark and Carla and Harry and a dozen others flashed through his mind. Painful memories struck like grenades lobbed from the past.

"Focus. Think black," he said, clenching his jaw. "The hot springs. Black."

Jade took long, deep breaths, emptying his mind of chaos and mistakes. A warm familiar dark pool. A shallow hot spring on a moonless night. His honeymoon. Two weeks of paid vacation.

Backpacking with his new bride.

The hiking trail they had followed for several days withered, then disappeared in the midst of a rocky meadow. They located a game trail, then followed as it wound over a pass and down into an isolated valley below.

The valley was breathtaking—but the peaks around them no longer matched those of their trail guide.

"Maybe," said Alice, "we should retrace our steps."

"Maybe," said Jade, "we should get lost."

They consulted their compasses, folded their maps and picked their way to the valley's floor.

"The fire trail," said Jade, "has got to be over there, beyond that ridge, a few miles to the south."

It grew dark and they scouted for a campsite. In the shadow of a granite overhang, they discovered a small, unmapped thermal pool.

"Look," Jade laughed, "how the overhang seems to jut from the cliff. It's almost like the hand of God, poised over the void and the darkness of the first day."

They made camp, stripped naked beneath the stars, and slipped softly into the steamy mineral waters.

"Like Adam and Eve," giggled Alice, "in the garden."

The soothing waters melted the fatigue of their hike and gently messaged their flesh in the faint warm currents of the natural spring. Their bodies floated in the thick, intoxicating sulfur steam, side by side, inches below the surface, an eternity below the stars. Suspended between the heavens and the rocks.

They drifted together for hours.

Jade rolled on the couch.

"Name an animal," said Alice, finally stirring the waters and rippling the silence between them.

"Why?" asked Jade, his eyes still fixed on the stars.

"Because that's your first job. God made Adam, and then he told him to name the animals."

"Are you sure? I thought our first job was to be fruitful and multiply."

She splashed him. "Come on, name an animal."

"Okay. That one up there, on the rock. It's a mountain lion."

Alice jerked to her feet in the water and frantically glanced about the cliffs.

"Just kidding."

Alice laughed, throwing herself naked across Jade's chest and pushing him under.

"You big tease," she laughed.

Jade stood, sputtered, and grinned.

"Who is teasing who?" he said, taking her in his arms.

Later, after making love in the pool, from her back Alice commanded again.

"Name an animal."

"You're serious, aren't you?"

"Yes."

"Why?"

"I'm not sure. It just seems like the right thing to do. Here we are, naked and alone in the wilderness. I want you to be my Adam, my first and only man. And I want to be your Eve. It seems like you should speak into the dark and name an animal. Something new. A name that has never been spoken. It feels like you should bring order out of the unknown. That you should establish some sort of dominion. Like you should create something here tonight."

"Perhaps," he laughed, splashing her belly, "I already have."

"Then name it," she whispered.

He searched for the Big Dipper, found it, then closed his eyes.

Jade rolled on the couch. "Why?" he whispered into the black, his eyes clenched in hangover throbs. "Why did we ever leave?"

He tried, as he often had in the years since that night, to resurrect the sensations of those warm, peaceful waters. He could see the black void of the overhang silhouetted above him in the white prickle of a thousands stars, could almost feel the melting jelly bubbles welling up through the pool from the rocks below.

But he could not stay still.

His body drifted about the pool. The soft current of the spring turned him in circles. It was hard to stay afloat.

He tried to steady himself. He imagined his arms stretched wide. But the shadow stirred. His body turned, turned more, then faster. He began to spin. Suddenly, he felt himself sucked into the throat of a screaming whirlpool. The stars stretched into comets, long tails, flaming heads slicing through the atmosphere, plunging toward him. . . .

The stars exploded like fireworks, flashes of light, then color, then images. A dizzy blur of scenes, letters, faces, and failures filling the sky. . . .

Jade bolted upright.

"Damn," he said, looking about the room. "What's wrong with me?"

He rubbed his temples, then yanked his hands from his face and rose to his feet.

He needed water.

He found himself filling a cup in the bathroom mirror. The light was on. His hair matted on one side, spiked on the other. Dark smudges and creases scarred his face. His eyes burned with the sullen shame of a beast behind bars. His crooked undershirt clung damp beneath his open collar. No tie. Couldn't remember taking it off. Must have left it at the bowling alley.

Just like he had left Harry's ashes in the mall.

Jade shut the faucet, closed his eyes and leaned over the sink. His forehead stopped against the cold surface of the mirror. He raised his knuckles and pressed them against the hard glass.

"My God," he whispered. "What's going on with me?"

He said it again.

"My God."

Jade slumped to his knees, his elbows above the counter, his forehead sliding down to the wet splashes on the edge of the sink.

"My God, my God, my God. . . ."

He whispered the phrase over and over. It was neither a prayer nor a curse. But he could not stop.

He knelt on the bathroom floor for several minutes, unable to focus, unable to move.

He thought of Alice, of his children. Of Harry and that woman in the bathroom. Of Harry and the ladies with tans. Of letters. Of Chris, naked again, as always. Of his brother Randy, dead and gone. Ashes. And of Karen. . . .

"God!" he shouted, rising to his feet.

Jade opened his eyes and glared into the mirror. He felt his hand coiling into an iron knot.

"God!" he cried.

"You stupid son-of-a-bitch!"

His reflection exploded in slivers that ripped his knuckles and shattered his face.

"You son-of-a-bitch!" he sobbed again. "You stupid son-of-a-bitch."

CHAPTER 18

Jade dropped his clothes into a pile. He stepped beneath the spray of the shower and rinsed the drying trickles of blood from his face, neck, and arm. He leaned over the edge of the tub, then used his towel to mop glass aside so he could step to the floor without cutting his feet.

He put on a robe, wrapped his hand, and found several bandages for his cheeks.

Then, carefully, he began cleaning up pieces of the broken mirror.

It was a miracle that none of the exploding glass had damaged his eyes. He had not blinked. The image of his distorted face shattering in the mirror flashed over and over through his mind.

Jade dumped the last of the glass into the wastebasket beside the sink, then used the toilet.

The garage door rattled shut as he reached the couch.

Alice was home early.

He laid down, pulled the afghan over his face and closed his eyes.

"Good morning," said Alice, her voice quiet.

He remained still.

"Jade, I know that you're awake. The toilet was still running when I came in from the garage."

He rolled to his side and opened his eyes.

"Good morning," he said. His voice was raspy and dry.

She gasped, staring at his face. "What happened?" His right hand twitched, hidden beneath the cover.

"I had a little accident. No big deal. I'm fine."

"Jade, you were sound asleep when I left. Tell me what happened!"

He studied her for a moment. She leaned toward him in concern, counting the bandages on his face, searching for indications of the injuries that might lay below. The nurturing instincts that made her a good nurse pushed her other concerns aside.

"Here," he whispered, holding out his bandaged hand. "I put this through the bathroom mirror. I kind of went crazy for a second. But it cleared my head. And my hand is okay, really."

Alice sank to the couch near his hip. She gently took his hand and examined it, shaking her head the whole time.

"Jade?" She lowered his hand to his stomach. "I'm frightened. What's going on?"

"I'm not sure. But we need to talk. We need to talk like we haven't talked in years. Like we've never talked before."

She bent forward and placed her right hand gently upon his head. "How about your hangover? Are you feeling any better from that?"

"A little." He tried to smile. "I'm sorry about last night. I don't remember everything, but I remember enough. I'm not sure what to say."

"I'm lost," she said. "For the first time in our marriage, I'm completely clueless. I've been plenty mad and plenty confused before, but nothing like this." She placed her left hand over his wrist. "Are you able to talk now, or do you need more time?"

"I can talk." Jade wetted his lips and adjusted his pillow. Alice retrieved a second pillow from the floor and tucked it beneath his head.

"Thanks," he said. "That helps."

Alice stroked his head and touched his bandages in silence. Her hand felt tender and unrushed. Jade thought of his mother, the way she soothed him as a child the time he fell from a tree and gashed his arm. He rarely compared Alice to his mother. For once, the comparison felt okay.

"You're not the only one who came unhinged today," she said

at last. "I drove the kids to school and went to the hospital, but I couldn't stay and deal with needles and doctors and bedpans, given the kinds of stuff that was running through my head. I told them that I was ill, and I came home. I needed to figure out what happened yesterday."

Jade looked into her eyes, uncertain, with no idea how or where to begin.

"For starters," he sighed, "I think that I almost drowned myself last night in beer. I've never been so beer-sick in all my life."

"You couldn't have been at the Grill," said Alice. "As drunk as you were last night, you never could have made it home that far in one piece."

"No. I was only a mile or so away. At that little bowling alley by the liquor store."

"Did you meet someone there? I've never known you to be much of a bowler."

He tried to smile. "They would agree with you. They said I was one of the worst bowlers they'd ever seen. I couldn't even tell you their names. Just five guys from the night shift at the dairy. I went in for a drink and one thing led to another, until. . . . Well, you know. You were here when I got home."

Alice fanned her fingers and ran them through Jade's hair. He was still damp on his temples from rinsing the blood.

"Jade," said Alice. "You never drink like that. What happened yesterday at work?"

"It was a strange day for me. One thing after another." He raised his hand to touch Alice's forearm against his shoulder.

"The big news," he said, "is that I told NightLight Books and Jeffrey Seinner to take a leap. Although not in so many words. I asked Chris to repack the books and to send the display back." Jade watched carefully for Alice's reaction to mention of Chris' name. He thought he detected a slight wince.

"Good, Jade. It sounds like you did the right thing. And how did Chris feel about returning the display?" It was Alice's turn to watch and gauge a response.

"Actually, Chris wasn't very excited about my decision. In fact, she called this morning to say the NightLight rep was in the store. She was trying to stall him until I could change my mind."

"What did you tell her?"

"Nothing. I didn't pick up when it rang."

"You didn't want to talk to Chris?" Jade couldn't determine the agenda in her voice.

"No," he said. "I didn't even want to think about Chris today. Chris has become a bit of a thorn in my flesh."

"Yes, I suppose she has."

Alice gave him several long minutes to continue. At last, she continued on her own.

"Jade, I have to be honest with you." She slid her hand down from his shoulder. "I spoke with Chris yesterday. Twice. And then again today."

He stiffened. "What?"

"I got your message yesterday at the hospital. When I finally got around to returning the call, Chris said that you'd already left. She said that you came out of the back room looking terrible, and that you were frantic about your briefcase. I was worried, so I called home. But you didn't answer."

Alice reached for his hand.

"Yesterday, when I got home and found that note on your computer, I freaked. I called Chris back at the store, and I read her the message over the phone." Alice squeezed his hand as he sat upright.

"Jade," she hesitated. "Chris swore that she did not write that note."

He lowered his head into his hands. Several moments later, he raised his head and faced her.

"Are you saying that you read the whole thing, word for word, over the phone?"

Alice reached to rub his neck.

"Yes. At the time, I thought she was the one who had written it. I was angry and I wanted to confront her and to find out what was going on between you two."

He shook his head.

"I'm sorry, Jade." She stroked his arm. "Maybe I should have come to you first. If you'd been home, I would have. I wanted to."

"How," he asked, "am I going to face her after this? After your call? After she heard what was in that letter?"

Alice shifted on the couch and bent low, to within inches of where he again buried his face within his hands.

"What about me, Jade? What about facing me?" She straightened. "Why did you send that message here? Did you plan for me to find it? Were you trying to punish me for something?"

Jade's shoulders trembled.

"I was going to tell you," he said at last. "Yesterday, when I left the store, I came home to tell you everything. But you weren't here." His voice cracked. "How much do you know? What all did Chris tell you?"

"This morning," said Alice, "I stopped by the mall store on my way home. Chris and I went to the back room to talk. Eventually, she admitted that she had been working on you. But she only opened up after I told her how screwed up you were last night and how you've been falling apart at home these past few months. She said that she's been lonely since her divorce, and that the single men that she's tried dating have all been jerks. She thought you would be the perfect man for a very discreet affair. Apparently, she's had affairs before."

"Is that all that she told you?"

"No. She admitted trying to seduce you. It was late one night while you were doing inventory, but you brushed her off. She said that you were too straight to fool around. And she confessed that she sent you several e-mails. But that's it. She denied that anything else ever happened, including the letter from last night. And I believe her. She had no reason to lie after what she already confessed."

"Alice," he said at last. "I'm sorry. I know this makes no sense.

But I promise, I have not touched Chris since that one night, and then, only for a moment. You are the only woman that I've slept with in my entire life."

He continued, again speaking into his hands. "Nothing happened yesterday in the back room. At least not as far as Chris is concerned. What happened was one-sided. Behind an unlocked door. Anyone could have barged in. . . ." He shook his head. "And you're right, that was not her note."

Alice gently pulled Jade's hands away from his face.

"Jade," she said. "Please, tell me about the e-mail. What's going on with you? Do you hate me so much that you would fabricate. . . ."

"No. That's not it." He turned to Alice, tears burning through the cuts on his face. "Don't even think such a thing." He began to weep. "I'm sorry Alice. I'm so sorry."

She held him for a long time.

When he at last regained his composure, Alice made no attempt to force eye contact. Instead, she looked to the floor. On the carpet near the couch was a peculiar prism of light that she had never before noticed. She traced the beam of light through the dust in the air back to the Regulator clock on the wall. Light was streaming through the picture window, bouncing from the coffee table to the clock, then reflecting from the clock's beveled glass to the floor beside the couch.

"There are things," he said at last, "that you don't know. Things about when I was growing up, and things about what goes on inside of me. Things I'm ashamed of. I try to be good, but sometimes it's too hard. Yes, I wrote that note. And others like it. But I wrote them for me, and for no one else."

She looked at him. "For you? You wrote that letter for yourself?"

"It was never my intention to hurt you. Or for you to know."

"Then why did you write it? Why would a sane man write a sick letter like that to himself? Please, tell me what's going on."

Jade slowly returned her desperate gaze. Yes, he would tell

her. If she was willing to listen.

"Are you sure that you want to hear this?" he asked.

"Yes. I think I have to."

"Where should I begin?"

"I don't know. Where do you think it begins?"

He thought for several moments.

"I guess I'd have to go back to Sixth Grade. To the beginning of the school year. The year that my mom and dad were in the midst of their divorce." He met her eyes. "Are you really sure you want to know?"

"Yes," whispered Alice. "I want to understand."

PART II

CHAPTER 19

Late August, 1970.
Grand Haven, Michigan

Jimmy walked to school alone.

Ben and Randy raced ahead on their bikes to join their old friends, but Jimmy was in no hurry for his first day of junior high.

For one thing, he didn't have any buddies left over from Fifth Grade that he was eager to see, and for another, he'd heard enough about junior high to guess that the next three years would likely be the worst years of his life.

He wasn't interested in adding another 10 minutes to the ordeal.

Jimmy checked his watch. It was a plain-faced watch, stark numbers strapped to a black imitation-leather band. He had saved his money for weeks, fearful that a tourist might spot the piece in his dad's case of discontinued gifts and snap it up before he accumulated the $8.50 he needed to buy it himself. Near the end of the summer, two days short of $8.50, the watch disappeared.

That summer, Jimmy practiced the art of not crying. The missing watch was the first real test of his not-crying skills. He was pretty good, but not perfect.

Then late that same night, while he knelt beside his bed reciting prayers, someone entered his room.

He felt her come and go.

He sensed a miracle in progress. His eyes squeezed tight as his mother tucked the watch beneath his pillow and quietly slipped from the room.

He had rarely taken off the watch since.

The watch now indicated that he needed to slow down.

He had timed the walk on three occasions during the past week. He memorized the school's schedule, as well as the locations of all of the halls, classrooms, offices and bathrooms. At the rate that he was walking, he would reach the school by the first bell. That would leave five minutes of standing around as one of the shortest, chunkiest targets at Harrison Junior High.

Jimmy slackened his pace. No way would he spend the five minutes there.

He looked around. The transformations of early autumn were everywhere. He inhaled the new season from the breeze off the big lake, and he detected the approaching days of frost in the changes of the clouds and sky. He scuffed a shoe through a clump of damp grass poking through a sidewalk crack. The humidity of summer days had begun wringing itself into cool morning dews that magically appeared upon grasses and leaves like the sweaty beads on the cold pop cans at his family's store. Above him, hints of yellows blushed among the branches of the maples that lined the streets. The somber green canopy was on the verge on an explosion of golds, flaming salmons and burning scarlets.

He could hardly wait.

If it weren't for school, this would be his favorite time of the year. The weather was neither hot nor cold, and an occasional early morning freeze all but eliminated the mosquitoes. Work slowed this time of year at the gift shop, which freed time for comic books smuggled from the racks beside the postcards, and which allowed undisturbed afternoons for counting boats from the pier.

Jimmy had done a lot of thinking over the summer. Especially near the final days of the beach season, when his parents began planning their divorce.

His parents had fought, stormed and stayed together through the end of the busy season, trying to control expenses until Harry could start his new job. He would begin driving a cola truck in mid-September, and he would move to Grand Rapids the day that his first paycheck was cashed. Jimmy's mom would keep the shop open herself during the off season, then when things got busy again, she would hire additional help if possible. The boys would be learning to take turns in shifts at the store. They would also have to learn to cook and clean at home.

The divorce was a mystery to Jimmy. He sensed that he was somehow responsible for it, but couldn't understand why it was necessary. He was the one who discovered his dad and Marsha Fenton having sex in the bathroom. If he had not fallen and made so much noise in the storage closet, his mother would never have found out. So the trouble was his fault.

On the other hand, he didn't see why one incident in the customer's bathroom was such a big deal.

Seeing that lady bent forward, her large breasts in front of the hole, his dad grabbing and leaning over her from behind, that bewildered Jimmy.

But the craziest part was his mother's reaction. People were always hugging and kissing on the beach in their bathing suits, which was practically the same thing as being naked, and he couldn't understand why having their bathing suits off was all that different.

"Listen," Ben had told Jimmy the next day. "Trust me. This is different."

"But why?" Jimmy asked. Ben was 14, and he could usually make things clear for Jimmy.

"Because," said Ben, "when you marry a person, you promise to keep your hands off from other people for the rest of your life. And from what you told me, dad had his hands all over the slut."

"I know, but why does that mean that mom and dad can't live together with us anymore? Can't dad just say that he's sorry that he broke his promise, and then swear that he'll never do it again?"

Ben put his arm over Jimmy's shoulder and leaned close to his brother's ear.

"Jimmy," he whispered. "Dad already promised mom that before. This isn't the first time. I know that I shouldn't be telling you this, because you're only 11, but as far as I can tell, dad's been screwing around behind mom's back for as long as they've been married. He's even been caught before. And always with a different lady."

"So?"

"Jimmy, dad wasn't just touching her tits in there. He was having sex with that woman. He was sticking his dick inside her."

"I know what having sex means," said Jimmy, frustrated. "But I never saw that part. Nobody else did, either. How does mom know for sure that dad had his dick in her? And besides, why would dad want to do a sick thing like that anyway? I don't think he really did. What person in his right mind would want to stick his thing in there and get smelly stuff all over his peter in the first place?"

Ben dropped his arm and laughed. "Sooner or later," he said, "we all do. Dad's just different from some guys because he goes ahead and does it, whether he's married to the lady or not." Ben shook his head. "And how do you know what it smells like? Do you know more than you've been letting on?"

Jimmy felt more confused than ever.

Ben stopped laughing.

"Jimmy, don't look so shocked," he said. "Your day is coming, too. Sooner or later, every guy starts seeing women that he wants to have sex with. That's only natural. It's just that if you're married, you're not supposed to touch them. No matter how much you want to. You can look, you can even think about it if you want to, but don't ever touch. That's the rule. Touching them unless you're married is a sin. You could go to hell for that."

"To hell? Just for touching a lady or having sex?"

"That's what the Bible says."

Jimmy kicked the dirt. "Okay," he said. "Let's just say that dad's dick was in that lady, and I'm not saying I believe that it was, I still don't see how that's something to get divorced over. I mean, if God wants to send dad to hell, okay. But why should mom divorce him for that? Dad didn't hurt mom any when he touched that lady. It's not like dad hit mom or something."

"Are you serious?"

"Serious. How come it's no big deal when dad kisses grandma when she comes to visit, but he's gotta get divorced for kissing the lady in the floppy hat?"

"But he wasn't just kissing her. He was fucking her with his peter. Maybe you're too young to understand."

"Maybe you just don't know any better than I do. Why is it so different to touch someone with your peter than it is to touch someone with your lips?"

"Man," said Ben, shrugging and walking away. "You are dumb."

Jimmy spent a lot of time that summer trying to figure out sex and his parents' divorce. He decided that if it was so hard for men to keep their dicks out of women, maybe guys shouldn't make promises about such things. That way, there would be no divorces and kids wouldn't have to imagine what it was going to be like when their dad moved out of their house and he wasn't around any more to keep things working and to tell everybody what to do.

As for himself, Jimmy was confident that he would never have a sex problem. The last thing he would ever want to do was stick his peter inside a girl.

He might be curious to see a lady naked, or to look at pictures of ones like the ones Ben kept under his mattress. Maybe even to squeeze a woman's boobs—after what he saw through the pinhole, his hands tingled just wondering what that would feel like. But there was no way that he would ever want to do the disgusting part that his dad had done. Jimmy was never going to push his dick up some girl's poop-chute.

No way.

The halls were almost empty when Jimmy arrived. Teachers were guarding their doors, smiling, helloing, and pulling students into their rooms like the migrant pickers filling their baskets with Granny Smiths.

"Good morning," said Mrs. DeBorst, giving Jimmy a gentle

shove as the final bell rang. "You must be. . . ." Jimmy started to answer, but was cut off. "Fine then. Please take a seat."

"Okay, class," she said. "The bell has rung and we are all in our seats." Several milling students attempted to finish conversations by the windows.

"We are all in our seats!" she repeated. The millers scrambled. "Very good," she continued.

Jimmy relaxed.

Mrs. DeBorst had the voice of a real teacher. Her voice would make short work of bullies so long as they were beneath her charge.

She also looked like a teacher was supposed to look: immaculately-combed gray streaks and a long skirt that eliminated any question of legs. Lack of legs was an important teaching asset. Jimmy was saddled in Fifth Grade with a teacher who looked like a nervous French model making her first movie. With long legs and short skirts. Fifth Grade had not gone well for Jimmy. The larger boys bullied him mercilessly, willing to do anything for more attention from that leggy teacher impostor.

"It is so good to have you all here this morning," she said. "My name is Mrs. DeBorst. I believe that I have met many of you already, as well as your parents, last week at our back-to-school junior high orientation night. I am confident that we are about to begin a very important and enjoyable year together. We all have much to learn, and with your cooperation. . . ."

Jimmy looked around. He recognized three quarters of the students and knew about half of them by name. He turned his attention back to Mrs. DeBorst.

". . . and I have here a list of the names of all of the students that are supposed to be in my class, which will be your home room for the entire year. As you all know, now that you are in junior high, you will be moving from room to room for some of your subjects. You will change rooms as a group, with the same students remaining your classmates throughout the year."

She glared at a distant seat, instantly silencing a boy who was about to whisper.

"This year, you will have the opportunity to experience differ-ent teachers for different subjects."

Mrs. DeBorst stepped to the front of the first row.

"For example, I will be your English teacher, but Mr. Nordyke will teach you math."

She stepped to the second row.

"While you are in his room learning math, Mr. Nordyke's students will come to my room to learn English. This will remain your home room for the whole year, which means that you will report here. . . ."

Jimmy noticed that the chalkboard was black.

Mrs. DeBorst had written her name on the board in white chalk. In elementary school, the boards were green; the teachers used chalk that was yellow.

Why did chalkboards come in two colors?

Maybe it had to do with reflection and glare, the contrast between the shade of a chalk and the color of the slate behind the letters. Perhaps yellow chalk on green slate worked better for big letters, while white chalk on black slate worked better for numbers and tiny letters. Randy warned him that the teachers in junior high would fill their boards with notes, and that they would ex-pect every student to copy everything into notebooks exactly as it was written on the board.

Students were standing and moving to the front of the room.

Jimmy quickly rose and joined them.

". . . very good. Okay, now as I call your name, please assume your chair. This will be your assigned seat for the first month until I learn each of your names. We will be seated alphabetically, which will assist me in calling roll as well as in collecting and returning papers and forms."

Mrs. DeBorst stepped to the front seat of the first row.

"Starting here," she said, pointing to the first desk, "Miss Janna Aardema." Mrs. DeBorst gave the girl time to begin moving to-ward her assigned seat for the next four weeks, then stepped and pointed to the second desk.

"Mr. Ronald Boerema."

A howl of laughter erupted around the room. Mrs. DeBorst smiled. She spotted the embarrassed boy.

"I forgot to mention," she said, sweeping a charitable gaze across the front of the room. "If you would prefer to be called by another name, please let me know and I will make a notation on my attendance sheet immediately."

She looked back at Mr. Boerema.

"Do you prefer to be called Ronald, Ron, or Ronny?" she asked with a smile.

In most communities, the name Vanderspyke would have placed Jimmy in the far back corner. Not so in western Michigan.

Western Michigan, and Ottawa County in particular, was settled in the 1800s by Dutch Reformed farmers from the Netherlands. The Grand Haven area schools were heavily biased on the front and back ends of the alphabet, with only a nominal sprinkling of southern European names scattered between.

The first two rows were anchored mostly with surnames like Brower, DeJong, and Dykstra; the last two rows with names like VandenBerg, Veltkamp and Zylstra.

Jimmy watched closely for where Vanderspyke might land in the room. Where a kid sat, and by whom, could make or break a student's year.

He judged by Mrs. DeBorst's position in the room, and by the names that he remembered of the classmates still standing, that he would settle in one of two seats. The first possibility was in the back seat of aisle four; the second possibility was at the front desk in aisle five.

He never fared well at the back of a room. He prayed for aisle five.

Mrs. DeBorst stood at the fourth desk in aisle four. "Mr. Thomas VanderPloeg," she said. Then, before the class could erupt, she hastened to ask, "Thomas, Tom, or Tommy?"

"Tommy," the boy blushed. The joke was growing routine for

the class, but for each child whose name was called, the experience was fresh and unnerving.

"So noted," she said.

Mrs. DeBorst moved to the very last seat in aisle four.

"Mr. James Vanderspyke," she called. "Do you prefer James, Jimmy, or Jim?"

He tried to answer. Couldn't.

No one had ever called him James. The sound of the word "James" startled him. He hadn't realized that his name could be interpreted in any way other than Jimmy or Jim. Where had Mrs. DeBorst even come up with such a monstrosity of a name? Surely his mother hadn't. . . .

"James, Jimmy, or Jim?" she asked again, impatient to return to the front of the room to finish the final row.

Jimmy took a deep breath. "J . . . Ji.. James."

"So noted," she said.

She stepped behind James' desk at the end of the fourth row and made her way up to the front of the room in aisle five.

"Miss Elenore VanderStarre," she said, pointing to Jimmy's lost seat.

Jimmy numbly made his way to the back of row four.

What happened? James? Where the heck had that come from? Why hadn't he just told her that his name was Jimmy? Now he would be stuck with James for the rest of the year.

CHAPTER 20

September, 1970.
Grand Haven, Michigan

Mrs. DeBorst lifted a flash card showing an outline of the state of New York.

"Albany, New York!" shouted Carla Mekluevich.

"Correct," said Mrs. DeBorst.

Carla did not wait to be told to advance. She stepped beside the next desk.

Darrel DeJong cowered in his seat, anticipating his imminent humiliation. Nobody ever beat Carla Mekluevich in "Around the Nation." No one.

The card flashed.

"Little Rock, Arkansas!" she cried.

Mrs. DeBorst nodded a yes.

"Carson-City-Nevada!" called Carla. Mrs. DeBorst had barely lifted the next card.

James studied Carla from his seat in the back of row four.

She had knocked him out of the game easily. Rather, she had never allowed him into the game. Carla approached, stopped, then passed him with ease.

Her seat was at the back of row three, next to James, on his left.

In "Around the Nation" a student would stand beside the desk of a challenger. The teacher would flash a card showing the shape of a state, including a star that designated the location of the state's capital. The first student to correctly shout the name of the state would win.

The winner would advance to the next desk, while the loser would remain in the seat of the challenger.

After several weeks of "Around the Nation," most of the students in Mrs. DeBorst's home room could quickly identify states like California, Florida and Alaska. A handful could even distinguish similar states, like Kansas and the Dakotas based upon the location of the stars.

Mrs. DeBorst then introduced an added challenge: students were to name the state's capital.

They were allowed to consult mimeographed maps on their desks for help. But as the fast-learning champions began to emerge, the maps became less of an aid and more of a handicap.

Carla dominated the game on the state level; on the capital level, she ruled.

The class became so demoralized by her brutal streaks of flawless play that students began doodling on their maps, passing notes and daydreaming. The class-wide mastery of American geography abruptly stalled.

Mrs. DeBorst started to flip another card.

"Boise, Idaho!"

Helen Dykstra slumped in her seat.

Mrs. DeBorst nodded. Carla moved on.

James watched Carla's eyes.

For her, this clearly was no game. She leaned toward each flash card, her eyes squinting to maintain a sharp focus. She was not smug in her victories. But each time she leveled a challenger, something happened to Carla's face. A brief twitch of emotion. He couldn't decide whether her blinks were those of satisfaction or of relief.

He wondered why winning the rounds was so important to Carla.

"Sacramento, California!"

James liked Carla.

She was the only girl he could talk to, and even though she

was the smartest student in his class, she seemed less complex and intimidating than most other girls.

James would watch his mother at the shop, trying to picture her as an 11-year-old in his Sixth Grade class. He would imagine his mom sitting with Helen Dykstra, Janna and the other girls, but the trick never worked. The other girls would remain as odd and baffling as always.

He could, however, picture his mom and Carla becoming Sixth Grade friends.

It occurred to James that Carla was a misfit.

"Austin-Texas!"

Carla was almost back to her own seat. Another fast lap around the room.

James studied Carla's thick, wavy black hair, her dark eyes, her large nose and coarse mouth.

Carla sometimes wore makeup. Not many girls wore makeup in Grand Haven in the Sixth Grade. When she did, it was always too thick in some places, and it never looked very smooth.

James glanced at Carla's challenger, Denise Hoekenstra.

Denise's hair was long, straight and blond. She had blue eyes and delicate features. Her build was tall and thin.

James looked around the room. Most of the girls looked a lot like Denise. So did most of the boys. Carla was, he decided, quite homely.

"Harrisburg-Pennsylvania!"

Then Carla dropped herself wearily back into her own seat.

The first few times that Carla circumnavigated the full course of the room, students clapped and gasped as she worked her way closer and closer to the end of the circuit. A few students even cheered as Carla knocked off her last challenger, Bobby Majers, then returned to her desk, unbeaten.

This time, many of her classmates didn't bother to lift their eyes.

"Very good," said Mrs. DeBorst, avoiding the use of Carla's name. The class was tired of hearing Carla's name.

"Today," she continued, "since that round went so quickly, and since we have some extra time, we are going to do something a little different."

There was a bit of stirring. Several students straightened themselves in their chairs.

"I have decided that it is time for a new way to test your knowledge of American geography."

At the word "test," a collective shudder of disappointment rose from every row.

"My concern," said Mrs. DeBorst, "is that some of you have stopped working on learning the states and capitals. I hope that I am wrong about this, but I need to find out to put myself at ease." She moved across the front of the room.

"I'm certain that many of you know this material by now, but that some of you are perhaps a little slow at shouting it out when we play 'Around the World'."

Several students glanced in Carla's direction.

Mrs. DeBorst lifted a stack of freshly mimeographed United States maps from her desk. She began passing them down each row.

"As you will notice, unlike the maps that we have used in the past for studying, these new maps do not include the names of the states or their capitals. It is your job to fill in this important missing information."

The recent sigh from the class echoed as a groan.

"The good news is, the better that you know your material, the bigger your reward." Students again leaned forward.

"As you know, class will be concluded in 25 minutes. That's when you will all leave for lunch. Today, as a special incentive and reward to those of you who have been working extra hard to memorize the states and capitals, I will allow students who finish this exercise early to leave for lunch as soon as they are through."

The class murmured in mixed reactions. Several students beamed at the thought of leaving early. Others shook their heads and grumbled. One boy muttered something about whether he would be allowed to go home for Christmas Break.

"The rules are as follows: Nobody may leave early unless they have correctly identified every capital and every state. I will check your work before you may go. Second, as always, spelling counts. An answer is incorrect unless the city is written out exactly as it should be. To save time, you may abbreviate the names of states by writing down just the first few letters. For New England states, you are encouraged to draw lines into the Atlantic Ocean and to place your answers there."

"Yes, Tommy?"

"What if we can't remember some of them?"

"Good question," nodded Mrs. DeBorst. "In 10 minutes, I will allow you to remove your notes from your desks, and then you may complete the remainder of the assignment by copying your answers directly from your practice maps. When you are unsure of the spelling for a city, I would encourage you to write the name lightly in pencil. That way you can go back later and make changes from your notes as necessary."

"Any more questions? Good. Please put away your practice maps at this time."

Mrs. DeBorst waited during the shuffle. Jimmy noticed several students taking last-second peeks.

"Again," she continued, "I will give you 10 minutes to work from memory, then another 15 minutes to finish while using your notes. You may begin."

The entire class bobbed in unison.

James hunched over his map, then dipped his nose to within inches of his desk top to inhale in a big whiff of the fresh ink.

This would be a fun assignment.

He loved maps. He found learning the shapes and names of the states an enjoyable challenge. Learning the capitals was a bigger challenge, which was why he had been so eager to tackle them and commit them to memory as fast as he could. A few challenges at school caught his interest and made things fun. Geography was one of them.

He glanced over at Carla.

She was scribbling, frantically, working her way through New England. James seldom beat anyone in "Around the World." Certainly not Carla. His mouth wasn't quick enough, even though he knew all the answers.

Carla glanced at him. She smiled, then dove back into her work. He could see that she was already moving into the mid-Atlantic states.

He decided to start in the upper left. A-n-c-h-o-r-a-g-e, Alaska.

Next, H-o-n-o-l-u-l-u, Hawaii. No, that wasn't right. James erased the back few letters of the word, then wrote out H-a-w-a-i-i. That looked better.

He glanced again at Carla. She was erasing a word as well. James went back to work.

O-l-y-m-p-i-a, Wash. B-o-i-s-e, Idaho. H-e-l-e-n-a, Mont. B-i-s-m-a-r-c-k, N.Dak.

This was fun, and he was picking up speed.

M-i-n-n-e-a-p-o-l-i-s, Minn. Tricky. But Minneapolis looked right on his page.

M-a-d-i-s-o-n, Wis. L-a-n-s-i-n-g, Mich.

He glanced at Carla. She smiled again, then went back to erasing. She had crossed the Mason Dixon Line and was moving south toward Florida.

H-a-r-r-i-s-b-u-r-g, Penn. A-l-b-a-n-y, NY.

James finished Maine and went back to the west coast.

S-a-l-e-m, Oregon. C-h-e-y-e-n-n-e, Wyo. P-i-e-r-r-e, S.Dak.

James swept faster and faster across the continent, moving left to right, working his way south in horizontal lines.

T-a-l-l-a-h-a-s-s-e-e, Flor. He double checked Tallahassee. Yes, that was the way it was supposed to look.

James lowered his pencil, his heart racing. He looked up.

Everyone in the room was still hunched over their desks, scribbling and scratching and poking their foreheads with number two erasers.

He glanced at Carla. She was not quite to the west coast.

James felt strange. He wasn't sure what he was supposed to do. He doodled in Puerto Rico off the coast of Florida with an arrow pointing down, added a star, then neatly printed S-A-N J-U-A-N. He looked up. Everyone was still busy.

He cleared his throat. Mrs. DeBorst continued correcting papers.

Meekly, James raised his right hand.

"Done!" said Carla, slamming her pencil to her desk.

Several students moaned. James looked at his watch. It had taken her under six minutes.

"Well," said Mrs. DeBorst. "Bring it up here and I'll check your spelling."

Then she noticed James' raised hand.

"Yes, James?"

"Should I bring mine up, too?" he asked.

"Are you finished?"

"Yes, ma'am."

Mrs. DeBorst seemed surprised.

"Well, okay you two," she smiled. "Bring your papers up here, and I'll give them a quick check."

James dropped sheepishly behind Carla as they made their way to the front of the room. He felt embarrassed, felt his face growing hot. Several of his classmates stared at him, then went back to work. Carla thrust her map into Mrs. DeBorst's hand.

"Uh-huh, uh-huh," said Mrs. DeBorst, working her way rapidly over Carla's map. "Uh-oh," she said. She circled *Cheyanne* and smiled at Carla. "I think you'll want to re-examine that one. "Okay, let's see . . . uh-huh, uh-huh. Yes. The rest look great."

She handed Carla her map. Carla looked at the map as James handed Mrs. DeBorst his paper. Mrs. DeBorst smiled at the addition of Puerto Rico, then began skimming through the states.

"Uh-huh, uh-hu. . . ."

"I got it," interrupted Carla. She shoved Wyoming into her teacher's face. "No a's in Cheyenne, right?"

"Carla!" whispered Mrs. DeBorst. "That was very rude. I'm checking James' map right now. You'll have to wait your turn."

Carla stepped back as if slapped.

James looked at Carla's crushed expression. For some reason, he felt guilty when Mrs. DeBorst returned to checking his answers.

He watched Carla bite her lip and stare as their teacher's pencil breezed over state after state. Mrs. DeBorst paused briefly in Florida, circled the capital, then finished checking the remaining states. When she looked up, she glowed.

"Very good, James," she said. "I didn't know that you were so quick, and such a good speller. I only have one question. It's a little hard to tell on your a's and e's in some places. Is the capital of Florida spelled l-l-a-h, or is it spelled l-l-e-h?"

James looked as his paper, then at Mrs. DeBorst. He glanced at Carla, who hovered nearby, holding her breath and squinting her eyes.

For once, James knew that he was the challenger who could topple the champion.

"I think," he said at last, "that it's spelled with an . . . ah . . . uhm. . . ." He looked again at Carla. There was anguish in her face.

"I think," he said again, "that it's spelled l-l-e-h."

Carla nearly exploded in relief.

"I'm sorry," said Mrs. DeBorst, "but that is wrong." She turned away.

"Carla, was there something that you wanted to change on your map?"

"Yes," she beamed. "Cheyenne is spelled with three e's. There are no a's in Cheyenne."

"That is correct, Carla. Very good. And James," she asked, turning to the short chunky boy from the back of row four, "was there something you wanted to change on your map?"

"Yes, Mrs. DeBorst," he replied. "Tallahassee is spelled with three a's, and only two e's, both stuck at the end of the row."

Mrs. DeBorst laughed. "I think," she said, "that you mean at the end of the word, don't you, James?"

"No ma'am," he smiled, looking at Carla. "I got it right the first time. Two e's stuck at the back of the row."

James and Carla left the room five minutes ahead of any other student.

They walked together through the empty halls in awkward silence. They headed toward the cafeteria, side by side, glancing at each other, then looking ahead.

Half way down the hall, James realized that his lunch bag was still in his desk. And he didn't have any money in his pockets to buy anything in the cafeteria.

He wasn't going to go back to the room to retrieve a brown bag. He felt hungry, but more importantly, he felt proud. He wasn't going to ruin the victory by going back into the room to face their snickers.

"You knew," said Carla, reaching for the cafeteria door, "that Tallahassee needed an 'a', didn't you?"

She continued looking straight ahead.

"How do you know," asked James, "what I know or what I don't know? You don't know everything, Carla. You know a lot, but not everything."

Carla laughed. "I didn't know that Cheyenne was spelled with all e's, I'll admit that. But you did. I think that you know a lot more than you let on. I think that you're a whole lot smarter than even you know."

She stopped, turned, then faced him.

"Why," she asked, "did you tell Mrs. DeBorst a lie? Why did you let me win?"

"I didn't know that it was a race."

"There you go," she laughed. "Lying again."

She grew serious.

"James," she said, "you've got a big decision to make here in junior high."

"What's that?"

"Either you've got to stop lying, or you've got to learn how to do it right. If you keep going at it the way you are right now, you're only going to make a fool of yourself."

"How can you tell I'm lying?"

"Your face, James. It gives you away. When you lie, you look as guilty as sin."

James blushed. Some from anger, mostly from embarrassment.

"Anyway," laughed Carla. "Thanks."

James looked her in the eyes.

"Since you want to be so straightforward," he said, "now you answer me a question. How come winning is so important to you? I just don't get it. You act like if one of us ever beat you, you would die for shame."

Carla began walking again. James fell beside her, matching her stride for stride. She headed toward the open hot lunch window, then began reaching for her money. She stopped and faced him again.

"James," she said. "Have you ever heard the saying, 'If you're not Dutch, you're not much'?"

Of course he had. He heard it his whole life. Kids said it around school all the time. He even heard adults cracking the joke on the streets of Grand Haven and in his family's store.

"Yes," he replied, guardedly.

"Look at me," Carla demanded.

She scooped together a fist full of her hair and shook it. "Do I look Dutch to you?"

She dropped her hair and began walking again toward the hot lunch counter. James stood for a moment, then hurriedly rejoined her.

"Look at me," James demanded, stepping in front of her.

She stopped.

"If you're not thin," he said, "you ain't in."

He frowned, then grabbed a roll of baby fat through his shirt and shook it. "Do I look thin to you?" He let go of his stomach. "You ain't so special being different, Carla Mekluevich, so stop acting so smug. I'm just as weird as you are, and you know it."

Carla smiled. And then she laughed.

She laughed so hard that James thought she might swallow her tongue. He once read that such a thing was possible. He thought of that from time to time when he was tempted to laugh too hard. The Dutch kids and their parents that he knew never laughed hard enough for anyone to have to worry about them swallowing their tongues.

"Okay, James," she said, finally catching her breath. "That's what you meant about two e's at the end of the row, isn't it? You and me, a couple of odd eggs at the ends of rows three and four, huh?"

"The thought crossed my mind."

"You're pretty clever for a sixth grader," she grinned.

James blushed.

"Well," she said. "Are you going to buy some lunch, or am I going to have to sit alone?"

"I'll sit with you," he smiled. "But no lunch for me today."

"Why not?"

"I'm on a diet."

Carla looked at James with disapproval in her eyes.

"I'm serious," said James. "It's a new diet. I just started it a few minutes ago, when I forgot my lunch bag back in Mrs. DeBorst's room. I'll let you know how the diet is going in about 10 minutes, right after class is over and I can sneak back to my desk without making a fool of myself."

James arrived back at Carla's lunch table a couple of minutes after the dismissal bell, in plenty of time to help her with her dessert.

CHAPTER 21

October, 1970.
Grand Haven, Michigan

James straightened the watch that stretched between them on the kitchen table.

The two straps of the plastic band lay flat and stiff on the marbled-gray formica top, extended like the thin black hands that now stretched up and down indicating that supper was over and that their 6:00 study hour had begun.

"Okay," said James. "Page 175, right?"

"Right," said Carla. "15 minutes. At 6:15, we both stop and the quizzing begins."

"Let's do it," nodded James. "Go!"

A pattern had developed over their first few weeks of studying together. James would arrive at Carla's house after supper, and they would sit together at her kitchen table racing through chapters, then drilling each other from the questions at the end of each section. At first, Carla was a much faster reader. But James sometimes managed a better recall of names, terms, and dates. Carla was better than James in Math, and her favorite subject was science. James' favorite subject was English, especially literature. Carla could remember most of the details from the plots they read, but James would sometimes have to explain the subtleties to her—like why the boy was afraid to ride the bicycle—which he delighted in doing.

Carla squinted and hunched over the pages of her history book. Her head slid left to right and snapped back like the carriage on a typewriter.

James kept his distance from the text and blinked furiously at each sentence.

In Mrs. DeBorst's English class, James was introduced to the concept of speed reading. The concept seemed simple. Beginning readers read one letter at a time, adding the letters of each word together like an arithmetic problem, then pausing at the end of each word to tally the sum and read the total out loud.

Mrs. DeBorst said that better readers learned to recognize whole words at a glance as quickly as a beginning reader recognized the single letters.

A speed reader, she said, takes the principal another step. Instead of advancing letter by letter, or one word at a time, a speed reader absorbs entire phrases in a single blink.

For those who wished to pursue speed reading further, Mrs. DeBorst gave the class several simple illustrations and techniques to use when practicing on their own. James was intrigued. He listened carefully to the explanation of speed reading, or phrase reading, as Mrs. DeBorst sometimes called it, and he was surprised at how logical the examples all seemed.

Mrs. DeBorst had turned on a slide projector and instructed students to write down everything they could remember from each slide.

Her first slide simply showed the letter "a". Then Mrs. DeBorst dropped a card in front of the projector's lens to block the light. Every student in the class was able to write an "a" behind the number one on the first line of their worksheets. She quickly progressed to flashes of short words like "the" and "cat", and then to longer words like "management" and "automobile."

James found some of the longer words familiar enough to recognize immediately. Others slipped from the screen faster than he could work them out in his brain.

Then Mrs. DeBorst switched to short phrases.

James had no trouble with the first few. "The cat."

He wrote it with a smile.

"The house." Easy.

"Big bad wolf." He was doing it. He was reading phrases at a single blink.

Then the screen flashed: "The . . .ed boat sank." James wrote what he remembered.

Next, "without a clue" blinked on the screen. At least he recognized that one. He wondered if Mrs. DeBorst had a sense of humor after all.

And then "breaking a . . . cup" flashed and disappeared. Then ". . . was a . . . ed".

James shook his head and gave up.

But later, he kept returning to the exercise and thinking through the concepts. He decided to do some experimenting on his own. It seemed like a worthy challenge.

He had done very little extended reading in his life, so he had very few deeply-entrenched habits that needed to be overcome. After several weeks of practice, speed reading began to work for James. The time that he saved by reading clusters of words at a single glance gave him more time to review difficult words, names and dates. He was reading faster, and he was coming away with more.

James glanced at the watch. It was almost 6:15.

He quickly turned back to page 182.

His history book was the easiest to read. It was loaded with pictures and the columns were so narrow that they made phrase reading almost automatic.

The chapter dealt with the Civil War. James forced his eyes to move more quickly down the columns. Rapid blinking was hurting his eyes and slowing him down. He stopped blinking, but he tried to keep his eyes moving through phrases without slackening his pace.

The adjustment worked. By skipping the blinks, he was reading faster than ever.

"Time!" shouted Carla.

James put his finger where he'd left off and looked up.

"How far did you get this time, Carla?" he asked.

"I almost finished," she said. "How about you?"

"I got to here." He pointed to the middle of a paragraph.

"Good job," smiled Carla. "I got to right there."

She reached over and pressed her finger to the end of the same paragraph that James had been reading. "You have really gotten fast. Did you give up on speed reading? I glanced over at you a minute ago, and it looked like you'd stopped that silly blinking."

James smiled.

"I stopped blinking," he said, "but I didn't stop reading in phrases. I think that I'm finally getting the hang of this. When I just stopped blinking and relaxed, I think that I was whipping down the page like crazy."

Carla pulled her hand from James' book.

"I told you," she smiled, "that you were smarter than anyone knew. How come it's taken you so long to figure out that you can be good in school?"

"I don't know." James thought for a moment. "I suppose it has something to do with my family. Nobody in my family is much into books. We work quite a bit at the store and my brothers like to throw balls and stuff when they're not at the shop. I've always liked to read comic books and watch the boats. And watch TV. I love to watch TV, especially the movies."

"Oh, yuk," said Carla, scrunching her nose. "You watch TV?"

"Sure. What's wrong with that?"

"TV is for imbeciles. The 'marching morons,' as my father used to call them. We only have one tiny little TV in the family room and we hardly ever have it on. In fact, I'm quite sure that it doesn't even work. I can't remember the last time any of us even tried to turn it on."

James had never heard of such a thing. Everybody that he knew had at least a few shows that they watched every week.

"Gilligan's Island," said James. "I'm sure that you've watched Gilligan's Island before? Like when they show the reruns on channel 12 after school?"

"Never."

"How about the Brady Bunch? You must have watched the Brady Bunch?"

"Once. I was at my aunt's house. She doesn't have any kids. She couldn't come up with anything else for us to do, so she plunked me and my sister down in front of her TV. I thought that the show was utterly stupid. I can't believe that some people think that show is cool."

"I happen to like it."

"You've got to be kidding! What could be more stupid than perfect people like Mr. and Mrs. Brady having to marry each other after getting divorced? Who would ever divorce either one of them? They're both so kind, and funny and good looking. Neither one of them would ever have to worry about getting dumped."

"Carla," laughed James. "I don't think they were divorced. I think they married each other because their first spouses were dead. She was widowed and he was a widower. I mean, I'm quite sure that's what they want you to believe."

"Uhm. Well, maybe. I only ever saw it once."

"How about your mom?" James asked. "She's divorced, isn't she?"

"Yes. So what?"

"Why did she divorce your dad? Your mom seems nice enough to me. She sure is a good cook. I love it when she gives me supper. My mom hardly ever has time to cook like that."

"Actually, it was my dad who wanted the divorce. He fell in love with some blonde chick from work. It got pretty ugly when my mom found out, but she wanted to take him back. We're Catholic you know. Only he didn't want to come back."

"Where is your dad now?"

"He's living with the blonde back east. In Connecticut. His company transferred him, and his girlfriend quit her job and moved out there with him. I think that my dad is switching out of the Catholic faith just so that he can sleep with his girlfriend without thinking about going to hell all of the time. I think that he's becoming a Presbyterian."

Carla turned her chair to face James directly. "You go to a Dutch Reformed church, don't you?"

"How'd you guess?"

"Come on, I'm not stupid. With a name like Vanderspyke? Blond hair, living in this town? Besides, you blush all the time. Kids who don't go to church don't blush very often."

James felt his face reddening. "Come on," he whined. "That's not fair."

Carla laughed. "Sorry. I can't help it. Your face looks so cute in crimson. It makes me want to pinch your cheeks. Is your skin as hot as it looks when you blush?"

"How should I know?" said James. "All I know is that it feels hot inside."

Carla reached toward his cheeks with two fingers. "May I touch and find out?" she asked.

"Cut it out," laughed James, pushing her hand aside. "You don't see me trying to touch your black hair, do you?"

"What about my hair?"

"You've got the strangest hair that I've ever seen. It looks so black that it's almost blue. And thick. And kind of curly."

Carla pulled a lock of hair around to the front of her face and examined it closely. "Pretty unusual, huh?"

James felt his cheeks returning to normal. "At least unusual for around here, I guess," he said.

"And there it goes," laughed Carla, dropping her hair and pointing at James' face. "Once again, as white as an onion."

"Thanks," James smiled. "I've been called a lot of things, but that's the first time that I've ever been called a vegetable."

"Okay. How about, 'as white as an egg'? Is that better?"

"Much better. Thank you."

"You're welcome."

James glanced at his watch and was thoughtful for a moment. "Do you miss your dad?" he asked at last.

"Sometimes, yes. And sometimes, no. It depends a lot on how my mom is feeling. My dad writes us letters all the time. He wants me to move to Connecticut to live with them. He says that he's going to marry his girlfriend when her divorce is final, and that's when I should come out. I've never met her, but my mom has, and mom says that the lady is a real bitch."

"She really called the lady a bitch? Right in front of you?"

"Of course. My family can get nasty, but at least we tell the truth. You Dutch Reformed types try to sugar-coat everything, don't you?"

"Is that so? Well, for your information, we don't sugar-coat what we think of the Pope."

"The anti-Christ, right?"

"Maybe not. But he's going to hell, that's for sure."

"Just like Martin Luther." Carla shook her head.

"Who is Martin Luther?"

"Forget it. Maybe you're hopeless after all."

James was quiet for a moment. He hated it when Carla made him feel dumb.

"Do you think," he said, "that your mom will ever get re-married?"

"Naw. I think she hates men now. Maybe she hates women even worse. I'm not sure. My mom has gotten pretty self-conscious about her looks lately. Really down on herself. One day she'll spend hours in front of her mirror experimenting with makeup and new hair styles, and then for the next week she'll hardly look in the mirror even to brush her teeth. Actually, I think she's depressed."

"That's too bad. She seems real nice to me."

"Yeah, but she's not pretty. If you're not pretty, and then your husband dumps you for a babe, it's got to mess your head up pretty bad. How about your mom? Do you think that she'll find a new husband?"

"Not for a while. She's too busy. Unless the guy is really hooked on Twinkies and pop and decides to hang around the snack shop all day. Then she'd have time to talk. Otherwise, I don't think so."

Carla closed her text book. "Let's not study tonight. I'm not in the mood anymore. Besides, most of the other kids hate us enough already. Another A in history tomorrow will only make it worse."

James closed his book. "They hate us?"

"Sure they hate us. You mean that you didn't know? Kids always hate the eggheads. That's me. And now you. The two e's at the end of the row."

"I never really thought of myself as an egghead before. I mean, we've kind of joked about it, but deep down, I don't really think that I'm all that smart."

"Sorry. Welcome to the club. And now that you're reading so fast, it's only going to get worse. When it comes to academics, reading is practically everything. And the better you do in class, the more the other kids will make fun of you behind your back."

She pushed her book to the center of the table.

"I've even had kids trip me, you know, when I was walking up to hand in my tests and papers. There's nothing more humiliating than falling down in front of the entire class, and all the A's in the world don't make it feel one bit better. Sometimes, I wish that when somebody tripped me, that I'd just bang my head and get stupid like everybody else. Present company excluded."

Carla leaned toward him. "James, are you saying that you really haven't noticed how kids resent your intelligence?"

James grinned. "You've got to remember, Carla, that I've been getting this sort of treatment for as long as I can remember. I just assumed that they were giving me a hard time because I was short and chubby. Little did I suspect that the other kids were actually harassing me out of an intuitive insight concerning my slumbering intellect."

"Wow," said Carla. She punched his shoulder. "Listen to you all of a sudden. All those biiiiiig words. Where did you learn that kind of vocabulary? You never used to talk like that."

James began to blush. As he became aware of the heat building in his cheeks, he blushed even more.

"Sorry," said Carla, looking as if she really meant it. "I'm as bad as the rest of them, aren't I?"

She gently reached her right hand to his left cheek, then smiled.

Her fingers felt cool on his skin, and he liked them there. But it felt awkward.

He raised his own hand hesitantly to the waves of thick hair falling over Carla's left ear. He had ridden ponies at the Ottawa County Fair. Her hair reminded him of a pony's mane. Her hair even felt black.

Carla softly closed her dark eyes and pressed her cheek lightly into the base of his hand. After several moments, she opened her eyes, smiled again, then withdrew her hand from his face. James took that as a cue, and he withdrew his hand at the same time.

"Thank you," she smiled, her dark eyes looking deep in James' blue.

"What for?" he asked.

"For being my friend."

"Always," he whispered.

He returned her gaze for another moment, then had to turn away. He glanced at the back door and noticed several empty liquor bottles lined on the floor to be taken out with the trash.

"You're a pretty special guy, James."

His dad had given him sips of drinks from time to time. The liquor burned, almost like a cheek blush, only inside his mouth and down his throat.

His mind returned to blushing, and to Carla's hand upon his cheek. To the feel of her hair and face within his hand. He looked back at her.

"I can't believe that I just touched your hair." James laughed. It was a nervous laugh.

"That was the most romantic thing that has ever happened to me," smiled Carla. "You're the first boy that has ever touched me. Except maybe to trip me, or to spill my books."

James glanced at her, then quickly looked away.

"Romantic, huh?," he said, picking up his watch. "Maybe I'm starting to read too many books. Sitting with girls, using big words."

He began putting on his watch. "Every once in a while, something clicks in my brain, and then I think I even start sounding like a book. Randy and Ben caught me using big words with mom the other night. They teased me like crazy."

"Yes sir-ee, Mr. James," laughed Carla. "You and me had better stick together."

James cinched his watch band tight and threaded the strap through the loop. He adjusted the watch on his wrist and looked at the time. Carla watched him carefully.

"You know," said Carla. "I think that you're the only boy in Sixth Grade that wears a watch."

"I just like to keep track of the time," said James.

"Don't get defensive, James. I think it's cool."

"You do?"

"Yes," said Carla. "It makes me think that you've got places to go, people to see and things to do. Like you're someone who's going someplace in life."

James smiled.

He liked that.

Yes, he was going someplace in life.

CHAPTER 22

December, 1970.
Grand Haven, Michigan

James adjusted his weight nervously, which only made him sink deeper into the old couch. He was submerged over his hips in green cushions; if he wiggled any more, he worried that he might disappear.

He glanced at his watch without lifting his arm.

Carla's mother and sister were off getting groceries and Carla was in the bathroom.

In the four months of their friendship, he rarely sat anywhere in Carla's house other than the kitchen. He always entered the house through the front door and walked straight through to the kitchen. There, Carla and James would study and talk, and occasionally, he would join them for supper. The kitchen was bright, if not modern or particularly clean. He felt as comfortable in the kitchen with Carla as he did anywhere in Grand Haven other than his own home or the family store.

He had noticed Carla's family room off to the side of the living room on his way to the kitchen. Two or three times, he even stepped into the family room when Carla needed to retrieve a book or to show him one of her treasures.

But this was the first time that they had taken a seat together on the couch. When Carla jumped up to the use the bathroom the moment they sat down, James almost tagged along behind her out of sheer habit.

She insisted they sit for their talk in the family room because it was Christmas. And this was the room in which her family had planted the Mekluevich Christmas tree.

He studied the tree.

It was a mangy specimen of a fir, with dry needles, broken limbs, burned out lights, reused silver tinsel and so few presents underneath that he worried that Carla's mom had not yet found time to shop. And Christmas was only a few days away.

The room itself was dumpy and small.

James had never been critical or paid much attention to Carla's house. Carla's constant prattle and dramatic gestures always demanded his full concentration.

Now, in the conspicuous absence of her energy, sitting outside the familiar confines of their kitchen, the house seemed oppressively run-down and darkly silent, in spite of the season and the tree. Or perhaps because of them.

He counted three mismatched lamps hooded in shades that were dented and stained. Heavy, uneven dark drapes that were secured with yellow diaper pins blanketed the front windows. The drapes were coated with a dry foam of dust and cobwebs that cascaded from the top edge like a ghostly waterfall suspended eight feet from the floor.

Above him was a smudged peach colored ceiling. Tears of painted wallpaper curled to reveal the shadowed gashes of darker colors from previous owners.

The couch into which he sank was worn at the arms and smelled of untrained pets. The end table to James' right was marked in beverage rings from perspiring glasses and crumbs from plates that should never have left the kitchen.

It occurred to James for the first time that Carla's family was poor. The revelation was unsettling.

James' family was also poor. The Vanderspykes owned a store, but the store barely broke even, and they had teetered on the edge of bankruptcy for as long as James could remember. Mr. Vanderspyke's job in Grand Rapids was paying barely enough to cover his living expenses, and he was unable to send much money to Grand Haven to help.

Despite their tight finances, the Vanderspyke house was reasonably clean and livable. Carla's house, on the other hand, seemed shabby and neglected.

"Okay," Carla smiled, bouncing back into the room. "That's better."

She plopped herself next to James and looked him in the eyes. James was relieved to see that Carla still appeared the same, though his perception of her house had changed.

"Subject," she said, "going to the bathroom. Challenge, complete this sentence. Here goes. Don't you think that it's awful when. . . ."

James thought for a moment. "Don't you think," he said at last, "that it's awful when," he paused, "someone leaves you alone in a strange place to run and use the bathroom?"

Carla laughed. "Nice try. No, what I was thinking was something else. How about this: Don't you think that it's awful when you want to talk to someone, but all that you can think about is how badly you have to go use the toilet?"

James smiled.

"I guess," he said, "that I shouldn't have given you that third Orange Crush at the store a while ago. It's just that you and mom were having such a nice talk that I didn't want you to leave. I figured that if you had another bottle of pop in your hand, then you'd stay a little longer. Which you did. Thanks."

"It was fun," said Carla. "I'm glad that you finally let me spend an hour with your mom, even if she was on duty the whole time. Why have you been keeping me away from your house and your family so much? Have you been embarrassed about me?"

"Of course not!" James started to blush.

"Let me rephrase that question," said Carla. "Why have you been embarrassed about me?"

"I'm sorry," said James. "You know that you're my best friend.

In fact, you're the only best friend that I've ever had. It's just that you're a girl."

"So I noticed," laughed Carla, "at least the last time I checked. And that was only a minute ago."

James' red face deepened. "Why do you always have to say things like that?" he asked.

"Because I like shocking you. Because then you blush. Because nobody else around here says wild things like that, and I don't want to be like everybody else. Because I'm not afraid of saying what's on my mind. Because. . . . Shall I continue?" Carla laughed.

"No. I should know by now that you can come up with five answers for every question I ask."

"Okay," said Carla. "Then let me ask you one. What's the problem with me being a girl?"

"It's my brothers," said James.

"You don't think I'm pretty enough to show off to your brothers?"

"No," said James. "Stop being so paranoid about how you look. It wouldn't matter how you looked. My brothers just don't understand why I'm spending so much time with a girl and not spending more time shooting baskets and stuff. They think that I'm becoming a sissy by spending so much time with you."

"What do you think?" asked Carla. "Am I turning you into a sissy?"

"Heck no! The opposite. To be honest, the only time that I really feel like a wimp is when I try to compete with other guys in sports. Then I start feeling like a lump or a sissy or something because I'm so uncoordinated and dropping the ball all of the time and all of that. But when I'm with you, I feel real good." James laughed. He lowered his voice. "You make me feel like a man."

Carla smiled. "Good," she said. "You make me feel like a woman, too. I can't tell you how lucky I feel that we've had a chance to get to know each other this year. I don't know how I would have made it through first semester without you."

"Well," said James. "We still have another semester to go. Who knows, maybe things will get even better."

Carla got up from the couch and stepped over to the Christmas tree. She fiddled with one of the dead lights for a minute, keeping her back to James the whole time. When she turned back toward the couch, her eyes were wet and her cheeks were damp.

"James," she said. "I've got some bad news. I haven't said anything sooner because I've been doing everything that I could to fight it. But I lost. My mom is sending me to Connecticut to live with my dad."

"What?"

"My dad married his girlfriend last month, and he wants me and my sister to come out to live with him. He says that we deserve better than we're getting here with my mom."

"That's ridiculous." James started to rise from the couch. When he saw Carla's face, he sat back down. He sank up to his waist into the old cushions and broken springs.

"James," she said. "I know that you like my mom, but there's a few things about her that I haven't told you. She isn't always easy to live with. I'm not saying that she's crazy, and I'm not saying that I want to move, but I'm worried about something happening to me or my little sister if we stay here much longer."

Carla began crying softly. She avoided James' eyes and glanced back and forth between her hands and the tree and James' knees.

"Look," she said.

She rolled her sleeve and held out her arm. Two inches above her elbow was an enormous bruise of brown, green and black.

"That's from my mom." Carla mustered a sad laugh. "I have others, but you wouldn't want to see them."

James felt numb. He tried to think of something to say. "From an accident, right? Your mom didn't do that on purpose, did she?"

"Of course she did it on purpose. That's what I'm trying to tell you. That's why I sometimes have to wear makeup to school."

She looked back at the tree.

"I don't hate her or anything, but I think that she's kind of messed up. I told you that she was acting depressed. That was putting it mildly. Ever since my dad left, even before he left, she's had a drinking problem. Mostly at night. But sometimes she's drunk even in the morning. She's gotten so good at being drunk that she can look as sober as you or me even after half a dozen drinks. You've seen her a few times when she's been drinking and I'll bet that you didn't even know."

James shook his head.

"My dad's sister, aunt Donna, lives here in Grand Haven. She's been calling my dad on the phone and telling him about how mom has been getting worse and worse, and how mamma has been blowing most of the money that he sends. My dad is flying into Chicago in two days. He's going to rent a small one-way U-Haul van to move me and my sister and the rest of his junk all back to Connecticut."

Tears were streaming over Carla's cheeks and dripping from her chin. Carla drew her cuff back down toward her wrist. She tried to wipe her face with her sleeve, but the sleeve was too tight, and all that she could do was dab her face with her forearm.

"James," she said, giving up on her tears and turning to face him. "I don't think. . . ." her voice cracked, "that I'm ever going to see you again."

James stared at Carla. He could not stand to see her this way. Could not stand to consider her words.

For the first time since he had known her, Carla seemed only his age, only eleven. Only a sad, frightened child. They had practiced talking and acting grown up together, but the truth was suddenly clear.

She began shaking.

James blinked at her tears, trying to read them as if they were just cleverly-crafted sentimental phrases on the page of another book that was rapidly approaching its climax and that would soon be over. But the blinking blurred his vision, and he couldn't see Carla very clearly at all.

When he stopped blinking, he could feel tears streaming down his cheeks as well. Carla took a step toward him. Her lower lip was trembling, and she began opening and closing her eyes, squinting and relaxing her wet eyes as if waiting for the next flash card, preparing herself to shout a simple answer that would advance her to the next desk.

James had seen this sort of scene in the movies. And he just finished a novel with a scene about friends parting at a train station in New York.

This was the moment where he was supposed to stand, take Carla in his arms and hold her as she sobbed into his shoulder and he stroked her back and whispered that he loved her.

But he had never hugged a girl before, and her tears frightened him. She suddenly looked too young to be hugged that way, in a train station or anywhere else. And he felt too young to hold her.

James closed his eyes. He felt a sob building within his chest until he could hold it no longer.

"No," he sobbed, raising his hands to cover his eyes. "No. . . ."

And then James felt the flow of the tears of a child, one who had abandoned the scripts of adults and who had given up on the advice of his dad and brothers. All that he could do was cry.

"James," whispered Carla from his side. She placed one tentative hand upon his shoulders. "James," she said again, "we're going to be okay."

He lifted his head and turned. Carla's face was still damp, but she was no longer crying.

Carla leaned very close to James' ear. "Thank you," she whispered, "for loving me. I will never forget you, as long as I live." Carla slid her hand down James' back until her arm was around him, and they sat, side by side, deep in the couch, quietly sniffling and thinking for a very long time.

When James at last turned to return her gaze, he was surprised by how different Carla looked. The frightened child that had stood weeping by the Christmas tree was gone. In her place, there now sat someone older, composed, tender and wise. Her face wore a subdued, sad smile, the sort of smile that children are unable to summon and that adults often struggle to hide.

Carla lifted her arm to James' face and held his cheek for a moment, then leaned and drew him forward until her lips gently pressed against his. James closed his eyes.

He had not expected that her lips would feel so soft, and they still carried a salty taste from her tears.

He sat perfectly still, unsure whether he should move his lips. He tried to remember what he had read and seen in the movies.

Then Carla pulled his head more firmly toward hers and pressed her lips harder. Instinctively, James raised his right hand to the side and back of Carla's head. He felt her thick hair in his hand, and he squeezed his eyes as he remembered the first time that he touched her.

She moved her lips very slightly. He tried to mirror the motion. The sagging couch rolled them together into a basket from which they could not easily escape.

James never guessed that kissing a girl would be like this. He was eager to discover more.

He forgot about her leaving and breathed through his nose and experimented with different pressures upon her lips for different effects. He began stroking her hair, running his right hand through her black waves and tangling her tresses in his fingers. He opened his eyes for a moment and saw that Carla's eyes were closed. Then he closed his eyes again and returned to stroking her hair.

His hand finally came to rest beneath Carla's hair, deep back on the side of her face. Her warm cheek glowed at the heel of his hand, and the soft bumps and ridges of her ear pressed lightly into his palm. His fingers cupped the side and the back of her head.

He pressed his lips more firmly into hers, pulling her mouth into his until his lips began to hurt. He savored the sensations, her mouth, the skin of her cheek, her heavy hair blanketing the back of his hand, and her ear searing its firm brand into the palm of his hand.

Carla let go of James' cheek and slowly raised her hand to his wrist. She softly grasped it where it disappeared beneath her hair, then gently pulled her mouth away from his. She drew his hand away from her ear.

As his hand slipped from Carla's ear, he opened his eyes. Carla turned her mouth slightly and kissed his palm good-bye. Her lips lingered in his hand. Then, suddenly, her tongue poked his palm with a quick wet jab.

Carla opened her eyes and tossed her head back with a laugh.

"Merry Christmas," she smiled.

James blinked, trying to laugh.

The spell was broken. But his palm still tingled, wet and strangely stimulated from the press of the ridges of her ear and from the moist jab of her tongue.

"I take it, "she beamed, "that this was your first kiss?"

James felt the familiar furnace flaring in his cheeks.

"Was I that bad?" he asked, trying to smile.

"How should I know?" Carla laughed. "That was my first kiss, too. Since I don't have anything to compare it with, all that I can tell you is how it made me feel. But I'd better not. Unless, of course, you want to blush even worse."

James smiled. "So you liked it?"

"It was fabulous!"

"Should we do it again?"

Carla frowned for a moment.

"I'd like to," she said. "But I don't think that we should."

Her eyes dropped and her subdued smile returned.

"If we hadn't kissed, I think that I would have kicked myself for the rest of my life, since that's how long that I'm going to remember you. But now that we have, I think that it's best that we call one good kiss good enough. I wish I wasn't moving away. If I was staying, I think that I'd sit right here and make out with you until my mom came home and threw you out the door. Then I'd kiss you again tomorrow in some closet after school."

Carla sighed. "But if we start kissing again, I'm afraid that I'll cry even harder when you leave tonight."

James was quiet.

He looked back at Carla's scrawny tree and the shallow pile of gifts beneath. He turned again to Carla's sad smile.

"That was the best Christmas and going away present that I ever got," he laughed, trying to sound cheerful. "I'll never forget that kiss. My first kiss, with my first girlfriend." James felt the searing brand of her ear and tongue in the palm of his right hand.

"Me either," she whispered back.

He tried to slide a few inches from Carla, but the couch wouldn't let him. When he tried to stand, the couch sucked him back down like mud tugging on a loose boot.

Carla laughed.

"Maybe," she said, "we should both stand up at the same time."

They rocked back in unison, then rose together, half facing and laughing themselves to their feet.

And then they were holding each other. They did not kiss, but they embraced, awkwardly and in silence, for a long time.

"Carla," said James, taking a step back. He lifted his arm and began to remove his watch. "I know that it's not a first kiss. But I want to give you something. Your first watch."

The strap unfastened easily within his fingers.

"It's the only thing," he said, "I can think of to give you that means anything to me. I know that the black wrist band is not right for a girl, but maybe you can make a prettier one out of something. Or maybe you can just put the watch in a box and think about me once in a while when you open the lid."

James finished removing the watch and held it in an outstretched hand.

Carla bit her lip. "Oh, James," she said. "I couldn't take your watch."

"It's all that I've got. Please, take it. It'll make me happy every time I go to check my wrist to think that somewhere out in Connecticut, you've got the watch, and that somehow, a small part of me is wrapped around you."

Carla began crying again.

"You've definitely been reading too many books," she laughed through her tears.

She took the watch, looked at it, sniffed it, then smiled.

"Here," she said. "Help me put it on."

A few days later, Carla was gone. Her mother left Grand Haven as well, and James never saw any of them again. James and Carla wrote long weekly letters at first, but gradually, the distance between their lives and their letters took its toll. One day James received a returned letter stamped: "Address Unknown."

He never heard from Carla again.

The time came when James could no longer remember the sound of Carla's voice. But there were other things that he could not forget.

He remembered her smile as she glanced at him across the kitchen table, and her eyes as she squinted and leaned toward the next flash card. And even though he forgot the feel of his arm around her waist, he never forgot the feel of the ridges of her ear and the wet jab of her tongue in his palm.

His hand remembered.

0955-CHEA

CHAPTER 23

Friday, March 22, 1996.
Lakewood, Colorado

Alice quietly stroked Jade's arm.

"So," she said at last, "that's why you liked the name Carla when I suggested it for our daughter?"

Jade opened his eyes. He adjusted his robe and raised himself from the pillows into a sitting position.

"I've always liked the name Carla," he said, tucking one of the pillows behind the base of his back. He turned to Alice. "I never would have suggested naming our Carla after Carla Mekluevich. But since you brought up the name and you liked it so much, I decided to agree."

Alice shifted in the couch.

"Does it bother you," he asked, "to know that there was another Carla before ours?"

"Not really. I'm glad you told me about her." Alice twisted a kink from her neck. "How are you doing, Jade? I guess that we've been sitting here for quite a while."

"I'm doing fine. It was nice to lie there like that, with you massaging my arms and shoulders. It brought back more memories than just those of Carla. We used to sit together on the couch quite often. I used to look forward to that after a hard day." He smiled. "How are you doing?"

"A little stiff. But I'd like to do some more talking, if you're up to it. Carla went to the mountains with Kimberly," Alice looked at the clock, "and Mark shouldn't be home for another couple of hours. We've got some time."

"You must be uncomfortable," he offered, "why don't you take a turn lying down. I need to sit up for a while anyway. Some of that beer is still in my system."

"Thanks. Maybe I will."

Alice propped a pillow against the arm at the far end of the couch. She looked at Jade hesitantly, then leaned back and swung her feet into his lap.

"Do you mind?" she asked.

It had been a long time since he had rubbed her feet. He smiled. Alice closed her eyes and settled her head into the pillow.

"Jade," she said. "That was a sad story. It's sad to picture you two young kids saying good-bye like that. Do you think about her any more? Like when you see our Carla, or when you use Carla's name?"

"Not very often." He removed Alice's white work shoes. He had not taken Alice's shoes off since Mark and Carla were in elementary school, back at their Maple Street home in Grand Rapids.

Alice's feet were smaller, more slender than he remembered.

"When Carla was first born," he said, "it was strange to say her name. I would tell someone about my baby Carla and it almost felt like I was talking about Carla Mekluevich. But as our daughter grew, and as I got used to her and to saying her name, she developed her own place in my brain. Right alongside you and Mark, in the family lobe." He smiled. "I guess that the two Carla's are now logged in two completely different parts of my head. I never think of Carla Mekluevich any more just by seeing or thinking about our daughter."

He began rubbing her arches.

"Except," he said, "when Carla was in sixth grade. There were times that year when I thought of the old Carla. Especially when Carla came home with stories that reminded me of when I was her age."

Alice's eyes remained closed. Jade studied her face, her mouth, her shoulders, her rising and falling breasts, her legs and her feet within his hands.

He closed his eyes. The refrigerator chortled to a stop and the house grew silent. He became aware of the faint ticking of the Regulator clock. The ticking grew louder and louder as he focused. Steady ticks, marking the time.

"Alice," he said.

"Yes?"

"Did you reset the clock?"

"Yes. It must have stopped last night. The funny thing is, when I went to rewind it this morning, it felt like the spring was still pretty tight. I hope that nothing's wrong with that old thing. I've never known it to stop on its own unless it needed to be re-wound."

"The clock is fine," said Jade. "I stopped the pendulum last night with my finger."

Alice opened her eyes.

"Why?" she asked. "The chimes didn't go off, did they? I'm quite sure that the chime spring is still completely unwound. I haven't turned the key on that side of the clock in years."

"It wasn't the chimes. Just the ticking. It seemed louder than usual. I was worried about getting to sleep."

Alice closed her eyes again.

"Do you remember," she said, "how when we first got married, the chimes kept going off and waking us up in the night? I can't believe how long it took us to figure out what to do, to just let the chimes wind down and then to leave them that way."

He grinned. "Not that it was always so bad waking up in the middle of the night."

Alice smiled, her eyes still closed. "No, it wasn't all that bad. Maybe we should have kept winding them a little longer."

"Sure," he laughed, "you say that now."

"You're right. Two kids are plenty. Can you imagine what a houseful we would have by now if we'd kept up at that early pace?"

Jade began massaging her toes.

"I was thinking of something else this morning," he said. "I was remembering our honeymoon. You and me floating together in that mountain hot spring."

He did not add how the water had churned itself into a frightening whirlpool.

Alice smiled. "Yes, I remember that night. It was lovely. Like Adam and Eve, I think I said."

"Why did we leave so soon?" he asked. "We should have stayed in that spot at least another day. We had the whole valley to ourselves."

"Oh, I don't know," she sighed. "Maybe we were low on food. Or maybe we were eager to see something else. I guess that we didn't realize how rare a good thing like that can be. Maybe we took it for granted."

They were silent for a long time.

"Alice," he said. "It was good, wasn't it? Between you and me, back then?"

"Yes. Not perfect. You always had a side that confused me, a part of you that I couldn't reach or know. But at times, yes, I remember that it was very good."

"When did it go bad? When did we stop enjoying time together?"

"We still do, don't we? Sometimes?"

"Yes. But we wouldn't be having this conversation if we weren't having serious trouble. Right?"

"Perhaps," she paused, "but then if we had more talks like this, our troubles would probably not be so serious."

"Touché."

"I've tried," said Alice, "to put my finger on the guilty moment when things went bad, or the event that marked the change. I thought that if I could find a simple cause, we could work out something to fix it. But I can't seem to isolate any one thing or one moment. I think it was gradual. I guess that it's not possible to undo a good thing in a single day. It takes a lot of chipping away to topple something that is this big."

"Many strokes fell mighty oaks."

Alice grinned. "Exactly." She opened her eyes. "Are you making fun of me?"

"Whatever gave you that idea?" he grinned.

"You don't like those little sayings of mine, do you?"

"Well, there's certainly some truth in them. But I have to confess, clichés have always bugged me. I guess it's the side of me that appreciates good literature and good thinking that wants to gag when I hear some of those adages popped off like they're so profound." He squeezed a toe. "But Hosea says that clichés have their uses."

"Hosea?"

"A guy I met up on the hogback. A real character. I'll have to tell you about him sometime."

How much should he tell her? Hosea was the kind of person that would have to be seen and spoken with to be believed.

Friday! It was Friday. Hosea would be expecting Jade at the cave tomorrow morning. Jade had been looking forward to talking with Hosea all week. He needed some advice about Harry's ashes. Of course, with Harry now in the custody of some stranger, the ashes were a bit of a moot point. But he still wanted to go. How could he justify another day off from work? To adjust the Saturday schedule, he would have to face Chris. Shit.

"So you think those sayings that I like are stupid?"

"Sorry, Alice. I just don't appreciate them the way that you do."

"Do you hate them?"

"Hate is a pretty strong word. Let's just say that they get on my nerves once in a while."

"Why haven't you said something sooner? Now I feel stupid. You should have told me how you felt." She grinned. "Not that I didn't guess. I've seen the way that you've curled your lip and brushed them aside."

"You could have asked me if I liked them. If it bothered you so much what I thought of them, you should have asked."

"I guess I wanted to. But more than that, I suppose that I

wanted you to say something to me on your own, without me having to drag it out of you. I think I was hoping that if I spread enough of them around, sooner or later, you would say something."

"So, in other words, you've been using them to goad me?"

"To some extent, perhaps."

He chuckled lightly. Alice joined him.

"We can both be pretty silly sometimes, can't we?"

"Silly or stubborn, I'm not sure which."

"Both. Probably both."

They grew quiet.

"Jade," she said. "There are still a few things that I don't understand."

"Go ahead."

Alice's voice went soft. "For one thing, that business about your dad. You've never said much about your father other than that your mom dumped him because of his fooling around. Now you're telling me that you caught him yourself having sex with a woman in the bathroom? That you saw the whole thing?"

"Yes. Not the whole thing, maybe, but I guess that I saw enough. And then my mom found out and that was it. The divorce came after that last time, the time with Marsha Fenton in the customers' bathroom."

"You make it sound so matter-of-fact. Discovering your dad having sex with a stranger must have been traumatic. Maybe more traumatic than you realize. I mean, can you imagine what it would have been like for your son if he discovered that you were. . . ."

She stopped.

Jade winced.

"I'm sorry, Jade. I didn't mean it that way. I wasn't talking about the e-mail that Mark found. I only meant that. . . ."

"You're right. I never thought about it quite that way. If that had been Mark seeing me in the bathroom with a naked stranger in the 1990s, some social worker would have ordered him into counseling, a few thousand bucks worth of professional therapy to make sure that he wasn't going to be messed up about it when he got older."

Jade looked toward the window and let the revelation sink in.

"And you're right," he added. "Sooner or later, I'm going to need to talk to Mark about the e-mail. One thing at a time, though. It's hard enough, maybe even impossible, to talk about it with you. Let alone with Mark. This is very personal, difficult stuff. Embarrassing stuff. And I haven't exactly been close to Mark lately."

"Or to me." She changed her tone. "Yet here we are, talking."

"Touché again."

"Jade, I'm not trying to score against you. I'm only trying to talk. To help us both get through this."

"I know. It's just that this feels pretty one-sided. It feels like I'm the one who's having to do all the squirming, the one confessing all the dirt." He met her eyes. "Alice, what is it that you will be bringing to the table?"

"What do you mean?"

"I'm not trying to be pushy. Or to start another fight. But I can't believe that our marriage has gotten to where it is simply because of me alone. Sometimes when we fight, we blame each other for things. I'm not trying to blame you for anything this time." He smiled and shrugged. "After all, I'm the one with the bloody knuckles. And with the e-mail to explain."

Alice straightened. "But?"

"But as you said, this is about chipping away, not simply about one or two things that can be pinned on me and my mistakes alone. I'm not going to accuse you of anything. All that I ask is that if you think of something about yourself, that you'll do a little sharing or confessing of your own, just like I'm trying to do."

"Confessing? Like what? What is it that you want me to tell you?"

"Oh, I don't know. Just think about it, and give me something if you can." He smiled faintly. "Okay?"

"I'll try. I think I see your point. But I guess you've caught me off guard."

"With your pants down?"

Alice laughed.

"No, thank goodness. I'll not have any confessions of that sort for you. Nothing as juicy as that. But I'll think about it. And, if I can, I'll bring something of my own. To the table, as you put it. When would you like it?"

"I'm not saying that I'll like it. I'm just feeling like it's important. And you can share things whenever you feel willing. With any luck at all, this will not be our last discussion. I think we'll be talking a lot for awhile. If you want to?"

"I do."

"Okay then." He patted her foot. "Back to Harry. My father. So maybe catching him doing the nasty with Mars was more disturbing than I realized. I'll have to give that some more thought. But there's something else about Harry that I need to tell you."

"Go on."

"He's dead."

"What!" Alice swung her feet to the floor and sat upright.

"Yeah. He died recently. That's what mom called me about the other night."

"Not to say that she was flying to Florida?"

"No. I mean, she was flying to Florida. That's what she told me when she called. It's just that when I told you about her call, I left out the part about my dad."

"Jade, I'm so sorry. Why didn't you tell me sooner?"

"It's complicated. And as you know, I didn't have a whole lot of respect for old Harry. It's not like I'm grieving or anything."

"His death doesn't bother you?"

"It just feels a little odd, that's all."

"Will you be going to his funeral?"

"Well, since you asked . . . that's another thing that I've been meaning to tell you. There won't be a funeral."

"No funeral?"

"He was cremated."

"Cremated?"

Jade stroked his neck.

Alice leaned toward him. She placed her hand on his shoulder. "How did he die?"

"Suicide. A shotgun."

"Oh, Jade." She drew back. "How awful."

"I guess."

"Why did he do it?"

"Who knows? Lonely? Broke? A guilty conscience? He had cancer, so that must have been part of it. But that's why I didn't tell you sooner. I guess I knew that you would have a bunch of questions and I really didn't want to talk about it. I have a hard time talking about this stuff. I've kind of made it a point all of my adult life to avoid thinking and talking too much about my past."

"So I've noticed. But this is ridiculous. You can't even tell your wife that your father died?"

"Not died. Killed himself. Blew his brains out. We're not talking about a heart attack, here. We're talking about a messy suicide. And there's something else. Another reason why I didn't want to mention his death, besides the suicide and all the questions it would raise."

"Yes?"

"His ashes. I knew that if I told you about Harry's death, then I'd have to tell you about his ashes."

Alice looked at him uneasily.

"Yes?"

"And I know how creeped out you get about these things, and I needed some time to think it through myself."

"Jade, tell me!"

"My mother sent his ashes to Colorado. I got them in the mail on Tuesday."

"My God."

"She sent them in a Frosted Flakes box."

"What?"

"The large family size box. Fat free."

"Frosted. . . ." Alice leapt to her feet. "Your dead father is in my house and you didn't even tell me?"

"Relax, Alice. I would have introduced you, but I hardly recognized him myself. I do remember seeing Harry toasted a couple of times, but this was the first time that I'd ever seen him frosted."

She wheeled on him.

"How can you joke about this? Where is he?" Alice glanced frantically around the room. Suddenly, she turned toward the kitchen. "Oh, no. He's not. . . ."

"Naw. Harry's not in the pantry."

She sighed. "Then where?"

"I'm getting to that."

She turned toward him again, her nostrils flaring.

"You brought some dead man's remains into my home, a grisly suicide no less, a troubled soul, and you didn't bother to tell me?"

Alice was again jerking her head in different directions. Her eyes paused on a track of mud near the front door.

"Don't worry," Jade grinned sheepishly, "I didn't spill him on the carpet. Relax. I've been stringing you along. Harry is no longer with us."

He laughed quietly. "I mean, he's no longer in the house."

Alice gathered her hair behind her neck, then let it fall. "Then, you already spread Harry's ashes someplace, or what?"

"Not exactly. I didn't exactly spread them. I misplaced them."

"Misplaced them?" Alice dropped herself in the chair near the couch.

"I was carrying the Frosted Flakes box around for a couple of days inside my briefcase. I couldn't decide what to do with the surprise prize inside. Fortunately, the stay-fresh liner. . . ."

"Your briefcase?"

"Yes. The briefcase that I lost at the mall."

"Oh, no. Jade. How could you? How could you lose track of your own father? His remains? The ashes of his dead body?"

Jade decided not to mention that he had lost the briefcase behind a trash can while watching Chris bend over at the mall.

"Alice. Please, lighten up. The ashes aren't toxic or anything."

Harry is dead and gone. We're talking about sand here, a few min-
erals, dirt in a box . . . dust."

"Lighten up?" She shook her head, rose, then left the room.
She returned a few moments later with a glass of water. She stood
for moment, then sat down next to him on the couch.

"I'm sorry," she sighed. "Maybe I'm over-reacting. But if my
father's ashes had arrived in a cereal box. . . ."

"Your father was nothing like Harry."

She sighed again. "Still, he was your dad, right?"

"Yes."

Alice took a few swallows of her water, then offered the glass to
Jade.

"Thanks." He took a shallow sip, then smiled.

"Okay," she said. "I'm under control. Thanks for telling me
about your dad. I wish I would have known sooner, but thanks for
finally filling me in. Even if this is a little late."

"I wanted to tell you sooner, but we haven't had much luck
communicating lately, remember?"

"True. All right. Where were we? What else?"

"That's about all that I can think of about Harry. I'll have to
wait to see if the briefcase shows up, but I'm not holding my
breath expecting to ever see Harry's ashes again."

"And you're not upset, shocked maybe, about his death?"

Jade swirled the water that remained in the glass.

"I'm not sure. Perhaps I haven't yet given it enough thought."
He took another sip, then handed the glass back to Alice. "I guess
that it did feel a little tragic to learn that Harry died alone, without any friends. My mom sent a few documents with the ashes.
Everything else that Harry owned is already long gone. It occurred
to me earlier this week that it was pathetic that Harry didn't even
have a swayed-back hound to leave behind. Nothing but his ashes."

Alice leaned forward.

"No," she said. "That's not true. Your father left behind more
than that. He left behind you. And your memories of him. And
your brother, Ben."

And Randy, thought Jade.

No, Randy was gone, too.

He was silent for a moment.

"Do you remember," asked Jade, "me telling you years ago about our other brother? Randy?"

Alice set down her glass and put her hand on his shoulder.

"Yes," she said. "I remember the little bit that you told me. You've never said much about Randy. He died during his senior year in a boating accident, right?"

"Right. His boat smashed into a dock on the bayou. It was foggy and the person driving the boat never saw it coming. They both died instantly. After the accident, I threw away my copy of the newspaper story about their deaths. I didn't want to be reminded of it. It was kind of a rough week for me."

"You never mentioned that two people died."

"Well, two people died."

Jade closed his eyes and leaned back.

"My dad saved his copy of the article. It was one of the documents that my mom sent. I'd show it to you, but it was in the briefcase with the ashes."

"And the other documents?"

"Nothing important, I guess. Copies of his marriage and divorce papers. A Detroit Tigers baseball program. A copy of the old snack menu from our store. And one photograph." Jade met her eyes. "The snapshot that my mom used for the divorce. It was taken the night that Harry stepped out of the bathroom with Mars. Mom used the photo as proof of Harry's infidelity, even though they weren't naked or anything in the picture. Harry never fought the divorce. He was caught and he knew it."

Alice looked puzzled.

"Why, of all things," she asked, "do you suppose he kept that photo?"

Jade hadn't thought of that. It was a good question.

"I mean," she continued, "that must have been an awful

memory for him. He must have felt sick to his stomach every time he looked at it."

"Maybe" offered Jade, "Harry didn't look at it very often. Perhaps he tucked it away with all of his other papers after the divorce and then forgot about it."

"Could be."

No, Harry would not have forgotten about the photo. A man would not be able to forget about something like that in a thousand years. He must have kept the photo for some other reason.

"Jade?" She stroked his back. "I hope that you don't mind me asking, but I'd like to know something else about Randy's accident. Did you know the other person who died, the driver of the boat?"

"Yes."

"Well, what else can you tell me? I mean, it was his mistake that killed your brother, right? Yet you've never said a word about the driver."

"The driver," said Jade, "was not a he. It was a her. Her name was Karen." He looked away.

"The person driving the speed boat," he added softly, "was my girlfriend."

Alice stopped breathing.

"We were in love."

"Oh, Jade. . . ."

"Karen was mangled so badly in the wreck that her family had to order a closed casket for her funeral." He looked at Alice, then turned away. "The accident was not her fault. It was Randy's. But he got his."

"What do you mean?"

"Randy's service," Jade's voice iced, "was held the day before Karen's. It was a much smaller service, with no casket at all. Just an urn."

"He was cremated?"

"Correct. Cremated. Like son, like father. You see, there was a small problem. The predicament was that Randy's head, like

Harry's, was a mess. At least what they found of it. It had been severed quite roughly by the underside of the dock. And then it had been soaking in the bayou for several hours before it washed up on the. . . ."

"Stop it," cried Alice.

Jade closed his eyes.

Alice shuddered.

"How," she asked, trembling, "can you talk about such a horrible thing that way? So coldly?" She shuddered again, then lowered her face into her hands.

They were silent for a long time.

Jade's mind emptied. Images of the accident pressed against his consciousness, were repelled. He stood, walked to the front door, opened it, then looked out from the entry.

The Dakota Ridge rose to the west, jagged browns and grays, blotches of black juniper and growth. He searched against ranges of mountains towering in the distance for the distinctive lower outline of the horse-head slog. He found it. Studied it. Projected himself into the rock. Felt the dank chill of the cave return as he had experienced it on Monday. When he had gone up in search of Hosea, and when he found the black abyss of the altar instead.

The dark hole into which he prayed. Into which he had impulsively crushed his watch.

He thought of the unexplainable exhilaration after his sacrifice, of his ride down the mountain in the darkening shadows, back to the road that led home.

For everything there is a season. A time to be born and a time to die . . . a time to kill and a time to heal.

He squinted toward the trough at the snout on the ridge. A billow of dust? A plume of smoke? It disappeared.

A time to weep and a time to laugh. A time to mourn. . . .

Jade turned back toward Alice on the couch. She sat motionless, watching him.

He closed the door and stepped toward her. He stopped, then came and sat at her side.

"I'm sorry," he said at last.

Alice's eyes were red and her face streaked.

"I don't understand you," she whispered.

Jade's hands began to shake. He looked down at them, then up at his wife.

"That was cruel. I don't know where it came from. It just welled up inside me and foamed out of my mouth. I wasn't trying to shock you. Or to upset you."

"I know. That's what frightens me." Alice slid to his side and took him in her arms. His whole body was shaking.

"Jade," she asked softly, "are you angry with Randy? You sounded angry, bitter for a mistake that he made, a mistake that already cost him his life. And Karen's. Are you still raging against your dead brother after all of these years?"

"All of these years? It doesn't feel like it's been that long. Right now, it feels like it was only a week ago, a week ago that. . . ." his voice trailed off.

"Jade, do you think of this often? Do you relive the accident over and over in your mind?"

"No. Almost never. After Karen's funeral, I pushed the whole thing from my mind. I let it go."

Alice squeezed his shoulder through his robe.

"Are you sure that you let it go? When people talk about death and the stages of grief, they say that it takes time. But they also say that a person must work through each stage, and that. . . ."

The phone rang.

Neither of them stirred.

It rang again.

The answering machine announced itself, then offered to take a message.

A woman's voice promptly piped through the intercom at full volume.

"Hello, Jim? Jade? This is Chris again. Look, I don't know what the hell is going on, but we're going to have to talk. That aside, the schedule is now all screwed up. Fortunately, Sally and I are working it out. She said that she would take the extra hours to make up for time she lost last week with the flu, so you're covered until Monday. I suggest that you get your act together this weekend and that you come in Monday morning ready to do some explaining. To the NightLight rep, to Mr. Seinner, and to me. I'm sure that I don't need to elaborate. I'll talk to you then. Goodbye."

The machine clicked.

After Chris's call, Alice excused herself to use the bathroom. Jade was thankful for the opportunity to breathe. He stood, retied his robe, then used the bathroom upstairs.

A few minutes later, they reconvened on the couch.

Alice sighed. Jade touched her lightly.

"This morning," she said, "has been overwhelming."

"Enough for one day?"

"I don't know."

"Me either. But I think that we're on a roll." He smiled. "Or a roller coaster?"

"Both," she smiled sadly. "It's been both."

"As hard as this is," he said, "I'm almost afraid that if I stop, I may not be able to do this again. To talk about these things. They've been bottled up for so long, and now they're starting to come out. . . ."

"You're right, Jade. We need to keep going. To keep plowing through this as far as we can."

"Yes. As long as we can stand it."

"Why now?" she asked. "After all of these years, why are you finally able to talk?"

He considered her question.

"Maybe," he said, "I'm talking because I finally have to. Because if I don't now, deep down, I know that later will be too late. For us. For this family. For me." He smiled. "Of course, it's also true that I seem to have been nudged by a few odd events this week."

"Nudged?"

"Mark's comment last Sunday. Mom's phone call. Harry's ashes showing up. Losing control in the back room at work. Meeting Hosea."

"The man from the hogback?"

"Right. But that's another story. Let's just say that this past week has included a conspiracy of coincidences that have knocked me out of my otherwise predictable orbit. Look at me, sick with a hangover, bloody knuckles, resistance down," He glanced at his lap, "and at home in my bathrobe with my wife on the couch when I should be at work."

"I have this feeling," she said softly, "that right now, you are exactly where you should be. Not at work setting sales records, but at home, working on this, talking with me. This seems far more important than another day at that mall. For me, at least."

"Me too." He reached for her hand, held it, then squeezed gently.

She met his eyes. Her hand stiffened lightly.

"Are you," she asked, "going to return Chris' call?"

"I don't think so. She was right. I need to use this weekend to get my head squared away. Chris and the store can wait until Monday. I've already got my hands full right here."

He squeezed Alice's hand once more, then released it.

"Thank you," she said.

She lifted her fingers to her eyebrows, stroked them, then turned back toward Jade.

"Why don't you," he offered, "lie back again and relax."

She did, slowly, awkwardly. She put her head against the pillow, swung her feet back to his lap and closed her eyes.

He returned to massaging her feet, waiting. Waiting for some of the tension to drain, waiting for a way to resume. He could feel it in his stomach and neck, and he knew it in his heart; if he didn't talk more now, it would only get harder.

"Why," she asked at last, opening her eyes, "why haven't you talked about Carla before? From what you said, that was a touch-

ing story about a young boy's first love. There wasn't anything
that I picked up from what you told me that you should be feeling
ashamed about."

She closed her eyes, then sighed. "I would have liked to have
known that side of you years ago." Alice's voice dropped softer
still. "And what does Carla have to do with what happened yesterday? With you, Chris, the phony e-mail . . . and you getting
drunk?"

Jade stopped massaging. He looked at Alice. Mercifully, her
eyes were closed.

"Well," he said, shifting his strokes to the balls of her feet,
"obviously, there is a connection."

He continued to gently knead one foot, then the other.

"Alice, do you remember me saying at the end of my story
that Carla and I wrote letters back and forth after she moved?"

"Yes."

"Well, I used to live for those letters. The first thing that I'd do
when I got home from school was to check the mail. Every day. For
years, even after I was sure that we'd lost touch. It became more
than a habit. I cherished Carla's letters, and she was a great writer.
I would read them over and over, slowly, tasting each word, picturing her talking and writing and laughing until it was almost as
if we were back together again sitting at her kitchen table. She
never really wrote anything that was downbeat, never told me about
bad things that might be going on. Just Carla at her lively best."

Jade shifted on the couch.

"As her letters slowed down, I became more and more discouraged. Without her help, I didn't have the guts to be a class egghead any more. I still loved to read, but I pretty much stopped
studying. I never dropped back down below B's, but I became a
classic underachiever. No special honors, and no enemies. But no
new friends for a couple of years, either."

He could feel her feet relaxing, her whole body surrendering
its fears and questions to his voice. To his decision to tell her more.

"I became addicted to novels. I asked my teachers for lists of good books and I read practically everything they mentioned. If I read them too quickly, I discovered that I missed the pleasure of the words and images, and the stories were over far too soon. So I stopped speed reading, and I started immersing myself in classics and thick pop-novels for long stretches of time, mostly just to escape into other worlds. And I loved those worlds, those fantasies. I've been a fast reader since sixth grade, but after Carla left, I never again practiced speed reading."

He glanced at the bookshelf beside the fireplace. A few of the books on the bottom row dated back to those years.

"So anyway, about a year later, when Carla stopped writing, I memorized all of her letters, and I copied the best parts from each one and strung them together into composite letters that I carried around in my notebooks and read silently in dull classes when I was bored."

He hesitated.

"Then," he said, "I started writing letters that I pretended were from Carla, but that I made up myself. She would tell me things in these letters that she was doing, and she would ask about what I was doing. She would always write about how much she missed me and how great it would be when she moved back to Grand Haven. Her letters became fantasies of a sort, an escape for me, a lot like the escape that I got from immersing myself in novels."

Alice stirred on the couch. Jade looked and saw that her eyes were open.

"Jade," she said. "That's not so unusual. I mean, at least it makes sense to me. A lonely boy, no friends, his only best friend moving away at a very unstable and insecure point in his life. Who else would you have to talk to? And everybody has to have someone to talk to."

"Thanks for trying to understand." He shook his head. "But it gets a little weirder. I started making up letters from her, and then actually mailing them to myself."

He tried to laugh.

"After a while, I could barely remember which letters were hers, and which ones were invented from my own imagination."

"Do you still have any of those letters?"

"No. I burned them all when I was in high school."

"Why on earth did you burn them? They were your last link to your first best friend."

Jade looked down to Alice's feet, then realized he had stopped rubbing. He wrapped both hands around her right ankle, then slowly began to massage.

"As I said, it got to the point where I could hardly tell where her letters left off and my fantasies began. As I got older, the nature of the letters changed. You know, puberty and all of that."

He closed his eyes.

"I started twisting Carla in my letters, and in my mind, started making her into something that she never would have stood for. I felt terrible about it, but I couldn't stop. The next thing I knew, Carla was trying out for the cheerleading squad. And then I had her growing up in my letters."

His voice thinned. "You know, changing her hair, wearing bras and that sort of thing. And, of course, I fantasized about her going on dates with me and making out with me everywhere that I could think of. I invented a whole bizarre world in those letters. I felt guilty about each letter, but I kept writing them anyway. Those letters became an addiction, an escape, an obsession that I couldn't shake."

He opened his eyes. Alice was again staring.

"So," she asked, "the e-mail that you invented, the one supposedly from Chris, that letter was a kind of extension of your fantasy letters from Carla?"

"I guess. Weird, huh? But it's not like I've been writing letters like that all of my life. I eventually stopped writing the Carla letters. And it was only recently, only after Chris sent a couple of real e-mails to our house, that I found myself slipping back into the old habit."

He began rubbing Alice's heels. Her eyes were again closed.

He studied her face.

"In Eighth Grade," he continued, "I had a growth spurt. All of a sudden, I started getting thinner and growing as tall as my classmates. My fat melted away. My legs were still short, so I was not a fast runner, but I discovered that I could play as well as most of the other kids. For the first time in my life, my brothers and the other kids started wanting me on their teams. When I got to my freshman year of high school, things really changed. I guess that I didn't need to escape so much any more. I decided to put chubby little Jimmy and dorky little James behind me."

"That," he sighed, "is when I started having people call me Jim."

Alice sat slowly, then leaned forward until her hand reached his. Her fingers paused where his hands rested on her ankles.

"Jade, you're telling me that you broke free of your secret letter writing in high school. But I'm not sure that I understand why you went back to creating such letters all of these years later, now . . . with Chris. I feel like a bomb has been dropped into my life, and it feels like you're changing the focus of all of this. Avoiding something. I'm not sure that I care why you changed your name from James to Jim. Not unless that's really part of what's happened this week."

She squeezed his wrist. "Right now, I can't get the Chris problem out of my mind. And I'm afraid that I'm still confused."

He closed his eyes. She wasn't going to let him off the hook.

"So am I," he said. "I'm a little confused myself. There's probably some pretty complicated psychology involved in all of this."

"There's a lot more going on here, isn't there?" she asked. "What parts are you leaving out? What aren't you telling me?"

"I'm not sure, Alice. I don't know what's important and what isn't. Really. This is difficult even for me to understand. I don't think that a woman, even my wife, could ever really understand this stuff. It's probably a man thing. Even if I tried to explain what I was talking about. . . ."

He felt himself talking in circles, felt himself unwilling to commit to any single direction in his thoughts or words.

She rubbed his hand.

"Try me. See if I can understand. You owe me that much. You're still my husband, and I'm still your wife."

He tapped her heel. "But for how long?"

"You tell me."

He looked back to her face. "At our wedding altar, I made a vow. With you, and with God. I promised to love you for the rest of my life."

"And?"

"Alice." He rolled her ankles beneath his thumbs, watching his own hands. "I'm not exactly sure what love is any more. I don't think that I really understood that vow when I made it." He squeezed. "But I'm still committed to you, and to our kids. And I don't want to lose you. I want to stay with you, I want things to improve between us. Deep down, I still love you, even if it feels different than it once did. I care about you, and I hate to see you suffer because of my mistakes."

She sighed. "I've made my share of mistakes, too."

He looked up.

"Alice, do you still love me?"

She met his eyes. "Sometimes, yes. Other times, I haven't been so sure. But right now, I feel like I love you very deeply. The moment that I saw your cuts and bandages when I walked in a little while ago, my heart almost stopped. I think that must mean something, don't you?"

He blinked, slowly.

"Yes," he said. "That must mean something. And when I think about the pain that I've caused you, and the way that I've treated you sometimes, I hate myself. That must mean something, too. Don't you think?"

She smiled. "Yes."

"But," she added, looking concerned, "it was you a little while ago who said that 'hate' was an awful strong word. You worry me when you say that you can hate yourself for something, even if that means that you care about my feelings. Hate is a strong word."

He thought for a moment. "Yes. It is."

They sat in silence.

"Tell me more," said Alice at last. "Let's keep going."

Jade sighed. "This is a lot harder for me than you might think. Part of me is freezing up inside. It's hard for me to concentrate on what I need to say and how to say it."

"Then start with what's easy, if that helps. I guess I've waited this long. Tell me about what happened after Carla. About your brothers and about when you changed your name from James to Jim. Take your time if you have to, as long as you're moving in the right direction. As long as what you tell me will help me to understand this man I married. This man I love."

She smiled, cautiously. "I'm all ears."

CHAPTER 24

August, 1973.
Chambers Park, Lake Michigan

Hot sand churned beneath his driving feet.

James was exhausted, but he refused to slacken his pace. He glanced beneath his swinging right arm.

He filled his mind with the vista in a snapshot glance, then replayed the image as his eyes refocused on the sand in front of his eyes.

Far below, at the base of the enormous dune, Lake Michigan stretched like a vast wash of water-paint blues. The pale aquamarines at the mists of the horizon deepened into rich cobalts several miles out, then feathered into teals and turquoises that splashed into a white foam on the beach a hundred yards below.

His focus returned to his pumping bare feet.

He was a machine. He felt no heat, no pain, no sweat stinging in his eyes, no knives stabbing in his calves.

Pump-pump-pump-pump.

His legs and feet were pistons that popped and recoiled in cylinders forged of unfeeling iron, charged and driven by the energy of his thinning body and determined will. Belly fat flowed as fuel to the chambers in which his legs exploded powerfully upward through the dragging sand.

He would not quit. He would not slow. He would ascend; he would triumph.

They would not laugh.

James shot a look up the steep grade of the dune, though he knew that the glimpse would cost him air.

He gasped as his breath was cut short in his throat by the angle of his tipped head.

Ben was almost at the top. Randy was half way to Ben. Their bare backs glistened in the hot sun, and their legs were caked below their knees with sand. Ben would easily beat them both. But James was gaining on Randy. There might be almost enough room to catch him.

James lowered his head and dug in.

The western face of the dunes at Chambers Park was steep, and the sharp incline of the bowl up which James was scrambling was free of vegetation.

Football players for two generations had called this V-shaped bowl "Ethel's Thighs." The tan bowl collected the heat of the sun's rays at its wide bottom, then funneled the heat in increasing degrees up its narrowing sides toward the only escape at its peak. At the apex, a dark triangular patch of grass and scrub trees encroached from the forest behind. Where the vegetation met the dune at the peak, a pleasant cloudless morning became scalding sands by noon. An inspired Grand Haven coach by the name of Thomas Diekensma had sent his loafing football team up the bowl one September afternoon in 1926. Two of his starters collapsed in the effort.

Grand Haven athletes had been clawing their way up Ethel's Thighs ever since.

James the machine was running low on oil. He felt his legs and hips creaking, his dry tongue clogging in the back of his parched throat. His eyes burned and his lips smacked dryly of the flying sand and salt from the sweat that streaked and evaporated from every pore of his face.

He stumbled, his toes sucked under by the sliding sand from the wake of Randy's swirling steps a few yards ahead.

James thrust his hands as he fell forward into the burning sand. But never slowed.

His legs continued to drive in hard pumps suddenly matched by the driving thrusts of his clawing hands. He continued scrambling forward and up, now like a sand crab fleeing from a wicked wave.

James heard and felt the churning of Randy's feet only an arm's length from his face. He could feel the quickened movement of air that marked the dune's top ridge. He could smell the grass and damp undergrowth that flirted with the hot sands at the pinnacle of Ethel's Thighs.

James threw himself blindly ahead. His right hand snaked forward and hooked Randy's trailing leg.

"You dog!" yelled Randy, falling to his chest.

James continued scrambling on all fours. He grabbed Randy's legs and pulled, climbing over his brother's body for better footing.

Beneath James, Randy rolled from his belly to his back. Randy planted his feet against James' stomach, then tried to launch James from the face of the dune.

James squirted sideways. He broke Randy's leverage and latched onto Randy's ankles as hard as he could.

They tumbled together 15 yards down the grade, rolling and laughing as they swore between mouthfuls of dune.

James released Randy and began scrambling again for the top.

They reached the grass at the same time. They fell together at Ben's feet, laughing, punching each other and spitting sand.

"Not bad, little brother," grinned Ben. "Last summer it would have taken you all morning to climb this hill."

James took several big gulps of air. His heart was pounding so hard he heard it in his ears. He was queasy with fatigue, but happy.

Randy was already catching his breath. "You cheating scum bag," he laughed. "If you hadn't latched onto my foot, I would have beaten you by a mile."

"Right." James swallowed more air. "If you were so far ahead," he gulped again, "how could I grab your foot?"

"A mere technicality. It has something to do with the pitch of Ethel's left thigh. The steep grade changes distances. On a flat beach, I was a mile ahead of you." Randy took several deep breaths.

"But when you lift one end of that mile almost straight up to make the dune, the person in front, namely me, is suddenly right above the person behind, namely you. That's why you could grab my foot, even though I was a mile ahead."

James laughed. "I get it," he grinned between open-mouthed pants. "It's like literary foreshortening."

"Huh?"

Ben slapped James on the back. "Don't be using them long words around us," he laughed. "You'll only get us confused."

"What could possibly be more simple than the concept of foreshortening?" laughed James. "It's a rudimentary technique employed essentially in situations in literature which require. . . ."

Ben grabbed James' arms. Randy lunged and grabbed his feet.

"No!" cried James. "I'll stop! I swear it!"

They hoisted him like a writhing hammock, then counted and swung together. "One . . . Two. . . ."

"Please. . . ."

"Three!"

They tossed him a good eight feet toward the lake. James did not hit sand for a long way. Adding in the number of times he rolled, he knew before he opened his eyes that he'd have a long climb back to the top.

In the past, he would have slid to the bottom rather than face them again. But James was 14 now and in a few weeks, he would be joining his two brothers in high school. Ben was going to be a senior and Randy a sophomore.

James headed back up the hill.

"You look like a sugar donut," laughed Ben, stretching his hand to pull James the last step to the crest.

"Thanks," said James, taking Ben's right hand with both of his own.

Suddenly, James dropped his rear to the sand. In the same movement, he yanked Ben's arm with all his might. Ben sailed over the top of James, screaming as he flew head long down the bowl.

Randy was only half to his feet when James tackled him. Again, James dropped his butt to the down side of the dune, planted his feet in Randy's chest and yanked. Randy was launched from the high side of the dune into the cool air rising from the lake.

"Damn!" screeched Randy as he passed over James' head.

James sat to catch his breath. He found a flat spot on a barkless log that had years ago been dragged from the wooded side to the dune's windswept crest. The sun-bleached hardwood trunk was wrinkled with decades of carved sketches, scratched initials, obscenities, cigarette burns and love notes. James ran his finger idly through the trench of a particularly deep message.

He glanced down as he traced the heart and letters that spelled the simple pledge of some teenager who had probably long since moved away.

Beyond the log, a long way down, James could see that Ben and Randy had finally stopped rolling. Each was half buried in the avalanche of sand that trailed them.

Except for the white sand, it was blues in all directions as far as James could see. Blue where the waves hit the thin strip of beach just past his toes, and blues up through the cloudless sky above.

Twenty feet behind him, the beach grasses of the crest merged with a band of scrub growth. Inland of the sand and scrub, a blanket of dark rotting leaves and dank humus covered black rolling hills of tall pines and hardwood forest.

But that was behind him, to his back. From the log, his senses were filled with the bright sand and pure water and clear sky. He watched his brothers slowly working their way back to the top, and he grinned down at them from his throne on the crest.

"What took you guys so long?" he asked.

Ben and Randy threw themselves on the sand before him.

"I was beginning to worry," said James. "If I had known that you two were so out of shape, I would have left you at home."

Ben looked at Randy. "What do you know," he panted. "Little brother is growing up."

"You know," said Randy, "we've got guys on the football team that couldn't have thrown either one of us off this hill."

"Hmm," said Ben. "Are you thinking what I'm thinking?"

"Maybe. Should we ask him?"

"Why not," Ben grinned. He turned to James.

"I know that this is going to sound strange," said Ben, "but you should try out for football in a couple of weeks."

James laughed. "No way," he said. "You know that I don't play sports. Especially football. A guy playing football could get killed. Or worse."

"Think about it," said Randy. "All three of us playing high school football the same year. Ben as the starting wide receiver on varsity, me as the starting safety on JV, and you as the second string waterboy on the freshman squad."

"That's what it would be," said James. "I wouldn't stand a chance of making the team."

"Yes you would," said Ben. "You might not be a starter, but you sure as heck would make the team. Look at you. You're stronger than lots of the guys. And you're twice the runt you used to be." He laughed.

James considered the idea. "What position do you think I could play? I'm too small to be a lineman and I can't throw or catch worth a hoot."

"How about trying out as a running back?"

"Yeah," said Ben. "You don't have to be big to be a running back."

"My legs are too short," complained James. "I'm not very fast."

"Short legs can be an advantage," said Ben. "A lower center of gravity and all of that. If you could put on some more muscle, you could make up for your lack of speed with guts and power. You know, bouncing and dragging tacklers instead of outrunning them."

James smiled.

Maybe, he thought. Just maybe.

For the next two weeks, James ran the dunes with his brothers every chance that he could.

He pushed himself hard, and he delighted in his increasing strength and endurance. Mrs. Vanderspyke was supportive. She said that maybe a year of football was just the thing that James needed to finish getting over Carla and to start making new friends. Since the tourist season was winding down, she was able to let the boys slip off for a couple of hours each morning, so long as they were back by 11:00 to help with the rush at lunch.

High school football rules stipulated that formal practices could not begin until the middle of August. But there were no regulations against informal "conditioning parties" that were organized by players and unsupervised by coaches.

Ben drove the old Ford wagon north out of Grand Haven, picking up more and more friends each day. Other players drove their own cars or peddled to the dunes on their bikes. Between runs up Ethel's Thighs, they played catch with footballs, drinking gallon-sized plastic milk jugs of water and horsing around on the beach. Once in a while, someone was tossed into the lake, and then everyone followed, diving into the waves, rinsing off sweat and cooling down. By the last weekend before the first official day of the season, most of Grand Haven's football players were back in shape.

Chambers Park stretched five miles north of Grand Haven on a quiet span of beach devoid of the tourists and the large Victorian beach homes that cluttered much of Lake Michigan's eastern coastline. The park's history was unknown to most of the athletes that trained on its dunes, and outside of the local sports teams that visited during conditioning weeks, the unimproved park was left mostly to seagulls and squirrels.

The baseball team favored the legend that the park was named after the wife of a wealthy lumber baron. Mr. Albert Chambers, they said, donated the park after his wife passed away without leaving heirs.

The basketball team held that Ethel Chambers was a prostitute. Years ago, when the state set land aside for the park, Grand

Haven businessmen had made good on their promises and given their favorite lady a touch of immortality.

Randy and Ben accepted the football account.

The football version said that Ethel had nothing to do with the naming of Chambers park. Ethel was just some ancient cheerleader who spread her legs at the top of the hill to motivate her boyfriend, who was out of shape with a scholarship on the line. According to football lore, the name of the park wasn't based on a person named Chambers at all.

Most of the park was hidden in the shadows and gullies of densely-wooded dunes that rolled for nearly a mile inland from the beach. But there was one area where the wooded hills of the dunes opened wide and flat to a low-lying field that sported only a smattering of oaks and maples.

The 10-acre field was pear shaped, the wide end butting inland against a county road and providing a limited amount of unpaved parking. The narrow end of the field stretched toward Lake Michigan. The only thing separating the field from the narrow beach on the other side was a single monstrous ridge of dune.

In an attempt to protect the fragile ecosystem of the park, the state tunneled holes through the sand ridge and installed three enormous culverts to link the parking lot to the beach. By using the eight-foot-wide culverts to reach the water, visitors were spared the exhaustion of climbing the dune, and the dune was spared the eroding effects of thousands of grinding and slipping shoes.

The three round culverts lay side-by-side, filled with carpets of sand creating level walkways through the cylinders. The culverts were almost 20 yards long, and at certain times of the day, they were dark and cool inside.

Shouts, whistles, and grunts bounced wildly within the tunnels, so some people called the culverts echo chambers. But the football team knew better. Chambers Park did not get its name with echo chambers in mind.

"You've got to be kidding," said James.

"No," said Randy. "I'm not kidding. Come Monday, when we

start wearing pads, the coaches are going to pile us all in buses and haul our butts down here. From Monday until the first day of school, every afternoon is going to include two sprints up Ethel's Thighs, plus twenty minutes in the chambers."

"How come you didn't warn me about having to run the hill in full gear? Barefoot and cutoffs is one thing, but cleats and shoulder pads is a whole different deal."

"Why do you think we've been coming down here every morning? Did you think that we were busting our asses just to get a good tan?"

James stood up from the log. Several boys had stopped 50 yards up Ethel to joke and catch their winds. Another group was just starting up the bowl, still scrambling at full speed. A dozen or so others were tossing footballs down on the beach.

"Okay," he said. "If everybody's got to do it, I guess I can, too. But what's this about 20 minutes in the chambers?"

"Yeah. You know, the Torture Chambers."

CHAPTER 25

Football Season, 1973.
Grand Haven, Michigan

"For those of you who skipped junior high football," barked Coach Smith, "and who therefore have never run the torture chambers, here's the way it works."

He surveyed the squad of 30 freshmen. With his feet planted wide and a clipboard tucked behind, Coach Smith was an imposing man. His arms and thighs stretched his gray sweats like the smooth skin of beech trees deep in the forest of the dunes. Neck muscles bulged from his shoulders to the tiny ears at the sides of the swells of his bald head.

James shifted awkwardly in his pads.

His shoulder gear felt top heavy. The thigh pads in his pants were creeping up and rubbing his groin. He pushed the pads with the heels of his hands, then glanced at the pants of the boy next to him. The other boy's pads looked different. James glanced around at the rest of the team and realized that he had stuffed his pads in upside down.

"Interior linemen go first," said Coach Smith. He brushed his flat nose with the back of one hand. "Backs go last. Everyone else, in between."

He glanced impatiently at his clipboard, then across to the other two culverts. The junior varsity and varsity squads were already in lines getting ready to begin.

During the bus ride, James overheard Smith joking with the other coaches. Smith bragged loudly of ramming squads through the culverts for 10 years, and said that every year was the same.

The chambers were great for building team spirit and toughening kids for their first game. And great for culling out the weenies. A few of the weenies always got hurt in the chambers, which was fine. A lucky break all the way around. That way the wimps had a good excuse to drop from the program right away, instead of getting cut later when they didn't measure up.

"I want all of the linemen over there." Smith pointed to a spot near the mouth of the open tunnel on the left. "Backs over there," he pointed toward James, which was as far from the entrance as he had dared to stand. "And the rest of you right here. If you're not sure what position you'll play, then you're probably a lineman. Okay, let's move!"

James stayed where he was, letting the rest of the aspiring backs join him. He glanced over his shoulder at the buses. Coach Beukensma, the assistant freshman coach, was still organizing the managers and water jugs on the grass in the shade.

James had hardly talked to any of the other boys all morning. The team leaders seemed relaxed and eager in the locker room, as comfortable putting on their jock straps and pads as James was scooping ice cream. Several were rowdy on the bus, full of predictions for the season and bursting with opinions about cheerleaders. Once off the bus, they teased the smaller boys and grinned sinisterly through the coated steel mesh of their face masks.

"Okay," bellowed Smith. "Here's what we're gonna do. You, Greg Dykstra. You'll go first."

James wondered how the coach already knew Greg's name. He didn't recognize the boy as anyone from Harrison Junior High.

"All you've got to do," Smith glared at everyone but Greg, "is to go stand 10 feet inside the chamber." He looked back at the boy. "Greg, do you think that you can handle that?"

The boy smiled, nodded, and stepped forward. Greg had at least six inches and sixty pounds on James.

"Good. Then the rest of you linemen will also go stand inside the chamber, one at a time, in any order that you want. Of course, since Greg is already in front, you'll have to slip around him."

There were several nervous laughs. "Greg's job is to let you through, but not to make it too easy. He'll just slow you down a little, right Greg?"

Greg grinned. He nodded again, turned, then trotted a few feet into the culvert.

"Once you've made it past Greg, pick yourself up from the sand, if you have to, and assume this position." Coach Smith dropped into a vicious-looking crouch, his knees and elbows wide, his fingers buried in the chest of his shirt. "Then it's your turn to make the next poor sucker pay."

He released his shirt and straightened his massive legs.

"Now, a few simple rules and suggestions. First, blockers may not use their hands. In a real game, if a ref sees the offense using their hands, it's 15 yards. In the chamber, you won't be so lucky. If you forget the rule in there," Smith shattered his clipboard against his thigh, "you'll break a few fingers. Or maybe a wrist, even an arm."

He dropped the last chunk of clipboard from his hand. "Such accidents happen when a kid smacks into cement. Bones go snap." He smiled.

A puff of wind caught one of the sheets from the broken clipboard. As the list turned in the grass, Smith squashed it with his right foot.

"Now, I know from experience that one or two of you morons are going to forget what I just said. Fine. Your choice. Maybe next time, when you come back from surgery, you'll remember and get it right. Hands in!"

He smiled again.

"Another hint. Mouth guards between your teeth at all times. Last year we had to waste half-an-hour sifting through sand for some kid's molars."

Smith nodded toward the culvert.

"Last thing. Remember where these tunnels lead. When we get to the other side, we'll be jogging over to Ethel's Thighs. You'll each get to take in some water, then up we'll go. And by the way, if you're not one of the first 10 men to the top, then you're a lineman and you'd better forget your little fantasies about scoring winning touchdowns."

Coach Smith brushed the remaining splinters from his sweats. "When we get back down," he bent to collect the scattered papers, "you'll drink more water. I don't want any babies drying out on me. And, since we're here, we might as well give old Ethel what they call 'a multiple.' Through the chamber again, both ways, same order, Greg leading."

Several players shook their heads.

"Then one more shot at Ethel, and we'll call it a day. All told—for you linemen who can't count—that makes three times through the chambers and twice up and down old Ethel. The last time through the tunnel, on our way back to the buses, no torture. You're free to walk through any way you want. Those unable to walk are free to crawl. And if you can't crawl, well then, we'll just bury you in the sand where you dropped."

Smith threw back his head and laughed.

"If you die a good death, maybe we'll send a few cheerleaders back with some flowers to mark your graves."

"Any questions?"

There were none.

"Oh, yeah," he added. "One more thing. No swearing in the chambers. I don't want no potty mouths representing Grand Haven High School on this year's championship team."

The first lineman charged Greg directly, making no attempt to dodge the collision. If his goal was to knock Greg down, he failed. As the lineman approached, Greg drew into his crouch like a turtle withdrawing into its shell. Then, a split second before impact, Greg exploded.

The charging lineman bounced back and landed face up, half in and half out of the culvert. His groans echoed loudly from the chamber's mouth.

"Get up!" yelled Smith. "We're all waiting for our turns. You're not the only man on this team, you know."

The boy staggered to his feet, shook sand from his helmet and brushed off his hands.

"Don't just stand there!" Smith bawled. "Try it again. You're supposed to be on the other side of Greg, not out here. What's the matter, don't you want a shot at Ethel?"

The boy charged again. This time, he swerved left a second before the anticipated collision. Greg sidestepped and cuffed the boy in the helmet with an elbow. The boy grazed past Greg and fell to the sand a few hard-earned yards inside the chamber.

"Next!"

James watched and chewed his mouth guard restlessly as players collided and banged their way one by one into the tunnel. Smacks, grunts, and blows echoed from deeper within. From what he could see, torture was not dolled out in equal portions. Some players were merely bumped or jostled, while others were smashed and hammered every step of their way.

As more of the team disappeared into the culvert, the knot tightened in James' stomach. His head throbbed. He glanced around. The backs were next.

Should he charge first? Show the coach some spunk? Should he go last, waiting for the linemen to tire? Should he stop after each impact, or keep moving and stay on his feet as long as he could?

"Okay backs, let's go!"

James started to move, but two boys bolted in front of him. One quickened his pace and forced the other to slow down so that Greg would have time to reset. The first back lowered his head and aimed his helmet for the lineman's chest.

Five feet to impact, the runner abruptly straightened and faked right, then left.

Greg shifted twice, then barely got a piece of the boy, who kept his feet and continued to weave his way into the chamber's shadows.

The second boy's fake was less effective; he landed face down in the sand only a few yards beyond Greg's feet. A third back, Mike, who James remembered from junior high, was already picking up speed toward the entrance.

James slid into the fourth slot, trotting nervously on Mike's heels. Mike slowed enough to let Greg set, then charged.

Meanwhile, the number two back regained his feet and disappeared deeper into the chamber for additional blows.

James focused on Greg and Mike, and on the timing of his own approach.

With the backs now running, the pace in the tunnel increased considerably. Mike was nearly in Greg's face.

Mike dodged left and spun in a fluid motion that left him unscathed. He accelerated and disappeared.

James was up.

He blinked, grabbed a deep breath, then hit the mouth of the culvert at full speed. He faked a move left, then felt his foot slip in the loose sand. He slammed into Greg sideways, off his feet, his full momentum behind him.

The force of Greg's forearm chop flattened him to the culvert floor.

He couldn't breathe.

The runner outside the culvert yelled for him to get out of his way. James tried to rise.

Couldn't move.

Coach Smith suddenly towered over him, shaking his head.

"Son," he said, "if you're alive, blink twice. If you're dead, just close 'em and leave 'em closed. I'm clean outta pennies."

James' chest and lungs ached, but he could feel himself breathing again. He turned his head and spit out his mouth guard.

"Okay," said Smith, "Enough of this. Can you stand, or are we going to have to drag you out of here by your heels?"

James slowly rolled to his hands and knees. His body felt as if it had been dropped from an airplane. He was dizzy, and he still had a hard time catching his breath.

Greg stepped to beside the coach. "Is he okay?" he asked.

"It depends," laughed Smith. "If it's a dog, he seems to be all right. If it's supposed to be a man, it's got some standing up to do. What's it to be, son? You a dog or a man?"

Legs gathered, fencing him in.

Several players asked questions; some made jokes. One of the boys muttered the name Jimmy. Another used the name James. They wore shoes with fresh laces and short padded pants.

Someone nudged him with a knee.

James thought he heard a snickered "pussy."

"You okay?" The voice dropped. "If you are, then you'd better get up." James recognized the voice as Mike's.

Another voice drilled from the other side. "What a woman. His first hit of the season, and he folds like a girl."

More knees. More laughter. Closing in. Surrounding him, ready to fall upon his back.

He couldn't speak. He squeezed his eyes and felt a butter knife in his fist, it's butt braced against a wooden deck. Realized that he was clutching sand.

And wished that he could disappear like an ant and crawl away.

A whack to the head.

Again, Coach Smith swatted him on the back of his helmet. "Is anyone home in there?" he asked.

James wet his lips. "Yeah," he whispered. "I just got the wind knocked out of me, that's all."

"Well, sounds like you finally got it back. Now stand up like a man, and let me take a look at your eyes. I gotta make sure you still got a couple of pupils, or I'll have to send you to the bus for the rest of the day."

Smith slapped his helmet a third time. "Come on," he said. "Stand up."

James willed himself to his feet.

He felt shamed and weak. He looked around. Several of his teammates were laughing openly. Others looked concerned. Smith grabbed his face mask and pulled his head close.

"Yup," he said. "You still got pupils. But they're pretty messed up. How many fingers do I got?"

"Ten," said James, closing his eyes to keep from falling.

Smith laughed. "Okay, smart ass, now how many do I got. Count 'em this time." He held up three.

"Three," said James.

"Close enough."

Smith glanced around at the rest of the team. "What are you all gaping at?" he shouted. "We're not done in there yet. Everybody, get back to where you were! We still have a few more running backs that haven't paid for a shot at Ethel." He leaned toward James. "What's your name again?"

"Jim. My name is Jim."

"Okay, Jim. There's nothing wrong with getting knocked down once in while. The big thing is that you always get back to your feet. Which you did. Let me see your hands."

Jim held them out.

"Good. Looks like you at least kept your hands in. Now let me see your teeth." Jim opened his mouth. "Very good. Looks like they're all still there. Except maybe you've got a cavity. Do you floss?"

Jim smiled.

"Good man." Coach Smith slapped him again on the helmet.

"You're going to sit this torture out. After we run Ethel, we'll see how you're doing. If you feel up to it, we'll give you another shot at Greg on the next round. You okay with this?"

"Okay."

"Good man."

Jim sat in the second seat of the old Ford, his eyes closed and his head pounding between his hands.

He had vomited twice. Once behind the log at the top of Ethel, when nobody was looking. The second time on the black asphalt alongside the Ford in the parking lot at school.

His entire body ached. He was raw in a dozen places from the rubbing of his pads. Over the past three hours, he had taken seven salt tablets and guzzled more water than he usually drank in a week. Jim shifted his hips and shoulders, trying to keep his back from getting any stiffer.

Through the hot Ford's open windows, Jim heard players joking their way through the outside locker room door, heading for their cars.

He lifted his head.

A few minutes later, Randy and Ben emerged, lugging their duffel bags and laughing. Jim opened the car door and forced himself to step out into the parking lot to greet them with a smile.

"Howdy," he shouted as they drew near. "What took you guys so long?"

Ben waved his hand. "How'd you get out here so fast? Didn't you take a shower?"

"Just a quickie." Ben and Randy reached him at the car. "I thought that we should hurry back," said Jim, "to give mom a hand at the store."

"Right," laughed Ben. "When we get home, the first thing I'm going to do is take a nap. Just wake me in time for tomorrow's practice." Ben opened the driver's door.

"Do you mean" said Jim, forcing a laugh, "that we've got to do this again tomorrow?"

Randy circled to the passenger's side of the car.

"Oh, yuk." Randy plugged his nose. "What happened here?"

"What's the problem?" asked Ben.

Jim climbed back into the car, trying to avoid Randy's eyes. Randy opened his door so that Ben could see down to the asphalt. Ben leaned over and took a quick look. He straightened and put the keys in the ignition.

"Did you do that?" he asked, glancing back at Jim.

Jim looked at Randy, who was gingerly stepping over the vomit to climb into the front seat.

"Naw," said Jim. "That's not from me. Some dog was hanging around the car when I came out. I had to give the mutt a kick in the ribs to get rid of him. That dog puke was just his way of saying thanks."

"Uh-huh."

"Cross my heart."

Ben started the car.

"Uh-huh."

"So, how was your first day of football?" asked Randy. "As if we don't already know."

"What did you hear?" asked Jim.

"We heard that Greg Dykstra about took your head off," laughed Ben.

"Oh."

Randy laughed. "Billy said that you took it kind of hard. He said that he expected to see tears in your eyes when you finally stood up."

Ben glared. "Back off, Randy. Give him a break. He made up for it, that's what counts."

"Right." Randy turned back toward Jim. "The thing is, nobody likes a baby. And since you got back up, nobody can call you a baby. And as long as the cheerleaders don't hear about it, maybe you've still. . . ."

"Cool it!" Ben shook his head. "The trouble with you, Randy," Ben put the car into gear, "is that you got too big of a mouth, too big of a dick and too small of a brain."

Jim smirked.

"Is that a compliment," asked Randy, "or a put-down?"

"Just the truth, brother. Take it for what it's worth."

The car started to move.

Randy looked at Ben, paused, then swung his arm over the back of his seat and turned to face Jim.

"You know," said Randy, "if that Dyskstra kid could remember a snap count and a blocking assignment, he'd be dangerous. Instead, the only thing that he can do right is play bouncer in the halls of the torture chambers."

"Yeah, don't feel too bad," said Ben. "Greg did the same thing

to Randy last year. Knocked him out cold the third day of practice. That's why Randy is giving you the hard time." He glanced
at Randy, who did not correct him. "I think that this will be Greg's
last year of football. I think that when a player turns 18, the rules
say he's gotta give up freshman football, whether he's still in Ninth
Grade or not."

Jim felt better. It helped to know a little more about Greg, to
know that Greg was a couple of years older than him.

Ben looked at Randy, then back at the road. Randy smiled,
then cleared his throat.

"We also heard something else about your first day," said Randy.
"The guys said that you had a hell of a run or two up Ethel's
Thighs. Second one to the top. Both times. Just behind Mike
Miller, right?"

"I guess," said Jim. "I really don't remember too much about
this afternoon."

"Yeah," said Randy. "But don't let it go to your head. You
were probably rested up from skipping that first run in the
chambers."

Jim groaned. "I wouldn't say that I exactly skipped it. At least
not the Greg Dykstra part."

"And," added Ben, "from what I hear, you survived your second and third tortures just fine."

"That's probably a generous way of putting it."

"So," asked Randy, "are you going to give it another try? You
gonna take the bus back to Chambers Park again tomorrow?"

"I wouldn't miss it for the world," said Jim, choking down his
third round of vomit. "Wouldn't miss it for the world."

CHAPTER 26

Jim lifted the lid of the white mailbox on the front porch of their small bungalow.

It was empty.

He pulled back a swollen finger and let the lid drop with a clang.

The soiled duffel bag in his left hand bumped softly against his knee as he turned and looked both ways down the sidewalk.

The century-old maples and oaks that lined their street showed hints of autumn in the long shadows of the early evening. A screen door banged across the street. Three young children played cowboys and Indians in the dirt front yard of another bungalow several houses west toward the lake.

Otherwise, the sidewalk was as empty as the mailbox.

An elderly couple in a blue Chevy sedan with out-of-state plates rolled by at trolling speed. They smiled and waved.

Tourists were like that. They treated the locals like animals in a zoo. Tourists seemed to believe that with the right gestures, they could prod the beach-town natives into swinging from trees. Jim faked a smile and waved back.

Don't bite the hand that feeds you. Without the tourists, the Vanderspykes wouldn't eat.

The mailman should have come by hours ago. Jim checked the sidewalk one more time, then forced his hand deep into the tight front pocket of his faded jeans.

The scabs on his knuckles raked painfully against the inside of the denim, and his fingers had trouble gripping his keys. He tried to adjust the angle of his elbow, then flinched as a stab of pain shot through his right shoulder.

"Shit."

He shifted his weight to his throbbing left ankle, which allowed some slack in his right pocket, and retrieved his keys. The door was already unlocked.

Jim swore again.

"Anyone home?" he called, stepping into the small living room entrance.

Randy called back from the kitchen.

"In here. Jim, is that you? Damn, you sound like an old man."

Jim dropped his duffel bag onto the frayed throw rug by the front door and hobbled through the house to join Randy at the kitchen counter. Randy was working on the second level of a triple-decker peanut butter, honey and jam sandwich.

"Save some bread for me," moaned Jim. "I hear that bread is good for a headache."

"Never heard that before," laughed Randy. "But you should know." He handed Jim his knife. "Man, Jim. You look like horse pucky. Maybe you should slow down a bit. Save a little of your body for next season, when the games start meaning something."

"Huh?"

"Nobody," said Randy, "gives a rat's ass about freshman football. Ninth Grade sports are just warm-ups for the real thing. To be honest, even JV football is kind of a joke. I mean, think about it. Who came to our first game? A couple of dozen parents, a few cheerleaders. That's about it. And that was with free admission."

Jim reached for the bread.

"On the other hand, varsity football," said Randy, taking a big bite and chewing. "Varsity football is whole different deal. People buy tickets and line up by the thousands to see a good varsity game. When a team is hot, it's almost like going to a college game. In fact, people from colleges come to varsity games to scout for guys to give scholarships to and all of that crap. Lots of the first string varsity players from Grand Haven end up with scholarships for college ball."

Jim looked up from the peanut butter.

"What's your point?" he asked. "Are you trying to cheer me up about losing our first game last week, or are you trying to coach me now on how football is going to pay my way through med school so I can become a brain surgeon?"

"Naw. Go ahead and feel sorry for yourself about losing the game. Losing is always a bitch. But what I'm saying is that you shouldn't kill yourself in practices as a freshman. Save something, you know, one knee and maybe a couple of fingers." Randy chewed another bite. "Just be smart and save a little of your body for the big games that really count in a couple of years."

"Is that why you spent half of your first game on the bench?" asked Jim. "You saving yourself for next year?"

Randy looked hurt. "Don't be such a prick. I'm only trying to offer some brotherly advice."

"Sorry. I guess I'm just pissed off that I'm out there busting my balls every day in practice, and then on game day, I hardly got to play at all. I've just been hoping that if I worked harder than anyone else during the week, the coach would give me a break. You know, a chance to play a little more."

Jim put the top on his sandwich. "Randy, I don't know why I'm making fun of you. Hell, you saw a shit-load more playing time against Muskegon than I did."

"Yeah. Sometimes it doesn't seem fair. Maybe you'll get to play more next time. We play Spring Lake in two days. Keep your fingers crossed."

Randy stuffed the last of his sandwich into his mouth. He chewed and swallowed.

"Oh," he said, reaching for more bread, "I know what will cheer you up. The mail came. You got another letter from Carla Mekluevich. I tossed it in our bedroom. It's on your dresser."

Jim shut and locked the door. Their room was so cluttered that he could hardly find places to step as he picked his way across the floor. Rumpled clothes, magazines and boys' junk littered every inch of the floor. But Jim spotted the white envelop immediately. It rested on the lid of a tan shoe box on the top of his dresser.

He gingerly lifted the envelope and turned it over in his hands.

After studying the envelope for a moment, Jim cleared a spot and sat on the edge of his bed.

He wedged his finger into the corner of the flap and ripped a jagged line along the address end of the envelope. He squeezed the top and bottom edges together, then blew a light puff into the envelope to separate the sides. He reached in and removed the typewritten sheets.

Jim looked at the letter for a moment, then laid back into his pillow and swung his feet onto the clothes piled at the other end. With the pages of the letter above him, Jim began to read.

Sept. 10, 1973

Dear Jim,

Congratulations on your first football game!

I know that you didn't play as much as you wanted, but I know that you'll be scoring touchdowns in no time. It's always funny when I think back to Sixth Grade. I can remember when you were still short and fat in junior high, and now . . . I'm dating a jock!

Karen Seinner (she's on the freshman cheerleading squad with me, as if you don't know), she says that she sits by you in English class. She says that she thinks that you're kind of cute. Karen says that you're real smart in English and that you've already read lots of the books that the teacher talks about. Karen's dad owns a couple of bookstores, so I guess she knows a lot about books, too.

I promise that I won't get jealous of Karen, if you'll promise to stop drooling over her during class. She says that when she wears dresses, you pretend to be reading, but that you're really staring at her legs.

Hey, if it's legs, or anything else, that you want to see. . . .

I mean it. You know that I'm all yours. Whenever you start feeling horny, you can get perverted with me any way you want! As you know, I'm always here if you need me.

Yours forever,
        but never,

            XXX Carla

Jim skimmed the letter again, then slowed for the last few lines. He re-read them deliberately, tasting the words, feeling his heart starting to race.

. . . if it's legs, or anything else, that you want. . . .

. . . feeling horny. . . .

. . . get perverted with me. . . .

. . . I'm always here. . . .

He rose from the mattress and double checked to make sure that the door was still locked. On the way back to his bed, he grabbed the box of tissues from his dresser. He unzipped his pants and laid down.

He tried to imagine Carla showing him her legs. Smiling at him. Flashing her cheerleading skirt back and forth, higher and higher, like a matador teasing in a bull. The legs were beautiful, smooth and tan. The wrists were slender, the fingers strong where they tugged at the skirt's hem. The waist was thin, the breasts large, swaying enticingly within the billows of the uniform top. The neck was soft, the face was. . . .

Jim squeezed his eyes.

Her face was. . . .

Blank.

Shit.

Jim opened his eyes. He skimmed the letter again.

He shook his head, unable to get or hold an image. Carla was thin, an eleven-year-old with toothpick legs.

He closed his eyes, then imagined a different pair of legs.

Beautiful tan legs under a desk at school. Shapely legs poking from beneath a cheerleader's short skirt. His third hour English class.

The tantalizing legs of Karen Seinner.

CHAPTER 27

As the football season progressed, Jim slowly established himself as a competent back.

By mid-season, he was playing nearly half of each game. He wasn't fast or strong enough to make many sensational plays, but when he was on the field, he threw himself into each play with such abandon that he earned a reputation as one of the best lead blockers on the team. The afternoon that his squad took sole possession of first place, everyone knew that it was Jim's block that sprang Mike Miller's game-winning bootleg.

In the locker room, Coach Smith smiled, thumping Jim so hard that he wished his mouth guard was still between his teeth.

"That was a heck of a block, Vanderspyke! I hope they got it on film. I'd like to show it to the new backs next season to illustrate how games are won."

"Thanks," said Jim, looking away. He wasn't used to being a hero. He felt himself blushing.

"High-five's!" said Mike, holding up his hand. "I saw that defensive end bearing down on me, and I thought I was dead meat. Then, wham! You blindsided that poor son-of-a-bitch. . . ."

"Uh-hum," interrupted Smith.

"Uh, sorry coach." Mike laughed and turned back to Jim. "You blindsided that poor son-of-a-women's-libber and took his head off! That was it man. The best block of the season. After that hit, the last 30 yards to the end zone was a cakewalk."

Other teammates swatted and congratulated Jim until he started wondering if it wasn't safer on the field.

A half hour later, clean, his hair still slick from rinsed sham-

poo, Jim walked with Mike Miller and several of the other starters
back outside to the playing field.

The junior varsity game was already well into the second quar-
ter. Jim's brother Randy was having a good game of his own. Jim
joined Ben beside the fence at the bottom of the stands.

"Good game," said Ben.

Jim cupped his hands to his mouth and shouted to the field,
"Nice hit, Randy!"

Ben grinned. "We might sweep these guys," he said.

"For sure," Jim grinned back. "You varsity guys will knock the
crap out of them. Feeling ready?"

"Can't wait. Maybe all three of us will have good games." Ben
raised his fist toward the sideline. "Come on Randy, let's see it!"

Ben glanced over his shoulder to the stands. Mike and the
others were already settled into the bleachers.

"Go sit with your friends," said Ben, nodding back toward the
stands. "I'll yell at Randy loud enough for both of us."

"You sure?"

"Oh yeah. No problem. You should sit down. Take a load off
and have a good time. You earned it."

The freshman starters were watching the game sitting in front
of the cheerleaders, half way up the stands. Between jokes and
anecdotes, they relived their game, play by play, savoring their
victory and each player's contribution. At JV half time, three of
the freshman cheerleaders joined them.

The girls were still in their uniforms, bubbling in the excitement of the win, still giddy in the afterglow of their own vaults
and cheers.

Jim knew two of the girls, but vaguely. He could hardly remember the name of the third. All three acted as if they had known
him for years. One of the girls grabbed his arm and laughed something about what a great game he played. As she spoke, her breast
brushed his arm as her breath steamed in his ear.

A few minutes later, two more of the freshman cheerleaders

spotted the group in the bleachers, then waved and climbed the stairs to join them.

One of the girls was Karen Seinner.

Jim glanced nervously as she climbed the steep bleachers, her thighs flashing beneath her pleated skirt. She dropped herself and her beautiful legs onto the seat beside him.

"You were great," she smiled. "I could hear the smack of that kid's helmet against the ground all the way on the sidelines."

Karen leaned around Jim to address Mike. "Good job," she said. "That was a great run!"

The cheerleaders stayed with the players until the end of half time, all of them talking and laughing at once.

Except for Jim.

He tried to think of something clever to say, but Karen kept smiling, and he kept snatching glimpses of her legs. Finally, he had to shove his hands into his pockets and check the scoreboard to keep himself from touching her.

When the JV team retook the field for second half warm-ups, the girls clapped and rose in a swirl of short skirts that left Jim dizzy. Then they bounded from the grand stands like a herd of whitetail does.

Mike leaned over and slapped Jim's knee as they watched them leave.

"You like her, don't you?"

"Who?" Jim replied feebly.

"Give me a break. Karen Seinner, who else? My God, Jim, I swear that you hardly took a breath the whole time she was here."

"I was nervous."

"That's okay. If she liked me, I'd feel nervous, too. Fortunately, that's your problem, not mine."

"What are you talking about?"

"Girls that gorgeous don't belong on freshman cheerleading squads. Girls like that should be in Hollywood making movies. Or else they should be tucked away in convents where they would not lead the rest of us into temptation." Mike pounded Jim's knee again and laughed. "High school football players like me and you have got way too many hormones to be sitting next to the likes of Karen Seinner. Hell, man, I could practically cream my pants just looking at her."

Jim forced himself to laugh. "What makes you think," he asked, trying to sound nonchalant, cracking his voice instead, "what makes you think that she likes me?"

Mike laughed. "Sandy told me. And her and Karen are best friends. Karen talks about you and that English class all the time. She thinks that it's cute the way you always blush. Like you did when she came up and sat next to you. Girls love it when they can make a guy blush."

"Do you blush?"

"Naw."

"Why not?"

"Who knows," shrugged Mike. "I guess I just don't got it in me."

"Hey mom," shouted Randy. "We're home."

Mrs. Vanderspyke emerged from the kitchen smiling and drying her hands as the three boys swarmed the room.

"I take it both teams won?" she said.

"Better yet," grinned Jim. "We both had great games."

"Good for you. I'm sorry that I couldn't make it. What with the long hours at the store, and then the women's Bible study tonight, there wasn't enough time. Next week, though, when you boys play under the lights, I'll make your games for sure."

Ben laughed. "Don't you worry about Jim-bo, mom. He don't need no mamma to sit with. When he's not out kicking butt on the field, he's up checking it out in the stands. I think old Jim has finally got himself a new girlfriend. And she is hot!"

Mrs. Vanderspyke shook her head in disapproval. Randy smirked.

"Karen Seinner, huh?" Randy liked his lips. "I should have seen it coming. Why is it that us dumb jocks have the pick of the bunch one day, and then the next day when some smart jock comes along, we ain't got squat?"

Jim laughed. "What are you talking about."

"Little brother," said Ben, wrapping his arm around Jim's shoulder, "are you telling me that you didn't know that Randy had the itch for Karen?"

Jim twisted from beneath Ben's arm.

"If I've got the hots for Karen," laughed Randy, "then so do you, Ben. And so does every other red-blooded stud in Grand Haven."

He laughed again. "Don't look so shocked, Jim. I'm not jealous. Me and Karen had a fight and broke up last week. We're history. She's up for grabs. So to speak."

Mrs. Vanderspyke wiped her hands again and cleared her throat.

"I'm glad that you two won your games. And it's good to see all three of you so happy. But let's not get so excited here that we forget what we're saying."

Randy ignored her. "Jim, to put you at ease, I hereby relinquish all my rights to Karen Seinner. Furthermore, I offer you my unqualified blessings. May you two bounce together like rabbits, and may you one day whelp together more bunnies than Ernie Bently has zits on his ass."

Mrs. Vanderspyke glared. Randy caught the look, then shrugged.

"Just kidding," he said. "I got carried away." He faked a serious look. "I lied. Karen has never been my girlfriend. Truth is, she ignores me completely. So, in the name of poetic justice, I figure that if I can't have her," he turned back to Jim, "my brother might as well. Have at her, James."

Randy and Ben roared.

"It's no wonder," their mother snapped, "that this Karen girl likes James more than Randy. You don't hear Jimmy talking like that, do you? Unlike the other men of this house, Jimmy's no pig."

Jim blushed.

"Randy," she continued, "I swear, sometimes you talk just like your father. Please, try to remember that this is my house, and that I set the rules. You are free to leave whenever you wish. This is not a locker room, and there is a lady present."

"Aw, mom," said Randy. "You know that I was only kidding. You're right. I should try to be more careful about what I say. But Jim's no choir boy, either. Just because he don't talk dirty, that don't mean he don't think it. He's just too bashful about such things to come out and say it."

Randy looked at Jim. "Ain't that right, Jim? Help me out here. You think about girls, too, don't you?"

Jim shrugged, blushing worse than ever.

"Now look," she said. "You've got James all flustered. That's what I'm talking about, Randy. Sometimes, the way you talk, you embarrass everybody within earshot."

"Not everybody," grinned Randy. "Ben?" he asked. "Are you embarrassed?"

"Terribly," said Ben. "I feel like the lobster that was caught with a case of crabs. But I'm hungry, so let's can this stupid discussion and let's uncan us some tuna." He laughed. "I've been craving a tuna sandwich all night."

"Fine," said Mrs. Vanderspyke. "I can see that this discussion is going nowhere."

"Not true," laughed Ben. "I'm not an ignoramus, mom. I'm not as smart as Jim-bo, but I got your point. You're a lot like my little brother there. You get embarrassed about sex, and I respect that. From now on, I'll try to be more careful about what I say in front of you and Jimmy. I promise."

"Me, too," laughed Randy. "I won't talk about tits or asses or legs or anything any more. And I especially won't talk about the way girls. . . ."

"That's enough!" She shook her head. "I'm warning you two, you're going to drive me crazy. And then who is going to buy all of your tuna?" She turned to Jim.

"Thank you," she said, "for showing a little more decency than your brothers seem to have the imagination to summon. There are certain things, certain words, that a lady should not have to listen to. Your father never understood that and we all saw what kind of man he turned out to be. Your brothers don't seem to understand the principle any better than Harry did. But trust me, in the long run, women appreciate courtesy. And it's the right thing to do. Self control is a virtue. Self discipline is divine."

She turned back toward Ben and Randy.

"And while I'm on the subject, let me say one more thing. If you can't respect women, please, at least show a little respect for God."

"God?" asked Randy. "What the heck does God have to do with what me and Ben say about women?"

She wheeled on him. "That's right. God!" She pointed her finger with unexpected fury.

"Remember," she demanded, "that after Adam and Eve sinned, God made them some clothing out of animal skins. He killed several of His own precious creatures in order to cover the two creatures that deserved it the least. Do not take such sacrifices lightly. Inappropriate nakedness and vulgar sex talk is sinful. Sex itself is necessary and even important in marriage. But when sex is treated lightly, it's an offense before our Maker. Even sinful. It says so throughout the Bible. Ask any preacher. Be careful, lest in all of your mindless joking and teenage horseplay, you inadvertently provoke the wrath of God."

She glared.

"You may be able to get away with toying with your mother, but your Heavenly Father might not prove to be so forgiving."

The boys cowered, stunned by her outburst. She looked at each of them again, then turned away. She adjusted her skirt.

"Okay," she said. "I've said my piece."

Randy was the one to break the silence.

"Sorry, mom," he said. "You're right."

She turned back to him, then smiled.

Ben saw the release and stepped forward.

0955-CHEA

"I'm sorry, too," he said. "I guess that it was all of the action and the hitting and yelling at the football game. It made us all a little wild. We'll try to remember to be more civilized the next time we get to talking like that. I promise."

"Thank you," she said. "I know that I may seem a bit old fashioned, what with this so-call sexual revolution that's going on, so thanks for putting up with me. But I have a responsibility to state my position, even if you find it odd. I would hate to see any of you turn out like your father on account of me lacking the courage to tell you the truth about these things, uncomfortable as the truth may be. I'm glad that at least we can talk these things out. Now help yourself in the kitchen and don't leave a mess."

She started to leave.

"By the way," she added, turning toward Jim. "Carla Mekluevich is in town."

It took Jim a moment to catch his breath.

"What makes you say that?" he stammered.

"Well, you got a letter from her today. It's not that I'm spying on you or anything, but I just couldn't help but notice something. Over there," she pointed, "on the dining room table. Take a look for yourself."

Jim slowly approached the white envelope. He recognized it as one that he had typed to himself a few days ago, the first in over a month.

He picked it up.

"Well," she said. "Do you notice anything unusual?"

Jim turned it over several times in his hands, then looked at her hesitantly. He wondered if it was possible that she had recognized the characters from her own typewriter on the desk in the dinning room.

"What?' he asked meekly. "I don't get it."

"The postmark," she laughed. "Look at the postmark. Carla must be in town, because the postage was canceled with a Grand Haven imprint."

Jim looked down.

Why, he cursed himself, had he never thought of that before? How was it that nobody noticed until now? Thank God that he usually got to the letters first.

"Don't just stand there," she urged. "Open it up. Find out when she's coming by. For all you know, maybe she was at your game tonight, waiting by the west gate to meet you afterwards. And then you never showed up."

"Oh, mom," smiled Randy, testing her mood. "You're so romantic."

Jim slipped his finger under the address end of the flap and opened the envelope. He removed the one-page note, then pretended to read.

"What's the matter?" asked Ben. "Is she okay? You look as white as a ghost."

"Everything is fine," he replied at last. "She's still back east. I guess that her post office must have forgotten to cancel the stamp. Someone at the Grand Haven office must have noticed, and then they just canceled it here, maybe so that nobody could reuse the stamp."

"Oh," said Mrs. Vanderspyke, not sounding altogether convinced. "I guess that I shouldn't be jumping to conclusions."

"If that's all," said Ben, "then why is it that you look like you're going to throw up? Are you sure that you're okay?"

"Sure," said Jim. "I guess that all of those hits from the game are finally catching up with me. Maybe I will throw up."

Randy stepped forward and reached for the note. "Here," he said. "Let me see that."

Jim jerked the note back from Randy's hand.

"What's the matter?" asked Randy.

"It's personal, that's all."

"How personal?" There was something in Randy's grin that made Jim panic.

Jim closed his eyes. A moment later, he opened them.

"Okay," said Jim. "If you must know. . . ." he began folding the note.

"Carla says that this is her last letter. She said that she's not going to write to me anymore. She wants to get on with her life. She said that she's found some new friends and that she hopes the same for me."

He wasn't sure if anyone believed him or not. He never was any good at lying, and he wasn't about to stand around getting even more tangled in some web. The less that he told people the truth about what he was thinking, the safer he felt. The less that he said, the better.

He turned and walked to his room.

That night, after everyone was asleep, Jim quietly gathered all of his hidden Carla letters and brought them outside.

There, in the moon shadows behind the garage, he burned them.

All of them, one by one.

CHAPTER 28

Friday, March 22, 1996.
Lakewood, Colorado

Once again, the house was quiet except for the ticking of the old clock.

Alice's breathing was so soft and slow that Jade suspected she was asleep. He gently slid from beneath her feet in his lap, then rose from the couch. His headache and nausea had completely abated, and he was beginning to feel hungry and thirsty.

Alice opened her eyes.

"Jade," she said. "While you're up, could you please get me something to drink?"

"Sure. Water, juice, cola? Something else?"

"Orange juice would be good." Alice stretched her legs and sat.

Jade stopped near the kitchen door. "Would you like something to eat?" he asked. "I'm finally getting a little hungry. I haven't eaten anything since the peanuts last night at the bowling alley."

She stood and walked toward him. "How about if you pour the juice and I make us a couple of sandwiches? We've been sitting for a long time, and I need to move around for a minute anyway. I almost fell asleep."

"Almost?"

"Don't worry. You won't have to repeat anything. I heard it all. But I'm not sure that I understood everything."

Alice removed a knife from the silverware drawer. Jade piled bread and fixings from the refrigerator onto the counter. He reached into the cupboard above the microwave and withdrew two glasses.

"If you're wondering about Karen Seinner," he said, "the answer is yes. Her dad and Jeffrey Seinner were one and the same. In Ninth Grade, I had a crush on my future boss's cheerleading daughter." He paused. "The same Karen who was driving the boat two years later that killed Randy. It was her dad's Chris Craft, one of the fastest on the lake. I didn't start working for Seinner until later, but I had a thing for Karen from my first week of high school all the way until. . . ."

"The end?" asked Alice.

"Yeah. The end. When Karen died. Our junior year."

Alice turned. "How tragic."

"Yeah."

Jade was silent for a moment. He began pouring juice.

"You're right. It was a real tragedy. Everybody knew her family, and everybody loved Karen. And not just because she was so good looking. She was special. Practically the whole school showed up for her funeral. There were so many cars strung through Grand Haven that they had to shut the town down for half-an-hour during the procession. Every major intersection was blocked and backed up by mourners."

Jade took a drink.

"Excuse me," he said. "I need to use the bathroom."

When Jade returned, Alice was waiting for him in the chair by the couch. She was holding juices and sandwiches on plates. He took a seat at the end of the couch nearest her. He lifted his sandwich and took a small bite.

"Peanut butter, honey, and jam?" he asked, smiling.

"Yes. I told you I was listening."

They ate their sandwiches in silence, avoiding each other's eyes. Alice finished first. She sat for a moment, then stood and disappeared into the kitchen. She returned with two paper napkins.

"Here," she said, offering one to Jade.

"Thanks."

She sat back down.

"The first half of your story, the parts about you and Carla in sixth grade, that was a lot easier for me to take." Alice refolded her napkin. "Those memories about an innocent young James and an insecure Carla clinging to each other for friendship and support, that was pretty dear."

Alice looked away and then back. "But I've got to be honest," she said. "It made me feel really uncomfortable when you started telling me about you unzipping your pants and fantasizing about Carla."

"I'm not surprised," said Jade. He looked at the crust on his plate. "Kind of crude and twisted, huh? I wasn't sure about telling you that part. I almost didn't."

He glanced at Alice, then quickly looked down. "That wasn't an easy thing to share."

"Then why did you? Did you want to shock me for some reason? I can't see what purpose was served by you sharing that explicit little tidbit."

"Hey," said Jade, suddenly feeling defensive, "you said when you sat down a few hours ago that you wanted to understand what was going on."

"I do. I think that we've got some important issues that we need to face and to work through if we're going to keep this family together. And I appreciate all of your effort and willingness to talk. I know this isn't easy for you. But I'm not asking you to tell me every little thing, like how you used to masturbate as a teenager, or what you were thinking about when you did it."

"Don't you see," said Jade, "that stuff is a big part of what's going on now. With Chris. It's all related."

"And Karen's legs? Is that part of what's going on now, too? You didn't seem to have any trouble remembering Karen's legs. In fact, you seemed to enjoy remembering Karen's legs. Is it her legs, or Chris', that you imagine while making love with me?"

Jade set his plate on the cushion beside him. He took another drink of his juice, then stood.

"I didn't think that this was a good idea," he said. "I should have known better. This isn't the sort of garbage a man should talk about, especially with a woman. You're the only one who knows about Carla's letters, about me writing them and sending them to myself. But so what?"

He stepped to the picture window, touched the drape and looked out at the street. "Who cares? This stuff is ancient history. It's better left alone. I never should have brought it out and messed your head with it. I'm sorry."

"No," said Alice. "I'm not saying that you shouldn't talk about what's relevant to your struggles. And I see the connection between Carla's letters and Chris' e-mail. I do want to understand, and I want to help you with the things that are important. I'm just saying that it's hard for me to listen to some of this."

She pushed her fingers through her hair.

"And I think," she said, "that maybe you don't need to tell me every little crass detail. Like how your friend Mike said that he could practically cream his pants just looking at Karen. I know that boys might talk that way in high school, but try to imagine how that sounds to a girl, or to a woman. To me. It makes me feel as if men see us like meat, like something to smack one's lips over and to chomp into when no one is looking."

"I already said that I was sorry." Jade angrily turned back from the street.

"Please, Jade, don't get mad. But the way that I was raised, in the church, we were taught that Christians don't talk that way."

"Or even think that way, right?"

"No, not if they can help it."

"And if they can't? If they can't keep those sorts of thoughts from their heads?"

"Then perhaps they need to make some changes. To find different friends, to stay away from the books or movies or whatever it was that gives them ideas." Alice shook her head and twisted her hands. "I don't know, Jade. But people weren't supposed to talk that way. At least not around women. Not like sex was so cheap, so . . . dirty. Not like women and physical intimacy was something from the barnyard."

"Women just don't get it," he snapped. "To all of you, guys are just a bunch of filthy animals. You all say that you want us to be honest, to share our feelings and to be intimate. And then when we do, women want nothing to do with us because we're too uncivilized or something."

He turned his back.

"Are we talking about 'men' and 'women,' Jade? Or are we talking about you and me?"

He spun toward her.

"Please," he barked. "Don't use that tone on me. This was not supposed to turn into a fight."

"Well, maybe we do need to fight. Maybe this is one of the few legitimate fights that we need to have. Maybe I'm wrong. Maybe you need to hang in there until you make me understand."

Jade began to pace.

"Let me get this straight," he said. "Our marriage is suffering because we can't get along. We fight too much, and we talk too little. And then when I try to talk, you can't handle it and it turns into a fight. And now, in the middle of a fight, you tell me that we should fight. I don't understand what you want from me. What do you want?"

Jade stopped and looked at her.

"Alice, sometimes, I don't get you. You just don't make sense to me."

"Jade," she said, her voice soft. "Please. Sit down. Let's try to work this through. I know that we don't want to fight. But I also know that working through some of this is going to be tough. I'll try not to be so judgmental. I'll try not to make it any harder for you than it has to be. I promise. Please. Take a seat."

He eyed her for a moment, tried to collect himself. Alice forced a smile. He tried to accept it.

"Come on," she urged, "let's try again. Think about all of the progress that we've made today. Let's not give up now. I'm sorry about the way I was acting. For a minute there, I know that my attitude got pretty conventional, even predictable," she smiled, "pretty clichéd, huh?"

Jade sighed, then smiled dimly. She was trying, he had to give her that.

"Okay," he said. "Sorry. You're right. We need to push through this. Let's try again."

He returned to the couch.

"It seems," said Alice, "that we've hit a touchy spot. We never have been any good at talking about our sexual histories."

"Or our sexual presents." Jade grinned. "Sorry. Let me try that again. No sarcasm or digs this time."

He looked at Alice and softened his voice. "It also seems to me that we have had trouble talking about our present sexual lives, not just our pre-marital experiences. I'm not saying that we have had a bad sex life. It's just that I've never felt comfortable talking about sex with you. Explicitly, I mean."

"Thanks for clarifying what you meant," said Alice. "It's hard for me to say some things, too. And maybe it's hard for me to listen, but I appreciate that you're finding the courage to put these issues out for discussion. We do need to talk about this."

Jade was not sure how to respond.

"Okay," he said. "Now that we've agreed that we need to talk about it, how the heck do we talk about it?"

"Beats me," Alice smiled. "When it comes to talking about sex, I think that I'm mostly still a virgin."

Jade laughed. "There," he said, "that's probably a good start. A little humor. And a real sex word instead of an indefinite pronoun. You said the word virgin."

"And?"

"And that gives me something concrete to respond to. An opening for further disclosures and confessions that may ultimately lead to deeper understanding."

"Brace yourself, Jade," she smiled. "My turn."

She cleared her throat. "If I am guilty of avoiding sexual discussions by referring to body parts and physical acts too discreetly, as if I was too embarrassed to say the words, then sometimes so are you. You can sound as much like a textbook as I do. Listen to yourself. 'Disclosures and confessions that may ultimately lead to deeper understanding.' Why do you talk that way?"

He thought for a moment.

"Good question," he said at last. "I guess maybe I start quoting textbook phrases because I'm as uncomfortable with the subject as you are. And because I am afraid of offending you."

He studied his wife, then plunged ahead. "Plus, I know that if I just came out and said a word like, say, pussy, instead of saying the politically correct term of vagina, you would rip into me."

"You know that for a fact, huh?"

"Sure. My mamma taught me good. And so did yours. This whole conversation started with you jumping on my case for quoting Mike Miller about creaming his pants. I know that you don't want to hear this, and I normally would never say something like this, but . . . the truth is, my mother would have reacted the same way that you did. She would have blown up if I ever quoted Mike Miller that explicitly."

Alice was thoughtful.

"Okay," she said. "You're right. So maybe I would rather that you used words like penis instead of dick, or breasts instead of tits. What's wrong with that? Can't we communicate using discreet words, as opposed to using gutter language?"

"Possibly," said Jade. "But then, that's where I get jammed up. Because the words and the messages are sometimes pretty much the same thing. And if I can't use certain words, then I don't think that I can really say what I need to say."

"Try to give me an example."

"The first example that comes to mind is with Carla and those letters. Why do you think that I never told you about them before?"

"Because you were embarrassed?"

"Right."

"So?"

"Why do you suppose that I was embarrassed?"

"Maybe," suggested Alice, "you felt embarrassed because after you outgrew the need for the letters, they reminded you of your pre-adolescent isolation from your peers? That if you'd had real friends, then you wouldn't have needed to make up letters from someone who had moved away? Or, I don't know, maybe the letters were reminders of the elaborately developed lie that you were flaunting for years in front of your brothers and your mom?"

"Wow," Jade whistled with a smile. "I never even thought of all of that. And who's talking like the doctor now?"

"What do you mean you never thought of that? Why do *you* think you never told me about Carla and those letters?"

"Because," said Jade, choosing his words with care, "because to me, those letters evolved into something sexual. The big issue, in my mind at least, was not about having a shortage of friends. For a couple of years, I think that I kind of enjoyed thinking of myself as a loner, sort of as a persecuted outsider."

Jade licked his lips. "For me, the big issue at puberty was sex. All I wanted was a flesh-and-blood girl that I could have sex with. All that I could think about was watching and touching girls. But I had to make do with my imagination. So I used my memories of Carla, and my phony letters, as my substitute for the real thing."

"Okay," said Alice. "I can follow that. And you didn't have to get crude to make yourself understood. Again, it makes me feel uncomfortable to think of you distorting and using a friend like Carla in your head that way, but I think that I see what you're saying. After all, I am a nurse. I've read about this. I realize that guys can't be blamed for some of that sort of thing when they hit puberty."

She followed his gaze toward the window.

"So how," she asked, "does this prove your point that the words and the messages are the same thing? That a man has to use uncouth language to communicate about his sexual issues?"

"Because," said Jade, "even though you just heard the truth, I still don't think that you really understand it. I think that by me using such stifled and understated phrases, you failed to really get the message."

He stood and paced back to the window. He spoke his words to the street.

"The real message," he said, "is primal and raw. Even painful. Based upon what I said a minute ago, you probably think that my shame over the Carla stuff was just some sort of developmental issue that I struggled with and needed time to work through."

"And you're saying that's not correct?"

"What I'm trying to say," he paused, "is that you were partially right, and pathetically wrong. Sterilized language, at least when it comes to sexual issues for guys, can sometimes muffle the truth until the truth is lost."

"Well," said Alice. "Then try it again. Tell me the unmuffled truth. I'll try not to act too shocked. Forget the clinical and understated phrases, and give me the message straight."

Jade looked away. "I'm not sure that I can," he said. He turned to meet her eyes. "Like I said, this is where true communication gets jammed."

"Would it help," asked Alice, "if I got you a pen and a piece of stationary? Then you could write it in a letter?"

He smiled. "No more letters, okay? But thanks for the offer. Okay. Here goes."

He squared his shoulders to Alice, then took a deep breath.

"I never told you about Carla and those letters because I was ashamed of them. And I was ashamed of myself. The thing is, I used to. . . ."

"Go on."

"I was ashamed, and I felt guilty about the letters because. . . ." Jade looked away.

"This is a hell of a lot harder to say than I expected. Now that you're finally willing to listen, I don't think that I can actually say the words."

"Is this important?" she asked.

"Yes. I think it is."

"Then say it."

Jade closed his eyes.

"I've never told you, or anyone else, the truth about Carla, because of the guilt and the shame that I feel about the whole damn perverted business."

His voice grew soft.

"It makes me want to puke when I think about what a twisted little bastard I was. It became an addiction."

The tone of his voice suddenly sharpened, became almost cruel.

"It was like an addiction, like alcohol or cocaine. I hated myself, but I couldn't stop. I used to play with myself and fantasize about screwing Carla practically every time that I read one of those letters."

His words began to tumble.

"Carla became a slut, a whore in my mind that I could fuck and jack off over whenever I wanted to. When I think back to Carla, I can hardly remember her without picturing her giving me my fantasy blowjobs, sucking me in my mind while I stroked myself with my own greedy hand."

Jade squeezed his eyes until they hurt.

"Even after all these years, when I think of her, I remember those images, and I remember the perverted release of my ejaculations, hundreds of times, over those sick letters. I just couldn't help it. And I still can't. Even now, as I stand here, when I start to think back, I can feel the stirring in my dick. I know that it's perverted, but I can't seem to help it. My cock, and my hand, the same one that Carla kissed . . . they still remember. After all these years."

Jade turned back to face the street.

"And after all these years," he whispered, "they still love the rush. Only now they prefer images of Chris. Like they did on Friday in the back room at work. Friday when I fantasized and stroked myself behind an unlocked door. This is the kind of worthless shit you married. . . ."

The room fell silent.

Alice gathered the sandwich plates and took them into the kitchen.

Jade could hear water running in the sink, then the splashing of the washcloth as she scrubbed the glasses and dishes. He heard the drying towel squeak, then the sound of china bumping ceramic as she stacked them on the counter.

A few minutes later, she walked back into the living room. She stopped, then approached Jade from behind.

"That speech of yours," she said softly, "was very disturbing." She touched his back. "I've never heard you say some of those words. Please, don't take this the wrong way, but I've got to tell you that what you said sounded dirty and degrading. It felt ugly, even wicked, for you to talk like that. And I felt violated and dirty by even having to listen."

She wrapped her arms around his chest and buried her face in his back. "And it killed me," she whispered, "to hear what you said about Chris." When they turned to face each other, they both stood with wet eyes. Alice spoke again.

"I know that must have been difficult for you," she said.

Jade nodded. "And I know that it was hard for you, too."

"But I guess hearing it helps," she sighed. "Let's sit down."

They sat together on the couch.

"How," asked Jade, "how does me shooting my mouth off like that help?"

"You were right. The words and the message are related. This stuff is not about Sunday school lessons or scientific laboratory notes. It's about who we are. People who, pardon the expression, fuck and poop."

Despite himself, Jade grinned.

She smiled faintly.

"And this is about people whose hormones and instincts sometimes drive them in ways that are utterly frightening. There was a rawness in what you said, a terrifying power in the words that you used. Words like cock and blowjob, they make me shudder. I can hardly even say them myself out loud without feeling like my mouth should be washed out with soap. But I think that, once in a while, they may need to be said."

Jade put his arm around her.

"I suppose," she said, "that I didn't really get the message until you used those words."

"And now you do?"

"I think so. It seems like your sexual struggles were like hornet nests stirred up inside your teenage body. Inside of your body and your head." She paused. "And that those hornet nests are still there?"

She tapped the outside of her thigh.

"When you used those words, the rough ones, I could feel the fire and the shame inside you. Anger and hatred . . . toward yourself."

Jade nodded.

"I think that you're right," he said. "The way that I feel sometimes about my life and who I am, it's just riddled with frustration, rage and self-hatred. Sometimes all I want to do is escape from it all. Escape in work, escape through bossing people around, escape in fantasies. . . ."

Jade met her eyes.

"Terry said something to me a couple of days ago at the Grill. He warned me that I was beating myself black and blue and slitting my wrists out of guilt."

"For once," said Alice, "maybe Terry is right."

"He also said that I should talk about stuff. You know, the painful things. He said that we never really can forget our tragedies, and that they can come back to haunt us if we're not careful."

"Are you being haunted?" asked Alice.

"Perhaps. I guess that I haven't been as good at forgetting things as I thought. I guess that I wanted to believe that out of sight was out of mind." He smiled at the cliché. "But it wasn't."

"How so?"

"Twenty years latter, Carla's ghost has come back. And she

brought her letters with her."

"Carla's ghost?"

"Chris Teller. And the e-mail."

"Right," sighed Alice. "Your new Carla."

"And other ghosts as well."

"Like Karen's and Randy's?"

"Yes. And the biggie. The one that showed up in the cereal box. The one that came packed as Harry's ashes."

CHAPTER 29

Saturday, March 23, 1996.
Dakota Ridge, Colorado

Jade hesitated on the ledge.

From around the bow of the cliff came voices, soft laughter and muffled dialogue escaping from the cave. There were three or four voices. Hosea's was among them.

Hogmen.

Hosea must have called a special meeting.

Jade checked his watch. 9:56 am. He inched closer. Hosea was describing last Saturday, how Jade suddenly appeared in the cave and how Hosea jumped and bumped his head.

Jade eased toward the entrance, then peered between a gnarled juniper trunk and a jagged outcropping. His eyes adjusted to the shadows within. Four men sat cross-legged around the altar. They had left a spot for him. Two men wore light jackets, ball caps and fanny packs. Hosea wore the same moccasins, sweatshirt and headband from the previous week. The fourth man looked taller and thinner than the others. He wore casual sports clothes and no hat. He was a good-looking man with thick black hair. Jade looked closer.

Yes, matted helmet hair. This was the owner of the red mountain bike stashed in the undergrowth near the trail at the top of the ridge. Jade pulled back from the entrance.

He felt odd. Strangely excited, strangely afraid. What would the hogmen think of him?

He almost hadn't come. He almost stayed home to talk more with Alice. But when she heard about Hosea, she urged him to keep the date. The appointment sounded important to her, as if Hosea and the cave were part of the fabric of this week that was changing their lives.

He weighed Alice's interpretation and advice. He recalled his experience at the strange altar. And he agreed that he should go. But now, he again wondered. What if this was some kind of cult? A dangerous one? For all he knew, these men were Satanists. Or perverts. This was crazy, strolling in among these strangers, these eccentric hogmen in this isolated, godforsaken place. Anything could happen. Nobody would know.

Hosea chuckled and the others joined in relaxed laughter. Jade stepped to the entrance of the cave.

"Good morning!" he called.

Hosea bounded to his feet.

"Good morning, Jade! Glad you could make it." He eyed Jade's bandaged cheeks. "A little shaving accident, eh? Well, we were just talking about you."

He reached for Jade's hand and shook it solidly, then turned to the others, who were rising to their feet.

"Well everybody, the man of the hour. This fellow was knocked out from some quarry near Holland, Michigan. But he's been here in Colorado long enough to count." Hosea laughed. "Did I get that right, Dutch?"

Jade laughed. "Close enough."

"Well, Dutch," Hosea winked, "I'd like you to meet a few of your fellow hogmen."

Fellow hogmen? Was he already a member of their group?

"This here," Hosea pointed toward one of the ball caps, "is Geek."

A short young man sprang forward and thrust a hand in Jade's direction. His grip was frail, though his small eyes had a grip of their own. He wore an earring beneath his 'Save the People' cap. A chain bracelet dangled from his thin wrist, and the back of his hand was tattooed with a serpent coiled around a cross.

"Geek," said Hosea, "is a real nutcase. He's been a Confused

Man of the Hogback all his life, even before he found our cave."

Jade glanced at Geek's left hand. No ring.

"Geek wandered up here after a church meeting. The services had been very enlightening, and Geek decided to keep the embers glowing. Roasted sinner. Sherried ham flambé."

Jade winced at Geek's ensuing laugh. "I was dressing for a hot night," cackled Geek. "If Hosea hadn't grabbed my matches, I would have made a hell of a hell on a hill. I was basted in gasoline and ready to flame." His cackle filled the cave. "And, man, I had found an absolutely awesome tureen. They would have seen me sizzling all the way up in Commerce City. The spot was right up top, at the peak between the spiked rocks."

Jade pictured the small plateau between the horse's ears at the top of the slog.

"Of course," he smirked, "I still think about that spot sometimes. I may yet have the opportunity to use it, if I ever get caught in one of those marathon revivals again."

"And this," said Hosea, "is Chips." Hosea pointed toward the other ball cap, a black one with a Rockies logo. Chips reached for Jade's hand and smiled broadly. His grip was dry and strong.

"Chips comes to us from the Park Service. Two years ago, he was mapping the Dakota Ridge Trail for a brochure. He noticed a faint path snaking off the main trail into the underbrush and he followed it here."

"Yeah," said Chips, "what a mistake that was. I found this cave, and then the cairn," he nodded toward the back corner. "I figured that if I put the cave on the map, then people would start coming. And if people started coming, then I'd have to haul out the trash."

He smiled. "Look at the size of that heap. There must be a thousand pounds worth." He shook his head at the cairn. "Needless to say, I left it off the map."

"How," asked Jade, "did you hook up with the rest of these guys?"

Chips lifted his cap, ran his fingers through his hair and

laughed. "Actually, they hooked up with me. I liked this spot, so I started sneaking down here for lunch breaks whenever I was working the ridge. One day I accidentally left a small bag of potato chips in the altar pit. When I came back, the bag had been crushed and thrown on the cairn."

Hosea grinned. "I didn't know how those potato chips got here. I figured they'd come from the devil himself, sent to seduce me into another five pounds."

"A note was stuck to the bag," said Chips. "It called me a coward for not meeting God's prophet face-to-face. It said I should come back Saturday at 10:00 am for a showdown, or I should never come to the cave again."

Hosea chuckled. "I gotta tell ya, Dutch. You've never seen a pilgrim pray so hard in all your life. By Friday, I was having nightmares, sleeping on a stack of Bibles and scared to death about what I'd gotten myself into with old Beelzebub."

Chips laughed. "I was so curious that I couldn't resist. Saturday morning, I made my way to the cave a half hour early, just in case something weird was going on. I was wearing my Park Service uniform and I'd brought along an extra-large bag of Nacho Red-Hots to pass the time while waiting."

"And then, at 10:00 sharp, up shoots this arm from behind the juniper roots. At the end of the arm was a huge silver cross, black fingers wrapped tight and waving it back and forth, and some half-crazed voice singing Jesus songs and reciting the Lord's Prayer over and over until I couldn't stand it any more and I started to laugh."

Chips snorted.

"Then up pops Hosea's face. The man takes one look at me with my chips, his eyes bug out, then he practically falls straight back off the face of the cliff."

Chips and Hosea howled. Geek cackled.

Jade's gaze shifted back and forth among them as he grinned.

"And this," said Hosea, wiping his eyes, "is Padre."

Padre's handshake, like his smile, was strong and lean. He had a spray of gray hair above each ear and a twitch in his left eye.

"Hello," he said. "Welcome to our cave. It's good to have you with us here this morning."

"Thank you," said Jade. He liked Padre immediately. Liked his rich low voice especially.

"Last summer," said Hosea, "I found Padre reading the Ten Commandments in a King James Bible on a log in Red Rocks Park. He looked so sad I told him that maybe he was reading the wrong book. He asked me what I recommended, and I told him to follow me up into the hogback where I'd show him something else that God had put in stone."

Padre smiled, sadly.

"You see, Dutch," he sighed, "I had recently lost my flock. Actually, they'd just thrown me out. One of the elders had a wife that was a snatch of heaven in bed, but she was a hell of a disappointment when it came to keeping secrets. One day she let it slip to a girlfriend that she knew me better than anyone else in the congregation. And then the two women got to quibbling, because the chairperson of the site improvement committee was positive that she knew me even better."

He looked down.

"Let's just say they both knew me, and I do mean that in the biblical sense. Before it was over, the two of them flushed out three other women in the congregation that I had also known."

Jade whistled.

"It could have been worse." Padre looked down. "They could have talked to one of the girls in our Sunday night youth group."

The cave grew still. Jade closed his eyes.

When he opened them, Hosea was holding Padre, whose eyes were flowing and jaw was trembling.

Hello to you, too, thought Jade.

"Well, then," said Hosea. He turned back to Jade. "I see that you're still here. That's a good sign."

Jade shook his head. "You guys don't waste any time, do you?"

"Life's short," said Hosea.

"So let's get started," said Chips.

They resumed their seats around the altar on the chamber's floor. Jade lowered himself awkwardly among them.

Hosea cleared his throat.

"As you see, Dutch, we're a rather informal group up here. We try to dispense with nonsense and forgo with pretense as much as possible, but we'll take whatever you give us. Feel free to be as frank or as modest as you wish. All that we ask is that you don't outright lie and that you allow us the freedom to say and do what we feel according to the same measure of grace we extend to you. Can you handle that?"

Jade hesitated. "I'm not sure," he said.

"Good answer."

They all smiled, including Padre, who was blowing his nose.

"Obviously," said Hosea, "the four of us know each other pretty well. You're clearly the novelty of the day and we're all eager to get to know you better. To keep things fair, though, you should be asking us questions as well. That'll give you a chance to breathe once in a while, and us a chance to feel like we're getting a little attention, too. Okay?"

Jade nodded.

"Very good. Then let's get started with an easy one." Hosea leaned toward Jade. "How was your week?"

Jade laughed. "I thought you said that you'd start with an easy one. This past week has been hell."

"Hell?"

"Listen guys." Jade looked around the circle. "I've been through the wringer. I'm emotionally and physically exhausted. I've had conversations, realizations and a package in the mail you wouldn't believe. Not to mention a hangover up around 7.9 on the Richter. I don't want to be rude, but I'm not sure how much of this I'm up for."

Chips cleared his throat. "Then why are you here?"

"Why are you here?" asked Jade, turning to the man on his left.

The cave fell quiet. Jade felt himself blushing. He had snapped the question back too quickly.

"Two reasons." Chips nodded toward Hosea across the circle. "First, because Hosea called me. He told me that he had a vision that something powerful was going to happen here this morning in the cave, and he said that he wanted my help."

"The second reason," Chips unzipped his fanny pack and removed a small brown bag, "is because it was time for me to make another sacrifice."

He poured a handful of plastic poker chips into his right palm.

"You probably thought my cairn name was Chips because of the Nacho Red-Hots. That's not it." He held the poker chips toward Jade. "It's because of these. Not these exact chips, but the real ones, from the casinos. I'm a gambler. A bad one. So far, it's cost me my wife, my kids, a car, and two jobs."

He let the chips slowly clatter from the side of his palm into the black altar basin. He stirred them with his left hand, mixing the colors thoroughly.

Chips closed his eyes and muttered a silent prayer.

The others watched solemnly as Chips shifted to his knees. He reached both hands to beside the altar, cupped the crushing stone, then jerked it from the cave's floor.

He looked at Jade, then raised the stone above his head.

"Into Thy hands," whispered Chips, facing up, "do I commend my vice."

Jade felt the crunching of the plastic as the stone reverberated within the rock of the chamber floor.

Jade closed his eyes, remembering the moment he crushed his watch on Monday.

Again, the rock was raised and dropped.

Then a third time.

He opened his eyes when he heard Chips scooping fragments of debris from the basin.

Chips rose, walked to the cairn, then let the waste and dust trickle between his fingers into the pile. He returned to the circle, sat, then turned to Jade. His eyes were damp.

"That," he said, "was the other reason why I came."

They were again silent. Jade noticed that Hosea's eyes were closed, and that his lips were moving soundlessly. He was praying. Jade closed his eyes.

Dear God. Be with Chips. Be with Chips. Please be with Chips. Jade prayed the refrain over and over. He was not sure why or for how long.

"Thank you," whispered Chips.

Jade opened his eyes. They were all looking at Chips, and the man was smiling. His cheeks were streaked.

Geek was the next to speak.

"I didn't bring a sacrifice this time," he said, looking at Jade. "Hosea called me, too. Not that I ever mind coming up here. This place, and all of the hogmen, are special to me. I don't know if I could make it without their help." He glanced around the circle, then back at Jade.

"My cairn name is Geek because I like that name when I'm up here. Kids used to call me Geek in school, but I hated it back then. Calling me Geek was better than calling me fag, or queer, or homo. But I still couldn't stand it."

He looked at the group.

"When the hogmen call me Geek, it feels different. There is no judgment or accusation in their voices. Just an acknowledgment, man, a simple acceptance." He smiled. "And maybe a dash of humor."

The others smiled.

"Hosea was right. When he found me up top, I was getting ready to kill myself. I was raised in a conservative home, and I've always believed in God. And I still do."

Jade noticed a thin cross around Geek's neck. Another small cross was crudely welded to a silver ring on his right hand.

"Lots of people think I'm gay. I'm not so sure that they're right, because, man, how does anyone know? I've never slept with a woman." He shrugged. "But if I had the chance and if she was kind and gentle, a good friend, then who knows?" He cackled. "It might be wickedly wild."

Jade felt uneasy. In the book business, he frequently dealt with gay clients. They were some of his best customers. This conversation with Geek felt categorically different.

Geek tugged his nose roughly, then abruptly dropped his hand.

"I've always looked kind of feminine, so some people assume I'm not really a man. The first time I was approached by a queer, I was shocked and confused. People had teased me, but there was never any question in my mind. But once that first gay man assumed that I was like him, well, that really shook me up. And then I couldn't get it out of my mind."

Geek stared into the altar.

"My first sexual experience came a few months later. It was with a man. Someone that I had known for a long time. It was in a hotel room, and he paid me money. More than I could earn in two weeks at the restaurant where I was learning to cook. A month later, he approached me again. Then he started seeing me regularly. Then setting me up with his friends. Even strangers."

He met Jade's eyes.

"I was only 14 years old, for God's sake. I hated myself, but I couldn't get my neck out of the noose. They treated me well, no pain or anything like that, and I liked the easy money. I even liked dressing up in the clothes they brought me. They made me feel popular for the first time, important to them, man, like they needed me. You know?"

Geek glanced at the others, then back into the pit.

"But I hated myself. The first time that I slit my wrists, my parents had no idea why. After some family therapy, then they understood."

He cackled softly, pathetically.

"Man, that's when my dad, my loving father, that's when he promised me that if I ever tried killing myself again, he would understand." Geek sighed. "He even offered to help."

He looked up. "So I moved out onto the streets for a couple of years. I got into body piercing, tattoos, heroin, you name it."

"My worst habit, though" he laughed, "was gospel revivals. I'd go to every one of them that I could find. They did for my soul what the needles and the strange men did for my body. I became a delightfully wretched pin cushion, inside and out."

"I would listen to the words of those preachers, and then I'd feel the nails of the cross sinking blow by blow into my own hands and feet. They would speak of the wrath of God toward perverts like me, and then I'd know that I deserved to die. I could feel the flames of the eternal inferno lapping at my soles. I'd crawl to their altars weeping and wailing, and I'd beg for mercy and I'd promise to change."

"Man, I absolutely made their days."

"But the next night, I'd find myself back in bed with another man. That's when Hosea found me, up here, ready to shake and bake and to fry in the sky. . . ."

He met Jade's eyes. "Sick, huh?"

"I guess." Jade glanced at Hosea, who nodded. "But it must have been rough." He hesitated. "And today?" he asked. "What is your life like since you've been coming here?"

Geek responded with a sickly laugh. "Better, I guess. I'm off the streets. I'm not turning johns anymore. I took the brass fishhooks out of my nipples. I've got a place with a couple of guys, and I've got a passable job in a three-star kitchen. But I still like to beat up on myself. Some habits are hard to break." He glanced at Hosea. "But I'm working on it."

Jade slowly looked around the circle. The others were quiet. He cleared his throat. They looked at him, patiently waiting.

"I'm not sure where to begin," he said. "You guys amaze me. I don't know how you talk so freely about your stuff, the bad stuff, particularly with a stranger. I had my first real conversation with my wife yesterday," Jade glanced at his bandaged knuckles, "and I told her some things that I hadn't had the courage to discuss in 20 years."

Geek smiled, then asked softly, "Did you hit her?"

Jade looked up. Geek was staring at the bandages on Jade's hand.

"No," he laughed. "I've never hit Alice."

"Then what?"

Jade grew silent.

"I hit the bathroom mirror." He sighed. "We're having it replaced on Wednesday."

Chips leaned forward. "Why?" he prodded.

Jade smiled. "Because the crew was already booked solid through Tuesday."

Chips wagged his head, looking disappointed. Jade felt stupid.

"I'm sorry," he said. "I guess that I hit the mirror because. . . ."

Why did he hit the mirror? He closed his eyes. He put himself back to the moment, stared again at his face in the mirror.

"I had a hangover," he said, "and everything was falling apart. Like I said, a week from hell. I saw my face in the bathroom light and I couldn't stand it. I guess I went crazy for a moment. It was like I was hitting my own face."

Geek sighed. "I can relate," he said. "I've been there, man. What else do you do to yourself, besides breaking mirrors with your fist?"

Jade looked at Geek, who was leaning toward him, licking his lips in eager expectancy, his queer little eyes glistening, piercing.

Jade felt his bowels knotting, churning with distaste.

He was not anything like Geek, had nothing in common with that effeminate cackling pin cushion. What did Geek mean, saying that he could relate? Asking what else Jade did to himself besides break mirrors?

Hosea's eyes were closed. He was probably praying.

Too bizarre. This hogman support-group thing was suddenly getting to be too much. These guys were sick, talking about their sleaze so openly, trying to outdo each other with their tales of perversity.

The others waited.

"That's it?" Geek asked. "One swat at the mirror? That's pretty lame, man."

Geek shook his head in disgust. "Dutch, maybe you're kidding yourself by coming up here. Maybe there's nothing wrong with you. Maybe you should just go get yourself a talk show where you can pass out advice and give help all afternoon, because if you don't have. . . ."

"That's enough," said Hosea. "Give the man some time. He's not used to this sort of party."

Jade's face burned.

He didn't need a fat little black man like this pompous Hosea to stand up for him. To fight his battles. He could close the mouth of that Geek fag with one swing. Linemen twice the size of Geek used to drop to their knees and roll out of the way when they saw Jim Vanderspyke lower his shoulder and charge.

Who did that scrawny twit think he was, anyway, hassling a man like Jade? A respected member of his church? A man who sold good books to little old ladies—not like Geek, who sold his asshole to whoever showed up. What did Geek know. . . .

What did Geek know?

Jade glared at the young man, who looked away.

Hosea was still praying, his eyes closed. Chips and Padre were doing the same.

Praying to whom?

God? As if God would really bother to listen to an overweight alcoholic or to a gambling addict.

Or to a fornicating preacher who had bedded every vulnerable woman he could snare between the sheets. In his home church, for crying out loud. Even a high school girl. Probably some cheer leader who. . . .

Jade shuddered.

Padre opened his eyes. He saw Jade looking at him, then closed his eyes again and continued to pray.

Jade never was very good at prayer. That hypocrite preacher had it down, though. Jade could see that. Padre was able to fool an entire congregation. Telling the men in the pews on Sunday that they'd go to hell for lusting, while the rest of the week, while the obedient suckers from the pews were off doing an honest day's work, he was slipping into their homes. Slipping into their bedrooms. Slipping into their wives.

Shit.

God didn't listen to Jade's prayers. Never answered, anyway. Never would.

And why were these strangers praying now, even as he judged them, supposedly praying for him? He didn't need the prayers of screwed up perverts to get his act together.

Jade stared into the shadows of the altar pit.

He wished that he'd never discovered the cave. He should have stayed up top, on the edge of the cliff, enjoying the view.

Feeling the whirlpool.

Enjoying his fantasies of a naked Chris.

Shit.

Jade softly bit his tongue. Then closed his eyes. Closed them as he had done last week. When he prayed for help, moments before he heard the sound of Hosea's shattering glass.

Shit.

"Should I leave, Lord?" he whispered. "Or am I supposed to stay?"

No answer.

As usual. Never would be.

His legs were cramping.

Jade abruptly raised himself from the cave floor. He needed to walk the stiffness from his thighs. They stared at him as he stepped from the circle. He started to speak, then turned his back and stepped through the junipers to the edge of the precipice.

The view was as he remembered. Red Rocks Park to the south, Mount Morrison opposite, Mount Vernon Creek below, cottonwoods. . . . Beautiful. He lifted his invisible harmonica in his left hand. He settled his thumb beneath his chin and his knuckle against his teeth, then cradled his left elbow with his right wrist and gently played five bars.

In the meadow below, around the cottonwoods, two horses galloped in tandem, graceful, stride for stride. Magnificent animals from this angle. Yet strangely distant, remote. He could not hear their hooves, could only see the wind in their manes and in the flowing of their long black tails.

Jade's mind flashed to his uncle's farm.

Uncle Bud raised a few horses. One paddock for the mares and geldings, another for the stallion. The stallion's name was Thunder. Uncle Bud charged $300 for stud fee.

Jade was there once. He had seen a mating.

Thunder had become crazed, running in circles, kicking up dirt clods and dust. A stranger held his mare, and Thunder performed.

It was a violent spectacle.

A rape.

The ground churned to dust, the mare and stallion neighed and cried horse screams, the owner lunged between white fence rails to keep from being crushed. . . .

Mrs. Vanderspyke had come yelling from the farmhouse, sweeping Jimmy into her arms, covering his eyes and ears, cursing Harry for allowing her youngest to. . . .

Animals.

She screamed that they were all animals.

Jade looked down.

The two horses disappeared beneath the cottonwoods below.

The cave was quiet. He turned to the four strangers gathered around the dark altar hollowed from ancient stone.

Hogmen.

They were all hogmen.

He rejoined them, lowering himself back onto the hard chamber floor. He slowly looked at each of them, starting with Hosea.

"I changed my name," he said softly.

"When I was young, everyone called me Jimmy. When I was

11, I caught my dad, Harry, with his pants down. Harry was having sex with a stranger in the bathroom of our bankrupt little store. My mom divorced him after that and I was raised by her. She was a good woman. Too good. She didn't know anything about teenage boys. She taught me that sex was dirty. Dirty even for animals."

He looked at Geek, then held his eye.

"Then, in Sixth Grade, I changed my name to James. I was short, fat and in love for the first time. Her name was Carla, and she was my only good friend. James was a geek, too." He smiled.

"I only kissed Carla once, but I never could forget it. She kissed my hand with her tongue. When I hit puberty, Carla was long gone. But in my mind, I paid her back by making love to her mouth a thousand times."

Hosea closed his eyes.

"In high school, my name was Jim. I was a jock. A football stud. My girlfriend was the best-looking girl in our class. A cheerleader. We fooled around, but we never went all the way. She wanted to have sex and so did I. Hell, I was ready to explode every time I touched her."

Jade slid his hands out to his knees.

"But I made a vow with God. I believed in God, everybody did where I grew up, and I figured that if I made a deal with God and held my end of the bargain, God would help me make it work. I vowed that I would never become like my father. I had learned that my father, Harry Vanderspyke, was a dirty animal. A sex fiend with no self control. Somehow, I wanted to be something else. What else, I've never exactly known. So I didn't make love to Karen."

Jade sighed. He closed his eyes.

"Throughout high school, I dreamed of the day when I would marry Karen. Then it would be okay. Then we could have sex, and it would be a good thing, not something dirty. Not a sin. I dreamed of making love to her on our honeymoon and of how beautiful it would be.

"Those were my daydreams." He shook his head. "Not my night dreams. Karen's body drove me crazy. In bed, alone at night, I didn't think about tender moments with Karen. All that I could picture was ripping off her clothes. And screwing her brains out."

He sighed again.

"Karen died in an accident our junior year."

He squeezed his knees.

"I never got to make love to my Karen. And I never got to screw her, either. In college, they called me by my initials, J.D. Later, J.D. became Jade."

He opened his eyes. Geek was watching. The other three hogmen were still in prayer.

"Names," sighed Geek. "They're clues. Jimmy, James, Jim . . . lost boys crying. Exiles longing to come home."

Jade looked into Geek's eyes. "Exiles?"

"Inner exiles. The missing players behind the man. Can you see them?"

"Maybe." Jade closed his eyes. Looked back, listened.

"I see James." Jade's voiced hardened. "He's a fat kid, still on his fat butt. He's stuck someplace getting off on fantasies, feeling cheated and empty about his girlfriend moving away. Feeling robbed for never getting to sleep with the good-looking cheerleader. And now he's stuck on someone new. Her name is Chris. James thinks about her all the time. She's his latest fantasy sex slave."

Geek rustled. "It's a start."

"You asked me, Geek, about what else I do to punish myself for being a pervert. I'll tell you. I bite my tongue. Nothing fancy, nothing complicated. No needles, no johns. Just my own back molars. When I think of Chris, I chomp down. I grind the back edge of my tongue until it bleeds."

Geek grinned. "Now you're cooking, James. What else?"

Jade smiled, thinking.

"In high school, I used to do pushups by the hundreds, forcing myself to continue until I collapsed. Then I strung a bunch of heavy car tires on ropes from tree limbs. I'd take my shirt off and run through the tires holding a football, believing that the pounding and the bruising of my body was making me a stronger halfback. An all-star stud who would never fumble the ball in a game. And I didn't. I set records and people loved me. That felt good."

"And now, man?"

"Now a days, I ride the hogback on a European mountain bike, pounding myself into the ruts, jarring my spine and skull until I can hardly see. Driving my arms and legs until they scream."

"And your soul, man? What do you do to punish your soul?"

Jade thought.

"Sorry, Geek. I don't do revivals." He smiled. "But I do go to church every Sunday. I especially like to listen to the reading of the law. I cherish the 'thou shalt not lust' sorts of passages. Those really make me squirm. They make me think of Chris, and then I have another chance to bite my tongue."

"Anything else?"

Jade raised his knuckles to his teeth, cradled his elbow against his ribs.

And then he saw it, clearly, for the first time.

He wasn't sure whether to laugh or to weep.

"One more," he said. "A big one."

Hosea open his eyes and met Jade's gaze.

"After Karen Seinner died, I took a position working for her father. For the past 20 years, I've seen her last name a hundred times a week. On the letterheads, on the invoice pads, on the sign over the entrance to the store. Even on my paychecks. It's always there, never letting me forget. Seinner Books. Karen Seinner. Seinner. . . ."

Jade closed his eyes.

"Not bad," said Geek. "Not bad."

CHAPTER 30

"Thank you," said Hosea, "for your sincere participation." He smiled. "And how do you feel?"

Jade opened his eyes. He wiped them. Looked around the group.

"Naked," he said. "I feel naked. And if I'm blushing, I don't want to hear about it."

"You did some good work," said Chips. "Thanks."

"I should be thanking you. You're the ones who helped me to find it, helped me to get it out. Why are you thanking me?"

Chips smiled. "It's a mystery. Who knows how it works. All I can tell you is that confessions are empowering. After watching you wrestle with the truth about yourself, I feel stronger about who I am. And about who I want to be. It always seems to work that way."

"Is it," asked Jade, "like this every time you guys get together? Ripping open your stomachs and spilling out your guts?"

Geek cackled. "Unfortunately, no. Sometimes it's pretty sane. We were lucky Hosea got you to come. We were overdue for some fresh blood."

Hosea shook his head at Geek, then turned back to Jade. "We always do some confessing. We check up on each other and we hold each other accountable for what's happening in our lives, good and bad. What Geek means is that a lot of what we talk about gets repetitious. Each of us has his own demons, and those demons keep regrouping and hitting us from new angles. But certain themes repeat."

"And," said Chips, "it is getting harder and harder for Geek to shock us with his stories. In fact, in another year or two, he may even have to concede that he's almost back to normal."

"No way, man," he cackled. "I'm still as screwed up as ever."

Chips smiled. "Perhaps."

"In a way, though" said Hosea, "Geek is right. We never really seem to change completely. The boys inside us, the Jimmy, the James, the Jim, the whatever-their-names, they're still there, even if we make them hide. They're inside, calling to be heard. Crying to be embraced. So we do what we can. We keep working on our stuff, setting new goals, and sometimes doing better."

"That pile over there," Hosea nodded at the cairn, "is mostly symbolic. But every time that I crush a liquor bottle, it's another sort of confession. A confession before myself and my God about who I am as a man, and about how I'm doing at the present time."

"What happens," Jade asked, "after your confessions?"

"On a good day," smiled Hosea, "God whispers back."

"And what does God tell you?"

"He just whispers the words, 'Good enough.'"

"That's it? Good enough?"

"That's plenty."

Jade was thoughtful.

"What do you make of that, Padre?" Jade asked. "You know the Bible. As someone who has listened to sermons all of his life, I'm inclined to believe that none of us are ever doing good enough. Does any of this make sense to you?"

Padre shrugged. "The healing powers of confession are biblically and psychologically well supported. The part about what God whispers back to Hosea is a bit more tricky."

Padre looked at Hosea. "Some people say that we are all born with an innate sense of justice and shame. Others say that we learn those things as we mature. Either way, most of us end up feeling bad because we often fail to behave mentally or physically according to our own highest standards. Traditionally, that's called feeling guilty for having sinned."

Padre turned back to Jade.

"Whatever it's called, it's almost universal. Almost every one of us feels his own personal form of sin and shame. Most religions use these feelings to their advantage. One of the things that got Jesus into trouble was his suggestion that trying to live up to super high expectations was a little bit irrelevant."

"Irrelevant?"

"Jesus claimed that none of us could live up to God's standards, which were the only standards that ultimately counted. No matter which people we hung out with, no matter how much we studied sacred texts, or even how hard we prayed, we would never meet God's standards."

"And then Jesus floored them all by saying that God loves us anyway."

Padre smiled. "It was a radical idea. The leaders of the day knew that it could be trouble. They feared the worst. After all, with a message like that, what was to keep people from going wild? You know, stealing, murdering, or sleeping with the wives of their friends?"

Padre shook his head and looked into the altar. "So, when Hosea stands here and says that God whispers a word of acceptance, in spite of a man's rancid guilt and shame, Hosea stands on shaky ground. Many folks would say that the man is crazy."

"And you?" asked Jade. "Do you think he's crazy?"

Padre looked up.

"He's crazy, there's no question about that." He smiled. "And I pray to Jesus that he's right."

Chips shook his head in agreement.

Padre said it again, in a whisper. "I pray to Jesus that he's right."

"Any more questions?" grinned Hosea.

"Hundreds of them," said Jade. "But I'm not sure how much more my butt can take. I should have brought something to sit on."

"You wimp," cackled Geek. "I would have thought that you would relish this sort of abuse."

Padre looked up and laughed.

"Break time!" said Hosea.

Jade and Geek were the first to their feet. The others rose more carefully. They stretched and shook their legs, then wandered to the junipers overlooking the valley. Geek produced some trail mix from his fanny pack, and they shared water from Hosea's gear bag stashed in the roots.

"So," asked Jade, "why is it so hard for me to break out of my fantasies about Chris?"

Chips leaned his shoulders against the cave's entrance.

"Who knows?" he said. "Obsessions are mysterious things. And the less that we understand our obsessions, the more power they seem to have."

Chips plucked a juniper berry, studied it, then flipped it with his thumb over the edge to the talus below.

"Obsessions are more than bad habits, though," he said. "When I was little, I chased my sister's cat. That was a bad habit. When the cat died, I stopped. No big deal. My gambling addiction is completely different."

"How so?"

"Gambling does something to my gut. The casinos are a sensual feast—you know, the smells, the lights, the sounds of slot machines, the feel of the green tables and the dark oak stools. It's overwhelming. Better than sex."

Jade laughed. "I've enjoyed myself the couple of times I've been to Central City to play blackjack, but I'd never say that gambling was better than sex."

"Maybe that's because you didn't have any side bets riding while you played. I've got stacks of them. Memories of huge wins in Vegas, of crowds gathering around to see how high I could go, memories of paying off debts with a single flip of a card. And then memories of my losing streaks, of times that I couldn't pull myself away from the table until my wallet and my credit cards were empty. Times that I missed work, missed my kid's Christmas pageant, hocked my television set, fought with my wife, you name it."

"Every time that I think of gambling, I get this instant rush of all of that, all those images and sensations and memories. It's a mood-altering drug for me. It sweeps me off my feet and carries me away from the mundane hassles of my life, away to a place where I can instantly go insane with mind-boggling stimulation."

Geek laughed. "If it sounds like Chips is having an orgasm, he probably is. Remember, he's the one who prefers gambling over sex."

Chips laughed. "And, like women, gambling provides its own special torture. I've been down that road all the way to the flames, and eventually, it does become a hell."

"Knowing that," asked Jade, "you still worry about getting sucked back in? Even though it brings you hell?"

"As the Bible says, I'm like a dog that returns to his own vomit. Or a freshly-washed pig that scampers back to roll in the mud."

Jade laughed. "You're pulling my leg, right? That's not in the Bible, is it?"

"Sure. In Proverbs, and in one of the letters from Peter. I guess that they had hogmen back then, too."

Jade raised a knuckle to his teeth, settled his left elbow onto his right wrist. He knew the gut rush. The whirlpool. The irrepressible intoxication of surging adrenaline. Of the emotional battles against forbidden beaches and of the twisted satisfaction of secret orgasms. He knew all about the escape from the foot drudgery of life into those magical skies where he could fly.

He also knew the hell. The guilt. The shame. The explanations that he now owed his wife, his son, even the woman that he used as a canvas for his twisted dreams.

He was stuck in a loop that he couldn't escape.

Like a dog returning to its vomit. Like a cleansed pig returning to roll in the mud. Doing again the very thing he hated. He turned to Hosea.

"You seem to understand this obsession and guilt stuff pretty well. Help me out here, would you?"

"If I can." Hosea scratched his forearm.

"Why is it an issue of gambling for Chips, alcohol for you, women for Padre, self-abuse for Geek, and . . . I don't know, sexual fantasies for me?"

Hosea smiled. "Those are five different questions, with five different answers. Let's stick with you. If you think you're up for it?"

"I think I am. Tell me, what's the answer? Why am I stuck in this fantasy loop?"

"I'm not sure. But, deep down, you probably have the answers. There are undoubtedly logical reasons why sexual fantasies are your escape of choice . . . and why they are your Achilles heel. Those reasons can be understood, but only if you are willing to dig them up. And digging them up can feel a whole lot like whittling out chunks of flesh to pull the poison from a snake bite."

"How do I dig them out, the answers?"

"By asking yourself the right questions, one at a time. As you honestly face the right questions, you'll start to move in the right direction. Eventually, if you've got the courage to push yourself far enough, you'll uncover the sources of your so-called 'loop.'"

"What kinds of questions am I supposed to ask?"

Hosea grinned. He looked at the others, then nodded back into the cave. They filed back to their places in the circle around the altar, then resumed their seats.

"This," said Hosea, "will not be easy. Fortunately, you've already done a lot of this work, much of it apparently in the last week, and some of it yesterday with your wife. That will help, because it's usually best to move quickly while you can. A therapist would drag this process out for thousands of dollars. Since I'm doing it on my own time and not your dollar, I'm going to rush things along as fast as you can handle it. If that's what you want?"

"You sound like you have something in mind."

"I do."

"Am I your guinea pig?"

Hosea laughed. "Goodness, no. I've done this with dozens of others, mostly hogmen, but a couple of students as well. I've developed a bit of a knack for it, if I do say so myself. And besides, I have a hunch that your case will prove to be relatively standard."

"No rare psychosis?"

"I doubt it. But we'll see."

Jade grinned. "I assume that you have malpractice insurance?"

"No way. If I screw you up, then you'll have to take your complaints to God, not to my estate. I keep myself broke enough without having to pay insurance. Poverty is all the protection from lawsuits I'll ever need."

Jade smiled. "Okay, then. What do you have in mind?"

"I'm going to prompt you with a series of questions. Answer them audibly for the group, or internally for yourself alone. If you hang in there, you'll probably find a few answers. If you bail out, then you'll have something to look forward to at some future date."

"Sounds easy."

"It's not."

"Why not?"

"You think too much."

Jade shook his head. "Remind me, why are we doing this again?"

"Because," grinned Hosea, "you said that you wanted to do some soul searching. Because you figure that there are important reasons why you prefer fantasizing about one of your employees instead of seducing virgins or rolling the dice in Reno. Because you fear that there is some significance in the fact that you prefer the abstraction of daydreaming over the tangible pleasures of escaping into politics or whiskey. Because you are curious about why you bite your tongue instead of bending over to touch your naked knees while some stranger drops his pants and. . . ."

"Oh, yeah. Now I remember."

"Are you ready?"

"Yes."

"Again, it's up to you how far we go." Hosea took a deep breath. "Okay. First question: What day is it?"

"Saturday."

"Where are you today?"

"The Dakota Ridge Hogback."

"Are you married?"

"Yes."

"Do you have children."

"Yes. Two. Mark and Carla."

"Do you go to church?"

"Yes."

"Do you believe in God."

"Yes. Almost always."

"Have you ever heard or seen God?"

"I'm not sure."

"Where do you live?"

"Lakewood, Colorado."

"Where else?"

"What do you mean?"

"What do you think I mean? Just answer the questions. If you can't handle a particular question, then nod and I'll move on. The less that we debate the questions and the quicker we move, the better this will work. Do you want me to continue?"

"Yes."

"Again. Where else do you live, besides in Colorado?"

Jade thought for a moment. "In Michigan. In Lansing. In Grand Rapids. In lots of places."

"Where did you grow up?"

"In Grand Haven, Michigan. In a shabby little bungalow with two brothers and my mom."

"Where is your father?"

"Dead."

"Where dead? Back in Grand Haven?"

"Somewhere in Denver. In a stolen Frosted Flakes box."

Chips and Geek laughed. Jade grinned.

"Really," said Jade. "That was something that I was going to ask your advice about. My dad died recently, and he was cremated. My mom sent me Harry's ashes in the mail. She packaged Harry in a Frosted Flakes box. But I lost the. . . ."

"Why do you call your father Harry?"

"That was his name."

"What else? Why does a son call his father Harry?"

"Maybe a son calls his dad that because they're good friends. Maybe they're buddies."

"Was Harry your buddy?"

"No. Not even close."

"Why do you call your father Harry?"

"I . . . because . . . I want to dishonor him. The man doesn't deserve the title of dad. Or father."

"Why not?"

"Because he left his family."

"Why did Harry leave his family?"

"Because my mother threw him out."

"Why?"

"Because he was fooling around. I caught him myself, in the bathroom screwing a customer. What kind of man would. . . ."

"I'll ask the questions."

Hosea shifted. Leaned toward Jade. "What kind of man would screw a customer in the bathroom?"

Jade hesitated. "A weak man. A dirty animal. A pig."

"Why would a man screw a customer in the bathroom?"

"Because he didn't have any self control."

"Go deeper. Why would a man risk everything to screw a customer in the bathroom?"

"Because he was horny. Because the woman turned him on."

"Go deeper. Why else?"

Jade stroked his chin. "Because he wasn't getting enough sex from his wife. Because he wanted to hurt his wife. Because he wanted to get caught."

"Why would a man want to get caught?"

"To hurt his wife? To end the relationship?"

"I'll ask the questions. You bluff. Quickly. Off the top of your head. Why would Harry want to get caught?"

"To end it."

"To end what?"

"I don't know."

"Try again. To end what?"

"The lies. The secrets. The marriage. The misery."

"Okay." Hosea took a deep breath. "Are you married?"

"Yes."

"Why?"

"Because I fell in love. Because I wanted a family. Because people are supposed to get married."

"Why else?"

"So that I could have a friend who would always be there. So that I could have sex."

"Why do you have to be married to have sex?"

"You don't have to. But you should."

"I should?" asked Hosea.

"I'm not sure."

"Then who should?"

"I should. I should be married to have sex."

"Why?"

"Because that's what the Bible says. Because that's what good people do."

"Are you a good person?"

Jade faltered. He opened his eyes. He couldn't remember having closed them. He looked around the small circle. They leaned toward him, waiting.

"I'm not sure," said Jade. "In some ways, I'm good. In other ways, I'm not so good."

"How are you bad?"

"I fudge a little with the sales figures at work. I fudge a little more on my taxes. I should spend more time with my family. I sometimes think about leaving my wife and kids. I sometimes. . . ."

"Sexually? Are you ever bad in terms of sexual thoughts or behaviors?"

"Yes."

"Don't chicken out. We've heard it all. Remember, Geek is

one of our favorites up here. Tell us, tell me. What do you do that is bad in terms of sex?"

Jade hesitated. They were listening closely. He looked at Padre, the man who had slept with a half a dozen women in his church. He looked at Geek, who. . . .

Jade closed his eyes.

"I sometimes download dirty pictures from the internet. I like to play the nude scenes from videos on slow motion when my wife and kids are out of the house. And I fantasize about a woman at work."

"You fantasize?"

"I picture her, Chris, naked. I imagine that we're having sex. . . ."

"And?"

"And then I masturbate."

"Does it feel good?"

"Yes and no."

"How no?"

"It makes me feel guilty."

"Why?"

"Because it's not good to masturbate."

"Why?"

"Because it's wrong."

"Wrong?"

"It's a sin."

"Who says that masturbation is a sin?"

"The Bible."

"Where in the Bible?"

"I'm not sure."

"Did Jesus say that? Have you ever read in the Bible that Jesus condemned those who masturbated?"

"I'm not sure. I don't think so."

"But having sex with a real woman other than your wife is wrong?"

"For me, yes."

"Have you ever heard one of your buddies brag about getting laid after a date?"

"Yes. Lots of times. Especially when I was younger."

"Did you ever hear a buddy brag about going home and having a good time masturbating after a date?"

Jade laughed. "Of course not."

"How about you, Dutch? Did you ever masturbate when you got home after a date? Did you ever jerk off because you were ready to explode because you hadn't allowed yourself to go all of the way with a girl?"

"Yes."

"But you didn't brag about it later?"

He shook his head. "Are you kidding?"

"Why not? By your own definition, having sex outside of a marriage is unbiblical, and masturbating is not."

Hosea leaned forward. "Dutch, you're a good Bible-believing sort of guy. Why is it acceptable for a guy to brag about sinning with a woman, but unacceptable for a guy to speak about making himself feel good when no one else is involved?"

He had never thought of that. The concept was bizarre.

"I'm not sure," he said.

"Not sure of what?"

"Why guys can talk so freely about the one, but not at all about the other."

"Make a guess. Why is it so hard for people to talk about masturbation?"

"Because it seems dirty. Maybe it has something to do with the way that our parents treated us when we touched ourselves when we were little."

"That's your parents. What about your culture?"

"The culture says that sex is great. The media is full of it. Most of the books that I handle rely on sex to sell."

"And masturbation?"

"Hardly a word."

"Why?"

"I don't know. Maybe our culture respects the fact that it's too personal to exploit."

"Dutch, are you talking about the same culture that I am? The same culture that produces movies suggesting that a handsome man and an attractive woman are required by some unwritten Hollywood law to have sex simply because they find themselves together in the same room? Are you saying that this culture thinks that anything is too dirty to mention?"

"I'm not sure."

"Think about it."

"Hosea, are you saying that the media should give equal time to masturbation?"

Hosea laughed. "Not at all. But I want you to see something else, something about yourself."

"What?"

"About what a good man like you is up against when he tries to be good in this crazy world of ours, where the messages that we get from around us are so convoluted that. . . ."

Padre cleared his throat. "Uh, Hosea?"

Hosea laughed. "Thanks, Padre. You're right, no sermons. But Jade tricked me. He started asking me the questions again."

Padre smiled. "You're welcome."

"Back to you, Jade," said Hosea. "Where do you work?"

"Seinner Books. Two locations. One downtown, another at Westwood Mall."

Hosea paused.

"Tell me about Chris. Is that her name?"

"Yes."

"Whose name?"

Jade hesitated, confused.

"Whose name?" pressed Hosea.

"The name of the woman that I think about."

"Tell me again, using her name."

Jade sighed.

"Chris is the name of the woman that I think about."

"Is she pretty?"

"Very."

"What kind of body?"

"Terrific."

Geek snickered.

"Nice breasts?" asked Hosea.

"Very nice."

"Very large?"

"No. Just full. Perfect."

"And her pussy?"

Jade recoiled.

"And her cunt?"

Jade shrugged.

"You don't care about her cunt?"

"I'm not sure. I haven't really thought about it much."

"But you have thought about her breasts. Why is it that you can talk about her breasts but not her cunt? Her vagina? Her clitoris?"

Jade shook his head. "Who cares about that? That's not what I think about. I imagine what it would feel like to be inside of her, but I don't picture what her slit would look like."

"Why not?"

"I'm not sure."

"You can think and talk about her top, but not her bottom?"

"I guess."

"You don't want to talk about her pussy?"

"Correct."

"Why not?"

Jade lowered his head into his hands.

"It's dirty," he whispered. "That part is dirty."

"How many women have you slept with?"

"One. Just Alice. My wife."

"A strong football stud like you? I'll bet that you could have slept with lots of girls. Why only one?"

"Like I said a while ago, I made a vow with God."

"Why the vow? Tell me again about the vow."

Jade raised his head, then shook it from side to side. "No more, Hosea. That's enough. I've had enough."

"Are you sure?"

"Yes."

Hosea rose. "We've come a long way, Dutch. I hate to stop now. It'll only be harder to start over another time. Who knows, if we don't finish, you may even talk yourself out of ever coming back."

"So be it," Jade whispered. "That's it."

Jade shook his head, then looked up.

Padre stood, then walked to the cave's entrance. The others sat quietly, eyes mostly closed. Jade watched as Padre shuddered and prayed, half in shadows, half in light. At last, he turned.

"Jade," he said. "You need to continue."

"Are you sure?"

Padre returned to his seat. "Yes."

"This is hard."

"What did you expect?"

"Not this."

"Keep going."

Jade lowered his head.

Hosea rustled, then broke the quiet.

"Dutch, could you try just a few more questions?"

Jade glanced around the circle. "Okay," he sighed.

Hosea put his hand on Jade's back. Chips and Padre closed their eyes. Their lips quivered. Geek stared, unblinking.

"Name the one important person in your life," whispered Hosea, "that Chris reminds you of the most."

Jade thought hard. Not his mother. Chris was absolutely nothing like his mother. Not Alice, either. Chris was much less inhibited than Alice, Chris was much more free. Certainly not Karen. Karen.

He thought about it.

Karen and Chris were both attractive. Both free-spirited. Sensuous. They both liked to tease him, to make him blush. They both made him feel alive, virile. Both made themselves available to him. . . .

"Karen," said Jade softly. "Chris reminds me a lot of Karen."

"Okay. Next question. A tough one. Forget Karen and focus on Chris. Lots of women are beautiful, but Chris has seized your imagination. She reminds you of Karen, but there is more to it than that. There has to be. Obsessions are complicated, but they are important. They tell us about ourselves. This is not about Chris, it's about you. If you look hard enough at your Chris, you will see something about yourself. Think hard."

Hosea closed his eyes.

Jade closed his eyes again as well.

"Tell me, Dutch. What is it about Chris that you crave? What does she have that you want, that you wish that you could take into yourself to make yourself more complete? You are restless and Chris has something that you long for. What is it? Think about her. What do you like the most?"

He pictured Chris. She was smiling. She was working in the store. Efficient. Clean. Well dressed. Attractive. A quick sense of humor. Attentive. Intelligent.

He appreciated all of those things, not any one of those things alone. No one thing stood out above the others.

He shook his head.

Hosea sighed.

"Try harder," he prodded. "Think about Chris. Why do you enjoy her so much? Why do you keep going back to her instead of someone else?"

Jade tried again.

Chris was smiling at him. Doing her job very efficiently. Ringing lots of sales. She was turning from the register to smile at him, sexy and inviting, wearing a thin white blouse. Several of her buttons were loose, and he could see into her top. He could see cleavage, could catch a glimpse of the smooth fullness of her breasts rising and falling, cupped in the lacy frill of her bra. She caught him peeking, then smiled. She reached to her breast, then touched herself lightly.

He could feel her breast in the palm of his own right hand. Her breast was soft and full, her nipple hard. She raised her hand to the back of his hand on her breast, then pressed his palm more firmly, drawing his palm and fingers. . . .

Jade bit his tongue.

"What's the matter?" whispered Hosea.

"The whirlpool," said Jade, his eyes still closed. "It's happening again."

"What is happening?"

"I'm feeling myself being sucked into the fantasy. It's a whirlpool that sometimes overwhelms me. I fight it, but I sometimes lose."

"Do you enjoy your fantasies when you lose?"

"Yes. But they're wrong. And they make me feel weak and dirty afterwards. Ashamed. I feel like hell afterwards."

"Are your fantasies more exciting than remembering real sex with your wife?"

"In a way, yes. Most of the time, the fantasies are very exciting. They're everything that I want to have happen. Except for the guilt."

"Dutch, tell me. If Chris became your wife, would it be as good with her in your real-life bedroom as it is in your fantasies?"

"Maybe. I'm not sure. At first, I'll bet it would be as good as I imagine." He paused. "It might be that good for a couple of nights."

"How often do you think real sex would be as good with the real Chris as it is right now with your fantasy Chris?"

Jade hesitated, confused. "What?"

"In real life, how often would Chris be as good as like you imagine?"

"I'm not sure. I guess the real Chris would have a hard time measuring up to the one in my head."

"Measuring up?"

"You know, always performing to please me. Being ready every minute at the drop of a hat. Always wanting to have sex no matter what. Doing stupid things to please me."

"Can you see, Dutch, that in one sense, your issues are not about the real Chris at all?"

"Then what are my issues about?"

"You tell me, Dutch. What do you think that you're real issues are all about?"

"I have no idea."

"Do you want to know?"

"Yes."

"Then let's ask Chris. The imaginary Chris that you create in your mind. The one that answers all of your desires and wants. Your answers will rest with her, if you want them. Shall we face her . . . together?"

"I guess."

"Then let her come to you, Dutch. Don't fight her. Don't be afraid of her. Let her into your mind."

Jade shifted uneasily. "Right now, Hosea?"

"Yes. Picture her. Can you see her?"

Jade tried. She started to appear, then faded. He squeezed his eyes. He imagined her rising from a beach blanket, walking slowly toward him with a smile."

"Can you see her?"

"Yes."

"What is she doing?"

"She's smiling at me."

"What else?"

"She's reaching inside of her bathing suit to touch herself."

"What else?"

"She is encouraging me to touch her."

"So what's the problem?"

"If I touch her, then I'll want more."

"So what? You said that she was pretty."

"If I let myself touch her, then I'll get hard. I'll want to masturbate. Or I'll want to have sex with her."

"Does she know what she's doing to you?"

"Yes."

"How do you know?"

"Because she enjoys watching me squirm. She smiles. She likes to make me blush. She likes to tell sex jokes and to tease me. She helps me to touch her body, even when I don't want to. And she enjoys seeing me get hard for her."

"What kind of woman does that to a man? What kind of woman is Chris, anyway?"

"She's a good woman. Intelligent, efficient, classy. . . ."

"Bullshit. Come on, Dutch. You can do better than that. What kind of woman smiles at a married man while she encourages him to touch her body?"

"A temptress."

"Not good enough. Another word."

"A tease. A nymph. A slut."

"Is Chris a slut?"

"No. She's just a single woman. Maybe she's a little lonely, and maybe she likes me."

"In your fantasies, then. The Chris that drives you crazy, the one that you create. Stick with her. When she teases you, when she takes off her clothes and dares you to look, dares you to touch her, dares you to ram yourself deep inside of her when she spreads her legs . . . is she a slut then?"

"Yes."

"Can you say it?"

"Say what?"

"Can you tell me what kind of woman Chris is?"

"She's a little on the wild side."

"Let's hear it," said Hosea. "Go ahead. Get mean. We'll never tell. What's she really like?"

"She's a God damned little tease. She's a slut."

"A slut?"

"Yes."

"Dutch, tell me. I need to know. What exactly is a slut?"

"It's a woman who is loose."

"What does that mean? What does a loose woman do?"

"She runs around like a camel in heat."

Jade heard snickers. His eyes remained closed.

"What else?" asked Hosea. "What else does a slut do?"

"She dresses provocatively. She walks and talks dirty. A slut is a woman who screws practically anyone she likes."

"Anyone?"

"If she wants to. If she feels like it."

"What is a slut like in bed?"

"She goes nuts. She has orgasm after orgasm."

"How is that possible?"

"It just is. It's the way she's wired. She loves sex. She tries anything and everything, and she likes it all."

"What else? What else does a slut do in bed."

"Anything that she wants to.

"Does she make noises?"

"She laughs. And she giggles."

"Why?"

"Because she's having fun. Because it feels good. Because she's uninhibited."

"Is that it? She just laughs and giggles?"

"She also moans and groans. Sometimes she screams."

"What does she scream?"

"She just screams. Out of pleasure. Like an animal."

"Listen to her, Dutch. What is she screaming?"

"I'm not sure."

"Listen to her. What is she screaming?"

"She's screaming the word fuck."

"That's it?"

"No. She's screaming, fuck me."

"And then she stops?"

"No. She keeps screaming."

"Screaming what?'

"She screams fuck me, Jimmy."

"What else?"

"Fuck me harder, Jimmy, harder! Fuck me, Jimmy, please!"

Jade buried his face in his hands.

The cave grew quiet.

"Dutch," said Hosea. "Listen to me. We're almost there. The slut. Do you hate her?"

Jade opened his eyes. His head was still drooped within his hands, and his eyes stared into the black of the altar.

"Do you hate her, the slut?" Hosea prodded.

"I don't know. Maybe."

"Do you love her? Jade, do you love the slut, even a little bit?"

"I'm not sure. I must like her a little. I keep going back to her."

"How would you like it, Dutch, if you could trade places with her? If, just for one night, you could be the slut? Maybe not a woman slut, but just like her? Would you like that?"

Jade thought about it. He tried to imagine such a thing. Tried to picture himself talking and dressing without inhibition. Teasing women with jokes and flattery. Having sex with any woman that caught his eye. Not feeling guilty about anything. Seeing a beautiful woman and just doing it. Reaching out and grabbing her breast. . . .

Jade felt the whirlpool approaching.

But a slut wouldn't worry about whirlpools.

That would be nice.

He could grab that breast and not feel guilty. He could grab it from behind, he could cup it in his hand, could cup both breasts in both hands, could. . . .

No!

Harry had tried that.

Harry had been a slut.

Jade would not be like that. He could not be like that. He was different. He was better than Harry.

Jade became aware of the others standing around him. Their hands were on his shoulders and head, and they were praying. He felt himself cold with sweat. He looked up. Even Geek was praying.

He sighed deeply, then closed his eyes.

For one night, it would be wonderful to be a slut. He could go crazy. He could sleep with anyone and it wouldn't matter. He would do Chris first. Then that silly air head Nancy at the downtown store. Then some blonde that he would pick up at a bar. He would go crazy. Like an animal. It would be great.

He wished that he could be an animal.

If only for one night.

An animal.

He opened his eyes and stared into the dark abyss of the altar. Beneath the hole, deep within the mountain, were the fossils of thousands of animals stretching back millions of years. Animals that rutted and bred. Animals that kicked up dust and bore offspring, then raised their young and died.

Jade lifted his head. The hogmen were still around him, lips silently trembling in prayer.

He looked at their legs. He looked at their shoes and at their laces. Good laces, no knots or frays. But no one was laughing, and the knees stayed back.

Hosea broke the silence.

"How would you like to be a slut, Dutch? Just for one night?"

"I would," he sighed. "But then I would hate myself for the rest of my life. Alice would be hurt, deeply. It would probably cost me my marriage. I might get diseases, AIDS even. It would not be worth the price."

"I'm not telling you to become a slut," said Hosea. "You're right. Such a thing could destroy you. But until you come to terms with her, you're vulnerable. Because she's within the reach of your fingertips, within a slip of your thoughts. And you want her terribly bad."

"I want her?"

"You tell me."

Jade thought. Yes, he wanted her. He ached for her. He created her and slept with her every chance he could, even when he knew that he would awaken later in hell.

"What do I do?" asked Jade.

"First, you pray."

"I've tried that. God hasn't helped me at all. She wouldn't stay away. She keeps coming back. . . ."

"Wrong prayer. Try a new one, Dutch."

"What should I pray?"

"Pray that you may have the heart of Christ."

"I don't understand."

"Palestine was full of sluts and whores. And Christ loved every one of them. And Christ still loves the sluts of this world today. The Bible says that it is a sin to hate sluts. Or to judge them."

Hosea squeezed Jade's shoulder.

"You need to love that little slut that is inside of you. You need to learn to love that sexual creature as much as Jesus does. Pray to God for the strength and the love of Christ, because you're going to need it if you're ever going to accept her as she is."

"I can't accept her. I want her, but she's bad. She has to stay away from me, or at least to change. . . ."

"When did Jesus love the sluts of his day? Before or after they joined their local choirs?"

"Before. He talked with them on the streets between customers, but then he. . . ."

"Have you talked with the slut that's inside of you, Dutch? Or have you simply screwed her like she was a chunk of meat, then condemned her to hell? Have you been stoning the poor creature to death on the steps of the temple, without so much as asking her name?"

Jade tried to think. Hosea's metaphors were becoming confusing.

"Hosea, are you saying that I should talk with Chris Teller? That I should learn to love her?"

"No. This is not about Chris Teller. It's about you. This is about the slut that's inside of you, the one that your mind keeps creating and trying to embrace. About the sexual animal within you that wants to scream 'fuck me' to a thousand different women in a single night."

Hosea sighed. "You don't seem to know that side of yourself very well. That's where it gets its power. From its mystery, and from your fear. When the slut shows up, you go ballistic. You blush, your heart races and you feel the sort of rush that makes the real world seem dull by comparison. For you, she's the ultimate mind-boggling, mood-altering drug. It's no wonder you keep going back to her. Who wouldn't?"

Hosea sighed. "But the better you get to know her, the less power she will have to charm you out of your pants. And the more power you will have to resist her. Not out of fear or out of shame, but out of the strength of understanding, and out of the power of God's love."

Hosea took a deep breath. "You have a choice, Dutch."

"What's that? What choice?" asked Jade.

"It's about that mysterious and powerful slut."

"Yes?"

"Do you want her to rule your life? Do you want her to be your obsession, a goddess inside of you? Your refuge when you feel the need to escape from the chaos of life? Or do you want her to step down, for her to assume a place to one side?"

Jade thought. The answer seemed too obvious.

"I want," he said, "for her to get out of my life altogether."

"Not possible," said Hosea. "You can't just send her away."

"I have to."

"You can't. But you can talk to her. You can get to know her so that she will lose much of her power to control you. If you can grow to love her. . . ."

Jade shook his head. "But she's no good, Hosea. She's not even human. She's an animal."

"Look at me," demanded Hosea.

The others stepped back, watching. Jade met Hosea's eyes.

"You're an animal, Dutch. A pig." He smiled. "Just like the rest of us. We're a fraternity of hogmen and you're a member. You'd better accept it, or else don't bother to come back here ever again. Skin color, suit coats, ties, college educations, Bibles, or not. We're all hog-men. Me. You. Geek, Chips, and Padre. And those who are not here. Bankers, plumbers, lawyers, brick layers. Our brothers. Your father. My father. Our father's fathers. All the way back to the beginning of time."

Hosea's words stung.

They pained him with their truth.

Jade looked up through eyes that began to blur.

"Pigs," Jade whispered, "are bad, Hosea. We've got to do better than that. And we can do better, if we really try."

"You haven't been listening." Hosea shook his head. "Who made the pigs, Jimmy? Don't answer. Just think about it. Who made the pigs?"

God made the pigs.

"And who," asked Hosea, "loves pigs? Who is it that knows them better than anyone, and yet loves them all the same and accepts them just the way that he made them?"

Hosea's voice grew firm. "And who made Harry, Dutch? Who made your father, animal that he was?"

"God made him," protested Jade, "but Harry screwed up big time. I'm sure that God did not accept the fact that. . . ."

"And how about you, Mr. Perfect? How are you doing in the realm of righteousness? Are you measuring up to God's standards on a daily basis?"

"No, but. . . ."

"Let God and Harry worry about your father's mistakes, terrible as they may have been. You worry about your own."

"Yes, but. . . ."

"Do you have the heart of Christ?"

"I'm not sure. Probably not. But. . . ."

"Concentrate on that, Dutch. Put all of your judging, all of your self-condemnation, and all of your self abuse on hold. Go back to that retched puke of yours in a few weeks if you still want to be that kind of dog that can't resist its own vomit. But for now, try praying a new prayer. Try focusing on something worthwhile, something positive with power behind it. Immerse yourself in a new mystery. Try praying for the heart of Christ."

Hosea smiled. "Can you do that?"

"I'm not sure."

"Fair enough. But think about it, okay? Regardless of what you feel about Harry, sluts, or pigs, try praying for the divine gift of a loving heart. Concentrate on that for a while, and then see what happens. You've got nothing to lose, right?"

"I'm not so sure."

Geek laughed.

"Good answer," grinned Chips. "Good answer."

They left the cave one by one until only Hosea and Jade remained.

"Thanks for sticking around," said Jade.

"No problem. I figured that we might have a little more talking to do."

"Yeah. The whole experience was pretty intense. A gut-wrencher."

"I'm glad you thought so." Hosea smiled.

"That was the strangest interview in my life. Nothing comes close. You badgering me with those questions, me squirming in a pool of sweat. You guys praying over me while I talked about masturbation and thought about sex. A perfect finale for a week from hell."

"Don't say that," said Hosea.

"Say what?"

"That's the last time that I'm going to let you get away with calling this a week from hell."

"But it was. You have no idea. . . ."

"Stop right there." Hosea sounded angry. "Listen, Jade. You've been enjoying a seat at the center of the universe for over an hour. Everybody's attention, and everybody's patience. Now it's time to grow up a little, to assume your place a bit further out on the edge. God sits at the center. He's the King. You're a servant. He loves you, but you're not God."

Jade stepped back.

"I know," he said meekly, "that I'm not God."

"Then where do you get off calling the past seven days a week from hell?"

"It was a figure of speech. I only meant to say. . . ."

"Did you ever stop to wonder," asked Hosea, "why I didn't have any bottles to smash today? Why I brought so many bottles last week—enough to catch your ear I might add—but not a single one today?"

"No. I hadn't really thought about it."

"Of course not. All that you've had time for was to think about yourself. I suspect that you seldom have time for anything else. The answer to the question about my bottles is that two weeks ago, I had my week from hell. Only I don't put it that way."

Jade cringed. What was Hosea saying, accusing him of always thinking only of himself? What a mean-spirited thing to throw into. . . .

Hosea stomped back to the altar and slumped to the cave floor.

"Two weeks ago, things went to hell in my life. It was the worst time that I'd had in three years. Phone calls from my screwed up wife, stories from the newspaper that I couldn't shake from my head, feelings of inadequacy and fear. I got so discouraged that I stopped by the liquor store. Just one bottle, I told myself. Just one."

Jade stared.

"Well, you know how these things go. Instead of biting my tongue, like you do, I punished myself for the booze by going out and finding another bottle. Once I'd gotten nice and drunk, I started raging. At myself, and at God. 'Why Lord,' I screamed, 'Why are you doing this to me?'"

"The next thing I knew it was Saturday, and I was up here at the altar calling in another hogman with the sound of my tears and breaking glass. I'd had a vision that there would be an important response to my sacrifice, but little did I suspect that I'd be shattering bottles for you. But there you were."

Jade approached Hosea at the altar, then sank to the cold rock opposite him.

Hosea relaxed, then grinned.

"No empties this week," he said, "because I had something better to do for the past week. Something more constructive on my mind."

"Like what?" asked Jade.

"Like praying for you, Dutch." He smiled. "And for the heart of Christ. I'd like to believe that in my very small way, through my prayers and my concern, that I was somehow a part of what you now snivel about as a week from hell."

Jade was quiet.

"I figured," said Hosea, "that you were having a rough week. Especially the past few days. I kept getting images of you crying and hurting yourself. I was praying for you all week, and that's why I was so glad when you showed up this morning. That's when I knew that you were going to be okay."

"If you knew," asked Jade, "that my week was so rough, then why are you giving me a hard time for calling it a week from hell?"

"From hell?" Hosea shook his head. "Come on, Jade. Do you really think that this past week was the brainchild of someone from that side of the battle? Are you going to insult me by suggesting that I drank all of that liquor a couple of weeks ago just so that you could come up here to tell me that I'm in league with the devil?"

Jade furrowed his brow. "Are you saying that God set this whole thing up, starting two weeks ago with you drinking. . . ."

"I'm not saying anything. You make sense of your reality anyway you want to. I'll do the same for mine. But if you leave this mountain today with a couple of new insights and a worthwhile prayer in your heart, then maybe you should be a little bit more careful about who you give credit for what it was that got you here."

Jade shook his head. "I'm not sure that I buy your perspective."

"It's not for sale. You've got to want it, and then it's free. In my experience, that's how God works. Like earthquakes and plate tectonics. Pressure builds, rocks squeeze," Hosea made two fists and pressed the knuckles of each hand against the other, "then suddenly an earthquake, and up heaves a whole new level."

He jerked his right knuckles up, then held his fists together like a porch step.

"In my humble experience, God moves powerfully throughout my life, but I mostly notice it when His earthquakes hit." Hosea dropped his fists. "In your experience . . . well, you decide."

"So you're saying that this past week was an earthquake? That it wasn't from hell, but from God?"

"You decide. It's your life, not mine."

"Do all of the hogmen look at life the same way as you?"

"Jade," said Hosea, his voice not altogether kind, "you're a big boy. Act like it. There's a limit to how much of this I can do for you. Most of the time, I've got my hands full just making ends meet and taking care of my own problems. We're all hogmen, but not all men look at God, or life, the same. As Padre said, some folks would even say I was crazy."

Jade looked down. "I'm sorry, Hosea. The thing is, a little while ago you seemed so strong, bigger than life. As if you were a saint, or an angel, or even the prophet Hosea himself. . . ."

"Enough of that, okay?" Hosea smiled sadly.

"I'm just another guy, okay? Sometimes I'm close to God, and sometimes He uses me in special ways. Other times, things fall apart and I can't find Him anywhere. Then it's my turn to wallow in tears of self pity. A little while ago, I enjoyed the power-rush of asking a clean suburban white boy like you some painful questions that made you feel weak and ready to cry. If God uses that, then great. Maybe next time, you'll get to ask me the questions and I get to squirm, if you feel so led."

"Come on," said Jade. "Are you reversing yourself, telling me that what happened a little while ago was just an ego game of yours? A way to humiliate me so that you could. . . ."

"No," sighed Hosea. He dropped his head shaking into his hands. "You still don't get it, do you?"

He looked up.

"One of the first questions that I asked you," he said, "was whether you had ever seen or heard God. Your answer to that question was critical, and it was destined to determine whether or not we continued."

"Why?"

"Because if you said yes, and you really believed that you had seen or heard God beyond a shadow of doubt, then I would have had to turn the interview over to you. After all, how could I, a man of clay feet in leather moccasins, presume to help someone who believed that they pulled off what Moses himself feared would cause his death? A clear view of God would kill most of us mere mortals."

Jade protested. "But lots of people claim to have visions, or to hear God talking to them. You've talked about visions yourself. Even in my life, there have been a few times when I felt certain that God was there, helping me through. . . ."

"Of course. Me, too. Some of my best moments have come at those times when God seemed at my side, or even inside of my head or gut. And I believe those moments were real, that they were of God. In fact, I'm building my life around those moments and those beliefs. In faith, though. Not in certainty. At least not a certainty of the sort that some people can accept."

"What are you saying, Hosea?"

"I'm saying that your past week may or may not have been the work of God. You decide. Your father's ashes, or your talk with your wife, or even our little discussion about the sexual beast inside you, any or all of that may or may not have come to you this week as a gift from God. You decide."

"But you think it was?"

"In my heart, I believe that God has been very busy with you lately. But how should I know? Some people would cringe to hear me say it, but I've never seen a miracle that did not require faith. When Moses lifted his staff and the sea parted for the Hebrews, a wind was blowing at the time. The Bible says so. If I was an Egyptian survivor, I would have bitched to the widows back home about them damn lucky Jews. If I was a Hebrew slave, I would have praised the hand of God. Same event, two different interpretations. One physical, one spiritual. One based upon admittedly limited data, the other based upon powerful, life-altering internal convictions."

"But I know of people," said Jade, "who claim more certainty than that. They claim to have evidence stronger than mere internal conviction. There are people who talk about special healings and visions that have no logical explanations in this world, things that could not be anything other than special acts of God."

"It's all special acts of God," said Hosea. "God rules."

"Yes, but I'm talking about special, special acts.

"And that's great. Praise the Lord. I'm not in the debunking business, and I would slit my wrists faster than Geek if I ever had to be. It's just that I've never actually seen one of those sorts miracles first hand. I believe they're possible. I've even prayed for them. But that's not what God has given me so far in life. All that I ever get is a remarkable wind once in a while that miraculously parts the water at the exact place and the exact moment that saves my ass. I guess that's all the miracle I need. And on a good day, I whisper back to God what God whispers to me."

"Good enough?"

"Yes, Jade. Good enough."

"But those remarkable winds could be lucky coincidences?"

"No. They're divine miracles. Acts of God."

"But you said. . . ." Jade hesitated.

"Jade, do this for yourself, okay? Accept the fact that God is busy in your life right now. I believe He is, and I suspect that you do, too. Then pray the prayer that I told you about a while ago. Pray for the heart of Christ. Stop focusing on yourself, and start praying for the vision and the strength to focus on others. That's what God will do for you, if He chooses to give you the heart of Christ. He'll help you to focus on others. That's what love is all about. That's the sort of prayer that will keep your molars off your tongue for a while, and it might even bring a little joy and meaning into your life."

"A prayer?"

"Not just any prayer. The big one. Not just for yourself and what you want or need, but for whatever God sets before you."

"What if I have another week from. . . . I mean, what if I have another rough week? Is there any way that I can get ahold of you?"

"Here." Hosea reached into his pocket. He pulled out a sheet of paper folded into quarters. "Take this."

"What is it?"

"It's a phone list. A hogmen crisis line."

Jade took the sheet and scanned the names and numbers. There were almost 30 men listed in all, Hosea's among them.

"Are these all friends of yours?" asked Jade. "All guys who come up here on a regular basis?"

"Yes and no. Names come and go from the list. I update it once or twice a year. There were 12 names on the list when it was first handed to me many years ago. Some of these names belong to guys I've never met. I've called them and they're legit. But I've never shaken their hands. Maybe they're in hospital beds, or maybe they have found other groups that better fit their needs. But every name on there stands for someone who is ready to talk with, or pray for a fellow hogman."

"You mentioned other groups. What other groups?"

Hosea laughed. "We're all hogmen, Jade. How many times do I have to tell you? Lone Ranger hogmen don't last. They end up as barbecue, like Geek almost did. With or without this cave, men are getting together like this everywhere. Talking, praying, confessing, holding each other accountable. It's going on all over the place. Before board meetings. After football games. Sunday nights in church basements. Even Friday nights in fern bars."

Jade shook his head. "It's hard for me to imagine myself talking about sexual hang-ups in a church basement or a fern bar."

"That," laughed Hosea, "is probably why God led you to this cave. He must have figured that you'd need a little privacy and a womb-like ambiance to loosen up." He slapped his hand against the cold rock floor and laughed again. "But you figure it out. Maybe it wasn't God that led you up here at all. Maybe God doesn't listen to you, doesn't know you, doesn't answer your prayers. Maybe this past week was all one big string of upsetting coincidences. . . ."

"Okay," Jade grinned. "I get the message."

They met eyes and smiled.

"One more thing," said Hosea. "You know the cliché about coming down from the mountain top?"

"Yes."

"Well, sooner or later, it'll hit you. You've had a good time up here today, but the truth is, it'll be a lot harder than you remember once you leave here. It'll be especially hard to talk. Other folks won't understand what you've experienced, and the exhausting realities of every-day life will catch up with you all too soon."

Hosea nodded sadly. "And your fantasy Chris, she'll be back. I meant it when I said that she's going to be someone that you'll need to learn to talk with and love. Chances are good that some version of her will be hanging around off and on for the rest of your life."

"What should I do the next time she shows up? Or if I get lost in some valley at the bottom of the mountain?"

"Use the phone tree if you have to. Or come back to the altar by yourself. Bring a good sacrifice that will help you focus and sort things out. Talk to your wife if you can. The next time that we get together, maybe we can brainstorm a few additional strategies."

Hosea massaged his forehead.

"But whatever you do, first you should pray."

Hosea sniffed. "Don't underestimate that prayer. The heart of Christ is not a weak thing. Don't discount how far that will get you. Christ dumped over the tables of money changers in the temple, even though he knew such an act would be the last excuse the authorities needed to nail him. Christ has got a lot of guts."

Hosea's hand returned to his lap. "But the heart of Christ is also a gentle thing. When your fantasy Chris comes, sit with her for a moment and don't panic. Tell her that you love her, but that you already have a wife. That you would like to embrace her, but that you're not going to sleep with her. Tell her that you have other people that you must love besides just you and her."

"What other people?"

"You tell me."

Jade was silent. He thought of Alice.

He thought of Mark and Carla. Of the real Chris who he must face on Monday. Of Nancy at the downtown store. He was sometimes abrupt with Nancy, and several of his other employees for that matter. He thought of fellow hogmen, other faces, customers, friends, family.

Even the dead.

"I guess," he sighed, "there will be no shortage of people to love."

Hosea grinned. "Probably not."

"So," he asked, "I just pray this prayer every night before I go to sleep?"

"Yes. And every morning before you get out of bed. And at every meal before you take your first bite."

"Do I close my eyes when I pray it?"

"Either way. And every meal when you take your last bite. And every time that you catch yourself feeling angry with your wife. And every time you feel the whirlpool building. And every time you look at one of your children. And every time you see a stranger who looks happy. Or every time that you see a stranger who looks sad. And every time you drive past a police station or a hospital. Or whenever you see a housewife disciplining her child, a taxicab that. . . ."

"Whoa," Jade laughed. "You can't be serious? I'd be praying all day!"

"Without ceasing," grinned Hosea.

"Yes, that sounds holy and everything," Jade shook his head, "but how would I get any work done? I've got a job and I'm under a lot of pressure right now. Plus. . . ."

"And every time that you think about your job. Or your finances. It's up to you. You decide. Do you want the heart of Christ, or not?"

"Yes. But this is the real world."

"Christ is plenty aware of what it's like in the real world. He's been there. Done that."

"It's just that I've got a family to take care of and I've got responsibilities. If I start turning into some kind of religious fanatic that's so heavenly minded that he's of no earthly use. . . ."

"Relax, Jade." Hosea grinned. "This scares you, doesn't it? You're a good man. You know a lot more about the heart of Christ than you've let on. You've seen the potential implications of this sort of spirit before, haven't you?"

Jade sighed.

"One step at a time, Jade. Don't rush. Don't panic. Don't substitute a religious obsession for your sexual one. Don't expect huge changes all at once. But do expect small changes. Expect them. A little change here, a little change there. If it goes any faster than that, call me. Too much too fast could be a sign of trouble, and we'd need to talk."

Jade scratched his neck and shook his head. "This is weird," he sighed.

"Then don't do it," smiled Hosea. "Leave your life alone. Leave it exactly the way it is. Don't change a thing. Leave your relationships with yourself, your world and your God intact as they stand. Don't change your point of view. And whatever you do, don't change your heart."

Jade stared into the altar pit.

"Is it worth it, Hosea?" he sighed. "Tell me straight. No bullshit."

"I think so." Hosea closed his eyes. "Don't pray for the heart of

Christ because you think that's the 'right' thing to do. But pray because you realize that any other kind of heart produces a second rate soul, and because you want the best. Because you want the heart that you were meant to have before you were ever born."

Hosea opened his eyes. "Yes, it's worth it, Jade. Your life may not get any easier, and you'll probably start crying more than you have in years. But some of those tears will be tears of joy, I promise you."

He smiled. "When was the last time you spilled a bucket of those kinds of tears, Jade?"

Hosea stood, then stepped around the altar and stretched a hand down to help Jade to his feet. He took Jade's shoulders in his hands and looked up into his eyes from arm's length.

"Jade, that breed of joy is worth it. And you ain't lived until you've had that kind of cry."

"And what," Jade asked, "do I stand to lose in all of this?"

"Good question," grinned Hosea. "Good question."

CHAPTER 31

Jade prayed for the heart of Christ.

On his way down from the hogback, he rode more slowly than usual. He hardly noticed the difference, didn't think about it really, just hit the ruts more sanely, considered his life more deeply, shook his head and continued praying for the heart of Christ.

He discovered Alice at home reading on the couch. She glanced at him as he walked through the door. She appeared small, worried, even frightened. He sat beside her and they talked for a long time. He shared with her the drama of that morning in the cave.

He told her about the interview, of Hosea's questions and of his responses. Of his insights. Of the slut inside of him that Hosea challenged him to love. They wept together as he relived his confessions about the whirlpool and what it might mean that Jesus had loved the prostitutes of Palestine.

Alice could understand only parts of what he said.

But she listened.

He told her of the prayer that Hosea suggested, and she nodded that it sounded good.

They tried it together, holding hands, praying like they had not prayed in years.

Alice, too, prayed for the heart of Christ.

That night, they made love.

Their lovemaking was awkward, but sincere. They talked afterwards, discussing hurdles still blocking their way, of problems still far from being solved.

Jade fell asleep in prayer.

Sunday morning, Jade woke early.

Alice stirred beside him, stretched her hand to his arm, then drifted back to sleep. Jade studied her sleep-wrinkled face on the pillow only inches away.

He felt himself drifting into prayer.

Thank you, God, for this woman.

Please give me the heart of Christ.

Help me to rebuild this home.

Give me the heart of Christ.

Use me this day as you will.

The heart of Christ.

Make me an instrument.

The heart of Christ.

My children.

The heart of Christ.

My job.

The heart. . . .

Mark lumbered in late for breakfast.

Alice shelved the last of the cereal boxes as Mark slumped into his chair and scratched his jaw.

One ear glittered with a diamond.

Jade winced.

"It's Sunday," said Jade. "The sun was up early. The church will be packed."

"So?" Mark shrugged. "Are you worried about there not being enough room in the pews? Because if you are, I'd be happy to stay home."

"We'll find seats," said Jade. "Probably the front row. That way you can show off your new earring to the entire congregation while we march up behind the choir during the processional."

"Fine," said Mark. "I hope that the entire congregation likes it. They should. It wasn't cheap."

"How much?"

"I don't remember."

"You don't remember?"

Mark scratched the other side of his jaw. "Hang on there a second, dad." He rose and started to leave the table. "Since you're so worried, I'll go dig out the receipt."

Jade squeezed his eyes.

The heart of Christ.

He prayed it again.

The heart of Christ.

"That's okay," said Jade. "Forget it. I was just wondering. I see those sorts of earrings in the store all the time, and I was just curious about what a nice one like yours might cost."

Mark stopped. He turned back, puzzled.

"Are you going to let me wear it?" he asked. "To church?"

"It's up to you, Mark. It's your image, not mine. I wouldn't wear one to church myself. But then, I'm not 16, either. You decide."

Jade stood, lifted his cereal bowl, then placed it in the sink.

"Well," he added, "for those of you who'd care to join me, I'd like to leave for church in five minutes. If you need more time than that, then you'll have to find your own ride. Or maybe you'll just have to stay home. As they say, you can lead a horse to water, but if he's not thirsty, why bother?"

He smiled briefly.

Jade rinsed his hands, dried them, then stepped around his son. He walked through the stares of his family toward his jacket draped over a chair in the next room.

Mark looked at Carla, then shrugged.

"One more thing," said Jade.

He turned to face them.

"Things are going to be a little weird around here for a while. Your mother and I will be working pretty hard for the next few weeks to figure out a plan to stay in Denver. If you kids don't mind too much, we would like to drop you two off back here after church. We'd like to drive up to the mountains for lunch together by ourselves this afternoon, just so that we can concentrate better while thinking through our options."

Jade grinned at Carla.

"Does that sound okay with you, Carla?"

"Sure," she grinned back. "I can deal with it."

"And you, Mark? Can you live with a change in plans?"

"Whatever." He shrugged. "Yeah, sure. You two have a good time." He hesitated. "So are you saying that we're not going to move to Portland?"

"Naw." Jade shook his head. "Portland is a dead deal. It seems that I was the only one who wanted to move. I suppose that I could move by myself, but we all know that I'd get lonely up there in no time. It just wouldn't be any fun without you guys around to drive me crazy."

He grinned. "Besides, I hear that they're expecting another big earthquake up there one of these days." Jade laughed. "And who needs an earthquake?"

Mark and Carla shook their heads as Jade disappeared into the other room.

"It seems much warmer this week," said Alice. "Last Sunday, it felt cold enough to sit inside."

Jade lowered his coffee to their table beside the stream.

"Seven days ago," said Jade, "it was still winter. Today, it's the first weekend of spring."

She smiled. "It feels like spring."

"Yes."

Jade gazed overhead at the massive gray branches of ancient cottonwoods. The tips of new shoots were exploding green buds into tiny leaves and the sky was clear and bright.

He looked down into his brown coffee, then up to her eyes.

"Alice," he said. "We've been through a lot since last weekend."

She cradled her coffee in both hands, staring vacantly into a gray wisp of steam. He drew her eyes up to meet his.

"It was last Sunday," he said, "that Mark mentioned that e-mail from Chris."

Her attention dropped back into her cup.

"I hadn't forgotten," she said.

"That's over," he said. "Now that you know what's been going on, I don't want anything like that to ever happen again. And it won't, if I can help it." He looked at her. "If you can help me."

"If I can help you?"

"If we can continue to talk. To keep in touch about what's happening inside of us. You've been wonderful the past few days. I wouldn't have blamed you if you had slammed the door in my face. Instead, you listened. You sat with me and you stroked my head."

Jade touched the last of the bandages on his face.

"And then," he smiled, "last night you kissed me."

She smiled, timidly.

"Thank you," he whispered. "What more could a man hope for? Thank you for loving me," he hesitated, "and thank you for forgiving me."

God, thank you for this woman.

The heart of Christ.

Thank you for her patience.

The heart of Christ.

Help me to love her the way she needs to be loved.

The heart of Christ.

Jade's eyes were filling.

Thank you for the gift of love.

Alice lowered her cup and reached to touch him across the table.

"Thank you, Jade," she whispered, "for talking. For not running away from me. For finding the courage to tell me about what's been going on with you . . . inside and out."

She squeezed his hand. "The funny thing is, as much as all of this has hurt during the past few days," she wet her lips, "as much as this has hurt, it has also felt good. Through everything that has happened, I suddenly feel deeply reconnected with you. I feel like somehow I know you better now than ever before."

Jade sighed. "Yeah, you know me all right. You've got all of the dirt."

"If it's dirt," she smiled, her eyes growing moist, "then why is it that I suddenly feel more attracted to you than I have in years?"

He shook his head. It felt strange to be saying tender things to his wife, and to be hearing her say that she appreciated him. To be talking with so much love in their voices. It had been a long time.

"It's a mystery," he said. "But I guess that life is full of mysteries, huh?"

He removed a handkerchief from his pocket, then pressed it into her palm. The handkerchief was from the monographed set she had given him on his last birthday.

They met eyes, then smiled.

"This won't be easy," he said. "You know that it's going to take a lot of discussing and planning to figure out a way for us to stay in Denver. And for me to reconnect with Mark. We're looking at some changes. We've got some tough choices to make."

"Such as?"

"Well, such as my job. I'm thinking that I'll try to get Seinner to send Chris up to Portland in my place. Maybe I can convince him to hang onto both Denver stores with me still in charge. But I don't know if he'll buy it."

"Do you think that Chris will want to move?"

"In a heartbeat. For that kind of money and opportunity, she'd do anything."

Alice took another sip of coffee.

He waited.

"Jade," she asked at last, "is that taking the easy way out? Sending her away so that you won't have to face her anymore?"

"I'm not sure. Maybe it is. Realistically, though, if I'm not going to take the transfer, then she's as good of a choice as any. She knows the business, she has the right skills and she doesn't have any family to worry about disrupting by the move. What do you think?"

"I'm not sure either. I hate the thought of you continuing to work with her, knowing what I do about, well, you know, the way that you have thought about her in the past and everything. But on the other hand, it seems like you could be taking the easy way out for yourself. Perhaps at her expense?"

Jade laughed, softly. "Don't worry about Chris. If Seinner goes for this, she'll be thrilled. Yes, I owe her an apology, and I dread that conversation tomorrow."

He refilled Alice's cup from the carafe at the end of their table.

"But let's not forget," he said, "that Chris played an important role in this whole mess."

He refilled his own cup, then returned the carafe to its coaster. "Chris is not just an innocent victim. She played a big part in getting the flirting and teasing started, and she's the one who attempted the seducing that night during inventory. She's even the one who sent the first e-mail. I'm not blaming her. Believe me, I'm painfully aware of what has been going on inside me throughout this entire pseudo-affair. But Chris has troubles of her own."

He sipped his coffee, then leaned forward, still holding his cup.

"And, as I said before, I'm sure there is nothing she would like better than getting promoted to Portland."

Alice sighed. "It just seems too convenient, almost too easy."

Jade lowered his cup.

"If you're not sure, then let's give it some more thought. No need to rush. Maybe there is another answer. I'm done playing Lone Ranger." He smiled. "From now on, when it comes to the big decisions, I'll take all of the help and advice I can get."

"And what if Seinner still wants you to go to Portland, even against your will? What if he decides to sell the downtown store anyway? Maybe he's still mad at you for bucking him about the NightLight books, so maybe he'll give you a hard time about your new ideas."

Jade raised an elbow to the table and eased a knuckle to his teeth. He closed his eyes.

"I may have exaggerated a bit when I told you about how I

stood up to Mr. Seinner on the NightLight display. The truth is, I still haven't actually told him that I'm sending it back. I just let the deadline pass without doing anything."

"Passive aggressive after all, eh?" She grinned.

"This time, I guess so."

"So then it's not too late to salvage the situation? You can still assemble the NightLight display tomorrow?" Alice held her breath.

"I could. But I don't plan to."

She sighed.

"I'm still against the books. Perhaps even more so than ever. That's another conversation that I'm dreading on Monday. But I'm going to call him and I'm going to insist that the books are inappropriate for my clientele. That I don't want to. . . ."

Jade hesitated. Thought. Smiled.

"Do you know what?" he said. "I'm just going to call Seinner and tell him the truth. Point blank. I'm going to tell him that I can't move to Portland because it would be bad for my family, and that I'm not going to carry the NightLight books because I don't want to promote what those books represent."

He stroked his chin with his thumb. "I think that I'll also need to tell him that there are a few other books on our shelves that I will no longer be reordering. I may even remind him of his roots, that the Seinner Family Book empire was founded without the help of trash, and that it's kind of a shame that we've come to this. After all, what does it profit a man to gain the world but to lose his own. . . ."

Alice frowned.

"What?"

"Be careful, Jade. Don't compromise your soul, but don't be foolish, either. The Bible is filled with warnings about fools. Ecclesiastes 7:17 comes to mind." She smiled. "I saw it last month on a book marker. 'Be not wicked overmuch, neither be a fool; why should you die before your time?'"

She laughed. "Jade, I'm glad that you've recommitted yourself to good works, but think it through carefully before you say something off the top of your head that is perhaps overly simplistic or self-righteous. And something that would almost certainly cost you your job."

Jade grinned. "Fools rush in where angels fear to tread?"

She smiled. "Something like that."

"You're right. Hosea pretty much said the same thing. He cautioned me that if I prayed constantly for the heart of Christ, I should expect little changes. But he insisted that I should call him up right away if I found myself getting too carried away with big changes."

"Good advice."

"I'm still going to tell Seinner to count me out on Portland and NightLight, though. Of that much, I'm convinced."

"You know that I'm behind you, Jade. It is possible, though, that Seinner will give you an ultimatum. What then?"

Jade fiddled with the handle on his coffee mug. He closed his eyes.

"In that case, I'm not sure what I'll do. I guess that if I have to, I'll find a new job with a different company. There are worse things that could happen than me having to leave Seinner Books."

He opened his eyes.

"It's possible, you know, that by the time the dust all settles, I might be making less money. Who knows, maybe we'll have to make some major changes in our lifestyle. That's probably not a bad idea anyway." He smiled. "But something will work out. I'm sure of it. I can feel it in my heart."

She looked at him, curiously.

"Yes," she said. "I believe that you do. And I believe that you're right."

They were silent for a long time.

Their waitress picked up their carafe and replaced it with a fresh one.

"Alice?" he asked softly.

"Yes?"

"Can you listen just a little bit more? I feel like I need to tell you the rest. One more story. About Karen and about my brother Randy. About the accident that killed them."

She sighed. "I thought that there were things you must have left out. It didn't quite add up. If Karen was your girlfriend, I couldn't figure out what she was doing with your brother and not you in the boat." She met his eyes. "And why you were so angry with him. I knew that something else must have been going on. That you must have had a fight or something, otherwise you would have been in the boat with them. . . ."

"I was there. I was in the boat."

Alice covered her mouth and closed her eyes.

Finally, her eyes opened. "You were there?" She reached over the table and touched his arm. "You were involved in the accident?"

Jade nodded.

He lowered his forehead to the top of her hand where it rested on his arm.

"Yes," he whispered. "I was there."

She placed her other hand on the back of Jade's head as he began to cry, softly, like a child.

CHAPTER 32

Indian Summer, 1975.
Grand Haven, Michigan

"What's the matter, Jim-bo? You gonna be a mama's boy yer whole life, or what?"

Randy smirked.

He took another slug from his beer, then tossed the half-finished can through the window into the weeds along the ditch. He reached into the styrofoam cooler in the back seat of the Ford, then pulled out a fresh one.

"I'm not a mama's boy," said Jim. He squeezed the steering wheel until it hurt. "But we're still in training. We've still got a few more big games left in this season and I'd hate to see either one of us get suspended for drinking. Especially with a championship on the line."

Randy popped the tab of his third can.

"Lighten up," he grinned. He opened the car door and stepped out onto the soft shoulder. "Enjoy yourself. You've earned it. We both did."

Randy banged the door and took a long swallow.

"That," he said, leaning back through the open window, "was a hell of a game last night. Dad even said so. He said that it was one of the best high school games that he'd ever seen. Did we make him proud, Jim-bo, or what?"

Randy took another reckless draw. He looked at Jim and laughed. "Dad was bragging that at this rate, you and me would be pulling scouts up from Ohio and Illinois by the end of the season. What'd you hit, Jim-bo, 150 yards last night, or what?"

Jim shook his head. He looked for cars, then opened his door. He circled the front bumper and joined Randy beside the shallow ditch. A long leg of sand stretched empty between Lake Shore Drive and the surf. No other cars were parked along the shoulder and no other vehicles were on the road.

Still, it was only a matter of time before they'd get caught. The police and the Coast Guard patrolled this run of waterfront on a regular basis.

"You're the one," said Jim, trying to sound rowdy, "that did all of the hitting. And all of the intercepting. You were great." He sighed. "That's why I don't want to piss it all away by getting us busted for. . . ."

"Who would bust us?" laughed Randy. "We've become like gods around here. Even the cops wouldn't bust us after the way we've been playing this season. Half of Ottawa County turned out for our last game. Grand Haven hasn't had so many people buying tickets for that field since the Beach Boys were in town."

Jim shook his head.

"So why ruin it?" asked Jim. "Why ruin it by doing something stupid like getting smashed at the beach?"

Randy dropped the can from his lips.

"You're right, little brother." He started to throw the can toward a clump of grass in the ditch, then reconsidered.

"You're right, Jim-bo. This is stupid." Randy held the can above his nose, studied it, then took another sip. "Let's not get drunk by ourselves at the beach. Let's rustle us up some cheerleaders and do it in style. Let's find us a big boat and go get ourselves smashed out on the lake."

"No way," said Jim. He shook his head. "Count me out. The cheerleaders are in training, just like us. If any of them got caught drinking, they'd be suspended just as quick as a player would. It's bad enough that you. . . ."

"How about Karen?" asked Randy. "I'll bet she'd love to have a couple of beers with us. She's got a wild streak in her and you know it. And she's got the boat that we'd need, for sure. Her old man's boat is a beauty. She could sneak off with the keys, and we could cruise the channel and the bayou all afternoon. Maybe all night, depending how long the beer holds out. Depending on if you can keep up with us or not."

Randy laughed. "Hell, Jim, you might even get laid out of the deal. A couple of beers, and who knows what. . . ."

"That's enough," snapped Jim. "You leave Karen out of your stupid plans."

"Ohhh. . . . I guess I hit a nerve, huh Jim-bo?"

Randy snickered. "You still don't want to get laid, is that it? You still planning to save yerself for your honeymoon, huh?"

"That's none of your damn business."

"Well, Jim-bo. I guess that it ain't. Then again, I guess that it is. It all depends upon how you look at it."

Randy took another drink, this time from deep within the can.

"What," asked Jim, "is that supposed to mean?"

"Well, Jim-bo. It's not that I want to shock you or anything. But you ain't the only stud in Grand Haven that's got a stiff little pecker for that angel-girl of yours. And if you ain't got the balls to use yours, then maybe it's time that one of us other. . . ."

Jim launched his knuckles from his hip.

It wasn't Jim's best uppercut—Randy's wrist and the beer deflected the blow slightly from the center of his chin. Still, it was good enough.

The beer can flew 10 feet, end over end like a bleeding field goal. Randy caved backwards like a linebacker blindsided by a pulling guard. He landed butt-first in the sand. Then spit.

"Shit."

He looked up at Jim, massaging his jaw.

"What the hell," he added.

He turned and spat a plug of blood.

Jim stepped closer. He towered over his brother, his knuckles still loaded.

"Shove that beer," he said, "up your own ass. I don't want

anything to do with it. And I don't want you using it to get yourself laid. If Karen wants to see your dick, that's between you and
her. But show a little class, okay? Don't get her drunk before you
ask her."

Jim turned his back to Randy and stomped back onto the
asphalt. He glanced over his shoulder as he walked passed the Ford
and began to walk the five miles back into town.

Randy stayed on his butt, stroking his chin and swearing about
what he was going to do with a bleeding lip and a cooler packed
with iced beer.

The phone rang shortly after supper. Jim answered.

"Hello. Jim here."

"Hey, Jim. It's Mike."

"What's up, Mike?"

"Trouble, Jim. That's what's up. It's your brother."

"Shit."

"And Karen."

Jim stopped breathing. "What?" he asked.

"They've been cruise'n up and down the channel all afternoon. A bunch of kids saw 'em drinking. Randy and Karen were
holding up beer cans and throwing full ones up onto the shore to
anybody who wanted one."

"Damn."

"It gets worse. Tammy just called to warn me that her mom
got ticked off and called the Coast Guard. The Coast Guard is
going to send a boat out to pick them up."

"Shit."

"The coaches are going to hear about this for sure. I just thought
you ought to know."

"Yeah, thanks."

"Jim . . . do you want some help? Do you want me to come by
and pick you up? Maybe we can catch them by the old bridge at
the mouth of the bayou. Tammy said they were headed in that
direction."

Jim thought for a moment.

"Yeah," he sighed. "Good idea. I'll meet you out front."

Mike was there in five minutes.

Jim climbed into the car and they sped north toward the end of the channel. They merged with Channel Road about two miles south of the bridge, then slowed so Jim could watch and listen out the window for signs of Mr. Seinner's boat. It was hard to see anything through the black brush and the thick groves of trees.

Three quarters of a mile from the bridge, Jim spotted the uneven glimmer of the setting sun on what appeared to be the dying remnants of a boat's wake.

"Slow down," said Jim. "I think they're up ahead."

Mike slowed.

At the next break in the trees, Jim caught sight of Mr. Seinner's sleek Chris Craft. Karen was driving, one knee on her seat, dressed only in a white swimsuit. Randy was stripped to his blue jeans. The boat was weaving. They were shouting and singing, both clearly drunk.

"Take me up to the bridge," said Jim. "You can let me out there."

"You sure?"

"I'm sure. You're already too mixed up in this as it is. Please, not a word to anyone. I'll see if I can talk them into tying the boat off next to the bridge. It's getting dark, and maybe I can get them home before they get caught."

"Maybe I could help you talk them into. . . ."

"Listen, Mike. You don't want to get caught in the middle of this mess. Especially if the Coast Guard shows up and starts writing tickets."

"I guess," he shrugged. He leaned toward the window and gazed down the bank.

"You sure?" he asked. "I mean, you know how Randy can get sometimes. I'd be happy to. . . ."

"Naw. Thanks anyway. Just drop me at the bridge."

"If you say so."

Mike stepped on the gas and quickly shuttled Jim around the next bend and up to the shoulder beside the old bridge. He stopped and Jim climbed out.

"Are you still sure about this?" asked Mike.

"Yeah. If they won't dock the boat, then I'll just jog home. I'll need the air to cool off by then anyways. If they do pull over, then I'll walk them home to help them sober up. The last thing that you need is to get caught with a couple of drunk teammates in your car. You get your ass home and I'll call you later to let you know how things came out."

Mike shook his head.

"Okay. But if you need any more help, you call me, right?"

"Sure thing. You've been a big help already."

Jim slammed the door.

Mike hesitated, then put the car in gear and left.

Jim made his way through undergrowth down to the bank beside the old Channel Road bridge. By the time he reached the water, he could already hear the smooth purr of the boat as it eased around the bend.

Above the growing hum of the motor, he could hear the voices and laughter of Randy and Karen.

Jim stepped to the edge of the water and waved.

"Hey there!" he shouted.

Karen jerked her head clumsily in Jim's direction.

"Hey, look," she slurred to Randy, pointing. "It's Him. I mean, it's Jim." They both laughed.

"Greetings, li'l bro," Randy yelled. "Glad ta see that you've decided to join us. Lotsa beers left. I think." He looked down. "Yes. Plenty. We'll be right over."

Karen swung the boat toward the shore, then eased the throttle. Jim waded a few feet into the channel to give her a target and to catch the bow. Karen cut the motor, and the boat drifted into his arms.

Waist deep, he steadied the boat against the rocking of its wake.

"You two having a good time?" he asked.

"Yep," said Randy. "Great time."

"Yep," echoed Karen. "And it just got better. Climb it." She giggled stupidly. "I mean, climb in. We'll pop you a fresh one."

"Sounds fun," said Jim. "The trouble is, someone called the Coast Guard a little while ago."

Jim looked down the channel, west toward Lake Michigan. The sun was already well below the trees. A hint of fog was haunting shallow mud holes at the water's edge.

"I guess," said Jim, "that the Coast Guard will be coming up the channel any minute. I suppose they'll be looking for you two and this boat."

"Oops," giggled Karen.

"Uh-oh," echoed Randy.

"Uh-oh is right." Jim held the boat more tightly. "Here's what I think. I suggest we tie the boat right here. Then we can dump the beer as quick as we can, and then can we walk. . . ."

"Oh, no," said Karen. She sobered unevenly. "My dad would kill me. He loves this boat. I gotta get it back tonight, right away."

She hit the motor and fished for reverse, found it, then began moving away from the shore, back into the channel.

"Wait," shouted Jim.

He tried to hold the boat, but knew that he couldn't. Water splashed up to his chest, then his feet lost contact with the bottom and he bobbed under in a cold rush of frustration.

He managed to hang on, then pulled himself back up for air. "Stop, damn it!"

Karen eased off the throttle. Jim dragged himself up over the bow.

Randy grinned.

"So you changed yer mind, eh?"

Jim stood in the bow and squeegeed what he could of the channel off from his pants and shirt. Spent cans lolled about the deck. Several empties with unfamiliar labels mingled among the rest beneath their feet.

Karen quickly squared the boat. She shoved the throttle forward in the direction of the gap between the pilings of the low
bridge.

Randy thrust his hand into the cooler.

"Here li'l brother." He yanked out a beer. "It's on me."

Randy tossed the can to the front of the boat. Jim caught it,
read the brand, then pitched it over the side.

"I hate those," said Jim. "Toss me another."

"Damn, Jim-bo. Why you wasting a good brew like that? A
lousy party-pooper is what you is." He laughed. "No more for you
until you promise to join us."

"Jim?" Karen looked upset. "Were you serious about the Coast
Guard? Are they after us?"

"That's what I heard. Someone's mom didn't like it that
you were flipping beers to minors. She called in a report a little
while ago."

"Darn." Karen shook her head. She glanced down the channel
behind them, then slowed only a little as they motored beneath
the black-stained wooden bridge.

Once through, she stood and surveyed the bayou ahead. It
was quiet. The sky was darkening rapidly. A downy mantle of thin
fog had already oozed across both sides of their path.

She sat, then shoved the throttle hard ahead.

"Slow down," Jim yelled.

Karen shook her head no.

Jim started to climb back to her. The nose of the boat lifted
dangerously high as he moved, and he had to stop where he was.

"Randy," he yelled over the noise of the motor. "You come up
here and watch for logs and sandbars. You can bring your damn
beer with you. Let me help Karen drive."

Randy laughed. He pointed at his swollen blood-caked lip.

"Fat chance," he hollered back.

Karen cocked her head toward the water. She was having diffi-
culty seeing around the elevated nose of the boat.

As she focused up the bayou, Randy made a show for Jim of

staring into the halter of her swimsuit. He stared at her top, licked his lips, then turned back toward Jim with a grin.

"Randy!" Jim shouted. "Get your ass up here."

Randy flashed another look at Karen, then laughed.

"Why would I wanna move, Jim-bo?" he yelled into the wind. "The view is much better from here."

Jim shook his head and swore.

Randy laughed again. He slowly moved his gaze up and down the length of Karen's legs, then settled once again upon her breasts. He put his thumb over the top of his beer and shook the can wildly. Karen glanced at Randy and laughed. He pointed the can at her belly, then pulled back his thumb.

White foam sprayed across her bare stomach and thighs.

She swore something and giggled loudly. The boat veered, and Randy reached for another beer.

Karen straightened the craft abruptly, then met Jim's eyes. She stuck her tongue at him as he turned his back in disapproval.

He lifted himself and studied the route upstream. Karen was angling a little to the left. He motioned her to ease the vessel the other way.

He was worried.

The Seinner dock and boathouse were another four miles up the bayou. Here and there, houses with backyards extending down to the water were already bathed in the blue glow of Mercury lamps. The night air was cooling fast, and billows of fog were swiftly thickening along both banks, rising in eerie low curls and ghostly swells of hanging gray shroud.

He glanced back at Karen.

She smiled at him, her lips black from the cold and hair whipping wildly.

Her jaw was shaking. Randy's beer foam glistened on her tan like a skin of ice. Her outside elbow shivered in bumpy goose flesh from the wet spray of the speeding hull.

Despite himself, even from the front of the boat, Jim could

not keep his eyes from darting down to Karen's sharply-puckered nipples. Both were clearly evident through her damp white suit.

He glanced back at his brother. Randy was enjoying the phenomena from the best seat in the house. He must have discovered the effect of his beer on Karen's flesh earlier in the day. The show had probably been repeating itself off and on for hours.

Jim's eyes flashed instinctively at his brother's crotch.

A bulge was in the making. And Randy was making no attempt to hide it.

Damn him.

Randy took another hit of beer, then lowered the can to his thigh. He glanced at Jim, then shouted something at Karen, baiting her to look.

Furious, Jim quickly unbuttoned his shirt and peeled it from his wet skin. He wrung it as dry as he could, then turned his shoulders upstream and held the shirt forward over his head. The shirt snapped heavily in the wind inches above his face as he peered ahead into the darkening waterway.

The icy wind buffeted the skin of his bare chest, and his damp shirt quickly grew cold within his hands. He pulled the shirt down, turned his back to the wind, then held it tightly within his arms against his stomach to warm it as best he could.

He looked up.

Karen smiled, guessing what he was doing.

Randy tilted toward the cooler and reached his free hand down for a chunk of ice.

Jim shouted. "Here, Karen. Put this on."

He underhanded her the wadded shirt, keeping it low so that it could not fly past her and out of the boat.

The shirt opened like a parachute in the wind. She caught it easily.

"Thanks," she shouted back.

Randy looked up from the cooler. He glanced at Jim's bare chest, then at Karen as she slipped an arm into the shirt. He looked back at Jim.

"Mama's boy!" Randy grinned. "Party-pooper to the end!" He tossed his ice at Jim.

Karen glanced back and forth between the brothers, then shook her head. Jim watched as she lifted her other hand from the steering wheel in order to slip it into the second sleeve.

He turned his gaze upstream to check their progress. They were entering a dark bend in the bayou. Fog obscured most of the shoreline. The water ahead was black, and the sky above was a dark canopy of somber purples and blues.

Jim turned back to Karen to motion her to angle more to the right. She was looking at Randy, shaking her head emphatically that she did not want a hit from his beer.

Randy grinned. He sealed the beer with his thumb and once again began to shake the can.

"Leave her alone," yelled Jim.

Randy looked at him, then laughed. "Mama's boy," he yelled back.

Jim's knuckles tensed.

He caught Randy's eyes. "Leave her the fuck alone!"

Randy glared. "Fuck you," he mouthed. He flashed a middle finger and showed his teeth. "If you want her, then you come get her."

Karen stared confusedly at one brother, then the other.

Jim rose from his seat. He took a step toward Randy, then felt the nose lift.

He turned from a half-crouch for a final check upstream.

A huge dock loomed through the fog. Jim whirled and screamed, and Karen killed the motor and tried to swerve.

Newspapers said they hit the dock with a crash that was heard a half mile away.

Jim regained consciousness in icy water, dazed, struggling for air, his pants dragging thick and heavy about his legs as he flailed to keep his mouth above the water. He instinctively sucked a big breath, then allowed himself to sink below the surface.

He struggled to unbuckled his belt and to be rid of his shoes and pants.

He came up gasping, groping for the dock or boat.

What was left of the boat was 20 feet beyond his grasp, its top half crushed and wedged almost entirely beneath the dock at a sickening angle. Jim kicked and pulled his body back toward the wreckage.

"Karen," he yelled. "Can you hear me?"

He continued to swim.

"Karen! Randy! Are you all right?"

He swam passed the dock and reached the rear of the splintered boat where it jutted from underneath the steel dock joists. The hull was intact, but the top portion of the boat was crushed and sheared low. The motor was dead. He could smell fuel. And something else.

He reached out and grabbed onto the motor.

"Karen! Where are you? Randy?"

The motor was slippery, and it was difficult to keep his grip. Jim threw his right arm over the top of the motor and dragged himself up.

He nearly screamed and slipped back beneath the water as the skin of his lower stomach snagged and peeled open like a sardine can against the sharp edge of the propeller.

Jim squeezed his eyes.

God. Please, let her be all right.

He clenched his teeth and pulled himself back up over the motor and into the boat.

The back of the boat protruded less than a yard from the dock. Everything was black in shadows. He groped blindly, one hand steadying himself against the splintered remains of the boat gunwales, the other submerged within the boat.

His right hand found her first.

"Karen!"

He released his grip from the side of the boat and lowered his left hand to cup the other side of her head.

"Karen! Can you hear me?"

Nothing.

He ran his right hand around her face. It was oily. Greasy. Sticky. Hot.

"God, no!"

His fingers found a deep mushy gash that opened from her left eye and ran down over a broken fragment of exposed jawbone. The laceration disappeared into a sickening mire of cords and severed throat. Her neck and shoulders were greased with the nauseating stench of blood. Blood was still leaking everywhere. He tried to lift her, but her lifeless body was pinned between the dock and part of the boat. Her head flopped limply as he released his grasp.

Jim squeezed his eyes.

No!

He slid his right hand from her tangled hair and groped toward the other side.

"Randy," he whispered. "Are you here?"

He found his brother's arm, then ran his hand up to Randy's shoulder.

Randy's chest was squashed backwards, almost flat between one of the dock joists and the back of his seat. He must have been thrown forward into the dock on impact, then slammed backwards as the boat rammed beneath the joists.

Jim groped a sticky hand across Randy's shoulder. Groped until he came to the mangled flesh that should have been the base of his brother's neck.

"No!"

He recoiled violently, lost his balance and fell from the back of the boat.

The icy water felt good against his clenched eyes and lips. Jim stayed under as long as he could, fighting for a clear head, fearful of what lay above.

A floodlight flashed white as he surfaced.

Dogs were barking, and a woman was screaming, running toward the dock. Jim sucked another gulp of air and went back under.

The water was cold. Damn cold. He could feel it everywhere on his body. It felt good. Felt real.

The carnage above was the nightmare. He squeezed his eyes. Panicked for oxygen.

Realized that he was naked except for his underwear.

Stayed below, dizzy, kicking away from the blood.

Away from Karen's throat.

Randy's. . . .

He bobbed for a flash of air, then disappeared.

Continued to kick and pull.

What would people think? Him at the wreck, naked, Karen and Randy . . . slaughtered. . . .

Jim shook his head beneath the water, swirled his hands and fingers to rinse off the sticky. The blood. From their mutilated flesh. He kicked harder, staying under until his lungs took control and forced him up for air.

He surfaced for another quick breath, then dove back under. His mind began to clear. His next breath was more controlled. His strokes evened out and he began to swim like an athlete, above the water, then below, with direction and purpose.

He was beyond the yellow ring of the floodlight. He could hear them behind him, their panicked voices and cries drifting through the fog.

He swam and swam.

Downstream. Back toward the lake.

On and on, forever.

When his kicking feet tangled in mud and marsh grass, he dropped his legs and stumbled from the water onto the bank.

Collapsed.

Fell asleep.

Awoke a short time later.

Rose to his feet and looked around.

It was more than a nightmare. There was no other explanation for where he was and his nakedness. And his bleeding gash. He staggered up the bank, back to the road, then took a deep breath.

He needed to get home. To get clothes. To sleep. To never wake.

Jim began jogging toward his house, fighting the nightmares, images and pain.

Fighting the nightmares with numbers.

Numbers that he pounded into his ankles and knees.

One-two-three-four.

Left-right-left-right.

One-two-three-four.

He dodged approaching headlights and ducked into the shadows of trees and bushes.

Until he collapsed at home.

CHAPTER 33

Sunday, March 24.
Bear Creek Canyon, Colorado

"Are you two okay?"

Alice raised her cheek from Jade's shoulder. She had moved around the table as her husband began trembling during his story. She now looked up with eyes wet and red.

"Yes, we're fine. Thank you. We'll be all right." She slipped her arm down to Jade's waist, then squeezed gently. Jade raised his head from the cradle of his forearm in front of his coffee. He turned to face their waitress.

The woman leaned worriedly in his direction, the heel of her right hand propped against her hip.

"We've just been talking," said Jade. "Stories from a long time ago." He looked at the young woman more carefully. Her name came to him unexpectedly.

"You're Wanda , aren't you?"

"Yes. How did you know?"

"We met you here last week. You were wearing a hand-printed name badge. You've got Janet's old position, right?"

"Oh," she said softly, "I remember you now. I was still on probation last week. They gave me the position this weekend. I'll have a real name tag in a couple of days, as soon as they get one made."

Wanda reached into her apron, then withdrew a pair of fresh cloth napkins.

"Here. You two look like you could use a couple of clean ones."

Alice accepted the napkins and smiled gratefully.

"You two were the couple with the teenagers. A boy and a girl, right?"

Jade nodded, then wiped his face.

"Funny thing," she said. "We got a call here right after you left last week. It was Janet. She had a question about her last paycheck or something. Anyway, I answered the phone, and I mentioned that you were asking about her. Janet seemed real flattered. She remembered you guys right away."

Wanda smiled, kindly. "Janet said that I should treat you folks real well. That you were always good customers." She grinned. "And big tippers."

Jade smiled. "Thanks."

"For what?"

"For the napkins. And for saying hello to Janet for us."

"No problem." She leaned again. "So you two are sure that everything is okay?"

"Yes, fine."

"All right, then." She straightened. "I'll leave you two alone."

She started to leave, then stopped and turned.

"Be sure," she said, "to call me if you need anything, okay?"

Alice nodded.

Jade finished drying his face.

"She's not so bad after all," smiled Alice.

"Yes. Who would have thought?"

Alice moved a few inches away from his hip, then turned to face him.

"I'm sorry," she said softly, "about what happened. About what you've been through. What a terrible, awful thing. A secret for all these years?"

"Yes," he whispered. "You're the only one who knows I was there . . . that I was part of that accident. I've been running from that night for 20 years."

"What about your friend, Mike?"

"He may have wondered, but he never said a word. He was

probably too scared to ask. I mean, how could you ever ask some-one a question about something like that?"

Alice shook her head. "And the beer? Where did Randy get all of that beer?"

"Well, I guess that's the other part of the story. Randy was eighteen. Back then, eighteen was old enough to drink. He could have bought it himself." Jade sighed. "But he didn't."

He placed his napkin on the table. "The beer was a present. It was for both of us. A celebration gift after a great game."

"From?"

"From Harry."

Jade closed his eyes.

The heart of Christ.

Please give me the heart of Christ.

Please be with Harry.

"It was from my father," said Jade. "My dad was really proud of us boys. He drove all the way from Grand Rapids every chance he could to watch us. He couldn't stick around after the games because my mom and him would start fighting, but he always came up as we left the field to shake our hands and tell us how good we played."

Jade pushed the napkin to beside his cold coffee.

"That case of beer was dad's way of patting us on the back. He did the same thing for Ben once the year before, after Ben's last game of the season. I guess that dad didn't want me and Randy to feel cheated or anything."

He lifted his elbow to the table and turned to face Alice.

"Do you think," asked Alice, "that your dad knew, afterwards I mean, that it was his beer that, well. . . ."

"He knew. The article in the newspaper mentioned all of the empty beer cans in the boat. And a few of the witnesses from earlier in the afternoon gave the paper quotes about how they saw Karen trolling up and down the channel with Randy tossing beer to minors."

Jade shook his head.

"Harry, my dad, he didn't come to Randy's cremation service. I guess that it was too hard for him, having to think about facing my mom and me and Ben. And having to talk to everyone else in the community, when everyone knew that he was the one who helped Karen and Randy get drunk. My dad sort of disappeared after that. He quit his job in Grand Rapids. A week or so later, he left the state."

Jade ran his fingers through his hair. "My last memory of my father is from the Saturday afternoon of the accident. I can still see him in our front yard handing Randy that cooler of beer. Dad said he had an errand in Grand Haven and that he just wanted to stop by and surprise us with the main fixings for a party."

Alice looked down to the stream's edge. The water was running fast and high. There seemed to be a lot of melt-off coming down from the high meadows.

She turned back to Jade. "Weren't the police after your father for contributing to a minor or something?"

"No. Like I said, Randy was the only one contributing to a minor. Randy was of age. And besides, I think the cops realized there wasn't any one person to blame."

Alice looked at the table.

"I'm pretty sure," said Jade, "that some of the beer in that boat came from Karen's house. Maybe she smuggled it out of the refrigerator in the garage. Her dad, Jeffrey Seinner, he usually kept a few cases out there. Fancy brands, not the kinds of beers that folks like us could afford. I saw a few cans with expensive labels rolling around on the bottom of the boat when I first climbed in."

Alice sighed. "It must have been awful. I would have been in shock if I were you."

"I probably was. I remember wondering while I was swimming, wondering that maybe I should have stayed with them, even though they were both so clearly dead. But once I was out of there, away from the carnage, I just couldn't imagine how I could go back. I just wanted to get away as far and as fast as I could."

Jade watched a pair of motorcycles pull up and park on the

restaurant's dirt parking pad beside the road. He turned back to Alice.

"By the time that I got home, I knew that I would never be able to tell anyone. It was all too bizarre. Too unreal. I wouldn't know how to explain myself. 'Yeah, I was there,' I would say. 'I jumped out of the boat just before it hit. I swam around naked for a while, then decided to swim home. . . .'"

Jade's right molars softly nipped the back of his tongue.

He closed his eyes.

The heart of Christ.

Please forgive me.

The heart of Christ.

Help me to accept my mistakes.

The heart of Christ.

Thank you for your divine forgiveness.

The heart of Christ.

Please take care of Randy.

The heart of Christ.

Please take care of Harry.

The heart of Christ.

Alice slid back to Jade's side, put her arm around his back, then leaned her head onto his shoulder.

Softly, she prayed with him.

They paid their bill, thanked Wanda, then walked toward their car.

They were quiet, side-by-side. Somehow, Jade's hand found its way into Alice's. Their fingers felt strange interlocked that way. It had been a long time. Jade walked with her to the passenger side, stopped, then turned to face her. Their eyes met. He released her hand and they embraced in silence.

He opened her door, then circled around the car and lowered himself into the driver's seat.

Alice buckled her seat belt, then turned to him.

"Jade, is there anything else?" she asked.

He inserted the keys into the ignition.

"No," he said. He started the engine. "Not that I can think of right now." He turned to her. "Maybe something else will come to me later. But for the most part, I'm pretty sure I've told you everything. Not just about Karen and Randy, but about me. And about my secrets. Right up to last week in the store."

He smiled weakly.

She smiled back, tenderly.

"I've said it once," she said, "but you need to hear this again. This past week has been overwhelming. But I'm thankful for it. Somehow, through all of the pain and all of the confusion and all of talking, I feel like we're experiencing a breakthrough in our marriage."

"Me too."

"I've got to admit," she reached for his hand on the steering wheel, "that I'm feeling more hope and love than I have felt in a long time. You need to know that. And you also need to know that I haven't forgotten about what you asked me. You asked me the other day what it was that I was bringing to the table. I'm still thinking about your question. One of these days, when I can get my feelings and ideas sorted out, I'll be trying to share some of what's hidden inside of me with you."

Jade grinned. "Thanks. That would be good. We need to keep this as mutual as possible."

Alice squeezed his knuckles.

"I'm sure that you're right," she said.

"You know," said Jade, "next week is Palm Sunday. And then it's Easter. Let's think of something special to do this year."

"Like what?"

"Oh, I don't know. But something."

She smiled. "Okay. I'll give it some thought."

He set his foot on the brake, put the car in reverse, then turned back to his wife.

"I hope that you don't mind, Alice, but I've been thinking

about something else, too. I'd like to stop by the little artists' co-op in Morrison on our way home."

"Why's that? Since when have you been into pottery?"

He shrugged. "Never. But I feel like there's something that I need to do. I'd like to pick out a nice little hand-thrown urn or vase or something. Just in case Harry's . . . just in case my father's ashes show up. If I get my briefcase back, I'd like to get my dad's ashes out of that cereal box."

"You're not thinking about keeping him around the house, are you?"

"No. Not if that would make you uncomfortable. I'm not sure what I have in mind. It's just that I'd like to show my father a little more respect next time. If I get the chance. He deserves better."

The traffic cleared, and Jade backed out into the road. He put the car into drive and started down the canyon toward Morrison, and toward home.

"I got to thinking," he said, "about what it would be like if I were to die. What it would be like if you sent my ashes to Mark in a Frosted Flakes box." He shook his head. "And then Mark didn't even bother to keep track of it. If he just left my remains some-place in a mall."

Alice laughed, hesitantly. "Something like that would never happen with us. We love you more than that. You've never left your family."

She caught his eyes. "And listen to me, Mr. James Vanderspyke." She smiled. "You are definitely not your father."

Jim checked his mirror.

"Yes and no," he sighed. "Yes and no."

CHAPTER 34

Monday, March 25, 1996.
Denver, Colorado

Jade glanced at the phone ringing beside the cash register at the front of the store.

"It's okay, Chris," he called. "I've got it."

He dropped a roll of price labels onto a freshly opened case of Frying Fat Free, then hurried to the receiver.

The morning had been hectic. There was no time to talk with Chris, nor was there time to call Mr. Seinner. Jade barely opened the doors when a bustle of curious activity erupted in the mall. Moments later, security guards and police officers evacuated everyone from Jade's wing of the mall.

Around 10:30, things settled down and Seinner Books was allowed to reopen. The officer in charge explained that a potentially explosive devise was spotted by the bench in front of Jade's store. The bomb squad retrieved the object and drove it away in a special truck.

Jade reopened the store to a backlog of phone calls and a steady stream of customers and merchants wanting to speculate about the bomb scare and to pump him for what he knew. Which was nothing.

He answered the phone.

"Hello, Seinner Books. How may I help you?"

"Good morning. I'd like to speak with Mr. James Vanderspyke. Is he there?"

"This is James Vanderspyke. What can I do for you?"

"Good morning Mr. Vanderspyke. This is Sergeant Peterson

from the Lakewood Police Department. We have something of yours. A briefcase."

"My briefcase!"

"Yes. Apparently the same one reported last week as stolen. A security guard discovered it this morning in Westwood Mall. It showed up sometime between 9:00 and 9:30 am, before the mall opened. It looked suspicious, so he kept an eye on, then called us. The bomb squad removed it an hour ago."

Jade laughed.

"Is this funny?" asked the officer.

"I'm sorry. It's just that I never expected to see it again. Was there anything inside?"

"Yes, as a matter of fact. The bomb squad thought they had a live one. Their scan revealed the shadow of a box containing what appeared to be a slab of explosives. When they couldn't find a detonator, they opened the briefcase and found your business cards, a few documents, and the strangest box of cereal they had ever seen."

Jade laughed again.

"Are the contents," the man asked, "what they appear to be?"

"Yes," said Jade. "Those are my father's remains."

"Okay, just checking. Of course, there's no law against carrying around a cereal box filled with the ashes of a dead relative. But that seems a little weird, don't you think?"

"Yes. Very weird. Tell you what, sergeant. On my way to the station, I'll swing by my house for an urn I bought this weekend up in Morrison. We'll put the ashes in that."

The man laughed. "Sounds good."

"Anything else?"

"Yes. One more thing. Whoever took your briefcase obviously checked out the ashes as well. He left a note."

"What did it say?"

"Shall I read it?"

"Why not?" Jade grinned, curious. "If you don't mind."

"No problem. I've already read it to everyone down here." He chuckled. "The note reads:

> To Whoever you are:
> Please take this back. I was told this stuff is ashes from
> a dead person. I don't screw with ghosts, and I don't want no
> dead spirits haunting me. I don't know what kind of person
> carries ashes from a corpse around in a cereal box, but I want
> nothing to do with it. Or with you. Sorry. Please don't hex
> me or look for me or anything. You can have it back.
> The guy who found your briefcase."

Jade laughed again.

"Okay," said the officer. "We'll hold your father until you get here."

"Very good," said Jade, smiling. "I'll try not to keep you, or dad, waiting. I guess it's time I brought him home."

POSTLUDE

Saturday, March 30. Dakota Ridge, Colorado

Hosea rubbed his knees.

The meeting had lasted over two hours, and the others were now gone. Jade smiled across the altar.

"It's been interesting."

"Yes, as always."

"You doing okay, Hosea?"

"Yes. Pretty good. I'm kind of tired, that's all. How about you? Was the meeting a little less exhausting for you this week?"

"Sure, much easier. I was glad to be out of the hot seat this time. I'm still trying to deal with last week. Today, it was good to mostly just watch."

"I'm glad you came back." Hosea stretched. "That was a powerful gesture, shredding and burning your father's old divorce certificates. And that picture of him with his girlfriend. Good riddance. Too bad your dad didn't have the right friends himself to burn it with him years ago."

"Yeah." Jade shook his head. "I wish he could have held off a little longer." Jade looked at the hand-thrown pot near the back wall. "You know . . . maybe the two of us could have reconnected. Maybe I could have invited him to come to Denver. . . ."

"Naw," said Hosea. He brushed several grains of debris into the altar. "It doesn't work that way. If your father hadn't died, you'd still be the same old son who never cared in the first place. It's all related. Death and new life. Your father is gone, and here you are, a changed man. A good man working on all sorts of things and helping fellow hogmen. We're glad you've joined us. You have a lot to share."

"Eventually, maybe. But not right now. I'm still trying to figure it out myself."

"Wrong." Hosea shook his head. "That's exactly what your contribution should be. Your process, your struggle from day-to-day as you work to understand and survive. That's the stuff we need. People who think they've solved their problems and have everything under control are usually pretty boring. Either they've stopped living, or they've started lying." Hosea smiled. "Lying to themselves, mostly."

Jade grinned. "By the way, thanks for letting me stash dad's ashes up here for a while. Alice still feels weird about having them in the house. Besides, he preferred the outdoors anyway."

"Well, then," laughed Hosea, "maybe your father has finally come home."

"I thought about spreading his ashes on the cairn."

"And?"

"It didn't feel quite right. The cairn is refuse, bad stuff that we're symbolically rejecting. That's not the way that I feel about him anymore."

"So what will you do?"

Jade gazed to the sunlight breaking through the junipers at the cave's entrance. "I'm thinking about spreading his ashes down by the creek, among the cottonwoods and horses. That way I can sit up here and look down. . . ."

Hosea closed his eyes. "Sounds good. Give yourself a little more time, and if it still feels appropriate, I'd be honored to assist you in some kind of private ritual."

Jade smiled, subdued. After a few moments, he continued.

"A small service would be nice. With Alice, Mark, and Carla." He cleared his throat. "It's been helping, that prayer you gave me. Off and on throughout the day, every chance I get. Sometimes it's hard, and sometimes it's easy. Sometimes it's as if God is filling me with love and mercy, and other times, it's as if the prayer makes no difference at all."

Hosea nodded. "I know. I've been there. I still am."

"And always will be?"

"Probably. As long as I'm a hogman."

"Then what?" asked Jade. "What comes after being a hogman?"

Hosea laughed. "Once a hogman, always a hogman, until the day I die. The day my body collapses and settles into the dirt. Ashes to ashes, dust to dust."

"And your soul?"

Hosea smiled. "Maybe that, too. Once a hogman, always a hogman. Of course, a dead hogman is a clean hogman. One who no longer returns to the mud to wallow. And clean hogmen get wings. Who says that pigs can't fly?"

They laughed.

"How about your job," asked Hosea. "Have you figured anything out yet?"

"Well, I told Seinner that I wouldn't stock the NightLight books. And I told him that Chris Teller would be perfect for Portland, since she didn't have any kids to pull out of school or anything. I'm not sure what he's going to do." Jade raised his knuckle to his teeth and cradled his elbow into his right wrist. Hosea watched as Jade played several slow bars.

"And?"

Jade returned the invisible harmonica to his knee. "Well, it looks shaky. Seinner wouldn't commit to keeping the downtown store in Denver. He says he needs to crunch the numbers. The best he offered for now was a reduced salary for managing just the one store at the mall."

"I'm sorry."

"One store, of course, would mean less hours . . . which might be good, now that I'm trying to spend more time with my family. But I'm not sure that we could make ends meet if I took such a drastic cut in pay. It's all pretty confusing. . . . Who knows how it will settle out."

Hosea closed his eyes. "Something will work out," he sighed.

"Yes. I know you're right. I only wish things were easier. I wish that I could just pray, and that God would just give me a simple instant-and-easy answer."

"God loves you," Hosea opened his eyes, "more than that. If He made it easy, without any earthquakes or fires, you wouldn't change. You would die the same naive, marginally-useful adolescent that you were 25 years ago."

Jade laughed. "Life," he said, "is not going at all the way that I expected."

"Welcome to the real world."

"This job uncertainty is especially hard on me right now. Deep down, I guess that I always knew that relationships were tough. But I honestly thought that if I worked hard enough, harder than my dad ever did, then I would never have to fear the winter."

"The winter?"

Jade nodded. "Yeah, the winter. Hosea, do you remember the fable of the grasshopper and the ants? The one where the grasshopper played around all summer while the ants worked, and then when winter came, the grasshopper starved because he hadn't stashed enough aside?"

"Yeah, I remember the story." Hosea scoffed.

"What's wrong?" asked Jade. "In a way, I've kind of built my life around that fable. I've been a good ant. I've worked hard ever since Randy and Karen died. Maybe I haven't put as much into savings as I'd like, but I've built up some good equity in my home, and I own some nice things free and clear. I have some pretty good net worth. And I've tried not to squander my time or to be too foolish."

"You tell me, Dutch. What's wrong with that story? What has it gotten you?"

Jade hesitated. "I'm not sure."

"Give it some thought, then. I'm not saying that hard work and sensible living are bad choices. They can be good choices. But there's a whole different way of looking at our short time on this planet other than in terms of working and banking up our assets."

"Maybe. But it takes money to live."

"Seek ye first the Kingdom of God, and all of these things shall be added unto you."

Jade shook his head.

"Then try this," said Hosea. "Since you like stories so much, maybe this one will make some sense to you. It's a short little parable that comes from Jesus himself."

Hosea closed his eyes. "There once was a rich man who owned land that produced good crops. So good, in fact, that the man decided he needed to tear down his barns and to build bigger ones in which to store his increasing abundance. But God said to him, 'You fool! This very night you will have to give up your life . . . then who will get all these things that you have kept for yourself?'"

The cave grew silent.

Jade stared into the shadows within the altar. At last, he looked up at Hosea.

"It could be tonight, couldn't it? Me, you, Geek, Alice, one of my kids . . . any of us could die tonight, couldn't we?"

Hosea met his eyes. "Yes. Of course we could die. And some of us will die tonight. Around the world, thousands will die tonight. Every single hogman and hogwoman, even the hogkids, we're all waiting for that eventual call that tells us our time is over."

"Life sounds so short," sighed Jade, "when you put it that way."

"Life is short. And we're all living on borrowed time. In this life, that's all that there is. A few short years, and then, bam. It's over. And then all of the grain in all of our barns will no longer do us a lick of good."

Jade shook his head. "That's pretty discouraging, Hosea. Here today, gone tomorrow. And nothing really left behind from our coming and going, nothing but ashes."

Jade glanced at the pot beside the cairn.

"No," said Hosea, "not just ashes. Think of your father. The man behind the ashes. Think of your brother, and of Karen. Weren't their lives about more than that? About something bigger than flesh or ashes, things that are perhaps even eternal? Can you remember them, Jade?"

"I can. I've been remembering them a lot lately. I guess that I was even remembering them when I was trying to forget them."

"So they're not just ashes, Jade. They're eternal creatures, beings that are defined by the circles of relationships in which they move. Children of God, brothers and sisters that even now are somehow still around. Still here on earth, inside those with whom they built their relationships before they died. But also with a host of those who've gone ahead, those who've finally found their way home to God somewhere off in eternity. Someplace where you will eventually be with them again, all free of guilt and shame, filled with the heart of Christ."

Jade closed his eyes. "Yes."

"For now," quoted Hosea, "we see through a glass darkly, but then face to face. . . ."

"Now I know in part," continued Jade, "then shall I understand fully, even as I have been fully understood. And now these three remain: faith, hope and love. And the greatest of these is love."

Jade pictured Randy, Karen, and his father. He tried to picture Jesus holding them, smiling, welcoming them home.

And then another image entered his mind. A picture he had never imagined, though he'd heard the cliché all his life. Jade wasn't sure if the image was a self-induced joke or a vision.

But he smiled as he watched it play.

Pigs.

Thousands, even millions of them. Pink ones, black ones, tan ones, young ones, old ones, fat ones, thin ones. Pigs of all sizes. Rising from the sooty remnants of a scorched earth, their snouts pointed heavenward.

Sprouting wings to rise from the dust, above the mud and over the ashes.

The day when pigs would fly.

THE END

9 780738 815923

90000